THROUGH THE VORTEX

THROUGH THE VORTEX

Escape from the Bermuda Triangle

Terrance Alexi

Writer's Showcase
presented by *Writer's Digest*
San Jose New York Lincoln Shanghai

Through the Vortex
Escape from the Bermuda Triangle

Writer's Showcase
presented by *Writer's Digest*
an imprint of iUniverse.com, Inc.

For information address:
iUniverse.com, Inc.
620 North 48th Street, Suite 201
Lincoln, NE 68504-3467
www.iuniverse.com

ISBN: 0-595-13173-5

Printed in the United States of America

CONTENTS

CHAPTER I

▼

THE DORMANT MONSTER AWAKENS

"Mayday, Mayday!" screamed a desperate voice over the radio. Mike Thompson, a twelve-year veteran with the Department of Natural Resources was speeding along about a half-mile off the shore of Miami, Florida when the terrified voice on the radio startled him. Instinctively, he glanced at his watch. It was just past 2300 hours. The sky was cloudy and it was a pitch-black night. The date was May 5, 2001.

"Mayday," the voice repeated. "Can anyone hear me? Please respond."

"This is Ranger Thompson of the DNR," he replied. "What's the problem?"

"Don't know," was the response. "Bright lights everywhere, compass is spinning out of control. It feels like something is underneath my boat, trying to lift it out of the water."

Mike didn't reply right away. He could hear loud noises in the background. The bizarre transmission left him at a temporary loss for words. "Lifting out of the water," he muttered. "What type of craft are you piloting? What's the vessel's name? How many are aboard? What's your present position? Over."

"*The Shangri-La*," came the response, "40-footer. I'm alone, about three miles from shore directly east of Miami. I can see the tower of the First National Bank building." There was a brief pause. "Something's out here! Help me please!"

"I'll be right there," Mike replied. He was only about five miles from the spot the man identified and gunned the powerful engine of his 32-foot racing boat, *One Summer Dream*. Turning toward the source of the radio signal, he looked ahead for bright lights and turbulent water. He couldn't imagine what would be causing so much commotion in otherwise calm waters. Maybe there's an isolated, violent thunderstorm over there, he thought. He could see nothing like that ahead.

Once at top speed of over 70 mph, he glanced to his right at the Miami skyline. The First National Bank tower stood in plain view. At his present location it was a calm, peaceful evening.

Mike switched on the radar. There was an area on the screen that appeared as a complete void, as if something was blocking the signal from reaching it. That's strange, he thought as he turned straight for it. The first of many cold chills ran up his spine.

It had been about two minutes now since his last transmission from the stricken vessel and he opened up the microphone to try and resume contact. "*Shangri-La*, this is the Ranger Thompson, do you read me, over." Only a loud hissing sound came in reply. "*Shangri-La*, do you read, over."

A moment later there was another weak transmission. Mike could hear the sound of splashing water. This went on for several seconds before another sound came, a sound unlike anything he had ever heard before. At first it sounded like a long, distant, chilling scream. Then it sounded more like many screams, all in eerie unison. "What the hell is that?" he muttered.

The sound continued for several long seconds. It almost sounded like the desperate cries of doomed sailors being dumped into shark infested waters as their vessel made a quick plunge into the sea. At the last instant, Mike heard another voice join them; this one was the man who had originally placed the emergency radio call. "This can't be happening," Mike heard him cry out. Then his screams joined the others. A moment later the radio went deathly silent.

"What's happening over there," he said. "*Shangri-La*, do you read, over." There was no reply. At that moment the radar screen cleared and resumed normal operation for the first time in the last ten minutes. Mike looked at it and saw a lone vessel sitting idle in the dark water about a quarter-mile ahead. He flicked on the spotlight mounted to the *Dream*'s deck and cut the speed down to a fast crawl. Moments later, the white hull of a large boat came faintly into view. The name *Shangri-La* was printed in large black letters across the hull at the stern.

In the piercing light, Mike thought he could see smoke rising from the unlit vessel. As he drew closer, he realized it wasn't smoke, but steam. He cut the speed completely and drifted up alongside.

Rushing to the starboard railing, he looked around on deck for the pilot. "Anybody here?" he said. There was no reply. He glanced all around for any sign of fire in the hold. There was no flame or smoke, only steam that seemed to be rising from the entire deck.

As Mike reached for a rope to tie off he absently placed his hand on the deck of the *Shangri-La*. "Ouch," he exclaimed, pulling his hand away. The vessel was freezing cold. "What the hell?" he said. He stepped back and stood observing the vessel. The *Shangri-La*, listing slightly to port, looked lifeless.

Without thinking, Mike's right hand touched his chest and marked the cross, just like it had hundreds of times since he was a small boy. The same hand then grabbed the dangling microphone and held it to his mouth. "Coast Guard," he said, almost in a calm voice. "This is Ranger Mike Thompson, I need somebody out here right away." In less than ten minutes a cutter was on the scene.

Mike had always considered himself a levelheaded and objective individual. As a ranger with the South Florida Department of Natural Resources for the last five years, he had encountered drug smugglers, boat people from Haiti and Cuba, sharks, pollution, and numerous tourists taking dangerous chances in ill-equipped water craft.

He hated to hear someone refer to the ocean around Miami as the "Bermuda Triangle". Also called "The Devil's Triangle," this large area of the Atlantic Ocean

measuring some 144,000 square miles is roughly triangu-
lar in shape and bounded by Bermuda to the north,
Puerto Rico to the southeast and southern Florida to the
southwest. There have been more accidents, disappearances, abandoned vessel findings and unexplained
phenomena in this one area than any other compara-
tively sized piece of ocean on earth. Like many in his
field, Mike denied the Bermuda Triangle was anything
more than myth. The shipping traffic has always been
heavy here, he thought. Naturally, there would be more
accidents too.

Mike, thirty-one years old and single, was often called
by the nickname of "Skinny" by some of the other
Rangers. At six-foot even but only 160 pounds, he had a
lanky look about him. His black hair and brown eyes also
sometimes led people to mistakenly think he was
Hispanic, although he was of English descent and didn't
speak a word of Spanish.

He lived, alone now since the recent death of his
beloved dog "Fannie" to old age at thirteen, in a small
beach house along a waterway about a quarter mile from
the open ocean and a few miles north of the city limits of
North Miami Beach, Florida. Behind his home was a boat
house that held his pride and joy, *One Summer Dream*, a
32-foot racing boat with twin Evinrude inboard engines.
The sleek white craft seated twelve comfortably and featured a removable roof over its raised control platform.
He kept her in top racing condition, not for competition
purposes but for the need of getting to accident scenes as
fast as possible. His first love had always been sitting at
the wheel some ten feet above the water and feeling the
wind in his face while pushing the throttle forward. For

Mike there was just something special about the feel of riding in a fast boat.

In the last ten years, metropolitan Miami had grown steadily in population. During peak tourist season from Memorial Day to Labor Day, Christmas season, and late January in the years the Superbowl was held in Miami, accidents involving boaters, swimmers, skiers and fishermen happened frequently. Mike originally joined the Department of Natural Resources to monitor such things as beach erosion and pollution, as well as to protect the animals and plants from the ever-increasing encroachment of man. In the last couple of years however, his duties had been limited almost exclusively to emergency rescue. The local ambulance services were under-staffed and often caught in Miami's notorious traffic jams. The DNR has to do its part, and Mike found a fast boat to be his best tool in saving lives. He performed his job well, but he longed for something different, although he didn't know exactly what.

Mike got an unexpected bonus last year, when he met Jan Smythe. Jan was part of a crowd of bystanders one weekday who watched the capture of a wayward alligator in a city park pond during the lunch hour. The police had asked for a Natural Resources officer to come get the alligator before he began devouring the park's beloved geese. Mike arrived on the scene, assessed the situation and then called for assistance.

A few minutes later, and in front of a crowd of roughly fifty people, the team of officers snared the alligator and took him away in a truck to be released into the wild in a remote area. While Mike was helping wrap-up the operation, he noticed a beautiful young woman standing about forty feet away, talking to another woman. She was wearing a bright red blouse and dark blue skirt. Her long, straight blonde hair blew gently in the breeze. A moment later she looked at him and smiled. His heart skipped a beat.

He walked up to the two of them and smiled. "Would you ladies like to be placed on the waiting list to adopt the next alligator we capture?"

The two of them stopped talking and started at him, unsure if he was serious.

"They make great pets," he said. "They sleep in the bathtub and keep burglars away."

They both laughed. "It would keep me away too," the blonde in the red blouse said.

"I have to go," the other woman said. Then to Mike: "nice work officer."

"Thanks," Mike said. She walked away, leaving the two of them alone. Mike introduced himself.

"I'm Jan Smythe," she said. "You do this often?"

Mike felt embarrassed. "Introduce myself to everybody?"

Jan laughed. "No, I mean manhandle alligators."

"Oh. A couple of times a week I guess."

Jan was smiling, almost laughing. "I really should be getting back inside," she said. "I have a conference call at 1:30."

Mike stood motionless, looking into her blue eyes. Jan stood motionless as well, still smiling.

"I'd really like to see you again sometime," he said, suddenly realizing he was probably violating every rule in the book about how Natural Resource Department rangers are supposed to conduct themselves while on duty.

"I'd like that too," she said. She pulled out her business card and handed it to him.

"I'll call you," he said.

"I hope so", she said, and she turned and walked away.

That had been over a year ago. Now, they were in love. And on at least three occasions, they had talked in general terms about marriage.

About 25 miles off the coast behind Mike's house lay a tiny island called Seaway Island. Sometimes he and Jan ventured there with a picnic basket and spent the day swimming and combing the beach. The island was just far enough offshore to be out of sight of the mainland.

Pirates once frequented Seaway Island. One of them, a seedy eighteenth century swashbuckler named Captain Derrick, was hanged there by the British Navy. Derrick had made a good life for himself for several decades in the late sixteenth century through stealing, robbing and murdering. The British navy chased him down one day as he tried escaping to Seaway. Jan and Mike sometimes found relics in the sand on the island, slugs from ancient pistols and metal belt buckles, violent remains in a now docile paradise.

Mike noticed soon after moving to the area, that when travelling by boat between the island and the mainland, he could see both pieces of land for a brief time. When he reached one, the other was obscured by the horizon. Not that it took an experienced sailor to read a compass; Seaway nonetheless remained isolated and deserted, rarely visited by anyone.

It wasn't until after Mike had been visiting Seaway for over a year that Joe Sanders, one of his Coast Guard friends, told him that the island and all the water around it lay within the confines of the Bermuda Triangle. Mike replied with a chuckle. "You're kidding me, right?"

"No," Joe had replied with a hint of fear. "The Devil's Triangle runs right up to the Florida shoreline this far south. You've probably gone swimming in it and not even been aware of it."

The unexplainable disappearance of the pilot of the *Shangri-La* occurred the first weekend in May. The following Sunday morning a local disk jockey embarked on a fund raising endeavor to generate donations for a local children's hospital. Sponsors pledged to give a certain amount of money for each minute it took for him to make the trip by boat from the mainland to Seaway Island.

On that warm, sunny morning at 9:00, the DJ and his station manager boarded their boat amidst 40 or so curious onlookers at the city pier and prepared to race to Seaway. A welcoming committee had gone to Seaway and set up on the beach to keep the official time for the event. The two parties talked over radios to get everything coordinated, the official starter waved a checkered flag and the stunt was on. The crowd cheered as the boat sped away. Mike had the day off and was eating breakfast and listening to the radio when the event started. Jan came over about that time and joined him. The two of them read the paper and talked about going to the beach as the radio played in the background.

The DJs talked about the pilot, Jim "Machine Gun" Cary and his fabulous boat, the *Shondelle*. The station would play a couple of songs, break for a commercial, then come back and announce Machine Gun's progress.

"That's a nice thing they're doing," Jan said without looking up from the paper.

"Sure is," Mike said. "And a pretty neat way of doing it, too."

At around 9:40, the radio station came out of commercial and the DJ on Seaway Island announced that it would be any minute that the *Shondelle* would pop into view. The average listener may have hardly noticed the slightest hint of concern in his voice but Mike saw a small red flag in his mind.

Jan had just put the dishes in the sink and he was setting the sugar bowl in the cabinet. She put her arms around him and kissed him.

"Didn't those guys leave the mainland at 9:00 sharp?" Mike said.

Jan was puzzled. "Yeah, why?"

"Well, the guy on Seaway just said they haven't even spotted the boat yet. They should be able to at least see him a good ten minutes before he gets there."

"Maybe they had engine trouble or something," she said.

"With a couple of million people listening?" Mike said. "I hope they planned it better than that."

Jan kissed him again. "Calm down worry wart. They probably taped that last message half-an-hour ago."

"Oh, I didn't think of that," he said.

A few songs played, followed by the station I.D. and the start of their 10:00 program.

Mike went straight to the phone and dialed the studio-line number from memory. He figured he'd heard it a thousand times. The line was busy at first so he kept hitting redial. It continued to be busy and the songs kept playing.

"What's wrong?" Jan said.

"Hopefully nothing," he said, putting down the phone. "Wait a minute. I've got the list of all the emergency phone numbers of the local radio stations here somewhere." He started looking through the top drawers of his desk. "Here it is."

Jan stood watching in bewilderment as Mike dialed.

"This is Bill," the answer came over the phone.

"Hi Bill, this is Mike Thompson with the Department of Natural Resources _ _ "

"Mike, thank God," Bill said. "Something's wrong. I'm really worried."

"No word from the *Shondelle?*" Mike said

"No," Bill said. "And I'm getting a bunch of calls I don't want to answer."

"I'll call you back," Mike said and hung up the phone. He looked over at Jan.

"They're missing." He reached for his keys. "Let's go." They rushed to the *Dream* and Mike cranked her up.

Jan untied the boat and gently eased them away from the dock. Mike turned toward the mouth of the harbor and pressed the throttle forward. The nose of the *Dream* jumped up above the water. The loud rumble of the engine roared from just below the water's surface behind the *Dream* and several people here and there on the shore and in boats turned to watch.

Jan quickly buckled her seat belt as Mike stood behind the wheel with the wind roaring through his wavy, black hair.

For several long minutes they cruised at about 50 mph, following the course the DJ had taken, when up ahead the *Shondelle* came into view.

"Look there." Mike pointed ahead to the left and turned straight for it. When they got within a couple of hundred feet, he slowed down and cruised over toward the motionless boat.

"She looks abandoned," Jan said. "I see some smoke rising out of her too."

Mike cut the engine and the *Dream* drifted up alongside the *Shondelle*. "This has an eerie familiar feel to it," he said.

Jan tossed a line over the *Shondelle*'s railing and tied up.

Mike quickly jumped aboard. "She's abandoned," he said.

"They must have been picked up by another boat for some reason," Jan said.

Mike picked up the microphone to put in a distress call to the Coast Guard. It burned his hand with intense cold, almost forcing him to drop it. "Ouch."

"What's wrong?" Jan said.

"This microphone feels like it's been in a freezer." He reached up and felt the console. It was ice cold, in fact, the whole boat was. "Jan, something strange is going on here." He looked over at her and saw fear in her eyes.

"Look over there," she whispered pointing.

Mike turned and looked. A large pocket of greenish colored fog hung over the water about a hundred yards away. It was thick and opaque. They watched for a few seconds it expanded, faded and vanished.

"That was the weirdest looking fog I've ever seen," she said.

Mike still held the microphone in his hand. He placed a call to the Coast Guard and then resumed his search of the vessel. Everything he touched felt like it had been in a deep freeze. A few minutes later a police boat and a small

Coast Guard cutter arrived at the scene. They pulled up just in time to hear the *Shondelle*'s engines crank as Mike turned the key he had found in the ignition.

The *Shondelle* had been found in perfect working condition, but two days of searching for her two passengers turned up nothing, and neither of them showed up for work at the station on Monday morning.

The local media originally treated the incident as a possible kidnapping. Before long, newspaper articles began to label it a "Bermuda Triangle disappearance." Although such an explanation struck Mike as bizarre, the local population seemed to accept it with ease. One characteristic that wasn't factored into all the stories and news reports was the coldness of the boat when Jan and Mike found it. The media people didn't know about it and Mike sure wasn't going to tell them. He had no interest in being part of the wild stories and was already more involved than he wanted to be anyway.

CHAPTER 2

▼

THE VANISHING AT "THE LANDING"

One week later, Mike was out on patrol just south of the Seaway lane when he got an urgent call on the radio. About a dozen boaters had placed frantic calls on cellular telephones to the police all at once from a popular gathering spot about seven miles off shore called "The Landing". This abandoned World War II Navy fueling platform was a haven for pelicans and other birds that the tourists loved to photograph. The Coast Guard was sent to respond. Mike's best friend, Joe Sanders, radioed him from aboard an approaching cutter.

"Mike, how far from The Landing are you?" he said.

"About five minutes if I hurry," Mike said. "What's happened?"

"Two speed boats just vanished off our radar," Joe said. "About one minute later we got a barrage of calls. Apparently there were a number of witnesses."

"I'm on my way," Mike said. He turned the **Dream** to the northeast and hit the throttle.

As he piloted across the waves, Mike made mental notes about the current conditions. It was a clear, late spring Tuesday evening, 6:55 p.m.

When he neared The Landing, Mike spotted several small craft gathered in an area about two hundred yards from the rusting steel platform. He noticed that there were no birds anywhere near it, a rare phenomenon.

"Over here!" he heard several people shout. They were waving at him frantically. He rushed over to them and coasted alongside.

"What happened?" he said, trying to sound calmer than he felt.

There were maybe thirty people in a dozen or so different boats. All thirty of them tried to talk at once.

"Hold it," he said. "One at a time." Mike looked over the crowd and spotted a man that looked about forty. He was wearing a sailor's cap, a neat, tan-colored shirt and was smoking a big brown pipe. He looked to be the best available candidate as spokesperson. "You sir," Mike said pointing at him.

"There were these two speedboats, I guess they were racing because they were going really fast," the man said. "They went past me about two-hundred feet or so away. I watched them pass, and then went back to my fishing. A moment later the sound of their engines suddenly stopped. I turned and looked again and both boats were gone."

"Gone?" Mike said.

"Vanished," the man said, widening his eyes in disbelief. "One second they were there and the next they were gone."

A little boy in the boat put his arms around the man's waist and held tight. "It's okay, Benny," the man told him.

"That's what I saw too," said a heavy-set woman in one of the larger boats. Mike counted five youngsters and another woman moving about the deck of the small yacht.

"I had just gotten drinks for the kids out of the cooler when my little one said: 'Look mama, those men are racing.' We all stopped what we were doing and watched them go by. Like he said, they were really moving. I'd say they were going about sixty."

"You saw them vanish?" Mike said.

"No," she said, "but I heard them. The boats were real loud. Then, all of a sudden they were silent. I looked back and didn't see them."

"I saw them disappear", the little girl next to her said.

Mike looked at the little girl. She appeared to be about five or six years old. "Are you sure they didn't just fade in the distance?" he said to her. "You know, boats going that fast get away quicker than you think."

The little girl shook her head adamantly. "They became invisible," she said.

"Now we know that's impossible," Mike said.

"But they did," the little girl yelled. The force with which she spoke startled Mike.

"The two boats bounced up in the air," the child said. "Then they went into a cloud."

"A cloud?" Mike said.

"It was more a fog bank than a cloud," a young man of about eighteen in an old, pale green outboard said. "I looked the second after the sound stopped and all I saw was the two boats' wakes. They drew a straight line in the water to a point where they suddenly ended. It was almost like they had lifted out of the air at that point and flown away. But I think I saw a small patch of fog in the spot. I'm not sure because it was gone just a few seconds later."

"Point out exactly were that was," Mike said. All thirty people pointed to the same spot about fifty feet away. As they all watched from what seemed to be a safe distance, Mike eased over to the place in the *Dream*. "About right here?"

"That's it," said the man smoking the pipe. "Right there."

Mike looked down into the water and all around. There was no debris and no sign of gasoline on the water's surface. He spotted the approaching cutter in the distance and decided to call in with what he knew. "No wreckage," he said. "No sign of anything at all."

Mike looked over at the gathered crowd. They were watching him like they were expecting some kind of explanation. He didn't have one.

"Did anyone else actually see the boats disappear?" he asked. No one replied.

"Got cold," a little boy in a ski boat said. Mike stared at him.

"Oh yeah," his mother agreed. "For a few seconds there was this blast of really cold air."

That comment gave Mike the chills. Just like the other night, he thought. At that moment the cutter arrived on the scene. Mike thanked everyone for his or her help and then drove the *Dream* over to the Coast Guard cutter, tied a rope to her railing and climbed aboard. He then apprised the seven men aboard of the details.

"We just got a call," Joe said to Mike. "There were a couple of people on Seaway Island waiting for two speed boats that were racing from the mainland. They were trying to do the same thing the radio DJ was trying to do when he disappeared."

"You mean set some kind of speed record?" Mike said.

"Yes, apparently so," Joe said. "Once they were thirty minutes overdue the people on the island called us."

"Three incidents in the same month," Mike said. "This isn't good."

"Just coincidence," Joe said. "We'll put out a bulletin on the two boats. Maybe they'll turn up somewhere in the next few days."

Mike thought a moment. "Well," he said, "I guess we're done here." He said his farewells and went back aboard the *Dream*, untied her and cast off away from the larger vessel.

He sat without starting the engines and watched as the cutter pulled away. For several long minutes he contemplated the mysterious events that were starting to add up, all the while watching as the first of the evening lights appeared one by one in the distant Miami skyline.

"I think I'll swing past Seaway Island before heading for home," he said to himself. He turned on the lights and cranked the engines. Ten minutes later he was half-a-mile from the shore of the deserted, dark island. The sun had set and the first stars were beginning to appear in the sky overhead. He cruised slowly parallel to the island. At that moment, a strange sense of not being alone suddenly came over him. Seaway was a beautiful, exotic island during the day but a mysterious and eerie one at night.

Several years earlier, before he met Jan, he had tried to camp out alone on the little island. At about ten o'clock that night a cold wind started swirling and blew out his campfire. Above the sound of the wind through the trees, or perhaps within the sound, he could have sworn he heard human voices. The strange sounds terrified him. He had cooked hot dogs and consumed three or four beers, which might have explained the voices. Telling himself that did little to quell the panic.

Without pausing to take down his tent, he grabbed the sleeping bag and backpack and ran for the *Dream*. He untied it from the palm tree, waded out to it and jumped in. He then roared away from the island as fast as he could.

Once he got close to home the fright passed and he started feeling a little foolish. The next morning when he returned for his tent he found it gone. There was no evidence of his campfire or any other signs that he had been there. He never told anyone about the experience.

Now, as he sat in his boat and looked at the distant, dark island, Mike was glad he had left Seaway that night, even though he doubted there had ever really been any danger. Then again, perhaps his instinct pulled him out right before the forces of the Bermuda Triangle came ashore after him. He had never allowed himself to believe such forces actually existed, but now was starting to come to grips with the sickening feeling that maybe he had been wrong all along.

At that moment a bright light came from the direction of Seaway Island, startling and momentarily blinding him. He imagined that, once his head turned and his eyes focused, he would see a pirate ship, brightly lit, just sailing out of the lagoon on Seaway Island. On deck there would be a crew of skeletons in pirate clothing, rushing to their battle stations. They would come after him, overtake him, and drag him back with them to their watery graves some-where in the Bermuda Triangle. When his neck finally made the endless turn and his tired eyes focused, there was no pirate ship, only the full moon, now out from behind cloud cover, cutting through the night and making a narrow white path across the sea to the *Dream*.

"Oh, it's only the moon," he said, breathing a small sigh of relief. As he watched it slowly drift above the distant clouds he became aware of the same strange sound he had heard that night years ago on the island. His heart skipped a beat. The sound was barely audible over the steady hum of the *Dream*'s engines, but it was definitely there.

There's that sound again, he thought. Panic began to set in as he heard the faint human voices, speaking in unison, gradually growing louder.

"Help us, Mike," the voices said. "Help us please."

He looked at the console and realized with horror that the *Dream*'s lights had gone out. In the moonlight he could see the compass spinning around. With a trembling hand he reached for the ignition switch to cut the engines.

No, screamed a voice in his head. What if it won't restart?

I have to know if that sound is coming from the boat's engines or somewhere else, he thought.

His hand reached the choke button and pushed. Nothing happened. The voices got louder. "Help us Mike," he heard them chant. "Help us please!"

His panic level increased another notch. He pushed the choke button again and again. Suddenly the engines died. And the chanting voices, if they had really been there in the first place, went silent with them.

A moment later a large cloud obscured the moon. The only sound to be heard was the gentle lapping of the water against the hull. Mike reached for the light switch. It was in the 'on' position, yet the lights were off. He turned the switch off, waited five long seconds, and then turned the switch back on. The *Dream* lit up like normal.

"Thank you Jesus," he said, glancing heavenward. The compass was now still and indicated the boat was pointed due south. Seaway was still straight to port. Good, he thought. The compass on the boat and the one in my head agree. He turned the ignition and it cranked perfectly. Within seconds he was speeding for home at 65 mph.

He awakened the next morning feeling a little foolish for letting himself get frightened by his own imagination. He couldn't explain the disappearances, yet he knew the legend of the Bermuda Triangle was nothing more than a legend. Somewhere there was a logical explanation for everything. Even so, he decided not to tell anyone about his experience.

The next day Joe and Mike sat on the dock next to Mike's boathouse fishing. "Did you see the article in the paper this morning?" Joe said.

Mike cast out his line. "What article?" He kept his eyes on the little float some forty feet out from the dock.

"One of those supermarket newspapers is offering a thousand bucks to the first boater to do the Seaway run from the mainland in less than thirty minutes."

Mike glared at him. "You're not serious."

"As a heart attack," Joe said.

"Oh great," Mike said, not noticing that he had a bite. "Don't they realize that every fool with a fast boat is going to come out of the woodwork to try to get the money?"

"I think that's the whole idea," Joe said.

They fished quietly for several minutes. The idea of beer-guzzling boat owners turning the Seaway lane into some kind of maritime Indianapolis Speedway turned Mike's stomach. There could be collisions, fighting over the prize money, and even a fatality or two. The last thing the Department of Natural Resources needed right now was more media hype.

"When does this so-called contest start?" Mike said.

"According to the paper, it's Saturday," Joe said. "They're going to have their reporters stationed at the city pier and on Seaway starting at nine in the morning. I guess any fool that wants to can pull up to the pier, sign a waiver, log in their start time and take off for fame and fortune without ever getting out of the boat."

"That's really crummy." Mike pulled in a small fish. He unhooked it and tossed it back in the water.

They fished a few minutes longer until Jan drove up with Joe's girlfriend, Cathy, in the car. Soon, the four of them were on the *Dream* headed for a remote beach for a Sunday afternoon picnic. Mike managed to forget about the disappearances for a while.

That Sunday passed without any boating incidents of any kind. It was a peaceful day. That night Mike lay awake in bed thinking about the upcoming Saturday. It could be a nightmare if this tabloid reward money attracted the attention he feared it would. He chuckled as he thought how much it would frustrate those so-called journalists if someone accomplished the feat before their little contest even started.

One Summer Dream is one fast boat, he thought. It could do the trick easily and might even save a few lives in the process.

He knew his boss would never tell him to do it but Mike couldn't see him standing in the way either. The thought had uneasiness to it, mixed with a bit of excitement, the kind of excitement Mike found hard to resist. I'll do it, he thought.

The next morning he told Joe of his plans and Joe told several of the Coast Guard sailors on his vessel. Most everyone knew Mike, and while there was general concern, most agreed that it would be an effective way to prevent the upcoming Saturday from being a major headache for them all. Mike wouldn't get the thousand dollars, but hopefully, neither would anyone else.

Monday night Mike called Jan to make a date with her for Thursday evening. She wasn't home, so he left a message on the answering machine. They had been dating pretty seriously for some time now, and Mike had become accustomed to leaving her a message stating when he wanted to take her out and being reasonably certain that it was as good as planned. The same held true for her.

After saying that he wanted to go out for dinner Thursday night, he finished the message by mentioning a moonlight cruise on the *Dream* where he could discuss "something of vital importance," referring to his race against time in the Seaway lane the following day. He felt in the back of his mind that he really needed her approval to do something he considered risky, and wanted to talk it over with her first.

An hour later, Jan returned home and played back the message. Mike's voice held a hint of nervousness, something that surprised and intrigued her. After listening to the message twice more, she decided to call Cathy for a second opinion.

"Listen to the message Mike left me," she said excitedly. "Tell me what you think."

Cathy listened and reached the same conclusion. "I think he's talking marriage," she said.

"Do you really think that's what he meant?" Jan said. "He's kind of unpredictable. I don't want to get my hopes up."

"You know he loves you," Cathy said. "And he sure sounded nervous on that message."

"Yes he did," Jan said with a smile.

"I'm really happy for you," Cathy told her.

As the days passed, both Mike and Jan were so busy that they never had a chance to talk in person or by phone. Jan called him back and left a message confirming that she'd be ready when he came by at 7:30. She finished the message with the words: "I'm really looking forward to our boat ride. I love you."

The week passed slowly for Mike. Both the Coast Guard and the Department of Natural Resources were embroiled in the investigations into the disappearances. Several local libraries were consulted for research purposes, and one researcher turned up a startling fact. In 1966, there had been a local TV station owner that disappeared near the Seaway lane and made major headlines. The entrepreneur had just moved from New York and bought a local TV station. Just minutes after closing the deal, he and his wife and their two young sons went to a local marina, rented a yacht and sailed away, never to be heard from again. That disappearance occurred thirty-five years to the day before "Machine Gun" Cary vanished in the same spot.

One of the local TV stations reported that one of the two men that disappeared out by The Landing had a brother that lived along the coast of Lake Superior in Wisconsin. Five years earlier, he and six other fishermen vanished on the lake during a freak June snowstorm. The older brother's disappearance occurred exactly five years to the day before the younger brother's. Mike felt a cold chill run up his back when he read that.

These facts and many others were printed in the newspapers and continued on a daily basis. As the days passed, the stories got further and further from the front page, but something on the Bermuda Triangle appeared somewhere in print every day. Reporters hounded police and Coast Guard officials constantly for new information.

Some reporter with the Miami Herald was doing his homework. He discovered that the *Shangri-La* was built by McKenna Harbor Craft, Inc., a small boat manufacturing company that was a subsidiary of the company that built the *Cyclops*, perhaps the most famous ship ever to vanish in the Bermuda Triangle. The coincidences were beginning to pile up. Consequently, Mike's fears were growing as well.

On Thursday afternoon Mike hinted to Joe that he wouldn't mind not making the journey the next day. Joe reminded him that it was purely his decision and nobody would think any less of him if he changed his mind. Mike knew that wasn't entirely true. Everyone involved in the investigation was aware of Mike's plan and seemed to like the idea. Several of his coworkers were planning their Friday schedules around assisting him. They hated the tabloid newspapers as much as he did and were dreading Saturday too.

Mike soon began to feel that he was in over his head. His trip was less than 24 hours away and there appeared to be no backing out now. The only way he could save face and not go would be if Jan talked him out of it. He wasn't sure he wanted to cancel his trip, but if Jan really balked at it he would. He'd probably sleep better afterwards too.

That evening Jan opened the door with a big smile. "Hi," she said putting her arms around him.

"Hi Sweetie." He kissed her. After the kiss she held him tight a few moments longer. He felt safe in her arms. It was moments like this that he realized how much he really loved her.

After dinner, they drove back to Mike's place and boarded the *Dream*. The Seaway lane was just a little south of the inlet leading out of the cove that formed his backyard. Mike piloted away from the dock and through the inlet to the open sea.

Jan sat beside him, her long blonde hair blowing in the wind. Once they got out of the inlet, Mike steered north away from the Seaway lane. They rode a couple of miles out and Mike cut the engines. The *Dream* drifted to a halt under the bright evening stars. Jan walked to the back of the boat and sat on the big seat. A moment later he sat down beside her. He noticed that she was unusually quiet, and without speaking put his arms around her and kissed her.

"Jan," he said. "There's something that's been weighing heavy on me all week." He paused, as she remained silent.

"What would you say to my trying to make the Seaway run in less than 30 minutes tomorrow?"

Jan stared at him. "What?"

"Well," he said. "Somebody needs to do it before they hold that rat race on Saturday, and I seem to be the most qualified. I didn't want to commit to it, though, without talking to you first."

"Is that what you were referring to when you said there was something important you wanted to ask me?" she said. She rolled her eyes and looked up at the sky.

"Well, yeah," he said. "I really value your opinion."

"I thought we were coming out here to talk about something important," she said. "You could have asked me about all this in the living room."

"I guess I wanted to come out here to get a feel of the boat in deep water again before I even told you what I was thinking," Mike said. "I'm still not sure what I should do."

"Well, I sure don't know what to tell you," Jan said. "You're the one who's out in these waters everyday. And you're certainly the only one who knows what's going on inside your head."

"So you think I should just go ahead and do it?" he asked.

"Sure," she said. "Why not? I don't believe in the Bermuda Triangle anymore than you do."

Mike looked around. "You're right," he said.

"Can we head back in now?" she said. "It's getting chilly out here."

"Sure," he said. He started to get up but quickly sat back down and kissed her.

"What was that for?" she said.

"Do I have to have a reason every time I kiss you?" He returned to the pilot's cockpit and started the engine.

By the time they got off the boat and Mike had closed the door of the boathouse, he realized that he didn't feel any better about the next day than he had when they first got into the boat, in fact, he felt worse. The fears that had been circling in the back of his mind for the last couple of days had finally eroded his confidence. He was starting to get scared.

Jan's indifference to the whole thing didn't help. He knew she loved him but maybe she just didn't understand what he was going through at the moment. After taking her home and kissing her goodnight, he drove around for a while listening to Machine Gun Cary's old station. When he finally crawled in bed he felt incredibly alone. He awoke several times during the night from bad dreams, the details of which he couldn't recall afterwards.

Friday morning dawned clear and hot. Mike was standing ankle-deep in the water, staring out to the place where the sea and sky met when Joe walked up behind him.

"Good morning," Joe said.

Mike turned around and looked at him.

Joe's eyes grew wide upon seeing Mike's face. "You don't want to do this do you?" he said.

"Not especially," Mike said. "But if not me, who? If not now, when?"

"You're not obligated you know," Joe said.

"Yes, I am." Mike smiled slightly. "It'll be okay." He waded over to the *Dream* and climbed aboard. "I don't think you know Phil Stewart," Mike said. "He's listening on channel 26."

Joe spotted Mike's radio sitting on the dock. He walked over and picked it up.

Mike looked at his watch. "In thirty seconds it will be precisely 9:00 am. Tell Phil I'll be there in thirty minutes." Mike started the mighty engines, belted himself in tightly, and slowly steered the *Dream* out toward the middle of the inlet. Pointing toward the open sea he turned around for one last look.

"Ready?" Joe said.

Mike nodded. Joe got Phil on the radio. "Tell Mike I'll be here waiting," he said.

"Ten-four," Joe said. He looked over at Mike. "Good luck."

"Thanks," Mike said. He hit the throttle and the *Dream* roared out of the harbor. As Joe stood on the dock and watched, Mike and the *Dream* exited the waterway and poured on the speed. Moments later, the loud roar of the engines faded into the distance.

CHAPTER 3

▼

THE VORTEX

Mike pushed the throttle forward as far as it would go and the *Dream* sliced through the calm water toward the open ocean ahead. As the minutes passed, he began to relax. Soon, it began to feel like any other day, out on patrol. His mind began to put the thoughts that had kept him awake most of night into perspective. There is no such thing as the Bermuda Triangle, he thought. And the fact that Jan didn't seem concerned about his being out doing this was a good thing and not a bad one.

A few minutes later, the tops of the trees on Seaway Island came into view. The sight relaxed him even more. The *Dream* was cruising at eighty. Mike glanced at his watch. His time was good; he'd make it in less than thirty minutes with plenty of time to spare. He smiled. This was going to be a breeze.

As Seaway Island grew closer, Mike felt more and more exhilarated. He was about to render moot a silly superstition and score a victory over the tabloid newspapers that had hounded him and his fellow law enforcement comrades for the last several weeks. He couldn't believe it was this easy.

His eyes remained fixed on his destination. Seaway's beach would soon come into view. Just about five more minutes, he thought. The enjoyment was greater than he had anticipated. He had always gotten a natural high from fast travel in a boat, but this particular experience was euphoric.

As he stared ahead, the blurry water seemed to sparkle and twinkle, almost like a roadway of asphalt, dotted with small pieces of broken glass that reflected the sunlight in a multitude of color. Mike didn't notice anything out of the ordinary as the air temperature began to drop. Within seconds he was covered with goose bumps.

A thick, dark cloud suddenly moved in front of the sun and the surface of the water all around him began to turn bright white. The *Dream* increased its speed and began to bounce up and down on the water's choppy surface. "What's going on?" Mike muttered as he looked down at the speedometer. The boat was approaching one hundred, faster than it could possibly go.

Mike looked ahead. Seaway Island was nowhere to be seen. "Oh no," he said, realizing for the first time that something was seriously wrong. Then he looked around him. Walls of white water, sparkling with flashes of red, neon blue and purple color, were forming a tunnel on either side of the boat.

At that moment, the *Dream* began bouncing up and down, moderately at first, then violently. Within seconds it was bucking like a wild bronco. The speed dropped quickly as the bow slammed into walls of rough water. Mike was yanked forward, almost tearing him in half. The *Dream's* engines burst forward, straight into another wall of water. Mike reached for the throttle and pulled it all the way back in an attempt to stop. An instant later she plowed into another large wave, throwing him forward and tearing the seatbelt out of its mounting. Mike felt the steering wheel embed itself into his chest, knocking the wind out of him.

The rear of the boat began veering from side to side, fish-tailing as if the rudder had come off. Mike was desperately trying to hold on now, hands flailing for anything he could grab onto as he was being thrown about the boat's interior. Despite the fact that the throttle was in neutral, the engines were roaring at full speed. The *Dream* was completely out of control.

"What the hell is going on?" Mike screamed.

A cold rain began pounding his face as he realized with horror that his boat was now his enemy. The *Dream* bounced hard off the water and threw him back into the cockpit for a moment. He took the opportunity to reach over and hit the choke button to kill the engine. A moment after he hit it the *Dream* bucked upward and threw him several feet into the air. "No," he screamed as he tumbled skyward. His last view of the *Dream* was of it spinning like a top somewhere below him.

The next sound Mike heard was a loud blast. An instant later he hit the water and skipped like a rock several times across the surface before slamming into a large wave. The strong current pulled him under and he quickly sank into the rough water. Desperately, he reached upward with his hands, praying that they would find the surface. In sheer panic he flailed his hands as his lungs began screaming for air. At last, he made it and gasped for breath.

As he struggled to keep his face above the rough water, he noticed it was now bitterly cold. Each time he exhaled he billowed out in a white cloud. The sea was angry and violent, and large raindrops were pounding the top of his head. The sky flashed with lightning that made the surface of the water appear bright white for an instant. A loud crash of thunder that seemed to come from directly overhead almost burst his eardrums.

The waves were tremendous and the undertow powerful. He quickly realized his strength would last about two minutes before he'd tire and drown. For the first time in his life he felt the overwhelming fear that non-swimmers must feel upon falling out of a boat. He had always been an excellent swimmer. But now, he felt like a beginner.

In sheer desperation, he looked around for the **Dream** or some floating debris, anything he could use to keep himself afloat. There was no sign of his boat, which a voice in the back of his mind was telling him had exploded, creating the loud blast he heard just before hitting the water. He hoped the sound had been thunder, but he couldn't see his boat anywhere.

On the verge of exhaustion, Mike spotted a large wooden box of some kind floating about twenty feet away.

If I can just reach that thing I might have a chance, he thought. He started making his way toward it, but saw that it was drifting away from him faster than he was swimming. It seemed that for every stroke he made toward it, it drifted two strokes further away. He tried swimming faster, calling upon strength he didn't have, and fighting the mighty waves as they relentlessly pounded him in the face.

He got within several feet of the floating object and dove toward it. It eluded his outreaching hand. He swam a couple more strokes and reached again. A big wave moved it at the last second and all he managed to do was feel its wet slimy surface as his hand slipped away. He saw another big wave approaching and knew he'd better beat this one to it or he'd drown. Using the last bit of strength he could muster he dove for it and managed to grab hold. An instant later the wave got it and tried to wrench it from his grip. He managed not to let go.

He pulled the large wooden object underneath him and found that he could lie on it. It was made of several wooden planks nailed together and was covered by slimy, green algae. Gripping tightly with both hands, he rested and caught his breath as the violent surf tried to pull him into its deadly depths.

The rain pounded on his back and the massive waves threw salty water into his face. Overhead, a bright flash of lightning bolted across the dark sky followed almost immediately by a deafening crack of thunder. I must be right under the storm, he thought. When the plank crested a wave he had a brief moment to look all around. All he saw was the rough ocean and pounding rain. The water was a dark greenish blue, which indicated great depth. He couldn't help thinking about sharks.

Breathing heavily, he held on to the platform, feeling the ocean swelling underneath him. For the next two hours he just lay still, not knowing what to expect next. Later, the rain let up and the sea calmed a bit. Mike drifted into and out of a coma-like daze for the next several hours. Sometime later he came around to see some late afternoon sunshine. He looked ahead and saw the outline of land through the thick mist.

"The mainland at last," he exclaimed. Slowly, he started paddling toward the shore, realizing how sore his muscles were. The paddling seemed to go on forever.

Finally he got close enough to the shore that he felt he could swim for it. He abandoned the platform and started dog paddling. As he neared the shore he tried touching the bottom with his feet and couldn't. He struggled to get closer and was finally getting a little help from the waves. It wasn't until he was less than twenty feet from shore that his feet touched sand below him. "Thank you, God." His voice was cracked and weak. The elements were taking their toll. He staggered out of the water and up toward the beach.

Once he was well away from the pounding surf, he fell to his knees and sprawled out on the sand, still feeling the motion of the sea. His head was pounding and he felt very dizzy. Nausea overtook him and he realized that for the first time in his life he was seasick. He hoped he was far enough up the beach that the tide wouldn't reach him if it came in. Placing his head on his arms he began to drift off toward unconsciousness. "My boat," he moaned. "What happened to my boat?" He took a deep breath and drifted into a dreamless, deep sleep.

Sometime later he was awakened by intense thirst. His body was ordering him to get up and go in search of fresh water.

Night was falling and he would soon find himself in total darkness. "Water," he muttered. "I've got to find water."

He staggered to his feet and began trudging toward the thick jungle ahead. There ought to be a road close by, he thought, knowing that most of the south Florida coastline has condos or houses near it. He'd go up to the first building he saw and drink from the garden hose. This was no time to be civilized. The area looked unusually deserted. He continued to stagger along, into the jungle and its darkness under the dense trees.

Mike saw no buildings in the distance and no roads or even paths in the jungle. "Something's wrong here," he said. "This has to be the mainland. It can't be Seaway because the land is too big." The vegetation resembled Seaway but he knew this wasn't the familiar island.

Suddenly he heard the sound of running water and followed his ears to a small stream. He ran to it and hit the ground. Taking a handful of water, he quickly determined that it was not salty. He then cupped his hands and drank. He swallowed handful after handful of the wonderful tasting water. Then, after his immense thirst was satisfied, he washed the salt from his face.

With fresh water in his system, Mike felt renewed. He stood, looked around, and listened to the sounds of the jungle. Birds, insects and tree frogs could be heard in all directions. However, there was no sound that would indicate human inhabitance. "Where the hell am I," he said.

Mike stepped out of the jungle onto the edge of the beach and began walking. For the next fifteen minutes, he walked along looking for a road, a house, a store, any sign of civilization. There were none.

Darkness had fallen completely now and Mike began to wish he had stayed by the stream. He scanned the dark beach ahead and a faint light caught his eye. He headed for it, hoping it was a street lamp or some other sign of civilization. It soon became evident that it was a campfire. When he got close, he spotted a path into the jungle and followed it toward the fire. Upon reaching it, he saw a man standing beside it, piling on firewood.

"Hello," Mike called out.

The man whirled around and looked into his direction. "Evan? Is that you?"

"No," Mike replied. "The name's Mike."

"Mike," the man said. He watched Mike approach. "Friend or foe?"

"Friend I hope," he replied. Mike stepped into the firelight so the man could see he was unarmed and not dangerous.

"Oh, I thought you might be somebody else," the man said. "But you're too muscular and about thirty years too young. Plus, that would be too good to be true I guess."

"Sorry to disappoint," Mike said.

"The name's Roscoe," the man said, extending his hand. "Roscoe Mullins."

"Mike Thompson," Mike said. He shook Roscoe's hand.

"You're wet," Roscoe said, noticing that Mike's dark hair was matted against his head. "Stand over by the fire."

"Thank you." Mike stepped closer. The evening chill had started getting to him and the warmth felt wonderful.

"Do you have a boat?" Roscoe said.

"I did until a few hours ago," Mike said. "I got caught in some rough seas and was thrown clear. When I surfaced I didn't see my boat anywhere. Luckily, I spotted an old wooden pallet floating nearby and grabbed hold of it. It's a miracle I didn't drown."

"That is a miracle," Roscoe said. "You're the first live one I've seen come out of that ocean in a long time." He sat down on a wooden crate. "Have a seat."

Mike looked around for a chair of some kind but didn't see one.

"Try that steel box over there," Roscoe said pointing.

Mike walked several steps to what appeared to be a pile of discarded ship junk and spotted the dented, rusty box to which Roscoe was referring. He dragged it close to the fire. Once seated, he was able to get a good look at his host.

Roscoe looked to be around sixty-years-old. Piercing blue eyes protruded from a wrinkled face that looked worn from many years of exposure to sun and wind. His disheveled hair was long and gray, and his clothes tattered and drab. Both knees in his faded brown pants had holes in them. He reminded Mike of a homeless street person, in need of a shower and a hot bowl of soup.

"I can't stay," Mike said.

Roscoe looked up from the fire with a surprised expression.

"What I really need is to use your phone."

Roscoe stared at him a moment before smiling slightly. "I wish I had a phone you could use," he said.

That was a dumb thing to say, Mike thought. He could plainly see that this man was homeless. "I can find a pay phone. What part of Florida is this? I must have drifted a long way to have gotten this far from Miami."

"I'm afraid you're not in Florida," Roscoe said. "But you're right about having drifted a long way.

Mike stood. "I really need to get going."

"I'm afraid you're not going anywhere," Roscoe said. "Not without a boat."

Mike's stomach growled, reminding him that he hadn't eaten since breakfast. Hunger pains always left him irritable. "Look, uh."

"Roscoe," he reminded him.

"Roscoe," Mike said. "Just point me toward the nearest civilization and I'll be on my way."

"About a thousand miles," Roscoe said. "You pick the direction."

"Look," Mike said. "I don't want to sound rude. I just want to know where the hell I am."

"You want to know where the hell you are?" Roscoe said. "Then I'll tell you. You're vanished. Vanished in the Bermuda Triangle."

Mike stared at him and felt his knees weaken. He slowly sank back into a sitting position on the steel box. "What are you talking about?"

"Certainly you've heard of the Bermuda Triangle," Roscoe said. "Well, you're right smack in the middle of it. There are no phones, no roads, and no people here. I can't even tell you what day of the week today is. Hell, I don't even know the month or the year."

"Oh no," Mike said. "I've got to get back to Miami. I can't stay here."

"The ocean's right over there," Roscoe said. "Be my guest. I'd head north if I were you."

Mike looked past Roscoe toward the crashing surf. There were no boats or ships to be seen, no flashing lights from jets in the sky. There were no buildings in the distance or cars driving past on a distant roadway. The only light visible came from the campfire in front of him and the stars in the sky overhead.

"How long have you been here?" Mike said.

Roscoe stared into the fire. "Longer than I care to remember. I'd say eight years, maybe as many as ten. I really don't know."

Mike's eyes grew wide. "You mean we're marooned here?"

"I'm afraid so."

"But that's not possible," Mike said. "I never got more than a few miles from shore."

Roscoe nodded. "That doesn't matter," he said.

Mike's heart was pounding. "Marooned," he repeated.

"Yep," Roscoe said. "Sorry to have to tell you that."

"How large is this island?" Mike said.

"Huge," Roscoe said. "So big that I've never explored most of it. There's plenty of food and water but there's no way home. You might as well get comfortable because you may be here the rest of your life."

"I— I can't believe it," Mike said softly. He could do no more than stare at the ground beneath him. "I can't believe this has happened to me."

"Well, look at it this way," Roscoe said. "At least you got out of the sea with your life. Over the years I've found dozens of bodies on the beaches after storms like the one today. I suppose those people would feel very fortunate to have come out in as good a shape as you have."

"Are you trying to tell me I should feel lucky?" Mike said. "Because that's the last thing I feel right now."

"You're very, very lucky. Are you hurt? Do you have any broken bones?"

Mike took a moment to assess himself. Once he got a drink of water he found himself tired and hungry, but otherwise unscathed.

"No, I'm fine."

"Then you should thank your lucky stars," Roscoe said. "I have no medical supplies of any kind. If you were hurt you'd just have to suffer with your injuries from now on. You have your life and health. Trust me, you're the luckiest man I've seen in a long, long time."

Mike suddenly thought of Jan and realized he wouldn't be seeing her tonight after all. In fact, they wouldn't be together again any time soon. Maybe never! The thought devastated him. "This can't be happening."

"No reason to keep hanging around here," Roscoe said. "It looks like Evan's not coming. Let's go to my house and get some dinner cooking."

"You have a house?" Mike said.

"Not exactly. But you'll have much better accommodations than I had my first night on the island." Roscoe picked up a burning stick and led the way through the jungle. Mike followed in a daze.

After walking about a quarter-mile, they emerged into a clearing and Mike looked up to see an extraordinary tree house built into several large trees. Roscoe walked over to a campfire in the middle of the clearing and stirred the embers. He added a few pieces of wood and the fire perked up. He then dragged an old, rusty deck chair up to the fire and offered Mike a seat.

"We'll probably find your boat in pieces on the beach in the next couple of days," Roscoe said. "That's the usual scenario."

Mike cringed when he thought of the *Dream* destroyed. What bothered him even more was that he had no way to contact Jan.

"You hungry?" Roscoe said.

"Starving," Mike said.

Roscoe pulled some cleaned fish out of a bucket of water and ran a stick through them lengthwise. He had taken two Y-shaped tree branches and put them into the sand on either side of the fire. The stick with the fish on it fit neatly into the branches and held the fish above the flames. Within a few minutes they were enjoying dinner.

Mike found Roscoe to be very interested in conversation. He could tell it had been a long time since the old man had had any company. Roscoe seemed to be sensitive to his feelings and consoled him accordingly. Arriving here, especially the way he had, left Mike in a state of shock. Roscoe seemed to realize that and was giving him time to deal with it.

"Where's your friend?" Mike said.

"Who?" Roscoe placed more fish on the stick and put them on to cook.

"The guy you were waiting for when I came up. What was his name, Evan."

"Oh, Evan," Roscoe said. "He's a fellow that was here up until a few months ago. He built a sailboat and set out for the mainland. Said he'd be back for me as soon as he could. I don't really expect him to make it though. I don't even think he's still alive. But it's all I've got to hope for." He turned the fish to keep them cooking evenly. "When I first heard your voice I thought it was him. He's the one I built the signal fire for. I do that right after every storm"

"Sorry," Mike said. "I guess I'm not the only one who got a big disappointment tonight."

"Don't worry about it," Roscoe said. "There's always next time."

"Why didn't you go with him?" Mike said.

"I really didn't think he'd survive," Roscoe said. "Besides, I had to stay here—."

"Why?"

"Oh, I was just afraid we'd both end up dead," Roscoe finished. "I keep hoping a plane will fly over or a yacht will sail by. That's the only safe way to try leaving. The currents are treacherous out there and that water is deep. A hand-made boat just isn't going to cut it."

"Are there any other people on this island?" Mike said.

"No," Roscoe said. "Not at the moment anyway."

"You mean there used to be others besides Evan?"

"Oh sure. "People just like you that got stranded here by accident. They all had stories to tell, and they all sounded just like yours. They would go out for a boat ride and get caught by the Triangle. Some of them were travelling way out in the Atlantic and some were only a stone's throw from shore. It seems to make no difference; the Triangle can get you anywhere and usually with little or no warning. There would be the lightning flashes in a clear sky or the feeling of going through a tunnel of water. I've heard of people saying they were pulled by the sky right out of the boat. Only the lucky ones wind up here."

"Where are these people now?" Mike said.

Roscoe looked at Mike a moment. "Dead."

"All of them?"

"Yes, drowned by the surf or killed by the elements. Every time someone makes a raft and leaves the island

I find their remains on the beach within a few days. The ocean has no mercy at all. That's why I haven't tried escaping."

"But you think Evan might have made it?" Mike said.

"I suppose it's possible. He was smarter than most of the others. He had a shipbuilding background and took months preparing. He's the only one in all the years that I didn't find dead on the beach within a few days. I know it's not likely that he made it but I just have to keep hoping he did. Hope is about all I have left."

"All the others turned up dead on the beach?" Mike said. "That's pretty disheartening."

"Just a few weeks ago," Roscoe said. "There were these three guys that showed up one morning on the beach. I tried to get to know them but they were too intent on leaving. They spent three days building a flimsy raft and set out. I tried to warn them but they wouldn't listen to me. They kept to themselves the whole time they were here. I think they thought I was crazy or something. One of them at least came to tell me they were leaving the morning they left. I found two of them dead— worse than dead the next day on the beach. Don't know what became of the other one. I don't really care. They were stupid and thought they knew everything. They're fish food now."

Mike shuddered. "How did you get here?"

"I was on a day trip with my wife and two boys about ten years ago," Roscoe said. "A terrible storm came out of nowhere. We were tossed about for hours. I had no control whatsoever. It was all we could do to hold on for dear life. Finally, we got thrown ashore into a grove of trees on this island. I got thrown clear but my wife and kids were killed. I've been here, alone most of the time, ever since."

Mike stared at Roscoe. "That's horrible."

"More horrible than you can imagine," Roscoe said. There were tears in his eyes. "So you see, you're luckier than you thought."

Mike stared into Roscoe's worn face and pictured himself in the same place a decade from now. "I can't stay here," he said. "I've got a life and a woman who loves me back in Miami."

"I suggest you take your time and prepare well", Roscoe said, removing the cooked fish from the spit over the fire. "I don't know exactly how to say this but the rules are somehow different here. This isn't the same ocean that laps the shores of sunny Florida on a nice calm afternoon. You'll have to be smart to get away from here alive. Smart, patient and extremely lucky."

They finished off the fish in silence. "I'm glad I caught a few extra," Roscoe said. "They were really biting after the storm ended this afternoon. I guess they were as hungry as you were."

Mike finished the last bite and tossed the bones into the fire. "Dinner was great, Roscoe. Thanks."

"Want to see the tree house?"

"Sure," Mike said.

Roscoe picked up a homemade torch and led the way up some steps he had nailed into a tree. He stepped onto a platform that formed a small deck about fifteen feet above the ground and placed the torch into a slot on the railing.

"You waited until the right time to come," Roscoe said. "I just finished building my new bed last week, but my old one is still perfectly good. It's over there in the guest house."

Mike looked to his right and saw a small but elaborate hut with a cone-shaped roof between two large tree trunks. "Very impressive," he said. He walked over to the small hut. Inside was a single-sized bed covered with a quilt, sheets and pillow.

"Where'd you get all the furnishings?" he said.

Roscoe had gone into the larger cabin at the other end of the deck. "Salvaged it from the boat."

Mike walked back across the deck. It was some six feet wide and maybe eight feet across, and connected the two structures at each of its ends. The entire complex appeared to be in about six or seven trees. Roscoe lit another torch inside his living quarters. Mike stepped inside the doorway and saw that it was about the size of an average living room. To the left was a small closet. Inside, he saw pots and pans on the top shelf. On the next shelf were plates, dishes, cups and a box of silverware. The lowest shelf held a wooden box of tools. Inside were hammers, saws, a crowbar, paintbrushes, and screwdrivers. Next to that, Mike saw a toolbox full of hand tools as well as a jar of screws and nails.

Across the room were a bed, a rocking chair and a small table. Built into the wall was a long shelf containing a couple of books, seashells and other decorations. All things considered, it was quite luxurious.

"You salvaged everything from your boat?" Mike said. "Mine and many others," Roscoe said. "Made everything else. I think it's the most luxurious place this side of the Eye of the Needle."

"The Eye of the needle?" Mike took a seat in the rocker.

"The opening to the Bermuda Triangle. Everybody that ends up here goes through it. I think we're in a different dimension of some kind here. Anyway, I've always referred to it as the Eye of the Needle."

"Yes," Mike said. "I guess that's as good a description as any to what happened to me today." He looked over at a wooden shelf to his right and picked up a worn black and white photo of a young couple and two small boys.

"You haven't been through hell until you've had to bury your wife and children," Roscoe said. He crawled into bed. "If I can survive that I can survive anything."

Mike set the photo back where he found it. "Why do you live in the trees?"

"There are all kinds of creatures lurking on the ground," Roscoe said. "It took months to build this tree house. I've lived above ground ever since." He watched as Mike tried to get comfortable in the crooked, homemade rocking chair. "I know you aren't any happier being stuck here than I am," he said. "But it is nice to have some company again."

Mike looked over at him and tried to smile. He couldn't help but wonder what Jan was doing at that moment. The thought brought tears to his eyes.

"Hey who knows," Mike said. "Maybe I can get both of us off this island."

"I like pleasant thoughts to dream about," Roscoe said.

Mike looked up at the top shelf of the bookcase. There were a few seashells and a starfish on it, but one object stood out from all the others. "What's this?" he said. In the middle of the shelf was a gold crown. It was studded with jewels and was incredibly intricate. The crown immediately made him think of hidden treasure.

"Hey Roscoe," he said. He turned to see that Roscoe had fallen asleep. "Never mind. It can wait until tomorrow." He walked over to the other structure and plopped down on the bed. It was stiff and far from cozy but felt wonderful. He took off his damp clothes and shoes and sprawled out on the bed.

As Mike lay in the dark, listening to the insects, his thoughts turned to back home. He missed Jan. He started drifting off to sleep remembering the last time he saw her. She looked so pretty sitting on the *Dream*'s stern. "I love you," she had said.

"I love you too," he said. Tears were forming in his tired eyes. "I'm so scared I'm never going to see you again."

"Hurry back," she said softly.

"I will," he said. "I want you to marry me."

He bolted awake and sat up. "That's it," he said. "That's why things felt so strange on the boat last night. She was expecting me to propose."

Suddenly he felt like the world's biggest jerk. The last time he saw the woman of his dreams, he had blown the opportunity to do something he had planned to do all his life. "She would have said yes, too," he said to himself. "Now she probably thinks I'm not even interested." His heart began to race. "She'll meet somebody else and forget all about me in no time."

He felt a sudden urge to go back to the ocean and find the planks he had ridden to this island. Maybe they would take him back home, back to Jan. The sudden desire to get back to her overwhelmed him, and he had to fight the urge to run to the beach and charge foolishly out into the surf.

"I'll find a way back to you Jan," he whispered. "I'll do it no matter what it takes." He felt lonelier at that moment than he ever had in his life. Over an hour passed before sleep overtook him.

The next morning he awoke and walked outside.

Roscoe was standing at the table cutting oranges into eighths.

"Hi," Mike said.

"Good morning," Roscoe said. "Hungry?"

"Yes."

Roscoe handed him a piece of orange and Mike bit into it as he looked around. He noticed that the roof of the tree house had live grass growing out of it. "Is that a Swiss-made roof?"

"Yep," Roscoe said. "I once visited Switzerland and learned all about them. Perfect for a rainy place like this."

They ate the orange and then started on a bowl of berries Roscoe had gathered. "So you've been here about a decade?" Mike said.

"Roughly," Roscoe said. "Give or take a year or two."

"Was any of your boat salvageable?"

"No," Roscoe said. "It was totaled. Wasn't mine though, I rented it for a day. The wife and kids and I went out for an afternoon joyride to celebrate my purchase of a TV station. Always wondered what happened to the place after I never returned."

Mike thought for a moment. "A Miami TV station?"

"That's right."

"What year was that?" Mike said.

"1956."

"1956!" Mike said. "It's now 2001! Roscoe, you've been here a lot longer than ten years!"

"No I haven't," he said.

"Roscoe, when I left Florida it was June of 2001."

"I was forty-five years old when I disappeared," Roscoe said. "Don't I look to be in my mid-fifties?"

Mike looked at him for a moment. "Well, yes, but I don't know ages, you could be older."

"Maybe, but forty-five years older? Do I look to be in my nineties?"

Mike stared at him. "No, you don't look a day over sixty." Roscoe stood at the table and finished eating the orange.

Mike watched him reach for another one and begin cutting like he had probably done every day for the last ten years. His apparent calmness was totally opposite Mike's level of distress.

"Maybe my days of denial are over," Mike muttered, more to himself than to Roscoe. He knew now that the Bermuda Triangle was a real place where unexplainable things really do occur.

Roscoe produced a coconut he had split open and set it on the table a few feet in front of Mike. "Eat up," he said. "We've got to catch some fish today, but that can wait. First, we need to explore the east beach."

"Expecting someone?" Mike tried to smile.

"Expecting the unexpected," Roscoe said. "You never know what you may see or find. Most wind, rain and storms come from the east or windward side of the island. We're not as leeward here as we could be, but at least we're far enough from the beach that the wind isn't constant. This campsite was carefully selected."

"So the surf really throws a lot of stuff up on the beach?" Mike said.

"Constantly, and it seems that the smaller an object is, the greater the likelihood it'll make it here. Most boats or planes are destroyed coming here, people too. My family seemed to fit right into the averages. About one person in four survives."

Mike was once again harshly reminded of his predicament. "So you think getting off the island is a real long shot?"

"Damn near impossible," Roscoe said. "What I really can't understand is the number of destroyed boats that wash up. Sometimes the bodies don't make it but the boats almost always do."

"You bury the bodies when you find them?" Mike said.

"Yes," Roscoe said. "Only it's rare that the whole body is there though. Usually there are some parts missing."

"Oh."

"Sorry," Roscoe said. "Just thought you should be prepared before we go to the beach. We might find some things that are somewhat unappetizing."

Mike stared into the jungle toward the east beach about a half-mile away and wondered if he could beat the odds again. I could never spend the rest of my life here. If Jan were here maybe, but without her, no way.

Roscoe was watching Mike's face, perhaps reading his thoughts. "You have to take things one day at a time here," he said. "The name of the game is survival. You ready to go to the beach?"

"Yes, let's go." As they began walking, Mike remembered the gold crown he had seen on the shelf the night before. "By the way, was that gold I saw on the shelf in your cabin?"

"Yep," Roscoe said. "There's plenty of it here."

"Gold?" Mike exclaimed. "Maybe I should retire here."

Roscoe chuckled. "You might already have."

"Where'd you get it?" Mike said.

"Pirate treasure," Roscoe said. "There's a hidden cave on this island. I've got claustrophobia real bad so I don't go there except during hurricanes.

"I can't wait to see it," Mike said.

"All in good time," Roscoe said.

Up ahead, Mike could hear the pounding surf and smell the salty air. The trail led through a grove of stunted trees that were held to a limited height by the constant wind. The two men emerged from the thick shady cover and onto the hot sand.

"Looks like a boat over there." Roscoe pointed.

Mike followed his point and saw some kind of wreckage. His heart jumped into his throat as he thought about the *Dream*. They rushed over toward it and Mike quickly determined that it was not his boat. This one was considerably smaller than the *Dream*. It appeared to be relatively new, what there was of it. The engine had been pounded against rocks and the hull was smashed on the starboard side. It looked like it had been dropped from a great height. The only part of the boat that remained intact was the front-most part of the hull where the name was clearly legible.

"*Spear*. Pretty fancy boat," Roscoe said.

"I know this boat," Mike said. "It vanished a few days before I did. I wonder if it's a good sign that we both wound up in the same place."

"I don't know," said Roscoe thoughtfully. "Sometimes I think that there's a big vacuum cleaner in the clouds that sucks up anything going fast and spits it out here in this remote, forgotten place."

"Why here?" Mike wondered aloud. "Maybe…" He broke off, as they suddenly became aware of an approaching engine. "What's that sound?"

"It sounds like a plane!" Roscoe said. He stood a moment, aimlessly looking around in a panicked fashion. "We've got to signal it somehow."

Mike ran out to the middle of the beach and began scanning the sky. Roscoe hurried over beside him.

"There it is." Mike pointed.

It was about a half-mile away and heading right overhead. The two of them began waving their arms wildly and jumping up and down. It was hard for Mike to see the pilot in the cockpit but he thought he could see his head turned his way.

"I think he sees us," Roscoe said excitedly. "I've been waiting for this forever."

The plane flew directly overhead. A moment later it made a wide turn and came back for another pass.

"He does see us," Mike cried out. The pilot flew lower and Mike saw him wave.

All of a sudden Mike froze in his tracks. He stared at the plane, mesmerized and more than just a little frightened. The pilot looked right at him and gave him the thumbs-up. The plane seemed to move in slow motion.

Mike read the letters on the side, studied its tail, and almost counted the blades of the propellers. The two of them watched as it headed off into the distance.

Roscoe was elated. "He saw us," he said. "We're saved."

Mike just looked at him with a disappointed expression.

"What's wrong?" Roscoe said.

"He saw us, but he can't help us," Mike said.

"What are you talking about," Roscoe said. "He saw us. He's going to send back help."

"No," Mike said. "He won't be sending back help."

"Of course he will," Roscoe said. "That was a Navy plane. The pilot could see that we're stranded. Help should be along in a day or two."

Mike stood staring into Roscoe's blue eyes. He looked so much younger when he was smiling. He hated to burst the bubble.

"I don't know how to tell you this," he said, "but that plane is probably just as lost as we are."

Roscoe turned to him and the smile quickly faded. "What are you talking about?"

"Roscoe," Mike said. "That plane is from a different time. The U.S. Navy hasn't flown propeller planes like that one in over forty years. I wouldn't bet much on that pilot's chances of even getting home."

"But that plane looked brand-new," Roscoe said.

"Oh, the plane was new," Mike said. But that model went out of style long ago. Who knows, they may have actually sent out a rescue party to look for us. But that search would have taken place before I was even born."

CHAPTER 4

▼

THE PIRATE TREASURE

During the next few weeks, Roscoe continued to instruct Mike on the many survival techniques he had mastered over the past several years. With the exception of coconuts and nuts, virtually all food had to be gathered and eaten the same day. A couple of hours of each day had to be spent gathering fruit and catching fish, crabs and shrimp. Roscoe liked to eat, and Mike found that his knowledge of food, combined with the bounty of the island's natural produce, meant they rarely went hungry.

The gathering of food and the other daily activities helped Mike come to grips with his predicament. The frustration of being marooned and the inability to do much about it often left him feeling depressed.

Every time a storm came and went, he and Roscoe would go to the east beach to look for usable boat wreckage. They usually found nothing. Then, at sunset, they would build a signal fire, hoping Evan would come looking for them. Night after night, nothing happened.

As they were eating dinner one night Mike began to wonder aloud some of the things he had been thinking. "I'm scared I'm never going to see Jan again," he said. Roscoe didn't respond. "If there really is something to this time variation, then if I ever get back it may be a different year, or different decade for that matter. Jan could be old or not even born yet. Or worst of all, married to someone else."

"You're starting to sound like a broken record," Roscoe said. "As I keep telling you, you're going to drive yourself crazy thinking stuff like that."

"How can I help but think it?" Mike said. "There's no future here. It's like being in prison. My life is drifting by with each passing day." He put a log into the fire. "Maybe I should start building a catamaran. I could weave some sails out of sea grass."

"Now you're talking crazy," Roscoe said. "You need to stop thinking about Jan and what may or may not be happening back home. "Concentrate on getting home safely first. You can deal with the other issues once you get there."

"But the waiting is killing me," Mike said.

"I know," Roscoe said. "But if you let thoughts of what awaits back home cloud your judgment then the safety issues are going to start taking a back seat. And it's that very state of mind that has gotten all those other people killed over the years that I've been here."

Mike resumed eating at a slow pace. Roscoe was right and he knew it.

"Those other would-be sailors figured that even a poor excuse for a boat was better than no boat at all," Roscoe said. "You're smarter than that. What we need is an operational speedboat. A sail boat won't do the trick."

"But we're never going to get a speed boat," Mike said.

"Maybe not," Roscoe said. "But we have little choice but to wait until either Evan comes back or the parts we need to rebuild the *Spear* wash up on the shore."

"I just can't stand the waiting," Mike said.

"I know," Roscoe said. "But one look at the east beach after a storm provides all the proof anyone would ever need about what you'd face out in that ocean. Just because I'm still here after all these years doesn't mean I've given up hope. We've just got to be patient."

Mike finished eating in silence. It was easy to think that a good opportunity to leave may never happen and the thought terrified him. "There is so much time here," he muttered. "Too much time."

The following morning, the two of them ate a breakfast of bananas and oranges. Then Mike stood up and headed for the east beach. "Be back later."

Days before, they had pulled the wrecked *Spear* into the shade of the jungle and Mike had started repair work. The damaged hull could be fixed but additional material from another similar boat would be needed to repair the many holes in the sides and floor. The search for that other boat led him to the east beach at least once each day, sometimes more.

Roscoe had a large collection of tools he had recovered from the many wrecks, but a boat repair manual wasn't one of them. Getting the boat's hull repaired would be the easy part. Getting an operational engine and the gasoline and oil needed to run it was another story altogether. Mike had to keep reminding himself to take it one step at a time.

Mike's knowledge of boat engines was limited. He knew their hopes rested on finding a boat motor that was still operational. The possibility seemed remote, but his daily trips to the east beach continued nonetheless.

"Any luck?" Roscoe asked him upon his return to the campsite.

"No," Mike said. "I walked a couple of miles along the beach and didn't see anything. The *Spear* still has a long way to go. Until a similar boat washes up with plenty of usable parts we're stuck here." He took a couple of bananas from the basket on the table and sat down for a quick lunch. "I guess I'll have to wait on the next storm."

"It'll happen." Roscoe was holding a small burlap bag of gold coins. Mike watched him hold one up and admire it.

"So where's the cave?" Mike said. He had asked the question a couple of times before in the last two weeks and gotten no response. Roscoe stopped what he was doing and glared at him.

"Hey, I'm not planning to steal it," Mike said. "There's only one thing motivating me to get home and that's a beautiful woman with golden hair and a smile that can light up the world. She's the only treasure I care about."

"Then why all the questions about the cave," Roscoe said.

"Just curious I guess," Mike said.

"It belongs to Evan and me."

Mike didn't reply.

"Why shouldn't it," Roscoe said. "I've spent more of my life on this God-forsaken island than anyone else. I'm the one that fought claustrophobia to get it out of the cave. I found it, I've earned it."

"Then why are you planning to share it with Evan?"

"We found it together," Roscoe said. "He's coming back with a boat and we're leaving with as much as we can carry. Until then, it stays right where it is."

"Fine with me," Mike said. "I don't care about the treasure, I just want to go home." The two of them sat silent a moment as Mike tried to figure out what to say next. He needed to defuse this situation right now or else he might as well go somewhere and start building a shelter of his own.

"We don't have to let this come between us, do we?" he said at last.

Roscoe took a breath and sighed. "Of course not. Besides, we'd do ourselves a major disservice by not teaming up to survive. There are enough obstacles to living here without conflict between us becoming one of them."

"I agree completely," Mike said. He looked overhead and saw a few clouds gathering. "Maybe we've got a little rain coming. I think I'll take advantage of the coolness and go a little further down the beach to look for boat debris."

"I thought I'd do a little fishing", Roscoe replied. "Fresh catch for dinner tonight."

"Sounds good", Mike said. Without another word he stood up and headed for the beach.

The eastern end of the island extended for miles. Mike got out onto the beach and started walking, looking all around the beach and as far as he could see into the water, searching for anything that looked out of place. Before he knew it, an hour had passed. Up ahead he spotted some debris near the high water mark. He rushed to it and found about two dozen pieces of what had once been the hull of a boat. A short distance up the beach from that point lay several large boulders.

Looks like a boat came ashore here during a storm and hit those rocks, he thought. That's when he noticed that some of the pieces that still had paint on them matched the white paint on the *Spear.* "This is where the impact happened," he muttered. "The rest of the *Spear* then drifted down to where we found it."

Mike climbed up to the top of the boulders and stood looking out into the water. Hey, he thought, there's something on the bottom out there. He ran down to the water's edge and waded out to where the water came up to his neck. A short distance further out there was a large red object sitting on the bottom. He took a breath and dove down to find a six-gallon gas tank. The tank was dented but not punctured. It was also very heavy. He began dragging it along the sandy bottom, stopping to surface and breathe before returning to the bottom to drag it some more. Finally he got it into shallow water and picked it up.

Once on shore, he opened it and found it full of gasoline. All of a sudden he began to feel he was making real progress toward repairing and running the *Spear.* He went back to the boulders and stood looking into the water. There didn't appear to be any other debris. He decided to head back to the tree house. The gas tank was heavy and cumbersome. The return journey took about two hours.

When he arrived there, the smell of boiling shrimp overwhelmed him. He was starved. Roscoe had gathered some vegetables and was in the final stages of making a great meal.

"Soup's on," Roscoe said. The two of them sat down at the little table and stuffed themselves full. It was the best meal Mike could ever remember having.

After dinner, darkness fell around them. Soon, the only light was that of the fire and the stars overhead.

Roscoe stood up and went to get a couple of torches. A torch made of tightly wrapped tree bark would burn for an hour or so. He made several at a time and had a few in reserves. Grabbing four of them he returned to the campfire. "Would you like a tour of the cave?" he said.

"You sure?" Mike said.

"Yeah," Roscoe replied, taking a lit torch and starting toward the woods. "I did some thinking while I was fishing. Most of the people that I've seen come and go never cared about getting to know me, or even consider including me in their escape plans. You're different. I think that's worth something. I don't plan to keep all the gold to myself. There's plenty for both of us."

"Thanks," Mike said. The change of heart was very welcome to him. Somehow, he figured Roscoe felt the same way.

After a walk of about ten minutes they neared the cave. Roscoe turned and looked back. "I've never revealed this cave to anyone except Evan."

"How did you discover it?"

"About seven or eight years ago I was chasing a small wild boar. I had a craving for some roasted meat and that boar was going to be my dinner guest. He ran toward this hillside and into a dead end. When he didn't come out I knew there had to be a hiding place somewhere. I just kept searching until I found the opening."

He bent down and removed some tree branches from the cave entrance. Mike watched as he uncovered a hole about three feet high and four feet across.

"It's a bit tight the first few feet," Roscoe said. "But once you get in you can walk upright." He took the torch and paused a moment before crawling inside.

Mike entered right behind him. They crawled on the soft sand for about eight feet and then stood up.

Roscoe handed Mike a torch and lit it from the one he was holding. "Don't let your light go out," he said as Mike's torch sparked up. "It can be a real pain getting out of here in the dark."

"I'll bet," Mike said. He looked around and was surprised by the size of the cave. It was much bigger than he had anticipated. Roscoe took a moment to look around and Mike detected an expression of fear on his face. Mike was excited and ready to move forward. Roscoe led the way down a narrow passage with Mike right on his heels. About twenty feet in, Roscoe started down an incline and Mike noticed that the floor was no longer covered with sand but was solid rock.

"Where's the treasure?" Mike said.

"In a little room over there." Roscoe pointed ahead. They approached the far wall and Roscoe ducked through a narrow opening. Mike followed close behind. Once into the room, Roscoe held the torch high and the whole room lit up.

On the floor of the cave was a huge, ancient wooden box, or at least what was left of one. Filling it and spilling over onto the floor were gold coins, thousands of them. There were plates, saucers and platters, all made of gold.

Mike started running his hands through the horde as Roscoe held the two torches and looked on. There were small idols, cups, bowls and dishes. There were rings, necklaces and earrings. Next to the box were stacks and stacks of gold bars. Mike picked up one of the bars and almost strained his back. It felt like it weighed twenty pounds. The pile of gold bars covered an area the size of a car. Mike was speechless. The rotted wood of the crate looked centuries old. By comparison, the gold glittered like new.

"Not to sound greedy," Mike said. "But is this all of it?" "As far as I know it is," Roscoe said. "But I haven't explored the whole cave. There's a passageway that goes deeper in but I've never been in there."

"Why not? You've certainly had the time."

"Claustrophobia," Roscoe said. "That's where you come in."

"What do you mean?" Mike said.

"There may be more gold in here. The only problem is I can't bring myself to stay in here for more than a few minutes. I keep getting the feeling the whole place is going to cave in on me. I need someone that I trust to explore this cave completely and bring out whatever is inside." He looked over at Mike and gave him a sinister grin. "Then there'll be more for both of us."

Mike looked around to take in the whole view. He estimated there were about a thousand pounds in gold bars and maybe another three or four hundred pounds of coins and trinkets. There was enough gold here for dozens of men to become rich, far more than just the two of them would ever need.

"Why don't you pick out a souvenir of your visit to take back and let's get out of here." Roscoe looked around. "I'm getting edgy."

"Okay." Mike eyed a beautiful golden statue of the Virgin Mary. He carefully picked it up and followed Roscoe back outside.

Just before exiting Roscoe set the two unused torches down. "They'll be here for the next visit," he said. "I guess I should say: 'your next visit'." He smiled.

Once back at camp, Mike stirred the campfire to life and sat down. He held the little statue up in the light and admired its beauty and intricate detail. He pictured himself giving it to his princess, Jan. She loved beautiful things. Estimating its value was only guesswork, but he could easily see a store in Miami charging twenty thousand dollars for such a nice little statue.

"Let me see that." Roscoe took his seat by the fire.

Mike handed it over and Roscoe began examining the five-pound object.

"I guess I didn't dig around in that chest enough to find this before," Roscoe said. "It confirms that this gold is from a Spanish Galleon."

"Think so?" Mike said.

"Well," he replied. "The Spanish were the ones who mined most of the gold in the New World. With pirates and other European countries fighting over control of the seas, gold changed hands many times. A Spanish goldsmith probably in Mexico made this little statue. They set up some kind of refinery and melted down the gold to make coins and other items. They often made household objects out of the gold so it could serve a purpose on the ships during the long trip back to Spain. That's why you find it in the form of teacups, plates and stuff like that. This statue was destined for the queen I guess."

"Don't you think this gold is stolen," Mike said.

"How do you figure that?"

"Well," Mike said. "If the Spaniards had never lost possession of it, then it would either be in Spain or on the ocean bottom right now. But hidden in a cave? I'll bet this stuff was stolen and stashed here for later retrieval. Whoever stole it never got back for it. At least not yet."

"You're smarter than I thought," Roscoe said. "But there's more to the story than meets the eye."

"What do you mean?" He wasn't sure he wanted the question answered.

"Whoever stole and stashed this gold may come back for it," Roscoe said. "If they do then I want to be gone with it long before they get here." He stood up, handed the statue back to Mike, then yawned loudly as he stretched. "Keep those thoughts in mind tonight while you're falling asleep. See you in the morning."

"Good night." Mike studied the statue some more. Roscoe climbed up to the tree house and disappeared inside. Mike sat by the dying fire for a while longer and thought about the cave. After a few minutes he decided it was time to get to sleep himself.

Sometime during the night, rain started to fall. When Mike got out of bed the next morning it had stopped, but the sky was overcast. As usual, Roscoe was already up. Mike walked over to the bigger cabin.

"Hey," Roscoe said. "We'd better go gather up some fruit before the storm starts."

"I thought it already came through." Mike looked at the wet surroundings outside.

"I doubt it." Roscoe sat on the side of the bed and flexed his knee. "My knees aren't what they used to be and they get a little tight when the barometric pressure gets low. They're pretty stiff right now."

The two of them quickly climbed down and headed toward the "vineyard" area as Roscoe called it, the area nearby where fruit trees were abundant. As Roscoe gathered berries, Mike climbed into a tree to pick bananas. "Maybe this is just a shower," Mike said.

"Maybe," Roscoe said. "Can't take chances though. Hurricane season is coming soon. Since we don't have a calendar we can't be sure when the first one is due."

"You're right," Mike said. "There's no early-warning system here. We'll always have to be on our toes."

"And there are so many things in a hurricane that can kill you," Roscoe said. "Lightning strikes, large hail, falling trees."

"Not to mention flying debris," Mike said. "Hurricane-force winds can turn pine needles into flying nails."

They continued gathering food and soon had plenty. They then returned to the tree house just minutes before the pounding rain began. Roscoe watched outside as the storm went through. The wind blew hard enough to make the trees sway and the cabin rocked mildly back and forth.

"Is it safe to be up here in this storm?" Mike said.

"Reasonably so," Roscoe said. "We aren't all that high above the ground and there are many taller trees around us. There is no real safe place other than the pirate cave and I don't want to go there unless it's absolutely necessary. I'd rather be a little wet than a lot claustrophobic."

They ate and stayed alert. Within a couple of hours the weather calmed, and soon the warm tropical sun was shining brightly again on the strange island.

When they went back outside, Roscoe suggested scallops for dinner and presented a somewhat lopsided, homemade shovel and an old beat-up plastic pail. After two hours of digging on the beach, they had enough scallops for a feast.

"Why don't we eat dinner early tonight," Roscoe said. "Then maybe you can go explore the cave some more?"

"You coming?"

"I wish I could," Roscoe said. "You go have fun and tell me about it afterwards. I'll make some more torches while you're gone."

"I'll need them."

"By the way," Roscoe said. "Make sure you're extremely careful at all times. Any injury will be painful for a long time without any medical care available. And if you get hurt in there I may not be able to come get you."

"That's encouraging," Mike said. "Just thought I'd remind you," Roscoe grinned.

Later, after dinner, Mike took another torch and started for the cave. "Be sure to keep two torches burning at all times," Roscoe reminded him. "And take these with you." He reached into his pocket. "They'll help you if your torch goes out."

Roscoe held out a small rusty plate of steel, perhaps a tiny remnant of an old steamer's hull, and struck a flint rock across it. A spark flew off as the two objects hit each other. "It's real hard to get a torch lit from them, in fact I never have. But you can click them together and create sparks for emergency light."

"Thanks." Mike took the objects and put them in his pocket. A few minutes later he was crawling through the entrance to the cave. Once he got inside far enough to stand he held the torch up and gave his eyes a moment to adjust to the dim light. The room was small and there was no draft whatsoever. Mike figured the entrance was probably the only opening the cave had.

Picking up the two torches Roscoe had left on the floor the previous day, he headed straight back toward the unknown parts of the cave. Stepping into the treasure room, he took two handfuls of gold coins and stuffed both pockets full. Then, as he started into the unfamiliar parts of the cave he began dropping them on the floor as he went. Good thing my mother read 'Hansel and Gretel' to me as a kid, he thought.

As he got further back, he encountered a number of small indentations and open areas that branched off the main corridor. The cave went down hill for a ways, then uphill. The corridor got as much as twenty feet wide in places and so narrow in others that he had to turn sideways to get through. But it remained high enough to continue walking upright without having to duck.

Somewhere up ahead he heard water falling. As the corridor went around a corner he heard the sound getting louder. He proceeded carefully ahead, knowing that he could find himself with a wet and useless torch if he wasn't careful. He spotted the waterfall. It flowed out of a hole in the cave ceiling and fell about fifteen feet into a shallow pool. From there it disappeared into a hole in the cave floor. He couldn't help wondering if he was the first person to see this waterfall. He suspected he was not.

Walking past the waterfall and down the corridor another fifty feet, Mike soon found that the cave came to an abrupt dead end. The trail he had been following tapered off to a narrow crack that vanished into a stone wall. As he stood staring at the wall that formed the back of the cave his torch began to flicker. For a moment he was panicked, staring at the dying torch with no idea what to do next. Then he remembered the other torches and quickly lit one of them. The fresh one came to life just before the first one flickered completely out.

Mike decided to go back to the pool of water and find out if it was drinkable. He walked to it and kneeled down to give the water a taste. It wasn't salty but had a taste of calcium to it. He decided he could wait until he got back outside to get a drink of real spring water. He turned around and looked straight into an opening opposite the waterfall. The opening in the wall faced away from the direction in which he came.

His curiosity heightened. He stepped inside the opening and looked around. There were stairs built into the floor.

He slowly descended the stairs until he came to a level floor at the bottom. Holding the torch high above his head lit up the entire room. If only I had someone to stand here and hold this light for me I'd be fine, he thought.

Something in the corner of the room caught his eye. He walked over and saw that it was a small pile of clothes. Bending down he touched them, having them crumble to dust in his hand. Then he felt something hard and round amongst the clothes and immediately thought of a gold orb of some kind. He pulled it out and realized with horror that it was a human skull. He almost screamed as he

dropped it and jumped away, falling backward and dropping the torch. It flickered and started to go out, bringing
him quickly back to his senses. He grabbed it and held it
upright, praying that it would recover. The thought of
being alone with these human remains in the total darkness didn't appeal to him at the moment.

Once the torch returned to normal he leaned it
against the wall and looked back at the pile of clothes
and the skull. Slowly he reached over and pulled some of
the remains of the fabric away to reveal what remained of
a skeleton.

The bones had obviously been here a long time. Upon
closer inspection, Mike saw that one of the leg bones was
broken. He couldn't tell if the break had occurred before
or after death. Mike figured it probably happened while he
was alive, which would explain why the victim stayed in
here long enough to wind up in his present state.

What a terrible place to fall and break a leg, he thought.
"I must be the first person to come in here since you
died," he said to the skeleton. "I wonder who you were."

He looked around the dark room. Unlike the rest of the
cave, it looked manmade, almost as if someone had dug it
out with a bulldozer. The room was a perfect square with a
flat stone floor. Mike pulled at the rotting clothes and they
crumbled away in his hands. He began bunching them
into a ball when a key fell to the floor. He picked it up and
held it close to the torch. It was three inches long and
looked like it fit into a keyhole the size of a nickel.

"Well now," he said. "I wonder what you fit into." He
decided to continue looking around the room, hoping to
find a treasure chest or some other lock that went with the
key. There were some scraps of wood on the floor that

looked like it had once been part of a small table and chair. There was other stuff too, like a drinking cup and an old beat-up sword. Everything he saw indicated to Mike that this was once some kind of an office.

The torch began to flicker, making him realize he had left the last fresh torch up the steps by the pool. He rushed up the stairs as fast as he could and located the other torch, lighting it just scant seconds before the first one burned out. He still had the flints in his pocket for emergency but didn't want to have to use them to get out of the cave if he didn't have to. If he lost his light here, getting back out would be a difficult and dangerous endeavor.

As he stood atop the stairway he was torn between going back down and exploring the room some more and heading back toward the exit. His curiosity was piqued. He was dying to find the lock that the key fit. All the while, that voice of logic was screaming in his head to go for the exit immediately. He was on his last torch now, and logically should use it only for the purpose of getting out. But Roscoe knows I'm in here, he thought, and he stepped down the top step.

Then he remembered what he had said about the claustrophobia.

"On second thought—." He turned for the cave's exit.

A couple of times during the trip to the exit the torch flickered, mostly because he was walking too fast. Each time the light started to wane, Mike would freeze in his tracks and wait for the flame to recover. He kept walking, concentrating more on the torch than on where he was going. A moment later the torch flickered again and he stopped right where he was. This time it acted like it wasn't going to recover. "Come on baby," he said, careful not to exhale on the weak flame and blow it out. Several anxious moments passed as the flame slowly made it back to its normal brightness.

Once the light was normal again he looked around, suddenly realizing that he was in unfamiliar territory. The trail of gold coins on the floor was nowhere to be seen. The torch began to flicker again. Moments later it flickered and burned completely out!

Standing in total darkness, afraid to move, Mike was on the verge of panic. His mind began playing nasty tricks on him. He imagined rats, bats, snakes and biting insects. He even imagined the old skeleton, finding new life and getting up, staggering around on its one good leg and coming after him, working its cold fingers around his throat. He could hear his heartbeat pounding through his ears. He kept telling himself to relax. He stood as still as possible, breathing deeply.

Carefully, he reached into his pockets and pulled out the flint and the chunk of metal. The voice in his head reminded him not to drop anything. Holding the torch between his knees he took the flint in his right hand and the metal chunk in the left. Carefully clicking them together he got a momentary bright spark of light. He clicked them together again and again, inching his hands closer to the end of the torch.

He worked the sparks to the end of the torch and kept striking. Finally, on the hundredth or so attempt, a spark hit and a tiny flame broke out on the torch. He stood frozen and watched as it gradually encompassed the entire top end, eventually recovering to almost normal.

Holding the torch high, he began retracing his steps, trying to relocate the trail of gold coins. He was still near panic, rushing as fast as he could. The torch flickered with each step, daring him to go faster. He didn't. Finally he looked ahead to see a gold coin on the floor. He put the few remaining coins down in a pile and made a right turn. He could see now how he had gotten off track there, and would have to beware of the intersection the next time.

A short distance ahead he felt the incline and knew he was close to the exit. This brought a big sigh of relief. He saw faint light spilling through the cave entrance ahead and detected the scent of fresh air. A moment later the torch flickered out again and Mike knew this time it was for good. He crawled out the entrance to the outside and sat in the moonlight.

When he got back to the tree house he found that Roscoe had gone to bed. As he got a drink of water and climbed up to the deck, Roscoe came out of his cabin. "You just getting back?" Roscoe said. "Yes," Mike said.

"You've been gone quite a while. I was beginning to think something had happened to you."

"Something almost did. How long would you say I've been gone?"

"Well there aren't any clocks here. But I'd guess it's about three in the morning."

"Wow, I had no idea it had been that long. I almost got lost in there and once lost my light. I'm lucky to have gotten out at all."

"I don't think I could return to that cave again after something like that," Roscoe said.

Mike fingered the key in his pocket. "I'm going back in the morning."

Roscoe appeared to cringe, although Mike couldn't be sure in the dark.

"If I hadn't come back by morning you would have come looking for me wouldn't you?" Mike said.

"Well," Roscoe said. "I would have come to the entrance and called out to you. I'm afraid that would have been the best I could do."

Mike chuckled. "If I had made it to the entrance then I could have gotten out on my own."

"I tell you," Roscoe said. "My claustrophobia is so bad I never could have gotten you if you were deep inside that cave. It's all I can do to just get to the treasure room. Ten minutes in there and my nerves are frayed. I can't tell you how many nights I've laid awake and planned to explore deeper into the cave, only to get to the entrance the next morning and go into a cold sweat. The torch trembles in my hand and all kinds of thoughts go through my mind. If I got deep in there and the torch so much as flickered I'd go crazy. I can't think of anything that could be worse."

Mike pondered what Roscoe was saying. It was obvious that this thing known as claustrophobia, a concept he had never fully understood, held its selected victims in some kind of choke-hold.

"Look what I found." Mike held up the key.

"What's that," Roscoe said. "More gold?"

"A key."

"Key to what?"

"Don't know," he said. "But I'm going back in to try and find out."

"Good for you." Roscoe climbed down the steps and the two of them sat down.

Mike told him about the waterfall, getting lost and finding the skeleton.

"He must have been a pirate," Roscoe said.

"Whoever he was," Mike said. "He had the key for a reason and I'm going to find out what that reason was."

"I sure wish I could help you," Roscoe said.

"You can, make some more torches."

"I can do that," Roscoe said.

Mike yawned. "I'm going to bed.

When Mike awoke, the sun was high in the sky and it appeared to be near noon. A quick check of the other cabin told him that Roscoe was still asleep. Mike climbed down from the trees and immediately spotted four new torches lying under Roscoe's chair. Evidently he had placed them there so Mike would be sure to see them and where the chair would keep them dry if it rained. Mike quickly gathered some fruit for breakfast and admired the torches as he ate.

Finishing the last bites, Mike took the torches, flints and metal plate and headed for the cave.

Even under the shade of the trees, the hot sun made the temperature soar. Despite the heat, he walked briskly. With an armful of torches and the mysterious key in his pocket, he was heading for the cave with determination and certainty. Somewhere in the cave there had to be a lock that the key fit into. He would search as long as it took until he found it. He reached the entrance and crawled inside.

Holding a torch between his knees and working in the dim light just inside the cave, he struck the flints until he got one lit. The flame jumped to life and startled him. He had never had one light up so fast before.

"Wait a minute." He sniffed one of the other torches. The smell of gasoline was unmistakable. I can't let the gas get used up, he thought. Not if I want there to be any left

when we get the boat running. I'll mention to Roscoe to
go easy on it when I see him later.

He headed straight for the room where the skeleton
awaited. His curiosity, which had abated a little overnight,
was once again peaking. As he followed the trail of coins
on the floor he began to hear the waterfall ahead. Without
slowing down he turned and headed for the stairway.

As Mike descended the stairs, he noticed how much
more light the new torch emitted. It was a vast improve-
ment. From the top of the stairs he could see markings on
the wall that he hadn't noticed in the dim light the night
before. One of the markings indicated the year 1668.
There were other markings too but none were readable.

Once at ground level, he held the torch up and lit
another from it. The room was fully illuminated now and
he saw a lot more than he had before. The skull on the
floor was still smiling up at him and the pieces of wood
were still lying in a pile beside it. In the corner, which was
around a wall that obscured it from the stairs, was an
ancient skull and crossbones flag. The flag looked like it
had once hung from the wall, but had long ago fallen to
the floor in a small heap. Mike walked over toward it; eyes
fixed on a large object on the floor.

Before him was a very large empty wooden treasure
chest, or what was left of one. It appeared that someone
had taken an ax and pounded the top until it split open.
Small piles of dust that had once been wood chips were
scattered around it on the cave floor. Most of the wood
was rotted away by time, but Mike could tell exactly what
had happened here.

He pulled out the key and tried it in the ancient lock
that still held the front of the smashed chest closed. The

lock was much too big for this key to fit. He went back across the room and got the torch, which he had left leaning against the wall, and returned with it for a closer look. There was nothing inside the chest. He picked up the old flag and it crumbled in his hand.

Mike decided to give the old skeleton one more look. He reached down with his foot and moved the dusty pile. Underneath he spotted a small metal object. Maybe it's a button, he thought. He picked it up. "Wow," he said. "It's a slug from an ancient pistol."

Suddenly, the whole picture came into focus. Pirates often left one or two men behind to guard their treasure when they left it somewhere. This fellow had been the guard and someone had shot him for the treasure. Mike looked at the walls. He could see several dents in the stone that were apparently made by bullets. Looking around the floor for several minutes turned up five more slugs. Then he realized that the key he had didn't come out of the pocket of the skeleton, it had been in his stomach. Whoever stole the treasure had evidently hauled it to the front of the cave where it still sat to this day. "But what about the key?" he said. "There has to be another treasure chest here somewhere. But where?"

The two torches were burning down and Mike decided it was time to move on. Grabbing the unlit torches, he headed back toward the cave's main corridor. A few minutes later he lit a fresh one. When he reached the back-most part of the cave, he looked up and in all directions. There were no hiding places around, so he started back toward the entrance, checking as he went.

There were dozens of natural shelves and holes in the cave walls where a small treasure chest could be hidden, but each turned up empty. Eventually he progressed back to the spot where he had become lost the night before. In ten minutes he combed the entire small room there and found it empty as well.

He continued the meticulous search for another half-hour or so until he found himself at the entrance again. By this time he was very frustrated. "Where did you hide it?" he said. The echo of his voice carried down the corridors and back at him again.

He was getting tired and weary, yet the determination was still there. Grabbing the unlit torch and the lit one that was burning down quickly, he started for the back of the cave.

Mike decided to start anew in the room near the entrance that held the pile of gold coins and the stacks of gold bars. There was virtually nothing left of the old chest. The sea air was stronger here than in the back of the cave, which probably explained why there was so little wood left here when there was, still some toward the back. He looked over the gold and realized that it had not been in a treasure chest, but a wooden crate of some kind. The gold bars were stacked as if several men had made dozens of trips back and forth to the back of the cave, returning with one in each hand and stacking them here. The large crate had been left here to await a ship, but it never arrived.

But they could be on their way now, he thought.

Mike shivered as he headed to the deepest part of the cave again. There was something else here to be found per-haps the best treasure of all. He had the key. Now it was just a matter of finding the lock it fit.

Near the back of the cave, the torch suddenly began to flicker. Mike quickly lit the last one and discarded the dying one. He'd have to make this one count. If he was going to find anything he'd have to do it soon and save some torchlight for his exit.

There was also the gasoline factor to consider. Roscoe had gone to great lengths to give Mike the opportunity to spend this day in the cave, but the gas supply was limited and so was Mike's time. He needed to be doing other things to try to get back home. The cave adventure had been fun, but this visit really needed to be his last. Think like a pirate, he thought. As he walked slowly, he tried to imagine the scenario of centuries before.

Suppose the guard knew they were coming, he thought. And had a few minutes to hide something before swallowing the key. He came within earshot of the waterfall. The sound of rushing water in the dark seemed to call out to him. "The waterfall," he said. "It's the only place left that I haven't looked."

He rushed over to it and set the torch against the opposite wall, safely away from the splashing water. Walking over to the large pool of water under the splashing falls, he removed his shoes and waded in. The water was bone-chilling cold and came up almost to his waist. He had to be careful not to fall on the slippery bottom.

Carefully, he made his way over to the waterfall and the icy water poured down on his head and back, shocking him with its numbing cold. Suddenly his feet went out from under him and he fell forward. He reached out his hands to cushion himself from the wall behind the falling water. When his right hand reached the wall, a loose rock moved and fell away. Mike fell into the water and landed hard on his behind. He hardly felt the pain because he knew he had hit pay dirt even before regaining his balance.

Through the stream of falling water he could see a hole created by the cleverly placed rock.

He reached through the water into the hole and felt around inside. The back wall of the hole was another foot or so deep. He stepped closer to the water, reaching in as far as he could. The waterfall poured down on his head and he had to turn his face away to breathe. Reaching as far as he could into the hole, his hand came down on something hard and flat. Taking a breath and reaching in with both hands he felt a small box about a foot in length. Struggling for a foothold, he put his hands on either side of the box and lifted. He gently pulled it out and then carefully waded out of the water.

The box appeared to be made of iron and weighed maybe thirty pounds. The front of it was held tightly closed by a lock with a keyhole that looked identical in size to the key in his pocket. Suddenly the torch began to flicker and Mike saw his life pass before his eyes. He wasn't sure if the flints in his pocket would spark soaking wet. He rushed over and picked up his shoes and the torch. Holding the chest firmly under his left arm, he rushed as fast as he dared for the exit. About ten minutes later, with the torch flickering down, Mike reached the exit and crawled out into the warm tropical sunshine. Holding his shoes in one hand and the treasure chest in the other, he ran all the way back to the campsite.

He didn't see Roscoe upon his arrival so he hurried up to his cabin and sat down on the floor. He took out the key and inserted it into the keyhole. It was a perfect fit.

The lock wouldn't budge. He kept trying, but couldn't get to give an inch. When Roscoe gets back, he thought. We'll get it open if we have to smash it."

"Anybody home?" Roscoe called up from the ground.

Mike ran to the deck railing. "Roscoe, you won't believe what I found. A small treasure chest hidden behind the waterfall in the cave. Come on up and help me get it open."

Roscoe stood silently staring into Mike's face. "Sounds great but it'll have to wait. Another boat has washed ashore. It looks like it's in pretty good shape. Let's go check it out. We'll get into the treasure chest in the firelight tonight."

"This must be my lucky day." Mike pushed the chest under his bed before rushing down the steps.

When they arrived at the east beach, stepping from the shade of the dense trees into the bright sun, Roscoe pointed to a speedboat lying upside down on the sand near the surf. "Over there. We need to get to it before the tide comes back in."

As they hurried toward it, Mike quickly determined that it was a small craft, a sixteen-footer, with its outboard motor missing. He struggled to overturn the boat and found it to be too heavy. "Hey Roscoe—," he said. He noticed that Roscoe was about fifty feet away near a standing pool of water. He walked over for a closer look. The dead body of a young man was staring up at them through glazed eyes. "Looks like the Bermuda Triangle got another one," Roscoe muttered as he looked around. "I wonder if he was alone."

Mike couldn't take his eyes from the dead man. Although he had seen many over the last several years it always had an effect on him. This one was particularly disturbing because he appeared to be about Mike's age.

"Poor bastard," Roscoe muttered. "I'll bury him with the others. We're starting to get quite a cemetery."

Roscoe walked over to the boat and Mike followed. It had been damaged but seemed to be mostly still intact.

"You can probably get the wood you need to fix the *Spear* from this boat," Roscoe said. "Let's flip her over."

Together, they turned it upright and inspected the inside. There were some fishing poles attached to the sides of the boat, a tackle box under one seat and about twenty feet of rope coiled up in the storage area underneath the front deck. Roscoe looked into the glove box and found a pair of sunglasses, some sun block lotion and a boater's map of Ft. Lauderdale's coastline.

"Sun block lotion." Roscoe held up the brown plastic bottle. "I've never heard of that."

"It's designed to prevent any sun from getting to the skin, including the tanning rays," Mike said. "I think they created it because the Earth's ozone layer is being eroded by industrial emission and sun tanning isn't as safe as it used to be."

Roscoe grunted and shoved the lotion into his worn back pocket.

Mike put on the sunglasses and gazed out to sea. "Hey, these are nice."

Together they pulled the boat up underneath the trees and let it rest well above the high tide mark. Roscoe dragged the body of the unfortunate young man to the small patch of ground where he had buried another dozen or so such victims over the last decade. He would return with a shovel later in the day and dig a shallow grave.

Mike spent an hour or so fooling with the boat, determining that the damage it had endured was too great for it to be repairable. Even so, it would provide some much-needed material for repairing the *Spear*. It would take time, but eventually Mike would have a boat that could be seaworthy.

"Let's head back," Roscoe said. "I think we're in for some more rain." Together, they overturned the boat to keep the rain out of it and made their way back to camp.

During the walk Mike told Roscoe about the spent bullets he had found and the apparent murder. "It's obvious that the dead pirate hid the little treasure chest behind the waterfall and refused to tell his killers where it was," he said. "Then he must have swallowed the key. They killed him and then did an unsuccessful search for the chest."

"Whatever is inside the chest must be really valuable," Roscoe said.

"Must be," Mike said. "Considering how much gold is piled up at the entrance it would take something pretty special to make anyone search further. Anyway, I can't wait to get it open."

Minutes later they arrived at the tree house as the first drops of rain began to fall. It started raining pretty heavily as they stepped inside Mike's cabin. He pulled the chest out from under the bed and handed it to Roscoe.

"Wow," he exclaimed. Roscoe held the chest up and set it down on the bed. It was about a foot-and-a-half across, a foot wide and about ten inches deep. "It's heavy."

Mike presented the key and started trying the lock again. It was jammed frozen.

"Let me get some tools." Roscoe hurried through the rain across the deck to his cabin.

Mike grabbed the chest and followed. Roscoe reached into an old wooden crate in the corner of his room and held up a heavy iron strip. "I could pry the roof off a car with this."

"Where'd you get it?" Mike said.

"More boat debris."

They sat on the floor and Mike held the chest firmly between his knees while Roscoe began working on the lid. After several minutes of bending and bashing he finally had an opening big enough to get the end of the iron strip in between the chest's lid and base.

"Hold her steady." Roscoe pushed in and twisted. The chest began to groan and creak before finally popping open with a loud crack.

"Alright." Mike pulled the lid open all the way. The two of them looked into the chest, now open for the first time in perhaps hundreds of years. There were gold trinkets, a tiny ship with masts, sails and even a railing around its little deck, and there were golden earrings, bracelets and rings. There was a golden dagger, a miniature shield and sword. Many of the objects had rubies and diamonds in them. All told, there were about twenty golden objects stuffed inside the little chest.

"Wow," Roscoe said. "I can see why they kept this stuff separate. This is definitely the cream of the collection."

Mike held up the tiny gold ship. "Look at the detail of this thing," he said.

Roscoe looked at it with awe. "Amazing. It's unbelievable that a goldsmith could create such a thing without modern tools and techniques."

"I wonder why the crown wasn't in the chest too," Mike said.

"Probably wouldn't fit."

Mike noticed a small gold box on the bottom of the chest. He pulled it out and unclasped it. "Look. A book."

"Maybe it's a yearbook," Roscoe chuckled. "Pirate U., class of 1690."

Mike looked over at him and they both broke up laughing.

"I wonder if they had a 'most likely to walk the plank' winner in here." They both laughed again. At that moment, Mike felt that there may actually have been more good than bad in winding up here in the Bermuda Triangle.

Mike opened the book and discovered several dozen yellowed, hand-written pages.

"Look at that hand writing," Roscoe said. "It looks like some kind of old English."

"Maybe I can decipher some of it," Mike said. "Perhaps we can learn something. Sure won't be easy though."

Roscoe put all the other stuff back in the chest and slid it under the bed.

"Why don't we get comfortable and see what it says?" Mike said.

Roscoe looked outside. The rain had stopped and the sun was peeking out again. "I think I'll go try out those new fishing poles. Guess I'd better if we plan on eating tonight."

Mike continued to examine the ancient papers and Roscoe got up to go outside.

"I'll be at the lagoon," Roscoe said. Mike was too engrossed in the pages to hear.

"Hey," Roscoe said.

"Okay." Mike didn't take his eyes off his reading. "Call me if you need me."

Roscoe chuckled. Climbing down to the ground he headed for the lagoon for a relaxing afternoon.

When Roscoe reached the beach he could see a colorful rainbow a few miles out to sea. The brilliant colors started from oblivion somewhere over the horizon and gradually thickened as they approached the island, appearing to end somewhere behind him. "I guess the old myth is true after all," he muttered. "There really is a pot of gold at the end of the rainbow."

Meanwhile, Mike sat and read the pirate diary for hours. Most of the pages crumbled as he turned them. He knew he would probably only get one reading before the diary turned to dust.

The old English language was difficult to follow and interpret but Mike stayed with it, mainly because it was so fascinating. He hoped it might reveal something that could help them get off the island. It only stood to reason that visitors to the island from centuries past were just as aware as he was that things were not normal here. Whether they knew of the Bermuda Triangle or not, they had to have known something was amiss here. Mike was thrown here with no prior knowledge of what to expect, but it was possible that other visitors may have known more about the forces at work in this place and how to deal with them.

Sometime later, Roscoe returned. He rounded the corner and stood in front of the tree house. "Hello," he said.

Mike came running from the interior. "Roscoe," he said. "You won't believe it. The pirates went through the eye of the needle."

Roscoe stood silently, staring into Mike's face. "Does it say how to get home?"

"I don't know," Mike said. "There's still a lot I can't figure out. But this diary is definitely the most valuable thing to come out of that cave."

Roscoe smiled. "It is if you include the other contents of the chest too." He held up the two stringers of fish. "I'll get these ready to cook if you'll go gather some fruit."

"Sure." Mike quickly returned the crumbling diary into the treasure chest before climbing down.

When Mike returned with some fresh produce, Roscoe had the fish cleaned and cooking. They finished preparing dinner.

"The diary was written by the first mate of Captain Derrick's ship," Mike said. Roscoe wasn't familiar with Derrick so Mike filled him in about Seaway Island and the notorious captain that had died there.

"According to the diary," Mike said, "Derrick and his crew had traveled up and down the American coast attacking ships and stealing supplies. Evidently, they had been doing it for some time without any major success, just finding food and rum.

"Then one day they came upon a Spanish galleon. The first mate said they drifted within a couple of miles of it during the night. When Derrick saw the Spanish, he gave the order to run from them. He said the sailors on the galleon saw them and watched them leave without making any attempt to pursue. This struck Derrick as odd, since no ships in the Spanish, English, Dutch or French navies had ever ignored his pirate ship before. Still, he wanted to keep a safe distance away and ordered them to keep moving.

"As Derrick's ship floated away he kept the spyglass on the Spaniards and closely observed their every move. A few

minutes later, the galleon set sail due east. Derrick was a
very experienced sea captain and he told his men that he
suspected the Spanish ship was loaded with supplies, possibly gold, and that they were taking it home to Spain.
That would explain why they hadn't attacked. The ship
was too full of valuable cargo to maneuver and the
Spaniards had too much to lose. Derrick ordered the crew
to sail a good distance behind the galleon but well within
view of it for a couple of hours. He was thinking of making some kind of move on them around sunset.

"Derrick finally made the order and the pirates charged
headlong toward the Spanish as night fell. His men were
not very confident but Derrick screamed at them that they
would fight to the death if they had to. This was their big
chance, the one they had been awaiting for.

"When they got close, he ordered the cannons to get
ready. The two ships exchanged cannon fire for several
minutes without any hits before Derrick decided to charge
straight at them. The gamble paid off. The Spanish fired
time and again, always just missing the bow of the oncoming pirates. Derrick's ship got alongside the galleon and his
men jumped onto the Spanish ship and started fighting
hand to hand. Pistols cracked, men were sent overboard
both dead and alive. Sailors swung from ropes tied to the
masts and dropped onto the deck, swinging swords as they
came. The fight raged well into the night and both pirate
and Spanish blood poured over the deck and into the sea.

"When dawn came the next morning, Derrick suddenly awakened in a sitting position on the deck of the
Spanish ship. He had been hit over the head and knocked
out during the melee and had somehow not been killed
thereafter. To his pleasant surprise, seventeen of his men

were still alive and all the Spanish sailors had been killed. He looked out into the water and saw dozens of bodies floating around the two ships. The victory had been nothing short of miraculous. He got on his knees and thanked the Lord for his victory over the mighty Spanish. This had truly been his greatest victory. He organized his men and went into the hold of the galleon to inspect the cargo. He was thrilled beyond words when he discovered that the cargo was gold, and lots of it."

Roscoe served the food and the two of them ate. "This is where it gets hard to follow," Mike said. "The pirates set fire to their ship and took over the galleon. They turned back toward North America and headed for the mainland. Somewhere along the way, another pirate ship came along and started after the galleon of which Derrick was now the captain. Derrick was mad at himself for setting fire to his old ship because the smoke had attracted these other pirates. They spotted Derrick and approached quickly.

"These new pirates were still a good distance away when Derrick's scout spotted them but they knew it would be only a matter of time before they got close because the galleon was heavy and slow. Derrick knew they'd be no match with only eighteen tired men to defend the cargo, so he tried to think up something fast.

"Derrick was a gambler," Mike said. "Off in the distance he saw storm clouds and ordered his men to head right toward them. Hoping that a heavy ship would be easier to maneuver in a storm than a light one, he charged straight into the heavy surf and high winds. Derrick figured that either he would prevail or the storm would destroy both ships. He was willing to settle for a tie or a win but never a loss.

"The seas grew rougher and soon a heavy rain was pounding down on them. The other pirate ship had closed the gap considerably and was now within cannon range. Derrick knew they wouldn't fire though, the cargo wouldn't do anybody any good if it were on the ocean bottom. One of Derrick's men asked him to give the order to let them tie down the sails before the wind tore them off or blew the ship over. Derrick refused and ordered the sails left alone. They'd take their chances. Derrick was desperate to escape the other vessel and protect the horde of gold he had waited so long to get. The two ships, now only a few hundred yards apart, tossed violently in the storm. The other ship began firing at them, trying to knock the sails out. None of the shots came close however, and Derrick continued to run as fast as he could. The other captain knew there was something well worth having in the holds of the galleon and was pulling out all the stops to get it."

Roscoe was on the edge of his seat as Mike described the battle. "That's when something happened," Mike said.

"What do you mean 'something happened'"? Roscoe said.

"I think they went through the eye of the needle. The diary says they began to spin in a circle, slowly at first then faster. It felt like they were out of the water, spinning in the air. Then the spinning stopped all of a sudden and the other ship couldn't be seen. It was still raining but the surf had gotten calmer. Derrick looked in all directions and the other ship was nowhere to be seen. 'We sank her!' he shouted and the crew let out a cheer of victory. The other ship was nowhere in sight but Derrick feared it might be close by. He didn't tell the others but knew they had not caused the other ship to sink. This victory had come incredibly easily, too easily. All eighteen men watched the ocean until nightfall without seeing any other vessels approach.

"The following morning Derrick, never one to kick a gift horse in the mouth, wasted no time speeding for a safe haven. He gave the order to set sail west. The next day they came to this island and spent several days unloading the horde of gold into the cave.

"A few days after unloading the gold, Derrick sent his men out to explore the island. One of them returned to report that he had discovered a high cliff from which a man could see fifty miles in all directions."

"I know of such a cliff," Roscoe said. "I've always referred to it as the summit."

"Well," Mike said. "Apparently the lookout spent a good deal of time up there, and he wrote about some things that don't make any sense."

"Like what?"

"He described seeing smoke coming out of large chimneys on some of the ships he saw, even though steamers didn't exist for another century. He also wrote about big birds that didn't flap their wings and made buzzing sounds like giant bees."

"That's really weird," Roscoe said. "Planes didn't exist for centuries after that."

"Evidently he spent a lot of time up there and saw things that he didn't even tell Capt. Derrick," Mike said. "Maybe he was afraid of what the captain would think so he kept the sightings to himself until after Derrick and the others left the island. I just wonder if he was imagining things or if he was seeing one of the quirks of the Bermuda Triangle. He could have been seeing ships and planes that disappeared in our era. Whatever he saw, I'm now curious about this summit myself. I think it should be the next place I visit."

"Maybe you can learn something up there," Roscoe said. "That's what I'm hoping."

"Does the diary say what caused Derrick to leave the island?"

"Yes," Mike said. "A lookout went up there and saw numerous ships passing in the distance. When one of them headed this way he rushed to tell Derrick. Derrick assigned his first mate to defend the gold if the cave was ever found, and then the rest of them got aboard the ship and left the island. The first mate's last entry in the diary said that he went into the cave and hid in the big room. That's where the diary ended. Apparently the other pirates came ashore and when he heard them approaching he quickly packed the little chest and hid it in the secret place behind the falls. I guess he swallowed the key and died with the secret."

"A secret that remained hidden until you came along," Roscoe said. "Well done. Your detective work on this is nothing short of amazing. I've been here all these years and never imagined such a treasure existed."

"Well," Mike said. "I always have been the curious type." Once they finished eating, Roscoe stood up and tossed his scraps into the fire. "Let's go look through that chest again."

"Okay," Mike said, and they went back up the steps to the bed and pulled the chest out from under it.

Roscoe sat in the chair and Mike sat on the bed as he spilled the contents of the chest and began admiring each piece.

"Why do you suppose they went to so much trouble keeping these pieces separate from the rest?" Mike said.

"I guess maybe they were thinking about damage control. Maybe they figured somebody might find the rest of it and kept this stuff separate so the best of the collection would always be safe."

"That must be it." Mike admired the tiny gold galleon. "I guess the first mate knew they were going to kill him anyway, so not telling them about the hidden chest made no difference."

"Loyal fellow."

Mike stood up. "Why don't we put these things on display on your book case. That way we can enjoy them."

"I guess that would be okay," Roscoe said. "But if anyone else shows up here we hide them right away."

Mike took a moment to determine if Roscoe was kidding. He quickly concluded that he was not. "You aren't seriously worried about someone coming here and taking it, are you?"

"We can never be too careful," Roscoe said. "This gold is ours now, Evan's, yours and mine. I don't know about you but I want my part of it to be safe at all times."

Mike thought a moment about what Roscoe was saying. It was beginning to become obvious to him that Roscoe was a bit greedy. He hoped it wouldn't cause conflict further down the road.

"There's something else the first mate wrote about," Mike said. "He mentioned briefly that he and the captain shared a bottle of rum one night and Derrick got a bit talkative. The mate, who for some reason never mentioned his name, said Derrick kept talking about a 'vortex' in the ocean. Derrick claimed that this island, which is where they were headed when the conversation occurred, was the perfect hiding place for their treasure because the vortex was the only way to get here. He said the vortex was the secret of many of his escapes over the years. By using it he planned on never being caught."

Roscoe thought a moment. "I can see why the writer didn't want to use his name. If any other pirates found it and identified him as the author they'd torture him for such information."

"But what about this 'vortex'?" Mike said. "Do you think it means they had some way of getting in and out of the Bermuda Triangle at will?"

"Don't know," Roscoe said. "Sounds kind of far-fetched. Then again, it does sound like when they shook that other ship they slipped through some sort of invisible doorway."

"It sure felt like an invisible doorway I went through when I came here," Mike said. "The weather went from sunny and calm to stormy and cold instantaneously. And that plane we saw at the beach came from somewhere." They sat looking at the collection of gold before them, deep in their own thoughts.

"A vortex," Roscoe muttered. "What I've called 'the eye of the needle'. There is definitely some sort of different dimension here."

"It seems that you can get from one dimension to another by either going directly through the vortex or by travelling fast in its vicinity. What gets me is that the vortex is undetectable. I wonder how close to it you have to get to be pulled through."

"Not only that," Roscoe said. "I wonder how they kept finding it."

"Derrick probably knew more than he told the British before they hanged him on Seaway Island," Mike said.

"Well," said Roscoe. "From all the evidence we've seen, this Captain Derrick must have known the vortex's exact location because we know for sure that he died on Seaway."

"Wherever he was going, he was in a big hurry," Mike said. "All this time I thought he was running for the mainland to escape the British that were after him. Now I'm convinced it wasn't the mainland he was running for at all, it was the vortex. The British just got him before he could get there."

"If that's the case," Roscoe said. "there must be one of these vortexes near Seaway Island. That is of course unless it moves around."

"That would explain why the first mate was killed," Mike said. "The enemy had the gold but not the secret. He wouldn't tell them so they killed him."

"Imagine that," Roscoe said. "A ton of gold that they only had to kill one guy for and they still weren't satisfied."

"Evidently they never took the gold," Mike said, "because it's still here. I just wonder if they are out there somewhere, planning to return for it one day."

Roscoe didn't reply.

They went back down to the fire and stirred it to life. The sun had just set and the fire would soon be their only source of light. Mike guessed it was about 9pm. It had been so long since he had seen a clock he was beginning to forget what time meant. Mentally, he had grown accustomed to just dividing the day into morning, mid-day, afternoon and night. He slept when he was tired and ate when he was hungry. He was getting used to it. He still thought of Jan almost all the time. As he stared into the fire he was thinking of her again. The urge to get off the island always came over him at times like these.

"Perhaps that boat we found today has an engine that still works," he said. "If so, then maybe it's lying on the bottom somewhere near shore. I'll start looking for it tomorrow morning."

He looked over at Roscoe, who sat silently, staring into the fire. Mike shuddered to think how many years of his life the old fellow had spent doing just that. Mike had no plans of doing the same with his life. "Then I'll need to make a trip to this summit you told me about."

"Tell a little more about Evan," Mike said. "Do you think he was a bit of a weirdo?"

"Yes," Roscoe said. "He was definitely weird. He told me he was a lighthouse keeper before he got lost in the Triangle and washed up here."

"Which one of you was here first?"

"I was," Roscoe said. "By a long time. I had been working on an old fishing boat for at least a year and was hammering away when he walked up out of the clear blue and started talking to me. He just started telling me all the reasons that the boat I was working on would never get me off the island. We talked for ten minutes before he got around to introducing himself."

"He just walked up?" Mike said.

"Yeah," Roscoe said. "It was the weirdest thing. He said his boat had thrown him out about the same way yours did, and he managed to swim to this island. He seemed to know that he was marooned before I even told him. Then he started talking about building a boat and sailing for home right away. I told him he was welcome to help me with the fishing boat but he declined. Said he could build a better one from scratch. At first I thought he was insane, but within a few weeks I was convinced that he was a genius. You know, there is really a fine line between the two."

"He knew about the Bermuda Triangle then?"

"Yes," Roscoe said. "He had some strange theories about it too. He claimed that it was a big doorway to another dimension, and that we were on the other side of that doorway here. A few months later, he took his home-made sail boat out just hours before a big storm. After it passed, I found debris all over the place, but nothing with which I could identify him."

"You say he was a lighthouse keeper?" Mike said.

"Yes, he was a walking encyclopedia on lighthouses," Roscoe said. "He knew where virtually every lighthouse in the world was located, when they were built and by whom. He was so into lighthouses. He used to talk about the lighthouse that he had to get back to. Said it would be unlit without him and that ships and lives would be lost if he didn't get back."

"That is weird," Mike said. "He sounds a little like a crazy old man I knew when I was a kid."

"Evan told me that the Bermuda Triangle didn't have definable boundaries," Roscoe said. "He said that it moved around, sometimes extending further to one side or the other. He was convinced that the Triangle actually expanded and contracted. That's why in some years there will be no disappearances and in others there will be a whole slew of them. According to him, there were no two consecutive days when the Bermuda Triangle's dimensions were exactly the same."

Mike was once again staring into the fire. "I knew this old guy that ran a lighthouse about a mile from my parent's summer place when I was a kid. He almost sounds like the guy you knew. He knew everything there was to know about lighthouses."

"I can't believe there could be two people like strange old Evan," Roscoe chuckled.

"This guy was strange too," Mike said. "He was a loner in the truest sense of the word. All the people in the neighborhood used to say he was crazy and that he was best avoided."

"Did you avoid him?"

"Oh yeah, at first anyway," Mike said. "I feared him. That is, until one day when I was at the beach with my dog throwing a tennis ball. The tides are real strong at the Outer Banks of North Carolina and the current caught my dog as he was chasing the ball that I had thrown out too far. He was struggling to get back to shore but couldn't make it. I was so scared he was going to drown. I knew better than to go out after him or the current would get me too. I just started screaming his name. I was terrified that I was going to be responsible for drowning my own dog. I was really panicked.

"Mr. Jonnsen just happened to be fishing a short distance down the beach and heard my screams and came running." Mike was too intent on the story to notice the expression of shock that came over Roscoe's face when he heard the name 'Jonnsen'.

"Mr. Jonnsen rushed over, saw what was happening and used his rod and reel to hook Sparkey. On about the third try he got him and reeled him in like a big fish. A moment later Sparkey made it to the shore and came running up to me. Mr. Jonnsen had hooked him in the scruff of the neck and bent down to carefully remove the hook. Sparkey was bleeding a little but was so happy to be on dry land that he wagged his tail and licked Mr. Jonnsen's face as he took out the hook. He was a real hero that day. I thanked him for saving Sparkey and we started a conversation. We must have talked for an hour right there on the beach. We became good friends. It didn't take long for me to realize that all the things I had heard about him were unfounded. He was just a nice old man that kept to himself."

Roscoe stared at Mike with his mouth hanging open.

Mike noticed his expression and smiled. "What's with you? Is there a sea monster sneaking up behind me or something?"

"Did you say his name was Jonnsen?" Roscoe said. "With a silent J?"

"I guess," Mike said. "I think he was Norwegian."

"What was his first name?"

"I never knew," Mike said. "I was just a kid so I called him Mr. Jonnsen."

Roscoe sat quietly a moment gathering his thoughts. "This is going to sound crazy, but the guy who left here five years ago was named Evan Jonnsen. The lighthouse he had to get back to was on the Outer Banks of North Carolina. And he too was Norwegian."

Mike looked puzzled. "Maybe he was the son of the guy I knew. Only I was almost certain he didn't ever marry or have any kids."

"You don't suppose it was the same man?" Roscoe said.

Mike looked at him. "That's not possible."

"We don't know that," Roscoe said. "In this strange place where ancient pirates and modern planes cross paths, who knows?"

"Surely you don't think he sailed from here five years ago and ended up twenty years back in my childhood," Mike said. "That's crazy."

"What else do you remember about him?" Roscoe said

Mike thought a moment. "He told me he had spent several years lost at sea," Mike said. "He talked about getting a boat and going back out to search for the Triangle, but I just thought it was some of his crazy talk."

"Why did he want to do that?"

Mike thought a moment. "To go after something. But I can't remember what it was."

Roscoe watched Mike's face as he searched his brain for the answer. Finally, his brown eyes widened and he looked at him in disbelief.

"Gold," Mike said.

"You're joking," Roscoe said.

"No. He was going to buy a boat as soon as he got the money, and go into the Bermuda Triangle for his gold. That's what he told me."

"Then it was the same man," Roscoe said.

"It couldn't be," Mike said. "It just isn't possible."

"Where do you suppose he is right now?" Roscoe said.

Mike looked at him and paused a moment. "I'm afraid he's dead, Roscoe."

Roscoe's eyes grew wide. "What? How? When?"

"Old age I guess," Mike said. "Almost twenty years ago."

Roscoe remained silent as he stared into the fire. Mike thought he could see tears in his eyes.

"Dead," Roscoe said.

"I'm sorry, Roscoe," Mike said.

Roscoe was silent for several long seconds and Mike decided to share more about his friend from all those years ago.

"The lighthouse became my second home after the day he saved Sparkey from drowning," Mike said. "Sparkey and I would walk over to the lighthouse around sunset and help fuel the lamp. Sometimes I got to light it. We'd sit at the top railing looking out to sea and he'd tell me stories. Sometimes I'd stay quite late and my mother would bitch at me when I finally got home. We had two great summers together. The following year when we returned I learned that he had died the previous winter. It was very tough on me. Summers there were never quite the same after that."

"What became of the lighthouse?"

"They automated it. It was rigged up to switch itself on when it got dark and off again at dawn. I remember trying to get up into it once and found 'No Trespassing' signs everywhere. They had sealed it off so nobody could get up there. That summer was the worst one of my life. It proved the old saying to me about how you can never go home again. It was really sad."

Roscoe was quiet for a moment. "He used to tell me stories too."

Mike looked over at him. "Wait a minute, do you really think we're talking about the same guy here."

Roscoe looked back at him, sullen faced. "Yes we are. There was only one Evan Jonnsen."

Mike stared into Roscoe's face and sighed. "You're right."

"Did he ever tell you stories about the Bermuda Triangle?" Roscoe said.

Mike thought a moment. "Yes he did. He was obsessed with it. He told me the boundaries of it were undefined, that there are even some places where it extends onto land."

"Islands?"

"Yes, and even onto the mainland as well. Mr. Jonnsen believed that the Bermuda Triangle actually came ashore with the fog, sometimes spilling into the isolated woodlands and swamps of the rural American coast under the cover of darkness."

"Do you really believe that?" Roscoe said. "I always thought he had a few screws loose somewhere."

"I believed him," Mike said. "He tended to ramble a bit sometimes, but everything about the sea that he ever told me proved to be true and accurate when I experienced them first-hand years later. He knew things that only the most experienced sailor would know."

"So, what did he tell you about the Bermuda Triangle?"

"He told me about growing up in southeastern Virginia, near the coast. There's a huge swamp down there called the Dismal Swamp. A good number of pirates supposedly disappeared there during the sixteenth and seventeenth centuries. They'd enter through a secret passage that linked the swamp to the ocean, trying to escape the English navy. The navy sailors wouldn't pursue them because it was too dangerous. The pirates would go in and get lost. Legend has it that their ghosts can still be seen on foggy nights even now, aimlessly searching for a way out."

"I remember him saying he was from Virginia," Roscoe said. "But he never told me about the swamp."

"One night, he saw a ghost ship," Mike said.

"A pirate ship?"

"Yes," Mike said. He felt a cold chill run up his spine as he recalled the terrified look in Mr. Jonnsen's eyes the night he told him the story.

"Mr. Jonnsen's father liked to canoe at night sometimes when the weather was warm and the moon was full. One night, the two of them were out in the swamp when a fog bank rolled in and overtook them suddenly. Evan told me he heard a strange sound in the distance. It sounded like several people all screaming in unison. At first the sound was very faint, but then it got louder as it drew closer. Then he could faintly make out a large dark object approaching from the middle of the swamp."

"What was it?"

"A Pirate ship," Mike said. "An old, dilapidated hulk with creaking boards and a tattered skull-and-crossbones flag. Then he saw the pirates. They were skeletons, manning their posts, steering the ship through the dark swamp the way they had been doing for over a century."

"Oh, come on," Roscoe said.

"Mr. Jonnsen swore it really happened. He said one of the skeletons was looking through a spyglass. When it spotted their little canoe, it told the others and they all looked and started pointing in his direction. A moment later the big pirate ship turned and headed right for them. They were going to run them over."

"What did Evan's father do?"

"He tried to paddle backward and get out of the way," Mike said. "But the Pirate ship was coming on too fast. Evan said that, right before the ship crushed them, he closed his eyes tight and let out a loud scream. A moment later he opened his eyes and the pirate ship was gone. He and his father sat still for a moment and caught their breath. Then, without saying a word, his father turned the canoe around and rowed back home.

"Neither of them spoke until right before they walked into the house. 'Don't say a word to your mother,' his father told him. They never spoke about it after that and Mr. Jonnsen told me that I was the first person he ever told that story. He even asked me not to repeat it. And, until tonight, I never have."

Roscoe sat looking at Mike, then turned and looked toward the ocean in the distance. "Evan was a strange man," he said.

"True," Mike said. "But he was smart too. I think we would be wise to remember what he told us."

"Oh hell," Roscoe said.

"What?"

"Are you sure he's dead?"

"That's what the neighbors told me," Mike said.

CHAPTER 5

▼

HURRICANE SEASON

Just after dawn the following morning, a frantic Roscoe awakened Mike.

"Mike," he said. "We'd better go take cover in the cave. A storm is coming."

Mike slowly woke and came to his senses. Outside, a strong wind was howling. A loud creaking sound was coming from the dozens of nails that held the tree house together. He could feel the structure swaying a few inches from side to side.

"Wind this strong is very unusual this far from the beach," Roscoe said. "It's an almost sure sign of a hurricane. We need to head for the cave."

"Are you sure?" Mike said groggily. "Maybe it's just a thunder storm."

"Maybe," Roscoe said. "But this tree house isn't safe with all the wind. And I just heard some thunder in the distance. We need to take cover just in case."

Mike sat up and started looking around for his shoes. The lightning flashed and about five seconds later a loud blast of thunder shook the entire structure. "You may be right." He jumped up from the bed and hurried outside.

Once on the ground, Mike looked up at the purple wall of storm clouds overhead. A light rain was falling. All around, the palm trees were blowing about, showing the undersides of their leaves as they reacted to the near gale-force wind.

"We'd better get the skins filled with water and gather as much fruit as we can," Roscoe said. "Then we'll head for the cave."

"Okay," Mike said, "but first things first. We need to pull the *Spear* further into the jungle where the surf won't be able to come in and carry it out to sea."

Another flash of lightning came at that moment and the thunder quickly followed. The storm was getting worse by the minute.

"We don't have time for that," Roscoe said.

"We're going to have to make time," Mike shouted back over the loud wind. "If we come out of that cave a day or two from now and find the *Spear* gone then we're back to square one. I can't take that chance."

He started for the east beach. After a few steps he turned and looked back at Roscoe. "You coming?"

Roscoe looked up at the blowing trees. "Okay, but let's make this fast."

The two of them hurried along the path toward the beach. When they reached it, Mike looked out at the furious ocean. The noise of the surf was deafening, and the wind whipped up white caps as far out as he could see. Toward the southeastern horizon the sky was black. As he watched, a bolt of lightning struck the water a couple of miles away.

"Wow, look at that," Roscoe said. "We need to move fast."

Mike grabbed the front of the *Spear* and Roscoe hurried over to help him roll it over. "I think it'll be easier to drag if it's upright," Mike shouted over the raging wind. Once it was overturned, the two of them started dragging it further up into the jungle. The boat was heavy and cumbersome, but with Mike pulling and Roscoe pushing from the back, they were able to make pretty good progress in the soft sand.

Once they had the *Spear* fifty feet further from the beach, a distance Mike feared was nowhere near far enough; they went back to pull the other boat next to it. The effort was slow and time consuming, and it was raining hard by the time they were done.

"Hopefully a tree won't fall on them here," Mike said as they rolled the *Spear* over once again. "I just hope we've gotten them far enough from the water."

"It'll have to do," Roscoe shouted over the wind. "Now let's go get the water and some fruit before the rain drowns us."

"Okay," Mike shouted. They hurried to the rich grove of trees where Mike gathered some fruit while Roscoe filled two wineskins with water from the spring. Then they ran for the cave.

Once inside, Roscoe took a Plexiglas boat windshield that he kept next to the opening and covered the entrance with it. Pushing sand around the base of it created a tight seal.

"This old windshield will keep the rain out and still let in the light", he said. "At least that way we'll know when it's day and when it's night."

"Very resourceful," Mike said. "It feels good to be under shelter."

"It helps my claustrophobia to be able to see outside." Roscoe peered through the Plexiglas. "If I stay close to the entrance then it's not too bad. I can always run outside if I start to panic."

Mike looked out through the dirty windshield. It was quite dark now and the rain was pelting down. "Thank goodness for this cave. How long do these things usually last?"

"About a day or so. I was in here for three days once, but that's really unusual. I think the hurricane kind of stalled out over the island that time. Usually I'm back outside in thirty-six hours. This is the first of the season so far. I imagine we'll see four or five before the end of the year."

The two of them were sitting in the sand in the cave's entrance, leaning against the opposite walls. The faint light from outside was the only light source. Roscoe had made a couple of new torches and they were close by. Mike knew that they should try to use them as little as possible. The time would pass slowly in here and they'd have to try and make the best of it.

"So tell me some more about Evan," Mike said. "Maybe something he did or said could give me some enlightenment about getting off this island alive."

Roscoe thought a moment. "He was always busy. When he wasn't working on the sailboat he was exploring the island. Sometimes I wouldn't see him for a couple of days at a time."

"Did he ever find anything interesting, like traces of ancient civilizations or anything like that?"

"I don't think so," Roscoe said. "But he was convinced that this island was part of the ancient continent of Atlantis."

"Atlantis," Mike said. "Isn't that place just a myth?"

"Evan didn't think so. He strongly believed that the Bermuda Triangle defied time somehow. I didn't agree with that until you and I saw that old navy plane that day. Since then I've gone over the evidence in my head and I'm beginning to think that he may have been onto something after all."

"So maybe he wasn't that surprised when he got back to civilization and found it earlier in time than when he first disappeared," Mike said. "But what made him believe in the time differential while he was still here?"

"He claimed he had psychic abilities."

Mike looked at Roscoe in surprise. "Psychic abilities?"

Roscoe laughed. "That's what he said. He was serious about it too. It's like I've said, he was a bit odd."

"Did he ever read your mind or anything to prove he was psychic?"

"No." Roscoe laughed. "But he pointed out a number of things to support his belief that we were inside the Bermuda Triangle's confines. For one thing, the beaches are mighty clean. And we couldn't be more than three or four hundred miles from the U.S. mainland here, and yet we never saw any planes or ships. Except for destroyed ones of course."

"Did you two get along?"

"For the most part," Roscoe said. "He just did things that didn't make sense to me."

"Like what?"

"Well, the weirdest thing was his trip to the summit. When he came back he started talking all this crazy stuff about the pirates buried up there."

"Did he think the place was haunted?"

"Yes", Roscoe said. "That's what he said."

"Did he see ghosts?"

"I don't think he saw them," Roscoe said. "But he sure heard them."

"He did?" Mike felt a cold chill run down his back.

"He spent three nights up there," Roscoe said. "Actually slept on the ground near the graves. He said he had vivid dreams, and that he heard voices and weird stuff like that."

"Voices?" Mike noticed that his voice cracked just a little on the word. "What did they tell him?"

"I'm not really sure. He came back a different man than the one he was when he left. I know that sounds crazy but it's true. That place changed him."

"How so?"

"He claimed he communicated with the dead pirates while he was there," Roscoe said. "They told him how to get in and out of the Bermuda Triangle at will to escape danger or hide treasure. He kept saying that he now knew 'the way' and that he was 'enlightened'."

"That old pirate diary talked about such a passage-way," Mike said. "And we now know that Evan did make it back home."

"We know now that he did," Roscoe said. "But at the time I had only one conclusion to reach and that was that

Evan had lost it. He kept telling me that everything he had learned up there was too complex to discuss with me, that it would take more time to explain than we had in a lifetime. The things he was saying all of a sudden just didn't make sense to me. They wouldn't make sense to anybody. That's why I didn't go with him when he left. I thought he was off his rocker.

"I mean, don't get me wrong, I liked the guy and he sure knew how to build a sailboat. But some of the things he believed in were crazy. I really figured I'd find his dead body on the beach within a few days of his leaving. The fact that you knew him after he got back home is really hard for me to believe. I never thought he would make it. Not in a million years."

"Did he seem certain that he was going to make it home safely when he left?" Mike said.

"He was positive he would," Roscoe said. "That was another thing about him that made me afraid to sail with him. He was too cocky."

"Well you must have thought he made it," Mike said. "After all, you continued to build signal fires for him."

"I needed something to live for," Roscoe said. "Besides, when I didn't find him dead on the beach for several weeks, I began to become convinced that he really might have pulled it off."

"Do you regret not going with him?"

"Not really," Roscoe said. "Look where it got him. He died alone and poor in a dank old lighthouse."

Mike thought of his old friend that he had liked so much as a boy. He may very well have been Evan's only friend at the time. The thought made him very sad. "Evan was a brave man," he muttered. "He wasn't afraid to take chances and it looks like he beat some long odds."

"You're right," Roscoe said. "He was a fine sailor. But what he did was sheer lunacy. I guess he was just more willing to take chances than I am."

Mike thought about the summit a few miles south of where they were sitting. Like Evan, he too needed to learn the secrets of the island. At the same time, the thought of going there alone gave him the creeps.

The rain continued to pound the Plexiglas at the cave entrance all night long. The two of them woke the next morning to faint light outside. Roscoe removed the cover and stuck his head out. "The storm's over," he exclaimed with a smile.

They emerged from the cave to find palm branches and other debris everywhere. A number of trees had been uprooted and were scattered about.

"Time to go home," Roscoe said. "Let's just hope it's still there!"

CHAPTER 6

▼

A SURPRISE AT THE SHORE

They walked through the jungle to the tree house and found it still standing. There had been some minor damage, a few boards had blown off and there were some large branches lying on the balcony, but it had escaped intact.

"I can't believe it wasn't demolished," Mike said.

"I built here because the area is fairly well protected from the wind," Roscoe said. "There's no perfect place to build but I chose this spot years ago because of the large number of tall trees in the area. The trees are taller here than in any other place I visited, leading me to believe that hurricanes have done less damage here over the years."

"Sounds like good thinking," Mike said.

"Then again," Roscoe said. "If one of these tall trees does blow down it'll destroy the whole structure. Looks like I got lucky again."

About an hour later the sun came out. After a hearty breakfast, the two of them headed for the lagoon to fish with a quick stop by the east beach to search through the latest debris. As soon as they reached the clearing, Mike went to check the boats. He pulled away some blown debris and found both to be in good shape. He also noticed a tree lying right where the boats had been before they moved them.

"Mike, come here quick!" Roscoe shouted.

Mike looked up. Roscoe was out on the beach about a hundred yards away.

"Hurry!" he screamed.

Mike bolted for him and ran as fast as he could.

As he got closer he saw Roscoe pointing at an object floating in the water.

"Look," he said. "I think there's a person out there."

Mike followed Roscoe's finger and spotted an object of some kind floating some one hundred feet from shore. It looked like a young man holding onto a log and losing a battle with the rough surf. "I think he's alive."

Mike rushed down the beach into the water and started swimming toward the struggling man. The sea was rough and filled with seaweed that hindered his ability to swim. Luckily he was well-rested and full of energy, and quickly closed the distance to the log. Within moments he got to it and found a man of about twenty-five clinging to the wood and struggling to keep his head above the surface. He appeared so weak that Mike wasn't sure he even knew someone was approaching. Mike grabbed the other end of the log and the young man's eyes opened. The poor fellow seemed to be asking for help but was too weak to utter a sound.

"Hang on." Mike started swimming and pushing the log toward shore.

Within minutes, Mike was nearly exhausted. Luckily, the log was big enough for them both to hold onto and he was able to rest his arms on it as he kicked with his feet. The undertow was very strong and he wasn't able to make much progress toward shore. They were still at least a hundred feet from the beach and Mike couldn't seem to get them any closer.

Seeing this, Roscoe rushed to the woods and found a long vine. He grabbed a medium-sized stick and tied the vine to it, then rushed out a few feet into the water and began throwing the stick toward Mike. When he let it fly, the piece of wood landed in the water and floated there. It took several tries before Roscoe placed it within Mike's reach but when he finally did, Mike grabbed it and held on. Roscoe then started pulling them into shore.

Once Mike could make contact with the ocean bottom he let go of the log and took hold of the other man to carry him. The poor fellow didn't want to let go of the log but Mike assured him he would be okay. Mike carried him out of the water and up the beach above the high-water mark.

Roscoe rushed over as Mike set the man down on the sand. "Is he still alive?"

"Barely," Mike said. "Mostly dehydrated I bet. We'd better get him into the shade and to some water, fast."

Mike remembered the little stream he first found when he arrived on the island and decided the quickest way to get water would be to take him there.

"Help me carry him," Mike said. He and Roscoe each got under an arm and began carrying the man to the jungle.

He was a few inches shorter than Mike and weighed about one hundred twenty pounds.

"He's easier to move than the *Spear*," Roscoe said.

Once they reached the small pool of water they set him down on the ground and Mike began scooping handfuls of water onto him. This revived him a little and he made his way over to the water and began cupping it into his mouth. The young man gulped water for several minutes. Finally he laid back and gasped for breath.

This man was a few years younger than Mike, twenty-two or so. He had straight dark blonde hair that just reached his shoulders and steel-gray eyes. He was clean-shaven, at least for the moment. Mike couldn't help think that he might be too young to grow facial hair. We'll find out in a few days, he thought.

"Better now?" Roscoe said.

"Yes," the man said between deep breaths. "You fellows saved my life."

"How about something to eat?" Mike said. "You hungry?"

"Yes, very," he said.

Mike helped him to his feet and they led the way to the camp. The young man was still having trouble walking so Mike assisted him. When they finally reached camp, Mike sat him down in one of the chairs and he and Roscoe fetched him oranges.

Mike cut them into quarters and the young man sat and ate every one they brought him. Although he was a bit sunburned and obviously exhausted, he soon was recovering nicely.

"Well, at least you have a healthy appetite," Roscoe said. "I guess that means you'll be okay. What's your name?"

"Les," he said. "Les Harrison."

Roscoe and Mike introduced themselves.

"Where am I?" Les said.

Roscoe looked at Mike. "Sound familiar?"

"I need to find a phone right away," Les said. "Can one of you drive me to the nearest town?"

"There are no towns out here," Roscoe said. "No phones either."

"No phones?" Les said.

"No," Mike said. "We're marooned here."

Les tried to get to his feet. Mike rushed over and grabbed him before he fell to the ground. "Take it easy. You're still disoriented."

"I've got to get back to Miami right away," Les said.

"You're not going anywhere any time soon," Roscoe said.

Les stood and staggered a few steps toward the path back to the beach.

"I wouldn't go far if I were you," Mike said. "You sure don't want to get lost here."

Les stopped and looked back at the two of them. For several long seconds he stood reading their faces. Mike looked into his eyes and got the feeling that Les was reading some of his thoughts. That made him a bit uneasy.

"You guys are serious," Les said at last.

"Yes," Roscoe said. "Unfortunately."

Fatigue seemed to reclaim its hold on Les. He walked slowly back to the chair and sat down. "I've got to find a way back to Florida and fast."

"I know the feeling," Mike said. He and Roscoe then told him about the island and what predicament he was now in with them. He asked a lot of questions and they answered as best they could. About half-an-hour later he was fully up to date. Just as Mike had weeks before, Les found the news hard to accept.

"This can't be happening," Les said. "The Bermuda Triangle doesn't even exist."

"I'm afraid it does," Mike said.

"What's your story?" Roscoe said. "How did you get out there in those rough seas?"

"I'm not sure," Les said. "We were cruising along slowly in my fishing boat about ten miles off shore from Miami when the boat just accelerated by itself. I cut the engines and it just kept going faster and further out to sea. Suddenly the boat seemed to have a mind of its own. It bounced up and down, spinning around the whole time. The next thing I knew I was thrown clear into really rough water. I fought to reach the surface and almost didn't make it. When I did get to the surface I couldn't see the boat, or anything else for that matter. It was as if it and everyone on board had gone somewhere else without me. I guess it sank. If I hadn't happened to spot that floating tree trunk I would have drowned. I must have been out there on that thing for more than a day.

"Finally, I saw the land and figured it was the mainland. But whenever I tried to maneuver the tree trunk toward it and paddled with my feet the current kept pulling me back out. If you guys hadn't seen me and pulled me in I'd still be out there, probably forever." He shivered.

"You said 'we'," Mike said. "There were others with you?"

"Yes, two fishing buddies," Les said. "I don't know what happened to them. I lost track of them and the boat in all the turbulence. I hope they fared better than I did."

Neither Mike nor Roscoe offered speculation on what may have become of Les' buddies. Mike figured there was no reason to make speculations until a body or two washed up somewhere on the beach.

Les kept looking around. "I've got to get back to Miami. I'm supposed to testify in a court case on Tuesday. That's tomorrow isn't it?"

"You tell us," Mike said.

"You'll be here a while," Roscoe said. "I've been here every Tuesday for the last decade."

"What are you guys doing to get out of here?" Les said.

"I've been working on a boat," Mike said. "The hull was badly damaged but I've got her almost ready to float again."

"What about the motor?" Les said. "How close are you with it?"

"Not close at all," Mike said. "It was really banged up. I don't think it can be fixed. Do you know anything about boat motor repair?"

"Yes," Les said. "I own my own machine shop. If a motor can be fixed I can fix it."

"Sounds good," Mike said. "There was a second boat that washed up a couple of weeks ago. I've been using the boards from it to fix the first one."

"What about its motor?"

"Didn't have one," Mike said. "But I think it may be around somewhere. I found a gas tank in the water near the shore that I think came from the same boat. I've been combing the beach looking for the motor but haven't had any luck."

"We'll find it," Les said.

Mike smiled. "That sounds good to me." He looked over at Roscoe. He was smiling too.

The next day, Mike took Les to see the *Spear* and the other boat. Les assessed the damage and Mike's repair work. "Looks like you've done a pretty good job repairing the hull," he said. He examined the other boat. "I think there's enough material here to finish the job. I'd say we could have her ready in a week or so."

He then turned his attention to the *Spear's* badly damaged motor. "Uh oh," he said.

"Think you can do anything with it?" Mike said.

Les tinkered with it for a moment. Then he pounded on it with his fist and several small pieces fell to the ground. "This thing has had it," he said. "Back at my machine shop I would label a motor in this condition as 'totaled'. It needs a lot of new parts."

"I was afraid of that," Mike said.

"Where did you find the gas tank?"

"I'll show you," Mike said. They walked a few hundred yards to the spot and Mike pointed it out. "It was sitting on the bottom about thirty feet out there."

Les waded out and looked around. After a minute he walked back up the beach. "I couldn't see anything out there," he said. "For all we know, the motor could have come off miles from here."

"That's what I was afraid of," Mike said.

"We'll keep looking though," Les said. They walked back to the *Spear*.

"I might as well disassemble this motor," Les said. "Then it will be easier to determine which parts I can use."

Mike walked over to the other boat and began removing the boards from the hull with a crow bar. "I'll do the same thing with this boat," he said. They both got busy and spent the time getting better acquainted.

"So, did you grow up in Miami?" Mike said.

"No. I moved down from Atlanta after graduating from high school. What about you?"

"I was born in Staunton, Virginia and lived there until I was about twelve," Mike said. "Later on, we moved to Charlotte, North Carolina. My family used to take a vacation to the ocean every summer and that's where I fell in love with the sea. Not much work available along the Carolina coast however. That's why I moved to Miami."

There was a loud creak as Mike pried one of the seats from the boat. He tossed it aside and started removing nails from the floorboards.

"What was the date when you went fishing and ended up here?" he said.

"The first weekend in August," Les said.

"No, I mean what year?"

Les looked at Mike with a puzzled expression. "This year," he said. "1996."

Mike's eyes widened. "Oh no." He nodded his head. He felt his hopes of ever seeing Jan again take another dip.

"You mean you've been gone so long you've forgotten the year?" Les said. "I thought you'd only been here a few weeks."

"Yes," Mike said slowly. "But when I left it was 2001!"

Les smiled a little. "Not very funny."

"I'm not joking." This led to a long discussion that made Les briefly question Mike's sanity.

"Just goes to prove that the only constant around here is change," Mike said. "Time means nothing here. On this island it's just a figment of your imagination."

While Les continued his work on the *Spear*'s motor, Mike began telling him about Evan Jonnsen and the bizarre circumstances under which both he and Roscoe had met him. Surprisingly, it only took about twenty minutes to tell the story. Mike found Les to be a good listener. A large number of people had preceded them into this predicament and it would be foolish to disregard their accumulated knowledge without disproving it first. Les seemed to realize that fact and accept it.

"I'm done here," Les said. He tossed the screwdriver back into the toolbox.

"Are we even close?" Mike said.

"No. We've got about a quarter of an engine here." Les looked out at the ocean. "We've got to find the motor from that boat."

Mike was disappointed but tried to remain optimistic. "Why don't we head back to camp. I'm thirsty, and it's about time to start planning dinner."

"Yeah," Les said. "I guess we still have to catch and gather it."

They went back to camp and got a drink of water at the spring. Roscoe had been repairing the damage to the tree house, replacing some of the boards that had blown off in the storm. When Les and Mike sat in the chairs in the shade Roscoe decided to join them.

"So, Roscoe," Les said. "Tell me more about Evan. Are you certain you both knew the same guy?"

"Oh, beyond any doubt," Roscoe said.

Les asked many questions and Mike and Roscoe answered them, always in agreement with each other about the details. Roscoe then told Les about Evan's changed personality after his visit to the summit and the pirate cemetery. Roscoe added even more details to the information he had earlier shared with Mike.

"Evan spent a lot of time pondering his thoughts after his return from up there," Roscoe said. "He described it as being 'adrift in the dinghy of thought.' He wouldn't talk much at times. I began to figure that he had somehow gathered a lot of information in his sleep while he was up on that big hill and was now trying to sort it all out. Whatever it was, apparently it worked. Sort of."

"Interesting," Les said. "I guess there really is something to this Bermuda Triangle. And all this time I thought it was just a myth."

Later that day they fished and gathered fruit. Once darkness approached they got a good fire going and sat down to a tasty dinner.

As he ate, Mike observed Les' facial expressions as he stared into the fire. Once his train of thought seemed completed Mike asked him what was on his mind.

"Maybe I can find some more engine parts in the debris piles," Les said. "If you two will work on finishing the hull, I'll do what I can with the engine. I've been doing boat engine repair for many years and have a few nice little tricks up my sleeve. Eventually, I'll get a motor built that works."

"That's the best sounding news I've heard in a long time," Mike said.

"Yeah," Roscoe said. "I'm ready to blow this joint."

CHAPTER 7

▼

THE GIFT OF THE SIXTH SENSE

The warm fire crackled, Roscoe and Les started talking and Mike drifted into his own world of thought. He stared into the fire, seeing Jan's beautiful face clearly in his mind. He loved her so much and knew she loved him. A life without her would be an existence, little more. He had to try to get used to the fact that they could get home and find it years earlier than it was when he left. It could be 1996 again, the year Les left. If that were the case then he and Jan would not have met yet. Could he recreate the same scenario all over again? Would she fall in love with him again? Would she even give him the chance? The whole concept frightened him terribly. Now more than ever, he wished he had never embarked in the Dream for Seaway Island on that fateful morning.

As Mike's mind drifted back to the conversation between Roscoe and Les, his ears re-engaged to their voices.

"I hope the trial came out okay without me," Les said. "I'm afraid it may have been a lost cause though."

"What kind of trial was it?" Roscoe said.

"A child abduction that resulted in murder," Les said.

By this time Les had Mike's undivided attention. "A child was murdered?" Mike said.

"Yes," Les said. "A six year old boy. It was a senseless killing. I was the prosecution's main weapon."

"Tell us about it," Roscoe said.

Les paused for a long moment as he gathered his thoughts. "Okay," he said. "I have some kind of psychic ability. I don't really know what it is or how it works, but I was born with some special ability to investigate crimes using a sixth sense." He paused, perhaps to allow Mike and Roscoe the opportunity to express their doubts. Both were listening intently and neither was smiling.

"Most people don't believe psychic powers exist so I don't talk about it much," Les said. "But for some reason I've always had this ability I can't explain to obtain knowledge about things I logically couldn't possibly know."

"What kind of knowledge?" Mike said.

"Facts about crimes that took place hundreds of miles away from me", Les replied. "I've gathered critical evidence at crime scenes just by touching the victim's hand and picking up impressions from his mind. I know it sounds crazy but it's what happened in this case. The little boy's body was found in a grove of trees about twenty feet from a highway. Everybody in the county had been looking for him for a week when a jogger stumbled upon him.

"When the story broke I saw it on television and began getting a sensation that I might be able to shed some light on the crime. I contacted the Sheriff's department and

told them I was a psychic and wanted to help. He probably would have told me to get lost under normal circumstances but was catching a lot of flack from the public
about the lack of a suspect. He was in no position to turn
anyone away that could help him so he told me to come
right over.

"The next morning I showed up at the police station
and he drove me over to the scene. I walked around,
touched the ground where the little boy's body had been
found, and basically tried to open up my mind. I got a
very weak impression and knew what that meant. 'The little boy wasn't murdered here', I told the sheriff. 'He was
killed somewhere else and brought here for disposal.' I
walked around a little more and stood at the roadside.
'The killer parked his car right in this spot', I said.

"'How could you possibly know that?' he asked me.

"'I don't know', I replied. 'This sixth sense of mine
works in mysterious ways. If I could see his body I could
tell you more.'

"'He's in the morgue', the sheriff said. 'Let's go.'

"We drove back to town and went inside the morgue. I
had never been in such a place before and it really gave
me the creeps. Still, my sixth sense led the way and basically told me what to expect. I actually saw the little boy
in my mind before the Sheriff opened the drawer to roll
him out. I won't describe what he looked like because it
was quite disturbing. I reached down and took his cold
hand in mine.

"Immediately I got images from him, events began
rolling like a movie before my mind's eye. I found myself
in the back seat of a car. A man with long blond hair was
driving. I couldn't see his face but I could hear a terrified

child crying and moaning. I felt terror. The man driving kept yelling something but I couldn't tell what because of the crying. My eyes were filled with tears and I was trembling. The man was very nervous, angry, and driving fast.

"Suddenly he turned his head and looked back and I got a good look at his face. He had a sandy beard, blue eyes and a scowling expression. Then I clearly heard him yell; 'can't you shut that kid up!' Someone was holding me down, I couldn't move. A moment later the image faded but what I had seen stayed clearly in my mind. I opened my eyes and looked down at the dead boy. I was madder than hell.

"'I can identify one of the killers if you let me see some mug shots while the image is still fresh in my mind', I told the Sheriff.

"'Let's try the big station downtown in Miami,' he said, and we drove the thirty miles or so into the city. We got inside the police precinct and they took me straight to the files.

"Luckily, they had them computerized and I could narrow it down somewhat. They pulled up hundreds of photos of Caucasian males between twenty and forty years old with blue eyes and started running them in front of me. Most I could rule out right away, several I had to study a moment before eliminating. Then a photo came up and my sixth sense went off. 'That's him,' I exclaimed. A guy named Brad Stevens with a police record a mile long. They wasted no time going and getting him.

"At midnight they brought him in. I picked him out of a line-up and they immediately started interrogating him. He had no idea what led them to him and apparently feared someone had set him up. In almost no time at all he admitted to being the driver but not the killer. When the police began talking capital punishment he sang like a little bird and identified the triggerman. They got him the next day and quickly began unraveling the gory details.

"It turned out to be a kidnapping that went awry. They were going to try to get a ransom from the boy's wealthy father but when they strangled him by accident they dumped the body and fled. It probably wasn't going to be necessary to involve me in the trial since the driver was going to testify against the killer to save himself, but I wanted to be there just to make sure."

"Wow, that's unbelievable," Mike said.

"Yeah," Roscoe said. "But how did you become a psychic?"

"Well, I didn't exactly apply for it," Les chuckled. "But when I was a kid growing up, there were occasions when I knew things were going to happen before they did."

"You mean like the final score of the Super Bowl?" Mike said.

"Oh no, nothing like that." Les shook his head. "It was always on a more personal level."

"When did it first begin?" Roscoe said.

"One of the first incidents I can remember was when I was in grade school," Les said. "It was recess and I was out on the playground with the rest of the kids in my class. There was this bully kid I didn't like named Johnny. I don't think anybody else liked him either. Anyway, he really had it in for me for some reason.

"Johnny was at bat and I was standing between him and the backstop talking to a buddy of mine on the other side of the fence. I told my friend that I would get to bat in one more out, just seconds before Johnny struck-out. Suddenly a voice in my head told me to bend down and tie my shoe. I bent over and realized that they were both already tied. An instant later a bat sailed over me and hit the backstop with a thud. Johnny had thrown the bat at my head and I would never have seen it coming. I also would never have expected anyone to do something so dangerous, but if it had hit me it would have caused serious injury. I stood up and glared at him. He looked at me and called me a 'lucky bastard'. Then he said he'd get me later. I was really scared of him and he knew it."

"That fool could have killed you," Mike said.

"I know," Les said. "But after that I was really on my toes and my sixth sense was in overdrive. The next day, the class was walking single file down the hall and a vision jumped into my head of Johnny pushing me down the stairs. Mentally I noted exactly where it would happen. The class turned a corner and started down the steps. On the fourth step I suddenly stepped to my left. An instant later Johnny went sailing past me headfirst. He had thrown all his weight at me and was going to knock me into oblivion. When I moved he was in big trouble. He flew past me down the stairs and landed in a heap at the bottom. He wound up with a broken arm and a busted chin, which required twelve stitches.

"What made it even better was that the teacher saw the whole thing and I got none of the blame. School got out for summer two weeks later and I never saw him again. It was then that I realized my sixth sense was a special gift and that I should treat it with respect."

"That's quite a story," Roscoe said. "You sound a little like Evan. Have there been other instances like that?"

"Plenty," Les said. "More than I can remember."

"Sounds to me like you're really lucky to have this extra sense," Mike said.

"I'm lucky and at the same time cursed," Les said.

"What do you mean?" Mike said. "I can't imagine there being a downside to such a luxury."

"I've also gone out on dates with someone I really liked and half-way through the date had my sixth sense tell me she was never going out with me again," Les said. "Just out of the blue I would realize she was going through the motions until the evening was over. Luckily I didn't have to bother asking her out again just to be told 'no'. Still, it was discouraging."

"I still think you're blessed," Mike said. "At least you didn't have to ask and then find out she didn't like you like I did."

Les chuckled. "I guess you have a point there. Still, there are some things it tells me that I'd rather not know. But then again, there's more good than bad to it."

"I'm going to bed." Roscoe stood.

"Good idea," Les said. "I want to get busy on that boat early tomorrow."

"Do you have any idea where we should sail once the boat's ready?" Mike said.

"East I guess," Les said. "Why?"

"I thought maybe we should find 'the eye of the needle.' Maybe you can direct your sixth sense on it."

"Is there anything to go on?" Les said.

"An old pirate diary," Mike said. "It might tell you something."

"We'll go over everything before we set sail. I'm sure we can find our way out of here somehow."

"I sure hope so," Mike muttered. And with that, he went off to bed himself.

The following morning, the three of them began working on the *Spear's* hull. Using boards and nails from the other boat, the reconstruction went quite well. By mid-afternoon, the hull was about finished.

"We need to make some caulk for the cracks between boards," Roscoe said. "We can get some tree sap and make glue. We can also use it to strengthen the nailed areas."

"Great idea," Mike said. "Now if we can only find the motor from this boat."

"Keep checking the beach," Roscoe said. "Scour the edges of the woods, the shallow water and dig in the sand. The eastern shore of this island has had wrecks all over it. It's a virtual used-parts gold mine."

"No time like the present," Les said.

Roscoe said that he would start getting sap for making caulk and Mike and Les headed for the shore. They exited the jungle and emerged onto the hot beach. Les looked at Mike. "Which way to where you found the gas can?"

"Right," Mike said.

"Let's go left," he said. "I've got a hunch."

Mike agreed and they headed down the beach looking all around. Nothing in particular caught their eye. After going about a mile they came to an outcropping of rocks that caused Les to stop. The beach was littered with boulders and there was a short rocky cliff about ten feet high that ended at the water's edge.

"I've never been this far around the beach on this side before," Mike said.

Les walked over toward the small cliff. There was a narrow beach in front of it that only appeared for a few moments between each wave. The sea would come in and crash up against the rock wall, then recede, taking all the water with it for a few moments. The bare sand would reflect the sky on its shiny surface for that brief period before the next wave would loudly steamroll in and repeat the cycle.

Mike watched Les from some fifty feet away as he crept closer to the side of the cliff. The whole cliff only appeared to be about thirty feet across, but in order for a person to get from the beach on one side to the beach on the other; he would have to pass through that dangerous, wave-swept area in front of the cliff. Mike realized with horror that Les was about to attempt to do just that.

"Les," he yelled out over the noise of the surf. Les didn't turn around but Mike knew he could hear him. "Climb the cliff and go overland to get around. That way's too dangerous."

"I don't want to get around," he called back.

Mike rushed over to him as Les waited at the edge of the pounding surf. "What are you thinking?"

"I see something half buried in the sand over there." He pointed about twenty feet away. "Watch the spot where I'm pointing."

Mike followed the point and watched for a moment as they waited for the surf to roll back. Wave after wave came, keeping the spot under water continuously. There was a lull and the beach became dry on the spot. Mike could see a shiny red object of some kind sticking an inch or so out of the sand. Just as quickly as it appeared, it again vanished as a huge wave slammed the wall and spattered water in all directions.

"Maybe the tide will go out enough for us to dig that thing up soon," Les said.

"I think it's pretty low right now," Mike said.

"Think so?" Les looked up at the sky. It was still morning and the sun was to the east.

"I'll bet right before dawn would be the best time," Les said. "The sun will be pulling the ocean as far away from the spot as possible right then and we could probably get in there."

"I think you're right."

"Let's come back tomorrow morning," Les said. "But while we're here, let's walk a little further."

They climbed up over the top of the small cliff and got around to the beach on the other side. Then they walked along the shore for another hour or so, seeing the north side of the island for the first time. Mike couldn't help but notice how the environment on this side was vastly different from the beaches in the other direction.

Erosion was wearing away the island's sand at an alarming rate. Much of the shoreline had little or no beach at all. A large number of live palm trees stood tall with their trunks in the water twenty or so feet off shore. Further out were dead trees, submerged in water so deep that only the tops were above the surface. A whole forest of palms rolled into the sea.

The jungle came right up to the shore and some of the vegetation had its roots exposed. The constant motion of the waves was cutting away the shore bit by bit. The shallow water was pristine, free of tar, bottles or cans. It was the cleanest shoreline Mike had ever seen.

"I sure wish the waterfront back home still looked this clean."

"Yes," Les said. "It's amazing. This shoreline is so clean it's almost like it's from another century."

"Maybe it is," Mike said.

Les looked at the dead and dying trees. "I guess the island is just sinking. It almost looks like this side is at the edge of a continental plate that's being pulled under the earth's crust."

"Continental drift?" Mike said.

"Yes. You know, that's what scientists speculate may have happened to the continent of Atlantis."

You believe Atlantis really existed?" Mike said.

"Oh yeah. There's plenty of evidence supporting it. The ancient Greeks traded with somebody from the Western Hemisphere long before Columbus discovered America. And recent discoveries of ancient stone walls and roads under the waters near Bimini support the theory as well."

Mike looked around them. "Where do you suppose those inhabitants are now?"

"Maybe something wiped them out. Maybe this island is all that remains of a once-vast continent. Look at those trees out there. This island is going under the Caribbean tectonic plate. Who knows how long it'll be before it goes under completely."

Mike remembered some of the things he had read about Atlantis. He never really thought it existed because there were no artifacts or other tangible clues to prove, to him at least, that it did. On the chance that they were on Atlantis during its dying years, they would need to leave before it sank completely. He was confident that they still had a few years, maybe more than a lifetime.

"The Bermuda Triangle may have gotten them," Les said.

Mike looked at him. "Maybe it's going to come for us too."

"Let's keep walking," Les said.

Mike agreed. Once they were where they could get way out from the trees and see far ahead, they realized they were at the northernmost point of the island. Around the corner that slowly curved back to the left they could see empty beach for a couple of miles.

"Ready to head back?"

"Sure," Mike said.

"I think I could learn something in that pirate cemetery," Les said as they trudged along on the warm sand. "Maybe there's some supernatural force up there. If it communicated with Evan then maybe it'll communicate with us too."

The thought gave Mike the creeps. "Do you really think there's any reason to go to all that trouble just to visit a pirate cemetery?"

"Apparently Evan thought so. Besides, I always get impressions whenever I walk through a cemetery, especially at night. Sometimes I wonder if the dead are trying to tell me something. It can be really scary. But in this case, it could be informative too."

An hour or so later they walked back into the campsite.

"Hey guys," Roscoe said.

Mike saw that he was carrying a couple of wicker baskets and went over to lend a hand. One of the baskets had bananas, a little bag of berries and a couple of coconuts. The other was full of live crabs.

Roscoe handed the bag of crabs to Mike and he opened it and looked inside. There were a dozen or so big ones in there and each reached up with its large blue claw. Mike closed the bag and hung it on a tree branch. He then went to gather up some firewood.

Before long the preparations were done and they sat in their chairs around the campfire and ate.

"So Les," Roscoe said. "I've been meaning to ask you when and where you were born."

"Oh," he said between bites of juicy crabmeat. "Atlanta, February 2, 1970."

Roscoe thought a moment. "That makes you about thirty or so?"

"No," Les chuckled. "I'm twenty-five."

"Wait a minute," Roscoe said. "Mike tells me this is 2001. You're not twenty-five."

"Yes," Les said. "I was twenty-five earlier this year."

Les explained to him what he and Mike had discussed a day earlier. The time situation again hit home for Mike. He and Les had been born less than a year apart and yet he was now much older.

Roscoe and Les went on talking as Mike stared into the fire and thought of his beloved back in Miami. Tears formed in his eyes, as he thought of Jan in her pretty white bathing suit with the Miami Dolphin insignia over her heart. The one she was wearing the day he picked up the most perfect starfish he'd ever seen and gave it to her, telling her it was put on that beach on that particular day especially for the prettiest girl in the world. The same white bathing suit she was wearing when she took the starfish, smiled, put her arms around him and told him that she loved him.

The three of them finished eating.

"Roscoe," Les said. "I think we'd starve without you."

Roscoe smiled and finished his cup of coconut milk.

Les then filled Roscoe in on their discovery earlier in the day. "Just before dawn tomorrow morning when the tide is at its lowest we'll dig that thing up," Les said. "Hopefully it's the motor from that second boat you two found."

"Do you really think that's what it is?" Roscoe said.

"It's possible," Les said. "Most of the damage on that boat is in the front part. There's a place on the side near the back where it looks like the surf banged it against a hard surface, possibly those very rocks. If that's the case, then maybe the motor was jarred loose and sank right to the bottom."

"Then it may be still intact," Roscoe said.

"Maybe," Les said. "Plus, I got a really good feeling about it when I spotted it."

"Hey," Roscoe said. "We could be on our way soon."

"A nice stash of gold would make matters a lot easier financially for us once we get back," Mike said.

"Absolutely," Roscoe said. "After spending so much of our lives here we might as well go home rich."

All three looked at each other and smiled. The smiles became laughter.

Mike pictured himself placing the crown on Jan's head and pronouncing her his princess for life. It gave him a warm feeling.

The three of them sat staring into the fire for several more hours that night, each in his individual world of thought.

CHAPTER 8

▼

THE LEGACY OF GREED

The sun wasn't up when Roscoe woke Mike. Having slept as late as he wanted practically every day since arriving on the island, Mike had forgotten how difficult it was to get up early.

"I've done my part," Roscoe said proudly. "Now I'm going to bed."

Mike rested another minute or two and then caught himself trying to go back to sleep. That motivated him to get up and go wake Les.

Once he was dressed and outside, Mike noticed that the sun had still not made it to the horizon but the sky was blue and too bright to see any stars.

Les came out and they headed for the beach. "Let's grab something to dig with."

"There's an old coal shovel in the storage hut," Mike said.

"That should do," Les said. "Let's take a sword from the pirate collection with us also."

"I'll grab that little potter's shovel too." Mike retrieved the implements and they headed for the beach. When they reached it, they saw the sun halfway out of the ocean. By the time they got to the small rock outcropping there was plenty of light. The tide was out, which left an area of dry beach about ten feet wide.

"Wow," Les said. "Even at low tide there isn't much beach in front of these rocks." They quickly searched around and couldn't find any traces of the red object they had seen earlier in the sand.

"I think it was right about here." Mike began poking the sand with the sword. A few jabs later he struck something solid about six inches under the surface. "Here it is!"

"Let's hope this is the motor we're looking for," Les said as he began digging. The coal shovel was wide and flat, and progress was slow. "This is like digging with a snow shovel."

"It's better than using our bare hands," Mike said as he aided the process with the much smaller potter's shovel. Gradually, over the next half-hour, the dull red-colored object began to reveal itself. It soon became apparent that it was the battered remains of an old outboard motor.

"If this is what I think it is then we're in business," Les said.

"It's probably in terrible shape," Mike said.

"We can clean it up," Les said. "And maybe fix it with the spare parts from the *Spear*'s motor." Les took the sword and stuck the point under the object. He began pushing down on the handle, trying to pry it loose.

Mike continued digging around the edges and soon revealed the word "Evinrude" printed on its side. "Almost there," he said.

They kept digging and soon got the entire top portion uncovered. Still, the motor remained mired in the sand. A little more digging and the base began to come loose. The two of them got on opposite sides and tried lifting from the top. The motor wouldn't budge.

"Hold it steady and I'll dig some more," Mike said.

Les stood holding it and Mike reached into the hole and dug around the base. A moment later Les tried rocking it from side to side and got it to move slightly.

"Let's try pulling up on it now," Les said.

The tide was coming in now and they were already ankle-deep in water. Mike got back to the opposite side from Les and together they rocked and lifted. After a moment the entire motor came free. Only the propeller was missing.

"Hey," Mike said. "Maybe we have everything we need now." They dragged it away from the rocks and up onto the shore.

"Now comes the fun part," Les said. "I'll see if I can piece this thing together with what we already have and build a motor that will run."

"How about we haul this thing up to a shady spot where you can work on it later and then go get some breakfast," Mike said.

"Fine by me." They carried the motor up the beach and put it on the ground next to the *Spear*. Then they rolled a couple of logs together and set the engine on them to keep it off the ground.

Les pulled off the outer covering. Sand and seawater came pouring out.

"Is everything intact?" Mike said.

"I think so," Les said. "Let's let it dry out and then I'll see what I can do with it." They headed back to the tree house for something to eat.

Roscoe was excited by the news that a working boat motor could be theirs in just a few days. "Is there any more gold left in the cave beside the stuff at the entrance?" Roscoe said.

Mike took a moment to think. "No," he said. "The hidden treasure chest was the last of it. That is, except for the coins I left on the floor."

"What did you do that for?" Roscoe said. There was a slight hint of anger behind the question.

"To mark the main trail so I didn't get lost," Mike said.

"How about going back in and gathering them up?" Roscoe said. "I mean, when you get a minute."

"Why bother?" Mike bit into a banana. "We've already got more gold than we can carry. Let's just leave it."

"Just leave it," Roscoe said. "Those coins are valuable. We need all of them."

Les looked over at Roscoe with a surprised expression. "What's the big deal, Roscoe? We've got plenty of gold. Just forget about the coins."

"No," Roscoe said. "If you don't want them, fine. But I do. Mike, would you please go back in and gather them up?"

Mike glanced over at Les. "Okay," he said. "But why are you so interested in them. There are plenty more coins piled up in the treasure room."

"Because the coins are probably the most valuable pieces of gold of all," Roscoe said. "Not only are they made of gold, they have value to collectors because they are relics of the Spanish conquerors. When you consider how small they are by comparison to how much we can sell them for when we get home, they're priceless."

"Let me get this straight," Les said. "Are you telling me that you intend to take a boat-full of gold with us when we leave?"

Roscoe flashed a greedy smile. "Let me answer your question with another question. Would you even consider leaving here without it? Are you crazy? There's enough gold in that cave to make all of us rich. There's no way in hell I'd leave here without a substantial horde in my pockets. And in my shoes and my hat…"

"Roscoe," Mike said, "we aren't going to be able to haul a lot of heavy gold with us when and if we leave here. We'll be lucky just to get back ourselves."

"Now you're starting to sound like Evan," Roscoe said. "He used to say the same things about how there wasn't enough room on the boat for gold and provisions both, and how the gold would weigh us down too much. That's a bunch of crap. I know we can't take all those gold bars with us when we leave but we can at least take enough to set us up just fine when we get home."

Les stared at Roscoe. "Did you and Evan argue about this?"

Roscoe stopped chewing and glared back. "I wouldn't say we argued. But the issue did come up quite a bit during the last several weeks he was here."

"Did he tell you that you couldn't take any gold with you?" Mike said.

Roscoe resumed chewing before answering. "Yes. He gave me an ultimatum. No gold on the boat or I don't get to go."

"Is that the real reason you're still here?" Les said.

"Mostly," Roscoe said. "And it cost him too. If Evan is indeed the same person you knew as a kid Mike, then he died alone and penniless. I've already spent too much of my life on this lousy island. When I leave I have no intention of doing so a poor man. And if you two are smart you'll agree with me." Roscoe stood, tossed his scraps into the fire, and headed to the spring.

Mike and Les continued eating in silence. "He's got a point, you know?"

"Who, Roscoe or Evan?" Mike said.

"Both, actually," Les said. "But I was referring to Roscoe. We have no idea where we'll wind up when we leave here. Having a good supply of gold will certainly help us when we get wherever it is we're going."

"Yeah," Mike said. "But too much would weigh us down to a point where the boat could sink if the seas get rough. I'd rather come out of this alive and poor than rich and dead."

"So would I," Les said. "We'll just have to find a good middle balance."

Roscoe returned from the stream. "You guys are going to visit the summit before we leave aren't you? Evan learned a lot up there." He looked over at Les. "I think you would too, you being a psychic and all."

Les paused a moment. "Yeah," he said. "I think it would be a good idea to find out first-hand if there really is something to the place. Mike, let's you and me go tomorrow."

Mike paused a moment. "Okay." The thought frightened him but he kept his thoughts to himself the rest of
the evening.

CHAPTER 9

▼

STORMY SECRETS

"Wake up Mike," Roscoe said, shaking him. "There's another hurricane coming."

Mike's eyes popped open. It was already early morning. "Oh no," he cried out. He looked outside. Although it was after sunrise it was dark enough to be early evening.

"Les is taking the boat engine to the cave," Roscoe said. "He wants you to help him get it inside the entrance."

Mike was wide-awake now. He jumped up and hustled down the ladder to the ground. Rushing to the beach, he found Les struggling with the boat motor. He ran to assist, taking a brief moment to look out at the rough sea. The wind was blowing in so hard that the water sounded like a huge band of drums, all playing at once. He picked up the propeller end of the motor and together he and Les carried it off toward the cave.

"I got out here right after sunrise and made some real headway with this engine," Les said. "I kept noticing how the ocean was getting louder and louder. Then I started hearing thunder. We're in for a real storm."

Mike glanced up at the blackening sky. It definitely looked like another hurricane.

"I'm real close to having this thing ready to run," Les said. "Damn if I'm going to leave it out to be smashed by a falling tree."

"I heard that," Mike said. He held the bottom end of the engine behind his back as he led the way to the cave. It was a lengthy walk, especially carrying the heavy engine, but after a few minutes, stopping several times to rest their arms, they reached it. It took some doing but they successfully managed to get the boat motor into the cave.

They immediately headed back to the beach. By now the palm trees were bending violently against the strong gusty wind. They knew that any minute the violent rainfall would begin, probably to continue the rest of the day and all night.

When they reached the *Spear* they tried to decide what to do. There was no safe place to move it.

"I guess we'll just have to hope nothing happens to it," Les said as he looked at the overturned boat.

"Can't you use your sixth sense to predict the safest place to put it?" Mike said.

"I'm afraid it doesn't work like that," Les said.

They both stood staring at the *Spear*. It had once been heavily damaged, but their recent efforts had made substantial progress toward getting it sea-worthy again.

"I've got an idea." Mike pointed to a place about twenty feet from where the *Spear* now sat. "Let's move it over by that downed palm tree."

"Why there?"

"Because the last hurricane blew this tree down right here. What are the odds of a tree landing in the same exact spot in two consecutive storms? Let's move this tree aside if we can and put the *Spear* here."

"Sounds logical," Les said, and they quickly began dragging the heavy tree aside. Within a few minutes they had the *Spear* overturned on the selected spot.

"We've done all we can do except pray," Mike said.

"We'll do that when we get to the cave," Les said and they quickly headed up the trail. The first large raindrops were just beginning to fall now and the wind was howling.

They rushed back to camp and found that Roscoe had filled two wineskins with water and gathered a basket of fruit. They all grabbed what they could and headed for the cave. Deafening cracks of thunder roared from so close overhead that Mike actually felt the ground vibrate. As they ran through the jungle for the cave the rain started to fall in earnest. The loud pounding on the green vegetation could be heard chasing them through the jungle. It closed in and finally hit them just as Roscoe was crawling inside.

They passed the food and water through and Les crawled inside with Mike on his heels.

Once they were in, Roscoe pulled the old windshield over the doorway. They got comfortable and caught their breath. Mike looked out to see the rain spattering wet sand, which hit the Plexiglas and stuck in place. The hurricane had arrived.

"Where's the booty?" Les looked toward the back of the dark cave.

"Oh yeah," Mike said. "This is your first trip into Roscoe's secret treasure cave. Let's go look around." He lit a torch with the metal plate and a flint and led the way.

"Don't forget to gather up the coins off the floor while you're back there," Roscoe said.

"Oh yeah," Mike replied somewhat sarcastically. "Come on Les, you won't believe this."

Mike showed Les the room full of gold as well as the waterfall where the small treasure chest was hidden. Finally he showed him the room with the skeleton.

Before long they heard Roscoe hollering for them to come back to the entrance and save the rest of the torch. "We may need the light in an emergency," he said.

They gathered up the coins from the floor and returned up front. "You can't imagine how nervous it makes me when you two are deep in the cave," Roscoe said as Mike and Les sat down.

"Why?" Les said.

"My claustrophobia is so bad that I even get nervous for you," Roscoe said.

Les walked over to the boat motor and examined it for a moment.

"You want to try working on it?" Mike said.

"I'd like to, but there isn't enough light," Les said. He walked over next to Mike and sat down. "I don't suppose we have any video games to pass the time."

"No," Mike said. "Just our cutting wit and bubbling personalities." They were silent for a minute, listening to the raging storm outside.

"I think this one's a category five," Mike said.

"Could be," Roscoe said. "This one is a killer storm. Maybe we should name it 'Attila'." They chuckled and then went silent, the sound of laughter, however brief, echoed down the cave's dark corridor. Outside, the front wave of destruction from the storm began to crawl across the island, tearing everything it could to pieces. Vegetation occasionally flew past the cave entrance.

They sat and talked for the remainder of the afternoon. Roscoe told them a lot about Evan and the "ghosts" he encountered at the summit. That led to further discussion of some of the frightening experiences they each had had in their own lives prior to getting marooned on the island. As the day wore on, they learned a great deal about one another.

Sometime later, the rain outside abated. Then it stopped completely, somewhat suddenly. Within minutes, late afternoon sunshine was brightly illuminating the island.

"Hey guys." Mike looked outside. "I think the storm's over." He slid the Plexiglas aside and crawled out. The soaking wet sand stuck to his knees and palms but it felt good to get into the fresh air. Les and Roscoe followed him out.

"Man that storm ended quickly." Roscoe got to his feet. The sky overhead was a deep, clear blue and the winds were suddenly calm.

"Almost too quickly to be true," Les said. The calmness and serenity was very refreshing.

"The storm couldn't have just blown by like this," Roscoe said. "Wait a minute. The hurricane isn't gone, we're in the eye"

"No," Mike replied. "We couldn't be."

"I think you're right," Les said. "There's no way the hurricane could have passed this fast. We're right smack in the middle of it."

"Not many people live to say they spent time in the eye of a hurricane," Roscoe said.

"We haven't survived this one yet," Les said.

"Let's take advantage of the opportunity." Mike rushed into the woods for a bathroom break. Roscoe and Les agreed.

"How long do you think it'll be before the intermission ends?" Mike said.

"Hard to say," Roscoe said. "Maybe half-an-hour. Don't hold me to it though. The eye of a storm is only about thirty or forty miles wide. We need to be back in the cave real soon. Part two's coming and it's going to be really rough." He looked around at the damage. Downed trees were everywhere. "I made a couple more torches that I wish I had thought to bring with us."

Mike looked at him. "Where'd you leave them?"

"Under my bed," Roscoe said. "If I had had more time to prepare for the storm I would have brought them with me. That dark cave is murder on my claustrophobia."

"Why don't I run get and them?" Mike said.

"No," Les said. "It's too dangerous."

"It'll just take a couple of minutes," Mike said. "Besides, I want to see if the tree house has survived the storm."

"Don't do it," Roscoe said. "The storm will resume any minute and if you're out there you might not be able to make it back."

"I'll make it," he said, and he suddenly bolted up the path for the campsite.

"No," Les shouted.

"Damn fool," Roscoe said. He looked overhead at the clear sky. Around them, nothing stirred.

Mike ran as fast as he could and reached the tree house in less than five minutes. When he arrived he found the structure still standing but heavily damaged. The wind had taken tree limbs and thrown them like javelins in all directions. There was a medium-sized tree trunk protruding from the wall of his room. Once the wind started up again it would probably move the tree back and forth, destroying the walls and floor. He quickly surmised that the structure was doomed. It was a safe bet that the whole tree house would be coming down sometime that night.

He knew he needed to go in and get not only the torches but anything else he wanted to salvage as well. At that moment the late afternoon sun went behind the wall of encroaching clouds.

Carefully, he climbed the steps to the platform and went inside his bedroom. There wasn't much to take except the bedspread and the treasure chest. He grabbed them and hurried back out to the deck and set them down before returning to the main cabin to see what he could salvage from it. He rushed in and bent down to get the torches from under the bed. At that moment he became aware of a rattling sound coming from inside the room. His first instinct told him that there was a snake coiled up, poised to attack. He whirled around and looked in the direction of the noise. It was coming from the side of the room where Roscoe's bookshelf stood. He didn't see a snake or any other wild creature.

Cautiously, he walked forward and looked closer at the bookshelf. The absence of sunlight had darkened the room and he wasn't able to tell exactly where the sound was coming from. He looked closely at the shelf and spotted the little gold ship. It appeared to be rocking back and forth, making a bumping sound on the hard wood of the shelf. For a moment Mike stood and stared. It was almost as if it was experiencing an earthquake, shaking gently like the shelf under it was vibrating as the earth shook, except the shelf was completely still. Mike stared at the little ship in the dim light. There was no mistaking the sound. It rattled faintly.

There was a crash of thunder and the tree house shook violently. For an instant Mike thought it was going to fall from the trees. He grabbed the gold ship and held it tightly. It was warm to the touch. That must be what was moving it, he thought. The storm and the static electricity in the air are causing it to vibrate.

Mike could hear a wall of heavy rain moving toward him through the trees. He slid the gold ship into his pocket, took the torches, and ran outside to grab the treasure chest. He tossed the bedspread and torches to the ground below, took the treasure chest under his arm and climbed down. Once on the sand again he picked up everything and started running for the cave. The rain started an instant later and strong gusts of wind started pushing him from side to side as he ran down the trail. The rain intensified and he slipped a couple of times, quickly getting up and resuming his progress. After about ten minutes he reached the cave.

Les and Roscoe had gone back in and covered the entrance with the Plexiglas. Mike slid it aside with his foot and set the stuff down in the entrance. From inside a pair of hands reached out and took them. Mike crawled in and Les quickly closed the doorway behind him.

"You had us worried," Les said from somewhere in the darkness.

"Me too." Mike gasped for breath.

"How's the tree house holding up?" Roscoe said.

"Not good," Mike said. "It's still standing but really beat-up. I doubt it'll survive the night."

Roscoe was silent as Les lit one of the torches they had partially used earlier.

"I don't know if these other torches will be any good when they dry out," Roscoe said as he held up one of the soggy ones Mike had just brought in with him. The bedspread was soaked too and he tossed it against the wall in a pile.

"I figured I'd better grab the treasure chest too," Mike said between breaths. "The level of static electricity in the air is unbelievable. The gold ship was hopping across the shelf." He pulled the little ship out of his pocket and held it up.

Roscoe reached over and Mike handed it to him.

"Wow," Roscoe said. "You sure have warm pockets."

"It was that way when I found it," Mike said.

After Roscoe and Les had admired the golden ship as well as the other objects in the treasure chest, Mike took them and walked a little ways back into the cave. After a brief search, he found a level shelf on which to place them for safekeeping. He put all the jewelry and the diary into the chest and set them on the shelf. The crown was too big for the chest so he set it on the shelf. He then set the little ship on the shelf, inside the ring of the crown.

The golden ship sat upright. Mike hoped one day to have it sitting the exact same way gathering dust on a bookshelf in his and Jan's house.

Once that was done he walked back up front. He was soaked from head to foot and when he sat down the dry sand stuck to him. As he wiped as much of the wet sand off himself as he could, he slowly began to get comfortable. Roscoe handed him a banana and he ate it slowly. Outside, the wind blew the rain horizontal.

CHAPTER 10

▼

TROUBLESOME GOLD

As part two of the hurricane raged throughout the night, the three of them slept soundly on the floor of the cave. When Mike awakened sometime after dawn the next morning, he crawled over to the Plexiglas cover and moved it aside. The fresh air was heavy and wet but the rain had just about stopped. He slid the cover completely away from the entrance and the cool air came pouring inside.

"Maybe the storm's over," he heard Roscoe say from behind him. "The long, steady rainfall is usually the final stage. I'll bet we see the sun later today." He pulled out a bag of fruit and offered it around.

Les dug into the mango he had found in the bag and ate it quickly. "Maybe we can make the trek to the summit tomorrow," he said.

"Do you really think it's necessary to go up there?" Mike said.

"Yes, I do," Les said. "If Evan learned something up there that helped him get back home then maybe I can too." He was silent a moment. "I'm able to pick up communication signals out of the air sometimes. Living people emit such signals and sometimes-dead people do too. Anything that is strongly charged emotionally emits energy that my sixth sense can detect.

"Does that happen often?" Roscoe said.

"Not really", Les replied, "just time to time. When I was a kid I learned at an early age how to tell if my parents were mad at me about something, even before they said anything. Later on I could tell that about anyone. These signals travel through the air like radio waves. I guess I have a receiver in my mind that picks them up. But there are plenty of people who do it better than I do. I've just never heard of anyone whose ESP works the same way as mine."

"Are you sure you're not just imagining it?" Mike said.

"Quite sure," Les said. "It's as different as being awake is to being asleep. I know what's there and what's imagined."

"Does it ever fool you?" Roscoe said.

"I sometimes misunderstand the signals," Les said. "But it's basically pretty accurate. I feel confident that I can learn something by visiting the summit."

"I'm not sure what Evan really experienced up there," Roscoe said. "But he said there were a lot of dead pirates and a lot of secrets."

"How did he expect to learn anything from a bunch of dead pirates?" Mike said. "I thought dead men told no tales."

"He claimed to have psychic ability, like you Les," Roscoe said. "Whatever it was he learned from going up there he didn't share with me, at least not in a way that made any sense."

"I take it you two didn't communicate much after that," Les said.

"Not much," Roscoe said. "By the time he got around to going to the summit he had about completed his boat-building task. I wasn't going without at least a little gold, which he said, would upset the balance of the boat. Plus, the boat was a rather crude creation. I think he found my reservations about leaving with him insulting, as if I was questioning his abilities as a sailor. The summit trip really changed him and some of the conversations we had afterwards got rather heated. We didn't speak much the last week or so he was here." Roscoe paused a moment as though to contemplate what he would say next. "I do honestly feel we were friends when he left though."

"I still don't understand," Mike said. "I would think that after being here as long as you had you would have taken the first opportunity to leave that came along. I know I would have."

"He refused to let me take any gold," Roscoe said. "Not one speck. He said I was greedy, self-centered and narrow minded. I told him he was a fool for leaving such a treasure behind. He said that the gold would hinder our travels and would eventually lead to arguments and, if we were at sea long enough, perhaps physical conflict."

"You mean murder?" Les said.

"What makes you ask that?" Roscoe said.

"It's a known fact that pirates and honest sailors alike fight amongst themselves over gold and women," Les said.

"It's been happening since biblical times. Long periods of time together in closed quarters only aggravate the problem. I can kind of see his point."

"So are you saying we shouldn't take any gold with us when we leave?" Roscoe said. "That we should just sail out without so much as a bag of gold coins to use as money in case we need it? If you think that then you've got to be crazy."

"No," Les said. "I'm not saying I agree with his idea of not taking any gold along. But I do see where limiting the cargo would be a wise move. There are plenty of Spanish Galleons on the ocean bottom with all hands lost because the captain put too much gold into the cargo hold."

Roscoe started to say something but Mike cut him off first. "Maybe Evan got scared about taking the gold after going up to the summit," Mike said. "Maybe he was afraid of some kind of curse or something."

"Or maybe he was just stupid," Roscoe said.

"Or maybe he knew something about you, Roscoe," Les said. "He was here with you longer than either Mike or I have been. Maybe there was something about you and the gold that he feared was a bad mix."

"What are you saying?" Roscoe said. "Why don't we just come right out and clear the air right now."

"What I am saying," Les said in a somewhat calmer voice. "Is that Evan obviously knew something about sailing, probably more than all three of us put together. If he thought your lust for gold was a problem, then he must have had a reason. He's also the only person we know who successfully made it home. I'm not trying to insult you but I do have to draw some kind of conclusion from the facts presented."

"Yeah," Roscoe said. "You draw your conclusions. And then you think about what type of future we're going to have if we do get home and we have no food, no place to go and no money. Maybe we won't get as lucky as Evan did and find an old, abandoned lighthouse to go crawl into and rot. We can go die like bums on a back alley somewhere."

"Come on, guys," Mike said. "We're all friends here, remember? Let's don't spoil what we've accomplished before we even get the *Spear* ready."

"Okay," Les said. "But I'm afraid I'm going to have to lay down the law with you the same way it appears Evan did. When we get in that boat, I'm the captain. I've spent many years sailing everything from dinghies to catamarans to yachts. I know a lot about the sea and I plan to use that knowledge to get us home safely. All three of us."

"Fine," Roscoe said. "Just don't try to tell me not to come aboard with some of the gold. If the two of you want to go home poor that's fine with me. Just don't expect me to."

"You can take some of the gold with you," Les said. "Just don't plan on taking a whole horde because the *Spear* won't hold it."

"I'm beginning to see why you stayed behind," Mike said to Roscoe. "You figured another opportunity would eventually come along to leave and take some gold with you, so you decided to wait for the next boat home."

"That's exactly right," Roscoe replied. "Unfortunately, the occasional cruise ship or navy plane I was counting on never materialized. Eventually, I realized I would have to pin all my hopes on Evan. He said he'd be back for me and the gold as soon as he could. That hope is what has kept me going these last five years. At least, until you guys showed up."

"Then let's not let the gold hurt our friendship," Mike said.

"No," Roscoe said. "The friendship is more important. But, unlike Evan and those pirates, I have no intention of returning here once I'm gone. I'm not asking you two to risk our lives by taking all the gold. I just want to take all we can."

"I think we can work with that," Les replied.

"I think so too," Mike said. It gave him a moment to think of Jan and remember that he had more at stake here than the others. His heart was also on the line. "We'll work it out so we're wealthy and safe."

A short time later Les looked outside. The wind and rain had almost completely stopped.

"Anybody want to go outside for some air," he said. Mike and Roscoe quickly agreed.

There was still a light rain falling but it had been hours since the last loud blast of thunder.

"I think it's about over," Roscoe said as the three of them crawled out. "Now comes the fun part, assessing the damage."

"I'll go check the boats," Les said.

"I guess we'd better check the tree house," Mike told Roscoe.

"Yes," he replied. "Then we fish."

Les headed for the east beach while Roscoe and Mike made their way toward the place that had been home for so long. A couple of hundred yards up the trail they came to the campsite.

"Oh, no," Roscoe exclaimed.

Mike came up behind him. The tree house was destroyed. It looked like two of the main support trees had been blown down and the rest of the structure was pulled down with them. There was nothing left of it but a pile of wet, splintered wood.

"Hey guys," Les cried out from somewhere up the trail. "The boat came through without a scratch." He came running through the jungle with a big smile on his face, completely ignoring the destroyed tree house. "I've got to hand it to you, Mike," he said, holding out his hand. Mike absently held out his hand and Les shook it heartily. "Maybe you've got some of that magical insight yourself," Les said.

Mike was bewildered. "What are you talking about?"

"The boat," Les said. "Remember when we moved it and you told me where the safest place was?"

"Oh, yeah," Mike said.

"Well," Les said. "There's a huge tree lying right where the boat was before we moved it. If you hadn't suggested a new spot it would have been smashed into toothpicks. But it came through completely untouched where it was."

"All right," Mike said.

Les noticed the tree house. "Man, look at that."

"Yeah," Mike said. "I think our homeowner's luck finally ran out."

"Don't worry," Les said. "We'll be leaving soon anyway."

Mike walked over to the destroyed tree house and joined Roscoe who was rummaging through the debris. They located the wicker basket with the fishing tackle in it and pulled it free. Les cut down some bamboo and quickly rigged up fishing poles. Within fifteen minutes, the three of them were sitting in their familiar places by the lagoon fishing.

A couple of hours later they were holding the fish on sticks over the fire and preparing to eat them off plates of tree bark.

Knowing they'd be sleeping on the ground that night made Mike realize just how luxurious they had had it until now. "I miss the tree house," he muttered.

"When we finish eating, it'll be time to go to the summit", Les said. "The secret to finding the eye of the needle is buried up there somewhere, I just know it. Once we find it, we can make plans to leave." He looked over at Mike. "You coming?"

"Yes," Mike said.

"Roscoe," Les said. "You want to come along?"

"No," Roscoe said. He looked a little shaken. "I'll stay here and gather up supplies for the boat trip." A few minutes later, Les and Mike were ready to leave.

CHAPTER 11

▼

THE PIRATES SPEAK

"I'll go grab a couple of blankets for us," Mike told Les. "You get a bag of fruit and some wineskins of water."

Les agreed and Mike headed for the cave. Grabbing a couple of blankets, he rolled them up and used a vine to tie them so they could be carried on his back.

Saying goodbye for now to Roscoe, the two of them headed down the path. A short time later they emerged from the jungle onto the beach. The sky was almost clear and the noonday sun would soon make the sand broiling hot.

Mike's tennis shoes were getting pretty worn but were a far cry better than being barefoot. They decided to walk along the area just above the edge of the water where the ocean kept the sand wet and cool. The beach was firmer here and would make the long walk just a bit easier.

In the wake of the hurricane, there was debris everywhere. Large clumps of seaweed and driftwood could be
seen all along the beach. Here and there were dead fish
and palm tree branches. Offshore, the whitecaps extended
to the horizon.

"The ocean is still pretty turbulent," Les said. They
looked to their left as a mighty wave curled and crashed
toward shore.

"I'll bet if you walked out to where it's waist-deep, the
undertow would drag you down," Mike said.

Les nodded. The storm had long since left the sky but it
obviously still had a good hold on the ocean.

They walked along mostly in silence for about an hour.
Soon they neared the higher elevations of the island's
southwest side. Les stared at the summit with a hesitant
look on his face.

"Anything wrong?" Mike asked him.

Les didn't reply. "Les," Mike said. "Hey"

Les looked at him.

"Everything okay?" Mike said.

"Yeah," Les said. "My sixth sense tingled a little for a
moment. I think I'm going to learn a lot up there."

"I sure hope so," Mike said.

The long walk gave Mike plenty of time to explore his
thoughts. The loudness of the wind and sea reminded him
of a freight train. The contrast of the blasting surf on the
left and the stark quiet of the jungle on the right seemed to
divide his mind into two separate worlds, much the same
way this mysterious place contrasted with the world he
had known in south Florida.

Jan, Mike thought. The name was synonymous with all
that was good in the world, Mike's fantasy world.

He glanced over at Les, steadily trudging along beside him, obviously deep in thoughts of his own. It seemed it would be a rude intrusion to speak at a time like this, as if Les didn't want to be disturbed from his thoughts right now any more than Mike did. He glanced up at the summit ahead, getting closer.

His thoughts always seemed to flow full circle around to Jan. It had become instinct for him. He had been here long enough to realize what it felt like to have one's sanity start to erode away. He had to just follow his instinct now.

"I'm ready," Mike told himself.

"What?" Les said.

"The summit." Mike said. "I'm ready for it."

Les chuckled. "Good. How about a drink?"

"Good idea," Mike said. They stopped walking and shared a quick drink of water from one of the wineskins. The sun had warmed it, but it tasted great just the same. After a moment, they continued down the beach.

After 45 minutes, they reached the base of the cliff. They searched around for the best route to ascend and soon found a craggy hillside that featured a few stunted bushes and many footholds.

"This looks like a good place to start," Les said. "It seems to not be as steep here."

"Careful," Mike said. "Remember, no emergency rescue out here."

Les led the way up the steep incline. At times, he had to use the three points of contact rule, keeping one foot and both hands or one hand and both feet in contact with the hillside at all times. Mike watched his progress from a few feet behind him and simulated the moves as best he could.

"You're good at this," Mike said between breaths.

"I've done this before," Les said.

"I can tell." Mike glanced around. "It says something about Evan's physical condition for him to have done this too."

Slowly and steadily, they climbed until they reached the crest some 200 feet above sea level. The ascent took about half-an-hour. Once they reached the top, they took a moment to admire the view.

"Wow," Mike said. "If any ships passed by you'd be sure to see them from here." He walked to the cliff and looked over the edge. There was no beach at all below, just rocks and the loud, pounding surf. They sat down to rest and enjoy the spectacular view.

"Even though I knew it would be this way," Les said, "it still looks so strange to not see a boat, plane or even a swimmer from up here. It really makes me feel alone."

"Me too," Mike said. "Can you just imagine how Roscoe must have felt having this whole island to himself for so long?"

"Yeah, I guess it's no wonder he's going crazy."

Mike looked at Les and saw that he was kidding. They both laughed. Les started to say something about having a house on such a spot when he froze mid-sentence and stared out to sea. Noticing his shocked expression, Mike turned and looked too. Way out to sea, near the horizon, the front portion of a huge ship could be seen.

"I don't believe it," Mike said. "That's the first ship I've seen since I've been here!"

Les jumped up. "We've got to build a signal fire."

Mike stared at the distant vessel without moving. From where he sat and what he could see, it appeared to be a cruise ship. "Mike, are you paralyzed?" Les screamed. "Help me get some firewood."

"Wait," Mike said. "Look closely at that ship."

Les looked at it again. Only the front quarter of the ship was visible. Although it was a very long way away, there appeared to be a small patch of fog surrounding the area where the ship partially appeared.

"I only see part of it," Mike said. "Where's the rest?"

"Who cares," Les screamed. "It's a ship and it can rescue us, now come on."

"Will you stop screaming," Mike yelled. "There's something wrong here. Besides, it's at least twenty miles away, they won't see our fire."

"Well we at least ought to try," Les said. He stopped stirring around and looked back at the partial ship. It was slowly moving parallel to them from right to left. As if it were emerging from behind a wall, the ship gradually came into view. Porthole after porthole appeared from the fog. A moment later a second smokestack appeared.

"What the hell is going on?" Mike said. "Where the stern of that ship should be there's only ocean. I can see all the way to the horizon."

"It's almost like it's emerging from that patch of fog," Les said. He stood looking on. The ship continued to emerge as if from nowhere.

"It's coming through the eye of the needle," Mike said. "Right before our eyes it's moving from one dimension to another." As they watched, a third smokestack appeared, followed by the rear deck and a tiny flag fluttering in the breeze at the very back.

"I guess it wouldn't hurt to try building a signal fire," Mike said.

Before he could move, the bow of the ship started dis-appearing. "Look," he said. "It's going back into the fog."

"What," Les said. He stopped and stared at the distant ship. As he watched, the first smokestack vanished and porthole after porthole started slipping into invisibility. Within two minutes the tail end of the boat vanished as well. Moments after that, there was no more sign of any fog. Once again, the entire ocean was void of any hint of human existence.

The two of them looked at each other.

"Did that just happen?" Mike said.

Les scratched his head. "The eye of the needle must be right out there and that ship just sailed past the opening. If only we had the *Spear* ready we could hurry out there and maybe get through it."

Mike continued to stare at the last place he saw the ocean liner. "I wish there was some way we could sail to it."

"Hell," Les said. "I'd settle for swimming for it if I knew it would still be there when I reached that spot." He threw down the sticks he had gathered and sat down on the ground.

Mike sat next to him and the two of them continued to stare out to sea.

"I wonder if the people on board that ship even know they entered the Bermuda Triangle," Mike said.

"They may never know how lucky they are," Les said.

They rested in silence a few minutes more.

"I guess we'd better get moving," Les said. "I'm get-ting hungry."

They walked away from the cliff and into the woods, gently sloping downhill toward the interior of the massive island. Once in the shade, they quickly spotted a plum tree and a couple of wild apple trees. The storm had knocked a lot of the fruit off the trees and much of what they found was edible.

"It doesn't look as though the storm did as much damage up here as it did down our way," Mike said.

"The cliff probably shielded the trees from some of the high winds," Les said.

Mike bit into a shiny green apple.

"Better eat all you can hold," Les suggested. "It'll soon be too dark to go looking for food." For the next few minutes they foraged around and found more apples, plums and berries.

"What do we do next," Mike said.

"Explore the woods", he replied. "We'll walk around and hopefully my sixth sense will pick something out of what I see and hear."

Les walked deeper into the woods to look around. Mike followed a few feet behind, looking in every direction.

After they had walked a few hundred feet, Les slowed his pace. "This place is really strange. The sixth sense is starting to click just a bit."

Mike didn't reply but the statement made him a little nervous.

"Have you noticed the difference in vegetation up here?" Les stopped waking and stood looking around. "Down at sea level the trees are more of a jungle. Up here they're woods. I don't remember seeing any apple or plum trees down there and I don't see any banana or coconut trees up here."

Mike thought a moment. "Maybe the vegetation isn't the only thing that's different up here."

They walked a little further, Les leading the way. The sun's light was shining only on the tops of the trees now. Sunset was just minutes away.

"My sixth sense is stirring around pretty good now," Les said.

Mike was surprised at the calmness of the comment. Les seemed to know what he was doing. That eased his tension just a little.

Les spotted a clearing. When they reached it they walked out from under solid shade into the openness. Overhead, the planet Jupiter was visible in the evening sky. The stars would soon follow.

Les stopped dead in his tracks, causing Mike to almost walk straight into him. He stared at the wall of trees on the far side of the open area. Mike thought he saw fear in his expression.

"I definitely feel something with the sixth-sense now," Les said.

Mike didn't reply. He suddenly realized he was quite nervous, almost like they were being watched. He set the blankets down on the ground and Les absently laid the wineskins next to them.

"Is the sixth sense telling you anything?" Mike said. He wasn't even aware that he was whispering.

Les continued staring into the woods at the backside of the clearing, listening to the stark silence and hardly moving.

"Plenty," Les said. "This place is really giving me the creeps." Mike didn't like the sound of that. Then he realized that it probably meant they were onto something. Thinking momentarily about Jan he realized that having something happen up here, even if it was frightening, was probably good.

Les stepped back into the middle of the clearing and stood observing the surrounding trees. "Mike, I want you to walk straight back into the woods about fifty feet or so. Let me try to tell you what you see there."

"Huh?" Mike said.

Les pointed. "Walk straight back there. I'll describe what my mind sees and if it resembles what you actually see then I'll know I'm onto something."

Mike paused, wondering if Les were playing a joke or just acting crazy. "It's pretty dark back there."

"And getting darker by the minute," Les said. "I think Evan was right about there being something supernatural to this place. My sixth sense is really tingling now. If we're going to learn anything up here then it may be now or never."

Mike looked into the thick forest before them, swallowed and tried to build his courage. The pirate skeleton in the cave came to mind. "Okay, which way?"

"Go right in there," Les pointed.

Mike followed Les' point and headed on a straight path toward the woods. It got even darker when he got under the first line of trees.

After a couple dozen steps Mike looked back at Les and saw him standing with his face down and eyes apparently closed. "What in the hell is this all about?" he muttered.

"Keep going," Les said.

Now quite tense, Mike resumed walking slowly into the darkening woods.

"Stop," Les suddenly called out.

Mike immediately froze.

"I'm beginning to see the woods in my mind." Les paused and Mike waited nervously. "Evan was right," Les said. "I don't believe it. There really are secrets buried here."

Mike looked around in all directions; half expecting a collection of pirate corpses to suddenly emerge from nowhere and swarm all over him. All he saw was the darkening woods. All he heard was his pounding heartbeat.

"Look to your right," Les said. "See if you can spot anything that appears man-made."

"Okay." Mike looked to his right. It was almost too dark to see the trunks of the trees. "Nothing here," he said.

"Look a little further back," Les said.

"I don't see any," Mike began. A strange object caught his eye about twenty-five feet away. A bright white stick of some kind was stuck in the ground. In the fading light it appeared to be almost glowing. The top of it looked like a human skull.

"I see something," Mike called out. "It looks like some kind of marker."

"It may be a territorial stake of some kind," Les said excitedly. "Walk over to it and look straight back into the woods from there."

Mike paused and stared at the object. If it was a property stake he hated to think what might be on the other side.

"Hurry, before the light runs out," Les said.

"All right." Mike started to advance slowly. "Just don't get me killed here." When he got closer he saw that the object was a neatly carved little pole about two feet high. The top was as big around as a softball and had been carefully carved into a human skull.

"Oh, man." He leaned over for a closer look but was careful not to touch it. "It looks like some kind of a cemetery marker."

"Stand next to it and look straight back," Les said. "What do you see?"

Mike stood a foot in front of the marker and stared into the thick woods. "Nothing but trees." He was beginning to wish they had at least started a campfire before now.

"Keep looking," Les said.

"Looking for what?"

"A headstone, a marker, some kind of structure, anything that nature would not have put here. Think for yourself Ranger."

Mike paused. Being called "Ranger" was nothing new to him. Hearing Les call him that, was.

Mike felt certain he was being watched and it was pushing him to the verge of panic.

"Calm down," Les said.

Mike looked back in his direction. He couldn't see him through the trees and yet it was almost like Les could read his every move.

"Come on Mike, you're not trying."

"I'm scared, dammit," Mike said.

The outburst broke his train of thought momentarily. At that moment he spotted a pile of human skulls that formed a pyramid about twenty feet from where he stood. The grinning heads seemed to be looking right at him, beckoning him, bidding him welcome to some horrible party, a party with the dead. Mike cried out.

"Bingo," Les said.

Mike turned and bolted out of the woods and into the clearing. "What did you see?" Les said.

Mike hesitated to catch his breath before replying. "A big pile of human skulls, each grinning like they've been waiting for me."

"Those are probably the losers in the pirate battles over this island," Les said. "I think this area was the main battle ground. That pirate you found shot in the cave was probably the last one to die. I doubt he even knew the fate of the others." He looked all around at the quiet trees that surrounded them. "Yeah, this is where the real killing took place."

"What were they fighting over?" Mike said. "Territory?"

"Maybe so," Les said. "Gold. And maybe something else."

"If only these trees could talk," Mike muttered.

"Maybe they can," Les whispered. "Maybe they can."

Mike glared at him but said nothing.

"Let's start gathering up some wood for the fire," Les said. "It will be pitch dark in few minutes."

"Sounds like a good idea."

Les gathered some dry grass and started piling it up on the ground a few feet from the back of the small clearing. He then took some thin sticks and placed them over the grass.

"Come light this will you?" he said.

Mike walked over to the spot and dropped the load of wood he had gathered. Taking out one of the flints and the piece of metal, he bent down and started throwing sparks toward the pile of dry grass. A moment later one of the sparks caught and he started blowing into it, making the fire spread quickly. Once they got the fire going they unrolled their blankets and got comfortable on the ground a few feet away.

Mike found himself keeping his back to the fire and facing the woods.

"So you think we're in some sort of pirate battle-ground?" He didn't look away from the cool darkness of the forest.

Les looked around them. "Oh yeah. We're in the right place. There's a whole lot more buried here than a bunch of bones."

Darkness finished falling around them and the stars filled the sky. They talked a little, ate the few pieces of fruit they had left and finished off the first wineskin of water. Sometime later Mike went to the edge of the woods to gather what firewood he could find. As he got away from the fire he realized that it was not only very dark but quite cool as well. The air temperature felt like it was in the fifties. He managed to find an armload of dead wood and hurried back to the fire. Les had gathered some wood as well.

As they sat side by side, backs to the fire and looking at the dark woods, Mike glanced over at Les.

"You look to me like you're listening to music," Mike said.

Les looked over at him and smiled. "I'm reaching."

"What do you mean?"

"Going into the woods mentally," Les said. "I'm certain now that this is Atlantis. We're sitting on the last remaining land mass that once was the lost continent."

"Your sixth sense told you that?"

"Yes. That means that we've traveled back in time too. A long way back."

"There it is again," Mike said. "The time factor. It's the main characteristic of this strange island."

"I know," Les said. "It seems so impossible yet it's the only explanation for so many things."

"Yes," Mike said. "With all the shipping traffic that normally travels this part of the Atlantic, there would have to be at least a little trash or petroleum on the beach if this was our present day."

Les thought a moment. "Yes. I just wish there was more evidence that Atlantis really did exist."

"Even though there are no records among the countries of Western Europe of its existence," Mike said, "the ancient Phoenicians are known to have traded with people from a large island nation somewhere in the West Atlantic. That could very well have been Atlantis."

"There's just one factor that bothers me," Les said. "If Atlantis really did exist then how could it have vanished without a trace? An island nation that traded internationally would certainly have had a vast number of ships. Assuming many of them were at sea when disaster struck the homeland, why did they also vanish?"

"Who knows," Mike said. "Maybe they just moved in with their trading partners, thereby blending into the other country's culture. Maybe they just didn't bother to keep records. They were just happy to go on living."

They both looked around the land that surrounded them, covered in darkness at the moment.

"A lot of men died here," Les muttered.

"The sixth sense tells you that?"

"Yes," Les said.

"Think they fought over the gold?"

"Yes," Les said. "But that may not be what killed all of them."

"You think there may be some kind of curse to this place?" Mike said.

"Maybe. Look at all the wreckage and the dead bodies that wash up on the beach, the murdered pirate in the cave and those skulls back there. Man may have never been intended to be here. I think the only thing more frightening than what we're finding on this island is what we may find after we leave it. There's no telling what may be lurking out in that ocean."

"That's a scary thought," Mike said. "As bad as it is here, it could be much worse out at sea, where there isn't any dry land with fruit trees and fresh water springs. Out there is only ocean and sky, and God only knows what else." A breeze gusted, giving them each a brief chill. "I sure hope we can learn something up here. It may be our only hope of getting off the island alive."

"I hope so too," Les said. "I hope so too." He sprawled out on the ground next to the fire and closed his eyes.

Mike sat quietly and watched the fire crackle and burn. Its heat was very comforting. A few minutes later, he tossed on some more wood. As he sat back down and started to relax, he fell deep in thought. Mentally he began to weigh the danger of leaving against the safety of staying put. He had to at least try to get home, for Jan if for no other reason.

He looked over at Les who had been lying down beside the fire and was now asleep or very close to it. He decided to lie down as well, even though he didn't feel particularly sleepy at the moment.

Once Mike got comfortable his thoughts began to drift far away. He began to relax and his guard went down, which is probably why it took more than thirty seconds to notice the eerie sound coming from somewhere in the woods.

What's that? he thought, sitting up and straining to hear. From the direction of the strange stake in the woods, came a sound he had only once heard before. That night aboard *One Summer Dream*, just days before he left Miami for the last time. Just under the rumble of the *Dream*'s engine he heard voices calling to him.

Once he cut the engine the sound went away. But Mike was sure he had heard it. Now he was sure the same sound was coming from the distant woods. It was the sound of human voices, very faint, screaming in unison. Mike couldn't move. All he could do was sit and listen.

Les began to stir in his sleep. Mike's attention was diverted momentarily before the sound became louder.

Les began to mutter unintelligible words and move his head from side to side.

Mike looked into the woods, half expecting a group of walking dead to come at him from their graves. Anything could find him if it wanted to in the stark light of the fire. He wondered if he should awaken Les.

Mike started to reach over but paused to look into his face. Les' eyes were closed and his face wore an expression of terror.

Mike touched his shoulder and Les drew away without waking. "Wake up," Mike whispered.

Les continued to twitch and groan in his sleep. From the darkness the sound got louder. Mike was able to positively identify it now. It was that third voice that appears on top of simultaneous screams of two or more people. Only this time it wasn't just one extra voice, it was dozens.

Les now appeared to be convulsing, twitching uncontrollably. He sat up wide-awake. "No," he screamed. The sound of his voice echoed away. They sat looking at each other in the flickering firelight.

"Did you just hear something?" Les said.

"Yes," Mike said. "The sound of the dead pirates screaming in the distance."

"I heard them too," Les muttered.

"The sound got louder as your sleep got deeper," Mike said. "It's almost like they came in response to your dream."

The two of them sat and listened but now heard nothing. "Does the meter in your head register anything?" Mike said.

"I'm not sure," Les said. "I guess I need more research." He got up, got himself a drink of water from the wineskin and then poked the fire with a stick. "You want to try sleeping for a while? I think one of us should stay awake in case something happens."

"Good idea," Mike said. He sprawled out on his blanket next to the fire and lay flat with his eyes open. "What did you just dream about?"

"Pirates," Les said. "I think I got a glimpse of some of the bitter fighting that took place here so long ago. It wasn't pretty. Then again it may have just been my imagination."

Mike gazed at the stars above, trying to take himself mentally as far from this place as possible. He remembered a night ages before when he and Jan had first started dating. After an evening of dinner and miniature golf, they had gone back to Mike's house and walked out to the end of the dock.

During the conversation, Mike lay down on the dock and admired the stars. Jan asked him what he saw and he gave her a brief astronomy lesson about the constellation known as Vega. Before he had reached the halfway point of telling her about it, he became aware that she was lying down on the dock next to him. He tried to be cool about it and even managed not to break his sentence. He casually reached down and placed his hand in hers. She reacted by locking her fingers into his.

Mike lay staring at the same constellation. He wondered if she thought of him at night as she looked into the starry sky. She could be doing just that at this very moment. He closed his eyes, whispered that he loved her, and slowly began to drift off to sleep.

Sometime later, the strange sound began to emanate again from the dark woods. Les had been sitting with his back to the fire, drifting in and out of sleep when the sound caused him to jump. It was all around them.

Les, now in some kind of trance, rose slowly to his feet and walked to the edge of the woods. After a momentary hesitation he continued into the trees and walked toward the strange marker with the skull carving. Once he reached it he stood and faced the wilderness.

Lifting his arms, Les extended his fingers. The strange sound began to increase. More and more unseen voices joined the eerie chorus. Mike sat up screaming.

The sound startled Les and brought him back to reality. The sound from the woods ended abruptly and Les quickly rushed back to the protection of the warm fire.

Mike opened his eyes and looked at him.

"You okay?" Les said.

"I, I think so." Mike was covered in sweat and shaking.

"The noise in the woods got louder and louder while you slept," Les said. "I think you scared it away when you screamed."

"I screamed?"

"Yes. So loud that Roscoe may have heard you. You don't remember?"

"No, in fact, I don't remember dreaming." He looked up at Les. "Did you learn anything?"

"I walked back into the woods a ways and tried to reach with my mind," he said. "I felt them watching me, asking me who I was."

"What did you tell them?"

"I told them I was one of them," Les replied. "It's true when you think about it."

"Did they respond?"

"I got some kind of a message but it didn't make any sense." Les appeared to still be sorting it all out.

"Didn't you pick up anything?"

"Nothing useful," Les said. "I just kept hearing the same thing being chanted over and over, like hundreds of whispering voices trying to say something. For all I know it may have just been the wind blowing through the trees."

"What was the sound saying?"

"It sounded like two words," Les said disgustedly. "Just two stupid words."

Mike swallowed. "What words?"

"I kept hearing the words 'ship spins. Ship spins, ship spins, ship spins', over and over again. First there were just a few voices, then several and finally dozens. That's all there was."

"Ship spins," Mike said. "Don't they think we know that ships spin when they go through the vortex. My boat bucked like a wild bronco. In fact, it spun me around so much I was almost too dizzy to swim away from it."

"I know," Les said. "My boat spun too. But I don't think that's what they meant."

"Well what did they mean?"

Les paused a moment. "I wish I knew."

Mike checked the constellation Vega overhead. It had moved a bit. Maybe two hours had passed since he last checked it. "Do you think there's more to come?"

Les hesitated before responding. "No, I have a strong feeling that whatever it was we encountered here tonight is gone now. Maybe forever."

Mike poked the fire, added the rest of the wood they had gathered earlier, got a drink of water and laid back down. Before long they were both asleep.

Shortly before dawn, Mike awoke and shivered. The fire was now nothing more than a few glowing embers and the morning was quite cold. He quickly got up and gathered some more pieces of wood. After stirring the fire back to life, he sat close and relished its warmth.

Les soon awakened and crawled over to enjoy the fire as well. "How about we head for home as soon as it's light?"

"Sounds great to me," Mike said. "I've had enough of this place."

An hour or so later, there was enough light for them to gather some fruit for a quick snack. Then they headed for the cliffside. As they walked past the cliff they took a moment for one last view from the top. No vessels of any kind were visible.

"Great getaway spot," Les said.

They descended back down to the beach and started walking back toward home. The water was calm and sea birds were everywhere.

"Hard to believe the ocean can be so fierce one day and as gentle as a kitten the next," Les said.

Mike nodded in agreement. After that they hardly spoke as they walked along, the bright sun slowly climbing overhead.

By late morning they were in familiar territory again. They were getting close to the lagoon now; another twenty minutes and they'd be back to the campsite, what was left of it.

"Well," Les said. "I think we can manage to make it back alive. We'll get the boat running in a few days and go find the vortex."

"I sure hope so," Mike said. "Maybe the boat will start spinning around and we'll know we're close to the doorway back. Hopefully that will happen before the fuel runs out." He allowed his thoughts to wander back to Jan again.

Soon they reached the narrow inlet that provided the lagoon its opening to the sea. They walked around the backside of it and to what remained of the old campsite. "See Roscoe anywhere?" Mike said.

Les looked around. "No, let's go find him."

They searched around and soon found him in the grove of fruit trees. He had a wicker basket almost full.

"Hey, fellows," Roscoe said.

"Hey Roscoe," Mike replied. "Mind if I have a cantaloupe?"

"Help yourself," he said. "How was the summit?"

"Interesting," Les replied. "But we didn't learn much. How about we tell you about it tonight. I need to do some more work on the *Spear*."

"I thought I'd build us a lean-to that we can sleep in until we're ready to leave," Mike said. "I should be able to salvage some of the boards from the tree house."

"That should work," Roscoe said. "You'll notice the gold missing from the debris. I went through the mess and found what few trinkets there were."

"Where did you put them?" Les said.

"Just inside the cave entrance," Roscoe said. "Why don't we all go do what we need to do and meet back here to eat in two hours." They all agreed and the three of them went in separate directions.

Mike headed back to the smashed tree house to find some building material. After pulling out several boards, he found some of the old nails lying on the ground. He gathered them up as he went and put them into his remaining good pocket, the other one had a hole in it. Noticing this again made him remember that he would need new clothes soon.

He located two blankets and some pieces of the stove. This thing will never cook again, he thought. Like everything else that was left of the tree house, it looked like a giant foot had stomped on it.

Aside from the few recoverable items, the tree house was little more than scrap wood. He gathered up what was salvageable and headed for the cave entrance. He could lean the boards against the rock wall and the cave would be close by in case they needed a place to seek cover if the weather turned nasty.

He wanted to make sure the gold trinkets were safely hidden along with the little ship and the crown before he went on to his next activity, so he lit a torch and crawled inside the entrance. He found the trinkets right where Roscoe had said he left them. He then walked back to the place where the rest of the trinkets sat safely on the rock shelf.

Arriving at the spot, Mike noticed something was amiss with the little gold ship. He had put it inside the ring of the crown but was surprised to find that it was now lying on the floor next to the shelf. "That's odd," he said to himself. "I distinctly remember putting the ship inside the ring of the crown. How did it get on the floor?" He picked up the ship and placed it upright on the shelf so that the ring of the crown surrounded it.

He stood and watched it a moment to make sure it didn't fall on the floor again. After a moment he was convinced it would stay where he had put it this time. Once he had put everything else away for safe keeping, he exited the cave. He then returned for some of the boards from the tree house and began hauling them back to the cave entrance. About two hours later he went back to meet the others for a late afternoon dinner.

After eating, there were still a couple of hours of day-light left. Mike decided to get started on the shelter. About forty feet above the sandy jungle floor was an overhanging ledge that jutted several feet out from the rock wall. At ground level he could line up several boards along the wall, use a vine to tie them together and form a lean-to. The wall of the cliff jutted out just enough to form a natural roof. The shelter wouldn't have to be fancy or take long to build and would still provide plenty of protection from the elements. Mike figured they'd be here at least a few more days, and a nice place to sleep was essential.

"Can I help?" Les said.

"Sure, how about going to the tree house and gathering up the least damaged boards you can find."

"Okay," Les said and he headed back down the trail.

Mike started clearing sand out of the spot where he intended to build.

Les soon returned with a pile of boards and set them down on the ground.

"Great," Mike said. "Another stack like that and we'll be in business."

Les returned for more boards and Mike began putting the first ones into place. He stuck one end of the first board into the sand about eight feet out from the cliff wall and leaned the other end against the rock. Placing several other boards next to the first he soon had the beginnings of a lean-to with plenty of room inside and a peak height of about six feet.

He found a strong vine, cut it to the right length and started tying the boards together. Les came back with another stack of boards and helped add them onto the structure. After a few minutes they had a nice shelter.

"I'll add palm branches to the roof tomorrow and build a front and back as well," Mike said.

Les nodded. "I'll let Roscoe know we're sleeping here tonight. Just don't spend too much time building it. We aren't going to be here much longer."

Mike looked at him and smiled. "I can't tell you how good that sounds to me. Do you know where Roscoe went?"

"He was going through the scrap pile with me," Les said. "I think he wanted his comfortable chair."

At that moment, Roscoe came up the trail and admired Mike's handy work.

"Well," he said. "Looks like the new place is coming along nicely." He started gathering wood for a campfire and Mike and Les retrieved chairs for themselves. As darkness fell and the fire started to feel good, all seemed to be getting back to normal at the new campsite. "I'm sure glad you fellows are back," Roscoe said. "This place is no fun alone."

Les chuckled as he took his seat by the fire. "It isn't even that much fun when you're not alone."

Mike positioned his chair and laughed. "I don't know. I think I could be happy here with a nice house and all the amenities. As long as Jan was here with me too. I sure do miss her."

"Try to finish your work on the shelter quickly tomorrow," Les said. "There's still plenty of body work to do on the boat."

"You don't have to worry about me," Mike said. "Just wake me up when you're ready to start."

"Roscoe," Les said. "Did Evan really believe that this island is Atlantis?"

"Yeah," Roscoe said. "He talked about plenty of stuff that didn't make a lot of sense, especially after he returned from the summit. He said we are well south of Florida here, perhaps south of the Tropic of Cancer. I don't know how he knew it though. He also said that this island is all

that is left of a once-great nation and that it would sink
into the ocean a few years from now."

"Well he was right about the island sinking," Mike
said. "We saw evidence of that when we walked around to
the north shore. He must have learned more than we did
up there."

"He said something about there being a key to the eye
of the needle," Roscoe said. "Like there was a locked door
out in the ocean somewhere and one would need the key
to ensure safe passage through."

"Well, if he thought that then why did he leave without
one?" Les said.

"He thought he could find a way through anyway,"
Roscoe said. "Apparently he did, but it landed him in a
time and place he never intended to reach."

Roscoe looked over at Les. "What do you think? Can
we still get back without this 'key'?"

"Do we have any choice?" Les said. "We know the mainland United States has got to be east of here and that's the
direction we should sail when we get the boat operational.
Other than that, I don't really know anything."

"How close are we to being ready?" Mike said.

"Well," Les said. "I've finished assembling the motor
and I believe it will run. We won't know for sure until we
try it and we can't do that until we get a boat that floats. If
we crank the motor without it being in the water we'll
burn it up."

"You mean you think you've got the engine completely
repaired?" Roscoe said excitedly.

"Yes, I think so," Les said. "I suggest we all three start
working together to finish repairing the *Spear*. I'll just

keep working on the engine until it works right. Then we'll sail for home."

Mike stared into the fire and thought about the possibilities. They made him a little nervous.

"I just hope we can find the eye of the needle again," he said.

"I hope we can get home on so little gas," Roscoe said.

"We won't know if we don't try," Les said.

A slight breeze filtered through the campsite. The faint smell of the salty sea came with it. They all noticed it but no one spoke. The Bermuda Triangle was waiting out there like a dormant volcano. They all knew they would be taking an enormous risk sailing back into it.

The next couple of hours passed mostly in silence. Occasionally one of them would add a few pieces of wood to the fire, get a drink of water or talk a little. Now and then a sound from the jungle would catch their attention, a small animal would stir or a few birds would fly overhead.

Mike noticed Les was dozing a bit. Roscoe stood up and walked toward the lean-to. "Think I'll call it a night."

"I'm not far behind you," Mike said.

Roscoe went inside and took a couple of blankets to make a bed.

"We might as well all sack out," Les said. "Tomorrow's going to be a long day."

They went inside and found plenty of room in the lean-to. "The shelter's great," Roscoe said from his place in the dark structure.

"Thanks," Mike said. "I just hope it won't rain."

"I think we'll be okay," Les said. "Goodnight." A short time later they were all asleep.

CHAPTER 12

▼

THE *SPEAR* IS READIED

The following morning Les woke Mike at around dawn. "Why don't we get started on the boat before it gets really hot," he said.

Mike slowly got to his feet before realizing how early it still was. "It's not going to be hot for several hours yet."

"I know," Les said. "But I couldn't sleep and you're up now anyway."

Mike chuckled. "Okay, let's go." They headed down toward the shore and began working on the hull.

"I couldn't sleep this morning and lay awake thinking about this island," Les said as he held a board in place while Mike hammered it. "I keep trying to figure out what led Evan to be so convinced that we've traveled back in time and that this island is the lost continent of Atlantis."

"I've wondered that myself," Mike said, setting the hammer at his feet. "I keep wondering if there would be some kind of proof somewhere. You know, an old stone temple or something."

"That's what I was thinking about this morning," Les said. "In fact, I even felt my sixth sense tingle a little." He wiped the sweat from his brow. The sun was getting higher in the sky now and the temperature was rising accordingly.

"What would you say to a day hike toward the island's interior?"

"You want to explore the island some more? Isn't that going to take time?"

"I'm not talking about a lengthy trek," Les said. "Just a little exploring this afternoon."

"Well, Roscoe told me he never really explored the island's interior. I guess there wouldn't be any harm, at least not as long as we're careful. But what in particular do you want to look for?"

Les carried several boards over to the *Spear* and set them in a pile on the ground. "I'm not sure. Maybe if we just go hiking my sixth sense start directing me."

"I guess it wouldn't hurt," Mike said.

"Right now I'm ready for some breakfast, how about you?"

"Yeah." Mike gathered the tools together and covered them with a small plastic sheet to keep them dry in the event they got some rain today. He then led the way as they headed back to the lean-to.

They gathered up some fruit to eat and filled Roscoe in on what they were planning. A few minutes later they set out into the jungle in the opposite direction of the beach.

"I've never explored past the cave," Mike said as they walked along. "Sure is cooler here than the beach."

"We'll have to be careful," Les said. "Watch your feet so you don't fall or step on a poisonous plant. And don't walk into a spider web."

About a half-hour's walk past the cave dense trees replaced the palms as the two of them reached the island's interior. The white sand became just a memory as the uneven ground was now made up of hard brown dirt, littered here and there with large rocks. Ahead was the foliage of a tropical rain forest. Les spotted a tree with a trunk the width of a small house. It towered overhead like a skyscraper.

"This place is almost like the Amazon," Les said. He had stopped walking and was now just standing, looking in awe at the dark jungle ahead. "My sixth sense is starting to click."

For some reason those words made Mike a little nervous. Les seemed to be following a natural trail through the thick undergrowth and Mike followed, trusting that Les would be able to find their way back. Mike heard something move in the branches overhead. "What was that?"

Les didn't slow down.

"What?" Les said.

Mike heard it again. "That, listen."

Les continued walking and barely paid attention to what Mike was saying. "It's just birds or something."

The sounds continued and became gradually louder. The unmistakable noises of creatures hopping from limb to limb came to Mike's ears. There were many of them, following the two men's progress from the cover of the dense brush. Their numbers were increasing.

"Les, will you stop and listen."

Les halted, so did the sound. "What?"

"They're all around us in the trees," Mike whispered.

"Who?"

"Something we can't see."

"Are you losing it? Come on." He started walking again.

Mike hesitated and listened. Total silence. After a few seconds, He started slowly walking. An instant later, the movement in the trees resumed. It's me, he thought. For some reason they're only following me.

Les stopped and waited a moment for Mike to catch up. Mike came up to him and almost walked right into him.

"Stop," Les told him. Mike was trembling.

"You had to hear that," Mike said, a little out of breath.

"Yes," Les said. "I think they're sentries."

"They're what?"

"Sentries, guards. They're here to follow our progress, keep tabs on us. Probably protecting something."

"Like what?"

"That's what I'd like to know. The fact that their numbers seem to be increasing means we're getting close to whatever it is they're trying to protect."

"What could it possibly be?"

"I don't know but my sixth sense is going crazy and so is my curiosity." Les followed the trail a little further and then abruptly stopped. Something in the distance to the right of the trail had caught his attention.

Mike stopped right behind him and waited. "What is it Les?"

Les stood motionless, staring into the jungle ahead.

"What the hell?" Les whispered as he stared, walking slowly.

Mike stood his ground and watched as Les crept toward something that seemed to be beckoning him from the dark jungle. Mike took a breath and prepared to ask him where he was going. Before he could utter a sound Les held up his hand and shushed him.

Mike froze. After a moment, Les motioned for him to follow.

Les walked about twenty feet with Mike a few steps behind, both of them trying to be as quiet as possible. There was a line of dense brush ahead and Les walked up to it and stopped. Mike walked up and stood beside him.

"Listen," Les whispered.

Mike stood perfectly still. Ahead of them, past the dense brush, they could hear hundreds of tiny creatures moving about. They seemed to be leaping from tree branch to tree branch, hopping about in the bushes and scurrying around on the ground.

"There's something in there," Les said quietly. "It's just beyond these bushes." He suddenly parted them and plunged forward. An instant later dozens of birds scattered into the air, causing a loud crashing sound that startled them both. After a moment, the jungle returned to its normal silent state.

"Those birds are all around," Mike said as he scanned the tree branches above them. "And they're still watching us."

"They can't hurt us," Les said. "They're only birds." He parted several tall bushes and stepped forward. "Hey, look at this."

Mike stepped through the brush. He froze when he saw that there was a large, round boulder sitting on top of pile of rocks.

"I don't believe it." Les slowly approached and Mike stayed two steps behind, half-expecting a crowd of squawking birds to attack from overhead.

"What the hell is it?" Mike said. For a long moment the two of them stood and stared at the huge, perfectly round boulder.

"That can't be a natural formation," Mike whispered. "Who do you think carved it? Pirates?"

"No way," Les said. "I think it was here for centuries before the pirates ever arrived."

They stood and stared at the strange boulder. It appeared to weigh at least a ton and was perfectly round, seated squarely on a pile of rocks that held it up like some kind of display. Mike mentally noted that it would take a large crane to move something this big. He couldn't begin to imagine how it got here or why anyone would go to the trouble of putting it in such remote place.

Les walked slowly up to the base of the rock and gently rubbed its smooth surface with his hand. "Boulders just like this one have been found in remote jungles in the Caribbean and South and Central America. Some scholars think they may be some elaborate model of the solar system. And so far, nobody's been able to totally rule out possible extra-terrestrial origin."

Mike looked overhead and all around. "This place is really starting to get to me," he said. "You ready to go back?"

Les looked around. Sounds of movement continued to come from the trees. The wild creatures seemed to be watching their every move. "Yeah," he said. "Let's go."

They quickly started back for home, leaving the wild sounds of the jungle behind. An hour or so later they found their way back to the lean-to. "I need a drink of water," Les said. "Then I'll be ready for more work on the Spear."

"Sounds like a plan," Mike said. "I guess Roscoe's off fishing."

After a quick stop at the spring they headed for the Spear. The rest of the afternoon was spent repairing the floor and sides. "She's really coming along," Mike said as they put their tools away for the day.

"Yeah," Les said. "She's coming along fine."

Roscoe was just getting the cooking fire going when the two of them returned to the lean-to. Mike and Les used the last few minutes of daylight to gather up some more firewood. They then cooked up the fish and discussed the day while they ate. Roscoe was fascinated to hear about the round boulder.

"This island is getting stranger and stranger," Les said. "I'm now in total agreement with Evan's theory about this being Atlantis. We went out this morning looking for proof and I think we found it."

"Well, we know one thing for sure," Mike said. "The former residents of this island included a lot more than just a bunch of stupid pirates. A lot more." He paused. "I just wonder where they went."

"The Triangle may have taken them," Les said. "We can't worry about it now. Let's just stay focused on getting the *Spear* running."

Mike thought about the gold still tucked safely away in the cave. "Oh, by the way, whoever last looked in on the gold ship forgot to set it back on the shelf. I found it on the cave floor."

"Wasn't me," Les said.

"Wasn't me either," Roscoe said. "I haven't been in that cave since the storm."

Mike looked at the two of them in bewilderment. "Then how did the gold ship get on the floor?"

"Search me," Les said.

"Well it sure wasn't me," Mike said. "And I know we haven't had any earthquakes lately."

"Wait a minute," Les said. "That ship was really warm when you handed it to me after you ran back from the tree house during the hurricane."

"Yes," Mike said. "It was warm when I picked it up off the shelf. In fact it was moving a little when I found it. I figured it was because of all the static electricity in the air at the time, but that really doesn't explain it."

"No it doesn't," Les said. "Roscoe, didn't you say that Evan believed the eye of the needle could be found near hurricanes?"

"That's what he said." Roscoe nodded.

"And he also said something about there being a 'key' that he never found," Les said. "The eye is about as close to a hurricane as you can get and that just happens to be when Mike went and got the gold ship. And Mike, remember my saying that the impression I got from the summit was the words: 'ship spins'?"

"Yes." Mike thought a moment. "Do you think they were referring to the little gold ship?"

"Yes I do," Les said. "That gold ship may be some kind of talisman. And it could be the 'key'. Whoever made it may have used some kind of special alloy mixed in with the gold. An alloy that makes it detect atmospheric changes that occur when the eye of the needle is close by."

"Causing it to spin," Mike said.

"Yes," Les said. "It may have started spinning while on the shelf in the cave and spun itself right onto the floor."

"If that's the case, then all we have to do is wait until the ship starts spinning and we know we're near the opening," Mike said excitedly. "That would explain why the pirates hid the treasure chest so well. If their gold bars were stolen then they'd be broke. But if the little ship got stolen then they'd be stranded inside the vortex."

"Yes," Roscoe said. "And it would also explain why the pirate in the cave swallowed the key and refused to tell his killers where the chest was, even though they were going to kill him if he didn't tell. They could have just taken the gold bars and left if that was all they wanted. They must have been looking for the gold ship."

Les jumped to his feet. "Let's go to the cave and get that little ship!"

Mike jumped up and lit a torch. A moment later all three of them headed up the dark trail.

When they reached the cave entrance, Mike took the torch and crawled inside. "I'll be right back."

"Bring all that stuff out with you," Roscoe said.

"Okay," Mike said.

A couple of minutes later he was back out with the entire contents of the treasure chest. They immediately headed back to the campsite with it.

Back by the fire, Les found a flat piece of wood and set it on the ground. Mike placed the ship upright on the block and the three of them stared at it in anticipation, hoping it would move. It didn't. They sat down in their seats and continued watching it. The rest of the evening passed without the gold ship moving at all.

The next morning's rain awakened Les just after dawn. A few minutes later the rain stopped and he got out of the lean-to.

Mike heard him moving around and got up himself.

"Want to walk down and check on the *Spear*," Les said.

"Sure," Mike said and the two of them headed for the east beach. Les walked over to the *Spear* and started checking the hull for cracks. "We'll need to seal these tiny gaps between the boards. But for all intents and purposes, the boat hull is repaired."

Mike suggested they go look through the debris pile. "Maybe we can find something we can use to tap the trees for sap," he said.

There was a place where the island jutted out a bit, making it the eastern-most part of the land area. Roscoe's boat had crashed near there. It was also the spot where both Mike and Les first came ashore. Practically every piece of debris ever found on the island washed up near it.

When they reached the spot, Les walked over to the edge of the jungle and looked at all the scrap metal and wood scattered amongst the trees. There were pieces from twenty or more different vessels strewn around. They varied from bolts and screws, left behind when the wood surrounding them rotted away, to rudders, masts and miscellaneous boards from yachts and schooners. The whole area was a mass grave of missing ships, pieces from another time and place that had been tossed into a heap on the shore.

Les stood with his hands on his hips and looked at the scattered mess. "I'll bet every bit of this stuff passed through the eye of the needle. Lone, surviving remnants of once proud and mighty sea-going vessels, stripped of their crews, their identity and their dignity by the Bermuda Triangle, then thrown to the winds and tides that brought them to this forgotten island."

"You know," Mike said. "It reminds me of movie monsters from some of those old flicks of the fifties. There was always a pile of bones lying around somewhere that the merciless creature had discarded after eating his victims. This area looks like a big pile of boat bones, useless scraps left to rust away through the years. Heaven only knows how many human lives are represented here."

Les paused a moment. "Judging by the number of different vessels, I'd figure it to be quite a few."

They began rummaging around. After some searching Les found a long hollow round metal piece that could be cut into pieces. "Hey," he said. "We can tap the trees with this. By placing a collecting pan underneath the end coming out of the tree, we might be able to collect a good bit of sap over several days."

They looked around a few more minutes for anything else they could use but found nothing. A few minutes later they returned to the lean-to.

Les took one of the saws and began cutting the thin metal rod. One difficult hour later, he had four hollow tubes, each about six inches long.

Mike had gathered two of the biggest coconuts he could reach and cut them in half.

Taking the hammer, the three of them went into the jungle and found some suitable trees. Mike started by hammering a tube into a tree trunk a few inches, pulling the tube out and poking out the piece of wood. He continued doing this until he had a hole several inches deep into the trunk. He then inserted the metal tube into the hole, careful to aim it downward, then set a coconut shell directly underneath the end of the tube to catch the sap once it began to drip out.

After repeating the process in three other trees, they headed back to the campsite. "We probably won't get a lot of sap," Mike said as they walked through the jungle. "But we should get a little."

"Where did you learn that little trick?" Roscoe said.

"I used to visit my cousins in Vermont during spring break when I was a teenager," Mike said. "During March and April they tap Maple trees that way. The stuff really flows when the days are warm and the nights are cold. Since the climate here isn't like that we won't get a lot of sap. Hopefully we'll get enough to serve our needs."

When they got back to the lean-to, Les took a moment to put the gold ship on the board again to see if it would move. It sat motionless.

That evening during dinner, Roscoe mentioned the mysterious birds in the jungle again. "It gives me the creeps to think about those birds you guys encountered around that giant boulder the other day. I wonder if there's any significance."

"I don't think so," Les said calmly. "There might be some kind of wild plant growing in the jungle that makes them crazy when they eat it."

"I hope that's all it is," Roscoe said. "I've had some strange encounters with birds on this island before myself."

"How so?" Mike said.

"Something happened to me several years ago that I can't explain," Roscoe said. "Now, every time I hear a bunch of those bastards squawking my blood runs cold."

"Why," Les said.

"Not long after I first got to the island," Roscoe said. "Even before Evan got here, there was a thunder storm that lasted for three days. It finally let up late in the afternoon and I went to the east beach to see what had washed up. Remember my telling you about those three young men that kept to themselves?"

"Yeah," Mike said. "One of them came and told you they were leaving."

"That's them," Roscoe said. "Well, they had been gone for about three days at the time.

"The sky was thickly overcast and it was almost dark. When I got to the beach I spotted two bodies right away. One was facedown on the beach and the other was floating facedown in the water near the shore. With each wave the body rose and fell, inching closer and closer to the beach. I didn't have to go anywhere near them to know they were both dead.

"Then I noticed a huge flock of birds a hundred yards or so down the beach. They were all congregated in this one spot, evidently feeding furiously on something. I figured it was the third man, but I couldn't understand why the birds were all eating this one body and leaving the other two completely alone, so I decided to go take a closer look.

"I started walking closer. As I approached I could see that there were at least a hundred birds of all types and sizes, fighting with each other for territory, furiously tearing flesh and eating. When I got close some of the birds stopped what they were doing and turned to stare at me with their piercing black eyes, squawking at me, daring me to come closer. They all had blood on their beaks and seemed angry, dazed, maybe even possessed. I suddenly feared they would attack me if I got closer so I stopped and just stared. The sight was grisly, sickening, but my curiosity was too strong. I had to know what it was that they were eating; what was turning them into vicious, ravenous carnivores. I stepped closer, trying to see. Suddenly several of the birds moved aside and I got a clear view of what it was." Roscoe took a moment to collect himself. He wore a look of terror.

"Was it the other man?" Mike said. His voice cracked a little.

"No," Roscoe said. "It wasn't a man at all. It was some kind of sea creature. At first I thought it was an octopus or large squid, something with tentacles, but it wasn't. It had a long snout like a crocodile and a mouth full of sharp teeth. Whatever it was, I had never seen anything like it. It was something from another time, maybe another world. A vicious killing machine from the sea washed up on the shore and was killed somehow. The birds seemed to be attacking it more from hatred than hunger. It was a horrible sight.

"All of a sudden the birds stopped gorging themselves and turned their attention to me. They all turned and started hopping toward me like an army of little aviary attack dogs. I started backing away slowly, trying to distance myself from them as much as possible without actually turning and running.

"They started squawking and crowing, hopping closer and starting to spread out. All of a sudden they flew at me in a giant swarm, almost like someone had fired a starting gun to give the signal to attack. They swarmed at me with their bloody talons and beaks, coming at my face, trying to peck out my eyes and slapping me with their wing tips. I started screaming as I tried to fight them off.

"I began swinging wildly with my arms, trying to keep them away as I staggered toward the woods. Fortunately, they backed off as I got farther away from their gory meal. When I had managed to get a good hundred feet away, they backed off completely and returned to their feeding. It was like all the forces of nature had suddenly decided one of their own had to be publicly executed by the masses and any human interference was unwelcome."

"What did they do to you?" Les said.

"Luckily, they only scared the hell out of me. They scratched me up pretty good but there were no major injuries. I went and washed all the blood and dirt off my face and arms and was fine again in a few days. Fine physically, that is. Emotionally however, it bothered me for a long time."

"Did you ever go back to the place?" Les said.

"I somehow got the courage to go back the next day," Roscoe said. "I stayed in the woods and sneaked a look from behind a tree. There was no sign of the birds or their victim anywhere around. I walked out onto the open sand and tried to find any evidence of what had taken place the previous day. There was nothing left at all, not even a mark in the sand. It looked like the tide had come in overnight and swept the spot clean. Over the years I've tried to convince myself that it never happened, that somehow I dreamt the whole thing. I just can't seem to convince myself of that though."

"Maybe it was some ancient creature that is extinct in our day," Mike said.

"I don't know," Roscoe said. "But whatever it was I never want to encounter another one, alive or dead." He looked over at Les. "So, now you know why I don't go out swimming in the ocean. And why I stayed here through countless opportunities to leave. There may be more of them out there."

"I think you just don't want to leave without your gold," Mike said.

"Don't start that again," Roscoe said. "I'm no fool."

"We can discuss the gold later when we get closer to time to leave," Les said. "But as for the thing you think you saw on the beach that day, I wouldn't worry about it. It was probably just a dead, half-eaten turtle or something."

"You haven't been here very long," Roscoe said. "I don't think you respect the dangers of this place. Ancient mariners had many fears of the deep and I'm not so sure they were without merit."

"Well whatever it was," Les said, "it isn't going to change my plans to get out of here when the *Spear* is ready and that little gold ship starts spinning. I believe in giant squids, sharks and octopuses but I don't believe in sea monsters. And neither should you."

"I believe what I see," Roscoe said. "And if these waters are teaming with creatures like that one, then we've got a very dangerous voyage ahead of us. This Bermuda Triangle is a place where the rules are different. My seeing that creature just confirms that."

"Whatever or whoever we encounter won't be any smarter than we are," Les said.

"Tell us some more of the things that Evan told you about the eye of the needle," Mike said.

"Well, it's been a long time," Roscoe said. "I remember how Evan used to say that certain days of the year were better than others for finding the eye."

Les looked at him with a confused expression. "Certain days?"

"Yes," Roscoe said. "He waited several weeks after he got his sailboat built before he sailed. He kept telling me the time wasn't right, but that the day was coming. It's really too bad it took so long for him to sail. We argued a good bit those last two weeks."

"Over gold?" Mike said.

"Oh yes," Roscoe said. "He told me I could take one gold bar and one little bag of coins. There was enough room in that boat for a couple hundred pounds though. He got really difficult. Finally, we practically stopped speaking to each other." Roscoe looked up into the trees that surrounded their current campsite. "A day or so before he left we came to an agreement. I would stay here and guard the gold while he would try to find a way home. Once there, he'd come back for me with a more able vessel. Then, we'd load up the gold and sail for home, eventually splitting everything evenly."

"Do you remember the day and month when he finally decided to sail?" Les said.

"No," Roscoe said. "I've long since lost track of the days of the week and the month. I do remember him going out onto the beach everyday and looking up at the sun. He'd jab a stick into the ground and measure the length of the shadow it cast. Sometimes he'd make calculations of some kind in the sand. I'd stand in the shade and watch him. He looked like some kind of sorcerer."

"Did he ever tell you what he was doing?" Mike said.

"He said he was trying to figure out the latitude, where we were in relation to the Tropic of Cancer. He made comments like: 'the shadow is getting shorter' and 'it won't be long now.'"

"Sounds to me like he was trying to determine when a solstice or equinox would occur," Les said. "I wonder if that meant something."

"The night before he left, he told me that he was sailing the next day." Roscoe said. "He was real excited about it."

"Did you ask him why?" Mike said.

"No," Roscoe said. "He asked me again to go with him. I refused to unless he'd agree to take a hold full of gold. That's when we had one last big argument. I told him I wasn't leaving without at least a hundred pounds of gold. He laughed at me and said I was nothing but a greedy old pirate. I told him he was a fool and we almost came to blows. I'd have to say we parted on less-than-ideal terms."

"But you still were convinced he'd return for you," Les said.

"Yes," Roscoe said. "He wanted the gold too. But he was more convinced than I was that it would compromise his sailboat's sea-worthiness. Evan was a man of his word. He said he'd come back for me and the gold and I believed him."

"Was he right about you being a greedy old pirate?" Mike said.

Roscoe sneered. "Maybe. But whatever I am, it beats the hell out of being broke like Evan, living out his numbered days in a cob-web filled, dirty lighthouse and eating cold sardines out of a can. I'm either going to live out my days in the lap of luxury back home or die trying. Either way, I'm going to die rich."

Mike chuckled. Although Roscoe's greedy tendencies troubled him, at the same time, he couldn't really see why Evan or any other man would leave this island without at least a little gold in his pockets. Especially when he'd still need to buy a new boat upon returning home if he really did intend to return for Roscoe.

"No matter," Les said. "We've got the talisman to tell us when the time is right to try leaving. And we can take at least some of the gold with us. I think I'll go see if those sap collectors are working before it gets dark."

Mike stood up. "I'll come too."

Of the four trees they had tapped, only one showed signs of progress. Several drops had made it into the coconut shell and more was on the way. Of the other three, one had a drop trying to get out of the tube; the other two showed no progress at all.

Later that night, thick clouds gathered and a vicious thunderstorm struck. The three of them got inside the lean-to and debated whether or not to go in the cave.

"The surf looked pretty tame when I went and checked it," Roscoe said. "I don't think this is a hurricane but we'd best be on our toes."

As the pounding rain hit the lean-to and trickled down on them, Mike sat staring at the little gold ship he had placed on the flat piece of wood on the floor. The talisman that they all hoped would lead them home sat motionless. Somehow the thought that it would move on its own seemed impossible to him. Then again there was nothing to lose by watching and hoping.

Later, the rain turned into a steady downpour that lasted the rest of the night. The next morning brought warm sunshine.

Upon awakening, Les went to check the sap collectors again. There was plenty of rainwater in the coconut halves but all four of them had at least a little sap clinging to the bottom. One of them had quite a lot.

He went to the east beach to check on the boat and found it just as they had left it, sitting upright in the sand. Several inches of rainwater had filled the bottom, which was a good sign that it didn't leak very much. Les spent several minutes looking it over and pounding a few nails in here and there. Once the sap was applied to the hull the *Spear* would be in pretty good shape.

When he got back to the campsite, he found some straw and began making paintbrushes. By wrapping a vine around a handful of straw and cutting it to uniform length he was able to make a very functional brush. He then made two more. Once the tree sap got boiling they would need to apply it quickly. There would be no time to make additional brushes if they were needed.

After lunch that afternoon, Les built up the fire while Mike went to collect the coconut halves containing the sap. When he returned, they scraped the sticky gob into a pot and started it cooking. Once it became runny, Les poured it into three coconut cups and they headed for the *Spear* to begin applying it to the cracks and crevices in the hull, coating layer upon layer in any area that might leak. They also applied it to the areas that appeared solid to strengthen them as well. By late afternoon, a sticky, glossy, waterproof glaze covered the Spear's hull.

The next day, with a fresh supply of sap, they turned the boat over and coated the outer hull, being very deliberate to fill all the cracks. They coated the original parts as well as the new ones, waiting an hour for the first coat to dry, then adding a second. At the end of the second day the coating was finished.

"Tomorrow morning we'll see how well she floats," Les said.

The three of them stood back and admired the boat.

"It looks good," Roscoe said. The others nodded.

"Then that means he's never coming back for me."

Mike thought a moment. "No. I guess he isn't."

CHAPTER 13

▼

THE *SPEAR* SETS SAIL

When morning came, Mike lay awake for a moment and pondered what would happen on this day. Les and Roscoe had already gotten up and he was alone in the lean-to. The sap they had applied to the hull of the *Spear* should be dry by now and they would find out if the endeavor had been successful. As always, Jan was foremost in his thoughts.

He sat up and checked the gold ship. It sat motionless on the block of wood. He then got up and went outside to find Roscoe and Les. Neither of them were nearby so he headed down the path to the lagoon. When he arrived there he saw that the two of them had the boat in the water. The sight made his heart start pounding with excitement.

"How's it doing?" Mike said.

"Fine so far", Les said. "Come look for leaks."

Mike quickly waded out waist deep into the warm water and climbed into the *Spear*. Jumping up and sitting on the side, he swung his feet around and stood up. The boat gently rocked from side to side. It felt sturdy and seemed to be floating nicely. A moment later Les jumped in too. The two of them gave Roscoe a hand.

The old seats were weathered and worn but felt incredibly comfortable.

"When did you put these seats in?" Mike said.

"Roscoe spotted them under the debris pile," Les said. "We got up early this morning and put them in. They don't all match but at least they're comfortable."

"I'll say," Mike said.

They immediately began searching around the walls and floor for signs of leakage. There didn't seem to be any.

"It's as dry as a bone." Roscoe smiled.

"Same here," Mike said. He noticed that Roscoe was checking out the storage areas of the boat.

"Let's attach the motor," Les said. He got out and waded to shore. Mike jumped into the water and got in front of the *Spear* to push it toward the beach.

Roscoe meanwhile inserted his hand into a small opening in one of the sidewalls. "Here's a good spot," he muttered.

"Can you give us a hand here, Roscoe?" Les called out. He was lifting the motor as Mike steadied the *Spear* in the gentle waves.

"Sure." Roscoe stepped to the back of the boat and prepared to guide the motor into the mounts. Together, Mike and Les hoisted the outboard and carefully attached it to the back wall of the boat. Mike held it steady while Les firmly tightened the big screws that clamped it into place.

When the task was done Les and Mike stood back to admire their work. The motor required cooling by the flow of water as it ran. Therefore, they never had an opportunity to even try it out until now. The two of them stood looking nervously at the idle motor and at each other.

"Get in and start her up, " Roscoe said to Les.

"Think she'll run?" Mike said.

Les had done the repair work and to the best of his knowledge had done it correctly. "No time like the present to find out."

Mike got back into the boat and moved to the front. Roscoe moved to one of the seats behind the windshield. Les then pushed the boat further away from shore and climbed in. He had placed one of the seats back near the engine so he could sit comfortably and steer the motor from side to side.

"Did you add oil to the motor?" Roscoe said.

"It's mixed in with the gas," Les said. He hooked the gas line to the intake valve of the motor and pumped the fuel by squeezing gently with his hand. The worn gas line had a few patches on it that he had repaired with the sap and pieces from other hoses he had found. The patchwork, representative of the entire rest of the vessel, was home-made and crude.

"How much gas do we have?" Mike said.

"It's a six gallon tank," Les said. "Looks like we have a little over five gallons. I just have to hope there's no seawater mixed in with it."

"I've got my fingers crossed," Roscoe said.

Mike decided to cross his too.

"Well," Les said. "Here goes." The other two watched as he reached over and gripped the handle on the pull rope. He placed his other hand firmly against the motor and pulled as hard as he could. The rope was slow to come out and the engine didn't make a sound.

"I probably need to pull this thing a few times to loosen it up," he said. He wrapped the rope around the starter and pulled again. This time the rope came out a little more easily. He tried again and again. Gradually, the pull-rope gave less and less resistance but the engine still didn't make a sound.

Mike sat silently. He watched Les as he coiled the rope around the starter again and paused a moment to pump in a little more gas.

Les stood up and placed his left hand firmly against the engine. Gripping the starter rope handle tightly, he pulled. As the rope came free the engine coughed. Les looked at the other two with an excited expression.

"Almost," Mike said.

Les coiled the rope around the starter again and got back into position. When he pulled this time the engine sputtered, struggled for about three seconds, then died. Without a word, Les repeated the steps. This time when he pulled the engine came to life. He quickly reached over to the throttle and gave her a little gas. The engine sputtered a few moments longer, tried to catch, then died.

"One more time and she'll start," Mike said. "That last one was so close."

Trying to stay calm, Les repeated the steps and got ready to pull. He stood up, got into position and yanked the starter rope. The engine fired to life with a loud roar. The three of them sat for several seconds as the rickety old motor rattled and shook. A large cloud of exhaust smoke billowed out and slowly lifted into the air. The engine continued to sputter, then gradually smoothed out into a steady purr. All three men were thrilled but nobody cheered. Les sat down and let the engine idle for several more seconds.

"Here goes nothing." Les reached over to push the lever that would put the boat in gear. He slid the lever and the loud roar softened to a sputtering, vibrating rumble. Les turned the throttle on the steering handle gently and the *Spear* lunged slowly forward.

Mike turned and looked out the front toward the open ocean at the far end of the lagoon. Subconsciously, he expected the engine to die but it didn't. Les gave it more gas and the boat began to speed up as it sliced gently across the water.

I can't believe it, Mike thought. The wonderful exhilaration that he always got from being in a moving speed-boat came over him.

They felt the boat speed-up slightly as Les gave it more gas. He banked a turn to the left to keep from running ashore then pointed toward the outlet to the sea. Moments later they exited the lagoon and roared into the open ocean.

Mike couldn't help smiling as the *Spear* began topping the ocean's waves. He turned and looked over at Roscoe. He was smiling and looked ten years younger. Mike could almost see in Roscoe's face what he looked like when he was a young man.

Mike looked back at Les, sitting at the throttle and looking around as he steered. He was smiling just a little. His eyes said he was in control as he scanned the sea around them.

Les glanced over and made eye contact with Mike. Without speaking, Mike grinned. It was a confident, proud grin.

Les smiled and nodded his head slightly. Mike felt a strong wave of confidence sweep over him. He figured Les felt the same thing.

After riding around for several minutes, Les slowed down and turned them back toward the lagoon. Once inside, he steered for the shore and cut the engine. The *Spear* drifted up to the beach and came to a halt with the bow gently touching the sand.

"Wow," Roscoe said. "That was incredible. It's been half a lifetime since I've felt a thrill like that." He reached over and gave Les a hearty handshake.

Mike thought about how it felt to him. He had been in a boat as recently as three or four months ago and that seemed an eternity. "I've got to hand it to you Les, you've really outdone yourself."

"Thanks," Les said. "But this is just a start."

"A really good start though," Roscoe said.

Hearing the silence of the island return after Les cut the *Spear*'s motor made Mike a little sad. He wanted to restart the motor, ride the boat around the island, reach the cliffs in a matter of minutes instead of hours and begin the journey home. But every drop of fuel was precious. Their course had to be plotted carefully and conservatively. Like Les had said, it was only the beginning.

That night around the fire, the three of them seemed to find their friendship renewed. "We've got to be prepared to leave at anytime," Les said without taking his eyes from the flames. "Tomorrow morning we need to get wineskins of water ready and replace the water every couple of days. We need to put fishing poles in the boat. We need to gather nuts and anything edible that will keep for a while. If that little ship starts to spin at ten tomorrow morning I want us to be in the boat with the motor running at 10:01."

"You've got it," Mike said. "We'd better figure out how much gold we can carry and stow it away inside the boat too."

"Good idea," Roscoe said. "In fact, I'll handle that little detail myself first thing in the morning."

They sat around the fire for a while and tried to brainstorm ideas. "Oars," Les said. "We have to remember to take some oars." They thought of a few other minor details and made mental notes of them. Sometime later they all headed for the lean-to for a good night's sleep.

The following morning, a steady trickle of rain started just before dawn. It gradually got harder and poured until around mid-day when it stopped abruptly. The three of them chose to stay inside, hoping it would dry up before they got too hungry to wait any longer. Once the rain quit, they emerged and began preparing breakfast and readying supplies for the boat.

In the mid-afternoon, the three of them stood on the shore and admired the *Spear* floating at the end of the tie vine in the shallow water of the lagoon. Mike and Les waded out to it and found some water in the bottom. "I hope this is rain water", Mike said. He reached down and dipped his finger in the small puddle near the back of the boat and tasted it. "It's rain."

"Gentlemen," Les said. "It gives me great pleasure to declare the *Spear* seaworthy and ready to sail."

Mike felt the hair on the back of his neck stand up, even under the long locks that were fast approaching his shoulder blades. That night, they sat around the fire after dinner and watched the golden ship sit motionless on the board at Les' feet. Each time they set the ship down Mike would cross his fingers and hope it would start twirling around on its own.

Two weeks passed. As the three of them spent a sunny, breezy afternoon at the lagoon fishing one day, Mike found a shady spot on the bank and cast his line. He found himself staring at the *Spear*, floating idle. He began to go over in his mind the things they would need when they sailed. Water, food, oars, fishing tackle, were all stowed away. The gold, approximately one thousand coins, was crammed into the walls, along with several of the smaller trinkets. The crown, several decorative crosses and a jewelry box were wrapped-up in a burlap bag that fit nicely under one of the seats. After many debates, the decision was made to not even attempt to take any of the heavy gold bars. Although each was probably worth several thousand dollars, the risk of overloading the motorboat was too great to offset the gold's value. The *Spear* was ready and so was its crew. Waiting for the gold ship to start spinning was the worst part.

In the late afternoon they returned to camp and Roscoe built-up the fire. Les pulled the gold ship out of its hiding place and put it on the board on the floor of the lean-to. He then walked back out and accompanied Mike to look for some fruit for dinner. Les had exited the lean-to too quickly to notice the little vessel turn forty-five degrees and point itself due east.

About an hour later Roscoe called out that the shrimp was ready. Les and Mike were hauling in the night's supply of firewood.

"Great, I'm starved," Mike said. He walked into the lean-to to get a rag to clean off his hands and spotted the little ship on the wood block and nonchalantly reached down and thumped it. The ship spun around a couple of times and came to a halt pointing toward the east beach. Mike thumped it again and once again it came to a stop pointing in the same direction. He thumped it once more and again it stopped with its bow aiming east. His heart skipped a beat. Without taking his eyes from it he sat down beside the block of wood and moved it halfway around with his finger. The moment he pulled his finger away it circled slowly around and pointed east again.

"Hey guys! Come here quick!"

Roscoe stuck his head in the doorway and looked at him. "What is it?"

"Look at this," Mike said. He moved the little ship halfway around and took his hand away. The ship spun halfway back around by itself and again pointed east. Mike looked up at Roscoe and their eyes met. Roscoe's seedy grin followed a moment later. Les came strolling into camp carrying an armload of firewood. Roscoe and Mike were shaking hands and smiling. He dropped the wood and walked over.

"The ship's moving," Mike said.

Les' mouth fell open.

Mike moved the ship back around several more times and each time it turned.

"The eye of the needle must be in that direction," Les said. "It has some kind of magnetic pull that the front of the little ship points to when it's close." He looked up at the evening sky. "It'll be dark in half an hour. Do you think we should chance it in the dark?"

"Let's wait and see if it gets closer," Roscoe said. "Remember, Mike saw it twitching several weeks ago. Maybe it'll start spinning soon."

"Yeah maybe," Mike said. "Then again it might stop pointing all together if we wait. I say we go now."

"I don't know," Les said. "If it weren't so close to night-fall I'd agree. But there are no lights on the boat or the island and we could easily get lost in the dark."

"Plus there's not much gas left," Roscoe said. "I've waited more than ten years for this. Let's don't blow it by jumping the gun."

Mike tried to calm himself. "Of course you're right," he said. "Sailing right away would be dangerous." Once he thought about it, waiting until dawn seemed like a wise idea.

Les picked up the talisman and the block of wood and walked out to the fire. He then set it on the ground where they all could see it. They sat down to eat, each keeping an eye on the little ship.

When they turned in, Mike set the talisman down in the middle of the lean-to. Once again it turned to point east. "If it starts spinning it'll wake us up," he said.

"If it starts spinning then the last one to the *Spear* is a rotten egg," Les said. They all chuckled, then began drifting into an anxious, restless sleep.

Mike kept waking up and drifting back to sleep. Inspired by the thoughts of going home, his imagination kept taking him back to Jan.

"Wake up," he heard Les say. He opened his eyes. Early morning light was showing through the cracks of the lean-to.

"The ship's spinning like a carousel," Les said. "Let's hit the water."

"Hell, yes," Mike said. He jumped up, just missing hitting himself on the low ceiling and rushed outside. The first thing he saw was Roscoe picking up a basket of fruit and a wineskin and starting for the trail to the lagoon.

"Race you to the *Spear*," Roscoe said.

Mike burst out laughing. Roscoe couldn't outrun him if Mike was dragging a palm tree in each hand. "I'm right behind you good buddy," he shouted.

"Grab the blankets out of the lean-to," Les said. "I'll get the engine running."

"Okay," Mike said. "Where's the little ship?"

"Got it right here." Les patted his pants pocket. "See you at the lagoon." He quickly headed down the trail.

Mike got the blankets out and looked around quickly to see if there was anything they might have forgotten. He didn't see anything else they could take so he ran for the trail to the lagoon. When he was almost to it he heard the *Spear*'s engine sputter momentarily and then go silent. A moment later he rounded the corner and the boat came into view. Les pulled the starter cord again and this time the motor roared to life. Mike waded out to the boat and handed the blankets to Roscoe who was already seated inside. He then climbed in and sat down, feeling the vibrations of the idling motor gently shaking the seat.

Les reached into his pocket and pulled out the gold ship. He then placed it on the floor in the middle of the boat and the three of them watched it start to spin around.

The little ship spun faster and faster. Les looked up at the two of them and smiled broadly. "Here we go!"

He put the engine in gear and the *Spear* began to putter toward the opening of the lagoon. He turned the throttle slightly and the boat sped up.

"It's a bit chilly this morning," Roscoe said over the drum of the motor.

"It's the cold, clean smell of freedom," Mike hollered back.

Les drove them out of the lagoon and turned due east toward the rising sun. The waves bobbed the boat up and down, and Mike found himself holding onto the steering wheel with both hands. The wheel did nothing but give him something to hold on to, as Les was doing the steering from the back. There was no way to attach the *Spear's* steering system into the motor, so he had just removed it, except for the wheel that was now nothing more than a dashboard ornament. The cool morning air whistled through Mike's long hair and the great feeling of exhilaration from going fast in a boat came sweetly along with it.

In the middle of the boat's floor the gold ship spun so fast that Les feared it would hurt his hand if the tried to grab hold of it. "We're close now!"

Up ahead Mike noticed a strange looking pocket of fog in the air. There seemed to be a transparent wall in front of them and the fog on the far side of it was backed up against it, almost like someone had stretched a big, greasy window across an acre of ocean one-hundred yards ahead. Les saw the fog and headed right for it.

Mike felt a rush of adrenaline. He had a feeling of uncertainty, like they were approaching a blind curve. He looked over to see Roscoe holding on. A gold coin popped out of the sidewall and Roscoe struggled to hold one of his hands over the opening so no others would follow-suit.

Seconds later, the *Spear* plunged through the invisible barrier. The air temperature dropped considerably. The waves increased in size and the *Spear* began to bounce violently up and down. The fog bank thickened with each passing second and, within moments, visibility dropped to near zero.

Mike noticed that the little ship had fallen over on its side and was bouncing along the floor. He didn't want to risk letting it fall overboard so he reached down to get it with his left hand as he held the steering wheel tightly with his right. The gold talisman continued to slide around and elude him for a moment before he finally got a handle on it. Once he got it firmly in hand he noticed how warm it was, almost hot. He quickly slid it into his pocket.

The *Spear* topped a huge wave and plummeted down about ten feet on the other side. Mike had just gotten both hands on the wheel and for an instant they were the only part of him still in contact with the boat. Back at the rear, Les grabbed his seat and barely managed to keep from flying out. To Mike's left, Roscoe was struggling to hold on. He had reached down to grasp his seat firmly with both hands and almost looked to Mike like a cowboy, fighting to stay on a bucking bronco.

The bag of gold trinkets that Roscoe had so carefully stowed under his seat rolled forward and hit the front dashboard floor with a loud thud. An instant later it rolled back under the seat and out of sight. A few moments later it flew back out again with another loud thud. Both Mike and Roscoe looked down at it.

Mike took one hand off the wheel and tried to reach down for the wayward bag of gold. An instant later the *Spear* took a sudden abrupt rise, followed immediately by a violent drop. Mike felt his whole body being yanked off the boat but his right hand held fast to the wheel. He immediately put his left hand back on the wheel and tried to get his heart out of his throat.

The bag of gold started sliding from side to side as it hopped up and down on the deck. Mike looked up and saw a huge wave about to hit the bow. He gripped the wheel as tight as he could and awaited the next jolt. An instant later the wave hit. Water started rolling across the front and into the boat. The *Spear* popped straight up and sailed several feet into the air. Mike watched in horror as the bag of gold flew upward and toward the open ocean. The *Spear* came down and slammed into the water. Both Mike and Roscoe watched the gold drop from the sky and splash into the waves about ten feet from the boat.

Roscoe jumped to his feet and stood in his seat.

"What the hell are you doing," Mike screamed. He tried to grab Roscoe but was unsuccessful.

Roscoe dove headfirst over the side and started swimming toward the spot where the bag of gold had fallen into the water.

"Get back over here," Les screamed.

Mike couldn't believe his eyes. Days earlier he had stowed three old moldy life preservers between the seats and sides of the boat and he quickly pulled one out. He tossed it in the direction of Roscoe and saw it hit the water a few feet from him.

As several rather large waves could be seen approaching the front of the boat, Roscoe neared the spot where the bag of gold had hit the water and dove down out of sight. The *Spear* was yanked skyward by another giant wave. The boat went completely airborne and both remaining occupants barely held on. When the *Spear* hit the water again it almost threw Mike right through the floor. There was a loud thud when the boat came down followed by the stalling of the engine. The violent waves continued and Mike and Les were yanked from side to side while the sea tried to tear them from the boat.

"Roscoe," Mike screamed. "Where are you?" He was attempting to stand while still holding the wheel. Looking in all directions through the thick fog and rough sea he saw no sign of him. "Roscoe," he kept calling.

For the next half-hour they kept calling Roscoe's name and looking all around. There was no sign of him or the life preserver Mike had thrown out for him. Then the sea gradually calmed and the fog thinned somewhat. There was still no sign of Roscoe.

"I should have made him wear a life jacket," Mike said.

"He would have just taken it off before jumping in," Les said. "He had a bad case of gold fever."

"Has," Mike said. His eyes were filled with tears. "Roscoe," he called out again. "Where are you?"

He continued calling out Roscoe's name again and again as Les sat silently. Mike's voice gradually took on the sound of heartbreak and defeat.

"You're wasting your time," Les said at last. "He's gone."

"We don't know that," Mike said.

"Listen to me," Les said. "Roscoe's gone. It's time to move on. We've got to start thinking of ourselves again."

"He gave me the strength to go on living when I felt like killing myself," Mike said. "I think I owe it to him to at least try to save him if I can."

"Fine," Les said. "You want to jump in and look for him?"

Mike was silent. Neither he nor Les said anything for a long time. Over the next hour the sea calmed somewhat and Les tried unsuccessfully to get the motor started several times. The minutes dragged and they sat quietly in the rocking boat, looking all around and seeing nothing but foggy ocean.

Sometime later the fog thinned a good bit. The sky was still cloudy but visibility was pretty good. It appeared to be around four in the afternoon. Les looked up. "Hey, a ship."

Mike turned the direction Les was looking. It was a ship, but it was dark and appeared deserted. The very sight of it gave him a slight feeling of hope.

Les began pulling the starter rope on the motor again. The seas had calmed quite a bit and he was actually able to move about without having to hold on at all times with both hands.

Mike braced himself and stood up. He couldn't see anyone on the deck but hoped maybe someone would see or hear him. "Hey, over here!" There was no reply. The ship was still at least a quarter-mile away and appeared dead in the water. They could see no movement of the vessel itself or any signs of life on board. Mike decided to take out an oar and begin rowing toward it while Les continued to try starting the motor.

"I give up," Les said after a dozen more pulls on the starter rope. "I don't know if the motor is just flooded or what, but it won't start." He reached down and got the other oar that Roscoe had made just days before. The boat was cumbersome and slow.

"Oh, this is going to take forever," Les said.

"I know," Mike said not breaking stride. "But if we stay at it I think we can make it to that ship before dark. I sure don't want to spend the night out here in this little boat."

Les agreed and the two of them began to row at a steady pace, periodically glancing up at the ship to make sure they were staying on a straight line for it. Mike rowed a dozen strokes or so, glanced up at the ship, then rowed more. When he looked up again his eyes analyzed the approaching ship momentarily before he looked back at the water. He looked back up at the ship and stopped rowing. "Hey Les."

"Huh." Les didn't look up.

"Take a good look at that ship."

Les stopped rowing and looked up. They were only about one hundred yards off its port bow. The afternoon sun was shining brightly now and they could see their destination very clearly. Like Mike, Les was shocked by what he saw. The ship they were approaching was a galleon, out of the sixteenth or seventeenth century. Planks made up its hull and its huge wooden masts stood starkly against the sky. One of the masts had the unmistakable shape of a crow's nest near its peak. Just under the bow was the masthead of a young woman wearing a blue gown of some kind. Her painted face stared directly ahead with piercing blue eyes. The ship looked relatively new and in good condition. There was not the slightest hint of anyone on board.

"Do you think we should continue?" Mike said. "That ship could be dangerous."

"Not any more dangerous than staying out here," Les said. "Let's have a closer look. If we don't see anyone on deck then we'll go aboard."

The motor boat slugged through the water slowly and the two of them had to take frequent breaks to rest. From time to time the wind would gust and the old ship would lean to one side, making loud creaking noises that carried across the water.

Mike pulled out the little gold ship and set it on the floor of the boat. It didn't move. "Looks like our talisman has shut down for the day."

He resumed rowing and they gradually got close to the big ship. There was a rope dangling from the deck and Les kept rowing as Mike stood up and reached for it. "Got it."

Les put down his oar and joined him up front. "Hey, anybody on board?" There was no reply. He pulled out the *Spear*'s anchor and tugged on its rope. "Let me see if I can hook this over the railing." Mike watched as Les swung the anchor around a couple of times and let it fly. It slid up to the railing and stopped firmly in place.

"Nice shot," Mike said.

"You want to go first or do you want me to?"

"Be my guest."

Les handed Mike the end of the rope to hold for him and then began climbing. He was exhausted from the rowing and the short, ten-foot climb was very difficult. He reached the railing and pulled himself up. Once he was safely on deck he looked around. The ship was abandoned.

Les looked around and spotted a rope ladder lying on the deck. He took it and hooked it onto the railing, then lowered it. Mike tied the only piece of rope they had to the front railing of the *Spear* and then reached up to tie it to the dangling rope from the big ship. It was just long enough to make the connection. He tied it off and then climbed aboard.

After reaching the railing, Mike stood next to Les and looked around. The ship looked to be in remarkably good condition. The sails lay neatly folded at the base of the masts and four lifeboats were tied securely upside down on the decks. The wind gusted just a little and the big vessel listed to the right. For just a moment every board in the deck seemed to groan. Mike made a mental note that the sound almost resembled groaning sailors.

CHAPTER 14

▼

ABANDONED VESSELS-THE HORRIBLE TRUTH

"Let's look around inside," Les said. "And watch your step." He gave no hint of whether or not his sixth sense might have an opinion. The abandoned hulk gave Mike an uneasy feeling.

There were two cabins built onto the deck, separated by an open space in the middle. Each cabin had a stairway that led to its roof. The fore and aft masts were built into the two cabins and the mid-mast, the tallest of the three, stood right in the center of the middle deck.

Both cabins had passageways with the doors standing wide open. Les walked inside the front cabin and Mike followed. The cabin had large, dirty windows on either side and in front. Les looked out the front window at the large coils of rope and a huge, rusty iron anchor sitting out on the front deck. There was a console in the front of the cabin with a big round steering wheel jutting out of it. Mike tried turning the wheel and found that it did move a little but with great resistance.

"This ship is in sailing condition," Les said. "I just wonder what could have happened to her crew."

"The lifeboats are untouched," Mike said. "It's almost like the crew disappeared into thin air."

They walked back outside, crossed the mid-deck and entered the aft cabin. There was more rope coiled up neatly on the floor. In the middle of the cabin was a stairway that led down below decks.

"Shall we?" Les said.

Mike leaned over the railing. "Anybody home?" The echo vibrated away into the musty, dank interior.

The stairway was wide enough for them to walk side by side, so they started down together. There was faint light at the bottom that trickled in through the portholes that stood in a row, running the length of the deck up near the ceiling. The stairs ended into the galley. Both of them felt the floorboards give a little and creak as they walked slowly into the middle of the vessel's lowest deck. Along the floors stood barrels of water and salt, and there were cabinets on the walls and long tables with benches nailed to the floor in the center.

There were few supplies. Even the wood stove appeared to be almost out of kindling. Mike walked over to the ancient cooking device and admired its simplicity. He looked up above and spotted several crude lanterns hanging from pegs in the wall. Gently rocking one revealed the sound of fuel sloshing around inside.

Les walked farther back toward the stern and noticed the numerous bunks that ran along the walls. With an upper and lower row running along both inner walls and extending down half the length of the ship, the vessel could carry a crew of about fifty or sixty.

"I guess we might as well choose bunks and sleep here tonight," Les said.

Mike wasn't wild about that idea but then again, there weren't many options. There were many blankets lying on the various bunks and the two of them would probably be more comfortable here than anywhere they'd been since the tree house was destroyed by the storm. The place was dusty and the blankets were worn.

Mike spotted a doorway leading to a small room at the very back. He went to it and saw that the door had been dislodged from its hinges and was lying on the floor of the room. "That's strange. I wonder why the door is busted."

"Probably just old," Les said. He had followed Mike into the dark room. "I don't suppose you brought the flints in with you."

"They're in the glove compartment," Mike said.

"Oh great. What about the gold ship?"

"It's right here in my pocket," Mike said. "I'll go get the flints. Anything else you want while I'm down there?"

"The water and food," Les said. "It looks like when we went through the eye it got later in the day. I think it'll be getting dark soon. I guess we'd better get settled in here for the night."

"Be right back." Mike headed back topside. Once he got back out on the deck and headed for the railing he glanced around. He spotted another vessel floating a mile or so away. Although he couldn't be sure, this one appeared more modern, and it too appeared dead in the water. He quickly scanned the horizon and spotted the distinct silhouettes of two other ships. All were much too far away to tell anything about.

All of a sudden he got the feeling that he was being watched from one of the other vessels, or perhaps from all of them. He realized that he was out on deck in these creepy waters alone for the first time. The Bermuda Triangle at that moment really did look like some kind of ship graveyard, just like the stories all said.

But what about the crews, he thought. He glanced over at one of the lifeboats, still snugly moored to the deck in its normal inverted position. Four oars lay neatly stacked on the shelf beside it.

"You got the flints yet?" Les called out from below.

"Not yet. Be right back." He climbed over the rail and scampered down the rope ladder to the *Spear* below. He got the flints out and put them in the wicker basket with the bag of fruit and the wineskins of water. He then looped his belt through the handles of the basket and climbed back up to the deck.

He returned to the cabin. "I spotted several other ships out there."

"What kinds of ships are they?" Les said.

"The nearest one looks like a merchant with a steel hull," Mike said. "The other two are too far away to tell."

"Hopefully we can get the *Spear* running in the morning," Les said. "Then we can go check out the close one."

"Maybe we can find more modern accommodations while we're at it too."

Les chuckled. He opened one of the lanterns by removing the glass and revealed the wick. Striking the flints a few times, he soon got the lantern lit. They touched the flame to two others and got them going as well.

Mike took one of the lanterns into the captain's quarters and looked around. There was a nice big bed, a small chest of drawers and a couple of paintings on the wall. The paintings both pictured a harbor, perhaps the home of the former crew. "I found where I want to sleep tonight," he said. Les came in a moment later.

"Looks like that bed's big enough for both of us," Les said. Mike chuckled. "Okay, but stay on your side and no snoring."

"Don't flatter yourself." Les smirked. He took the basket Mike had just set down on the floor and pulled out the wineskin of water for a drink. He also fished out the fruit and they shared a skimpy meal. As they finished the last of the food, darkness fell outside.

After eating, Les suggested a walk around the ship. "I doubt we'll see any lights but it won't hurt to look."

They went up the stairs and out onto the deck. The sky had cleared and the moon, somewhere between first quarter and full, provided a good bit of light.

"There's the other ship." Mike pointed. Les looked at the dark vessel floating silently off the starboard bow a couple of miles away.

There was a slight wind gust and the ship listed to port. Loud creaks could be heard from below. "One night on this old tub will be enough for me," Les muttered.

"Well, if that other one won't do we have at least two others from which to choose," Mike said. "It's just too dark to see them now."

Les stared at the one other vessel they could see. It appeared as nothing more than a big shadow in the moonlight. "There's something out there," he said.

"Where?"

"That other ship. My sixth sense clicks when I look at it. There's something about that ship."

Mike stared at the distant shadow. It sat dark and motionless. Chills ran up and down his spine as he stared at the mysterious vessel. "I sure wish I knew what it is."

"We'll find out tomorrow," Les said calmly. "I'm going to bed."

"I'll be in shortly."

Les went inside, leaving Mike alone on the deck, alone with his ever-present thoughts of home. As he watched the moonlight swim in the calm ocean he couldn't help but notice what a beautiful evening it had become. The threatening clouds had scattered, revealing a clear, starry sky.

He pictured being on a cruise ship, walking along the deck hand and hand with Jan. He could almost hear music in the distance.

The image faded as his brain reconnected with what his eyes saw now. As he stared into the moonlight he felt the tears in his eyes. The breeze gusted again and the creaky old ship listed forward slightly. The sinking feeling that they were actually regressing seemed to be shrouding around him like the ocean breeze. Les was determined to get them home and every step got them closer. There was no logic behind any feelings right now, good or bad. But still they were there, and they were sad.

He decided it was time to leave the deck and go try to get some sleep. Taking one last look at the distant ship, he thought he saw a flashing light. His heart skipped a beat as he stared, waiting for it to reappear. It didn't. The ship was right under the moon and a trail of light led across the water to it. "Must be imagining things," he muttered.

He walked back to the stairs and still felt his heart racing as he descended them. There was a strong feeling of anticipation for that strange ship; he felt it just as Les had.

When Mike entered the Captain's quarters, he found Les sitting on the bed reading a dusty old book.

Les looked up and smiled. "Captain's log. Maybe we can get some answers from it."

"I hope so." Mike went to the bed, sat down and took off his worn shoes. As he looked around his eyes fixed themselves on the chest of drawers against the wall. Taking the lantern, he walked over to it and opened the top drawer. Inside were a couple of dusty old button-down shirts. There was also a pair of uniform pants and a non-uniform pair as well.

Mike was dying to know what was written in the logbook but waited patiently for Les to read it and then fill him in.

"Looks like this book was used as a ship's log but the captain apparently wasn't big on writing," Les said. "Either that or they hadn't been sailing for very long. Only about ten pages have been used. The writing is really sloppy."

Mike sat down beside him and took a look. The cursive handwriting was messy, but some of it appeared legible. "I think I can read some of this," he said.

"Knock yourself out." Les handed it to him and then lay out on the bed.

"Looks like the entry at the top says: 'Day Two since passing through the fog'." Mike looked over at Les.

"Must be referring to the eye of the needle." He lay staring at the ceiling.

Mike slowly read some more. "Fog bank caused long journey to—something mysterious waters. Ships here seem to be trapped. There were no signs of life anywhere.

"Day Three, seven men missing from ship. They seem to have left during the night. Two bodies seen floating today. Tried to recover them but could not. One sailor said he heard screams on deck during the night. Believe— something about a fight.

"Day Five, cannot identify other vessel that appears in the distance off port bow. Ship appeared to be moving but saw no sails. Fear of attack but no—something.

"Day Seven, almost all of crew gone. Men are afraid. Deck seems dangerous at night. Only eleven of us left, rest of crew has disappeared. Some of remaining crew members reported seeing several of the missing in the water behind the ship."

"Dead or alive?" Les said.

"Doesn't say," Mike said. "Crew said that they see men in the water behind the ship, then they vanish. Times are bad; I have never known such fear. All men now carry weapons at all times but weapons did not save missing crewmen. Hope to—something—something at dawn."

Mike looked over at Les who was now lying with his eyes closed. "Is there more?" Les said.

"A little," Mike said. "Day Seven, midnight, awakened by screams on top deck. Crewmen are disappearing in the dark. I can hear something of great weight moving around on deck. Heavy bumping against walls, floor and door. Maybe——."

"Maybe what?" Les said.

"Nothing," Mike said. "It ends there."

Les sat up and looked at Mike who was staring across the room. He followed Mike's eyes. They were locked on the large door that still lay on the floor where it was when they had first come aboard. Mike looked over at Les but didn't say anything.

"Do you think something came in here and got him?" Mike said.

Les stared at the door. It appeared undamaged but was off its hinges. "I think we need to look around some more." This time let's look for damage; smashed walls or floors, signs of a struggle, anything that might identify whatever it was that made those men disappear."

They got up. Mike quickly lit another lantern so they both would have one. He noticed his hand trembling. Once he got it lit they quickly began looking around below decks. Here and there were damaged places and loose boards but all could have been caused by normal wear and tear. After inspecting the inside, they went upstairs and out onto the deck. Again there were no signs of a struggle.

"How's the sixth sense?" Mike said.

"Quiet as a lamb," Les said.

After walking around a bit more, they went back down to the Captain's quarters. "Think we ought to keep a watch?" Mike said.

"I don't see why," Les said. "If anyone comes aboard we should hear them. Just keep your ears open." He stretched out on the bed again.

Mike sat down on the other side of the bed once again thinking of Jan. He lay down and found the old bed remarkably comfortable. He blew out the lanterns and lay in the dark with his eyes open. As he started to relax he tried to picture Jan's pretty face in his mind. It had been so long since he had seen her that the clarity was no longer there. The last conscious thought he had before sleep overtook him was the replay of the walk along the cruise ship deck.

Sometime later Mike stirred in his sleep. He began to awaken from his restful slumber to creaking noises that got louder and louder. Finally there was a loud creak from overhead that made him snap alert. His eyes popped open and he lay quietly for several seconds. After a brief period of silence that almost allowed him time to disregard what he thought he had heard and close his eyes again, another creak, this one softer, caught his attention. He suddenly felt certain that there was someone walking around on the deck overhead.

"Les," he whispered. He reached over and shook him gently. Another series of creaks came from the darkness above. "Les, wake up," Mike said, attempting to keep his voice down.

Les made some sort of grunting noise. "I heard something," Mike whispered frantically. "Wake up."

Les stirred and suddenly snapped awake. "What," he cried out loudly. His voice echoed softly.

The sound of a heavy, cumbersome body could be heard moving across the deck above them. It lumbered and skittered, making floorboards creak and snap loudly as it moved. The two men sat in the dark and listened as it ambled from the middle of the deck toward one of the sides and then went silent. An instant later, there was a loud splash as something large and heavy fell into the water. The silence returned.

"What do you suppose that was?" Mike was too scared to move.

"I don't know," Les said. "It sounded like someone in a golf-cart dragging a chain drove across the deck and into the water."

"Whatever it was, it was scared off by the sound of your voice." The two of them lay silently for several more moments, listening for more sounds.

"Let's go see if there's anything on the deck," Les said.

"Do you think that's such a good idea?" Mike said. "Whoever or whatever we just heard sounded large. Going up there could be dangerous."

"No worse than staying down here," Les said. "Down here we're cornered. At least up on deck we'll be out in the open. I think that would make our chances a little better."

"Okay," Mike said. "But let's be ready for anything." He fumbled around in the dark for the metal piece and a flint. Finding them, he got a lantern lit. They then went out of the captain's quarters, heading down the aisle toward the stairs. Leaving the lit lantern behind, they quietly ascended to the doorway that led to the deck. Mike carefully peeked around the corner and checked outside. It was still quite dark, but the faint light of the moon revealed that the deck was abandoned. "Looks like it's all clear."

Les hurried back down the stairs and got the lantern. A moment later he returned and walked out on the empty deck and looked around. They walked over to the railings along opposite sides of the ship and looked into the water. Although it was still dark, there appeared to be nothing there as well.

"Whatever it was is gone now," Mike said. "Thank goodness."

Les walked back to the center of the deck and sat down on a barrel. Mike sat down on an old crate a few feet away.

"It'll be another hour or so before daylight," Les said.

Mike sensed tiredness in his voice that reflected his own. He glanced up at the sky and then at their dark surroundings. The moonlight was faint and there were no lights to be seen. The other ship that they had faintly seen in the distance the evening before was not visible.

"There's something on that ship out there," Les said.

"Where?" Mike scanned the horizon again. "I don't even see it."

"I don't see it either." Les pointed "It's right over there."

Mike followed his finger but saw nothing. Somehow he felt some comfort in this sixth sense of Les'.

They sat in silence for a while. The early morning was cool and a little breezy. There were no sounds of birds or anything else. Only the soft splashing of the water against the hull and the breeze blowing through the tall masts broke the silence.

"What made you wake up?" Les said.

"Creaking boards," Mike said. "I'm sure glad I woke up when I did."

"Me too," Les said. "We need to try and find a nicer vessel than the *Spear* or this old hulk." He stamped his foot hard on the old wooden deck and they both felt the boards move slightly beneath them.

Mike stood up and strolled a little toward the boat's stern. Les got up and walked along with him. The sun was climbing quickly and any minute would come over the horizon to the east.

"I guess it's a lucky thing we all ended up on the island," Mike said.

"I'm sure there are plenty of people that disappear and don't get so lucky," Les said. "I just wish I knew where we are in time right now. Look at this creepy old ship. It's ancient. And what's more, it looks like it wasn't built all that long ago."

"That other ship is newer," Mike said. "It has a steel hull." He could vaguely see the other vessel now that the sun was almost up. It appeared to have drifted a little farther away during the night and now looked like a little purple drawing on a huge distant canvas.

"We also need to find out what in the world it is about that ship that makes my sixth sense click," Les said.

Those words left Mike to wonder, and he stood looking at the distant ship while Les went over to the lantern and put it out. "I'm going to get the talisman and the water," Les said. "I hope the only reason the *Spear*'s motor wouldn't start was that it flooded yesterday. If I can get it started we'll head over there."

He went down the stairs for the wineskin and whatever else he could find that might be useful. When he came to the wicker basket he found the gold ship to be the only thing in it; they had eaten all the fruit. He grabbed it, put the wineskins inside it and headed back up.

Mike stayed on deck and stared at the distant vessel. The other two ships were still visible but they were much farther away. As he stood at the railing he suddenly became aware of a sound coming from the back of the ship. He turned and looked in the direction of the stern. There didn't appear to be anything back there but as he stood looking, he heard something that sounded like a human voice. Roscoe, he suddenly thought.

Mike hurried to the back railing and looked down into the water. There was someone frantically splashing around. Although there still wasn't much light, Mike could clearly see the top of a man's head. He was struggling to keep from being pulled under by the waves. Mike saw him thrashing about, trying to make it to the side of the ship. He spotted an old rope and rushed over to get it. When he got back to the railing he looked down and spotted the struggling man. He was facedown and Mike couldn't tell if it was Roscoe or not.

Suddenly the man in the water turned his face up to Mike and smiled. It wasn't Roscoe. It wasn't even alive. The eyes were solid white and the face puffy and greenish yellow. Seaweed was crammed in its mouth. Terror overcame Mike as he realized this was a dead sailor from the ship, trying to get back aboard. Suddenly two more of them popped to the surface and began swimming toward the ship. One opened its mouth and tried to speak. A big blue crab crawled out from the toothless grin and plopped into the water. It held its big claw in front of itself and glared up at Mike.

The three dead sailors were now looking at Mike angrily. One of them had a gaping hole where an eye should have been. The other eye moved steadily from side to side, blindly wavering about.

When the lifeless men moved their mouths Mike heard that eerie sound again, the high pitched voice that becomes audible when two people scream at the same time. The dead sailors came closer to the ship and Mike could do nothing but watch them. He tried to back away from the railing but couldn't.

There was a gust of wind and the ship tilted, pulling Mike up against the back railing like he had been shoved from behind. When he hit the rail it broke and he fell forward toward the water and the waiting dead sailors below. Mike screamed as he struggled to grab hold of anything he could before tumbling overboard. He managed to get a hand on a rail support that held him momentarily. His feet dangled over the water.

A few feet below the three dead sailors reached up with their swollen, yellow hands. Mike felt one of them touch his foot. It brushed by, tried to grab hold and slid off. He looked up to see the rail support he was holding start to pry loose from its moorings. The huge rusty bolts that held it fast were slowly pulling out from the deck. "Les! Help!"

He looked down and saw that two more corpses had floated to the surface. Now there were five of them, looking up at him and grinning, beckoning him to come in. Tiny fiddler crabs crawled out of their hair and took little bites from the rotting flesh on their faces. Swollen hands with long black fingernails reached for his feet.

Mike looked at the rail support and heard the horrible cracking sound as the bolts continued to pull out one centimeter at a time. In just seconds it would pop free and he'd fall into the sea.

"Les!" he screamed. One hand slipped off and the other barely held him. He felt himself going faint. Slowly the other hand slipped off and his descent began. His life passed before his eyes.

Suddenly Les reached down and grabbed Mike's wrist just before he plunged into the water. Mike felt himself crash against the side of the ship but Les held firm as he tried to keep from being pulled toward the edge. The ship tilted back as the morning breeze rose to a gust, almost as if it were trying to toss them overboard.

"Pull Les, pull!" Mike screamed. He tried to pull his feet up as far from the water as possible. From below he felt things brushing up against his shoes.

Les strained and pulled. He was making little progress and his grip on Mike's wrist was slipping. Luckily, Mike was able to use his free hand to grab the rail support. Once he lessened the weight with which Les would have to contend, Les yanked him up a couple of feet and Mike slid onto the deck. He quickly crawled a good twenty feet from the edge before daring to relax.

"You saved my life." He gasped for breath. "Thanks man."

"You okay?" Les was smiling just a little. "If I hadn't been able to pull you in I would have lowered a rope for you or you could have swum around to the *Spear*. It's not like you would have drowned or anything. You know how to swim don't you?"

"They would have gotten me," Mike said.

"Who?"

"Who. Didn't you see them?"

"See who?"

"The dead sailors in the water!"

Les' eyes suddenly widened. He walked over to the edge and looked into the water below. There was nothing to be seen but the swirling waves crashing up against the ship's hull. "There's nothing in that water."

Mike stood up and cautiously walked to what remained of the railing. The water was empty.

"You must be seeing things," Les said. "Happens all the time to men at sea. We just need to get some good food into you, then you'll be okay." He walked back toward the port railing where the ladder to the *Spear* awaited.

Mike continued staring into the empty water.

"Mike, let's go." Les had untied the rope and was holding it up. "Get aboard and we'll shove off."

Mike rushed over beside him and looked down into the water. The only thing he saw there was the *Spear*. Carefully, he backed down the rope ladder and got in. He then held the boat in place while Les got aboard. Once he was in, Les pushed off with his foot and the *Spear* drifted away. Mike mentally noted that even if they couldn't get the *Spear*'s motor started, the last place in the world he wanted to go was back aboard that old ship.

"Thought we might need a change of clothes," Les said.

"Huh." Mike turned and looked at him.

"Clothes." Les held up the captain's shirts and pants. "I don't think the captain will be needing them." He chuckled.

"Yeah," Mike said, still a little dazed. "That was nice of the poor guy."

Les had also stowed one of the lanterns under the dashboard next to where Mike was sitting. "There was enough fuel to fill one light so I brought it with us in case we need it," Les said. "Now if I can just get this motor running."

Mike sat still and looked in all directions for any signs of things in the water. Les pulled several times on the starter cord but didn't even get it to turn over. Mike didn't speak but thought to himself that the boat may have already made its final successful run. Les pumped gas with the little hand pump and tried again and again. It seemed to Mike to be hopeless.

Les continued trying to get the motor started. He displayed patience that Mike found to be incredible. "We're not out of gas are we?" Mike said.

"Not yet," Les said. He stood up and yanked the starter cord again. This time the motor sputtered. "Almost there." He pulled again and the motor sprang to life."

"Thank heaven." Mike put his hands together and looked skyward. A moment later, Les put her in gear and the *Spear* began moving forward. He steered around the back of the old ship and Mike looked up to see the damaged railing that had almost cost him his life. There was no sign of his little sailor friends. Les pointed the front of the boat toward the distant vessel and hit the throttle. Soon, the massive ship began to take shape as they neared it.

This ship was larger than the other one. It had probably been built in the early 1900s and there were signs of rust here and there on the black hull. The name *San Mateo* was painted on the side. Like the other ship, it appeared dead in the water and there were no signs of life on the deck.

"If nothing else, maybe there will be some gasoline aboard this one," Mike called out over the sound of the motor.

"I hope so," Les said. "This will be our last destination if there isn't. We're running on fumes now." He kept the *Spear* pointed toward the rusting hulk and sped up. When they got about two hundred feet away the *Spear*'s motor sputtered and died.

"Looks like we row the rest of the way," Les said as they drifted to a standstill. Mike got out the oars and the two of them started paddling.

Once they got within shouting distance Mike called out to see if anyone was on board. He called several times and never got a reply. From where they sat, the deck appeared abandoned.

"Can you see a ladder or anything else we can use to climb aboard?" Les said.

Mike didn't see anything at first. "Look." He pointed at the bow. "The anchor is dangling from a chain. If we get directly underneath it maybe I can jump up and grab it."

"It's worth a try," Les said.

They began rowing for the very front of the ship. Once they finally got there they maneuvered the *Spear* directly beneath the massive, rusty anchor. Mike stood up and reached for it. It was about four feet above his out-stretched hands.

"I've got an idea. Hold the boat steady." Mike walked to the back of the *Spear* and got a running start toward the front. There was only enough room for about four steps, the last of which was on the front deck of the fifteen-foot *Spear*. Mike leapt as high as he could and clamped his arm around the anchor. It held him fast and Les watched as Mike swayed back and forth, feet dangling above the *Spear's* deck.

"Nice going," Les said.

"I'm not there yet," Mike strained.

Les paddled back a few feet so the boat was no longer directly underneath Mike.

"What are you doing?" Mike said.

"I'm getting the boat out from under you," Les said. "If you fall it would be a lot easier to go face-first into the water than it would to go face-first onto the deck of the boat don't you think?"

"Yeah, you're right," Mike said. "Sorry." He checked the water below him and didn't see any dead swimmers.

Mike worked his legs over the anchor and climbed up to stand on it. He rested a moment to catch his breath, then began climbing up the massive chain. The climb was pretty easy since he could fit his feet into the huge links. He made his way up another five feet, placed his left foot in the last link below the eyelet where the chain dropped from the deck, and hoisted his right foot over the side of the ship. He then reached up, grabbed the railing support and pulled himself up. A moment later he stood on the deck of the *San Mateo*. From below he heard Les clapping.

"Bravo," Les said. "Now lower a ladder so I can come aboard. I also need a rope to tie off the *Spear*."

Mike looked around and spotted a rope. He picked it up and threw one end down to Les. Once he got hold of it Mike looked around for some kind of ladder. About halfway back on one side of the ship he saw a ladder built into the deck. Its handrails curled over the side railing. "There's a ladder a little ways down the side"; he called out to Les. "I'll pull you around."

Les tied the end of the rope to the front railing of the *Spear* and sat down in the back to steer it while Mike walked along the deck of the ship and pulled him back toward the ladder.

"Might as well forget it," Les called out. "I can't get up that thing."

"Why not?" Without letting go of the rope, Mike walked to the top of the ladder and looked down. Just below the deck the ladder ended. He could see holes in two straight rows going all the way down to the water where a ladder had once been, but was now completely removed.

"It looks like somebody took a blow torch and burned the ladder off," Mike said. "Now why in the hell would anyone do that?"

"To keep somebody from climbing aboard," Les said. "See if there's a rope ladder of some kind on deck." Mike looked around. A few feet away he saw one heaped in a pile against the wall. It had hooks at the top that would fit on the railing.

"Found one." Mike tied the rope to the railing and then went to get the ladder. He picked it up and pulled it over to the side of the ship. It was made of chains and had wooden steps neatly tied about a foot apart. He hooked it onto the railing and lowered it down the side. A moment later Les climbed aboard and set the wicker basket down on the deck against the wall.

Once they were both on board, Les looked around the deck. The *San Mateo* was a huge ship, maybe three hundred feet long and at least forty feet wide. Wires extended from the cabin roof to the smoke stack and they whistled loudly when the wind gusted. There were no flags flying on the flagpole, only an old, torn, white undershirt.

Les looked toward several lifeboats lying upside-down on the deck. Each appeared to have not been touched since the ship left port. There were six boats all together. "Do you see any signs that any lifeboats were deployed?"

Mike walked up the metal staircase to the roof and looked around. "Yep. There are two more places for boats up here and they're gone. There definitely are two lifeboats missing."

It didn't take long for them to determine that this was a merchant vessel, used to haul large cargoes back and forth across the ocean.

"This ship probably had a crew of fewer than fifty men," Mike said. "I wonder where everybody went."

"Anybody here?" Les called out. There was no reply. He walked up the steps and joined Mike on the top deck. The ship they had left earlier was now a dark spot in the water a few miles away. The other two were still visible in the far distance.

"We'd better be careful," Mike said. "There's no telling who or what could be lurking on this ship."

"I heard that," Les said.

"What about the sixth sense? Anything?"

Les paused a moment. "I don't detect anything. I guess whatever it was I detected last night isn't here at the moment."

"At the moment." Mike looked around.

There was a large cabin on the top deck with windows along the front and sides. There was about fifteen feet of deck between the cabin and the railing of the ship. Les walked over to the cabin's doorway and entered. There was no door but there were huge hinges where a door had once been. He had a passing thought that perhaps the constant warm weather had given the men reason to remove the door entirely. Somehow that didn't make sense. He didn't see the door, which was probably a heavy metal slab that would match the walls.

Les picked up the wicker basket and walked up front toward the controls. He reached the console and studied it.

Mike stepped in and joined him. "You think you can get the engine started on this thing?"

"Let's see." Les looked at the many controls. "I think this switch marked 'pump' would be a good place to start." He flipped the switch to the 'on' position. "If it's working then it'll put fuel in the engine. Then I'll try starting her up." After a moment he turned the key that was in a slot marked 'ignition'. From below decks a loud, grinding sound could be heard for a few seconds before going quiet again. "Almost," he said. "One more try ought to do it." He repeated the routine and again the loud grinding sound came, followed by the noisy starting of the engines.

"All right." Les put the ship in gear and it sputtered momentarily before stalling. A repeat of the process got the same results a second time. Les looked over at Mike with a defeated look.

"Something's wrong," Mike said. "It sounds like the propellers are trying to turn and can't. I wonder if something is caught in them."

"I think you've got something there," Les said. "But what could have clogged the propellers?"

"Maybe a loose rope or fish net got tangled in them," Mike said.

"I don't know. A ship this size has huge propellers. They would cut right through most of those things before they'd become ensnared. Maybe they picked up a steel cable somehow."

"That would do it."

"If we could figure out a way to free the propellers then we could get this ship moving," Les said. "There's still plenty of fuel and electric power."

Mike looked around the cabin. There was a picture on the wall of two men holding up a large fish. One was an older fellow and the younger one, who looked to be in his early twenties, may have been his son. "I guess we should be sure there's nobody on board alive or dead before we just take off and sail away."

"And while we're looking maybe find something to eat," Les said. "I'm starved."

Mike liked that idea. They had eaten the last of the fruit some time early the evening before and his stomach was growling constantly. He felt like he could eat a piece of the railing if there was enough mustard on it.

They found the stairway to the lower hold and carefully descended. Like the top deck, this area was eerily silent. When they reached the bottom of the stairs they found a hallway with many open doorways.

"This must be the crew's quarters," Les said. He looked up at the light bulbs protruding over the doors, each of which was on.

"I can't believe the power is on and the ship abandoned," Mike said.

"This whole thing is really strange," Les said. "My sixth sense is tingling just a little. Something is very wrong here but I can't figure out what it is."

They made their way along the corridor. Each doorway led to a small room, each with an upper and lower bunk bed built into the wall. There was a small table, two chairs and a chest of drawers in each room as well. Clothes were scattered about. Most of the bunks were unmade and many of the sheets and blankets were hanging from the bunks or lying on the floor. All the rooms had one thing in common that stood out above all other similarities: the doors were open, missing or heavily damaged.

"Man," Mike said. "Every room looks like it was evacuated under urgent conditions. Maybe they had an emergency of some kind in the middle of the night and everyone had to go topside in a big hurry."

Les remained silent a moment and looked around. Every single compartment looked as though its occupants had awakened in the middle of the night and rushed out. "The sixth sense suddenly upgraded to a chime," he said calmly.

They stepped a little farther down the hall and looked into the next compartment. The furniture was lying on the floor. The chest of drawers, which was made of metal, was bent badly. "Jeez," Mike said. "That thing looks like it was dropped five floors to the ground."

"Either that or thrown," Les said.

Mike stepped into the room and looked around. When he looked back he noticed the door. The metal slab that had once been a door was off its hinges and lying against the wall. There was a huge dent in it the size of a basketball. "It looks like someone drove a car into that door," he said.

Les ventured farther down the hall. "What do you think could have caused all the doors to burst open like this? Do you think there was an explosion that blew them all in suddenly?"

"Maybe," Mike said.

Les walked into one of the cabins and tried to lift the door that was lying on the floor in the middle of the room. "Help me put this back into the doorway. Maybe if we reconstruct the scene we can figure out what happened."

Mike got on the other side of the heavy metal door and together they dragged it to the doorway. Once they had it in place they were able to figure out what had happened.

"These doors were bashed in from the hallway," Les said. "Somebody or something smashed it's way into each cabin."

"What in the world could have done that?" Mike said. "This is a strong steel door that's designed to be waterproof and withstand heavy pressure. It's bent up like it's made of tin."

"And look at the walls," Les said. "They're completely undamaged, no powder burns or marks of any kind."

They continued down the hall to give the rest of the cabins a quick visual inspection. Several compartments looked as though the occupants had placed the furniture in front of the door prior to its being blasted open. Some of the tables were crushed and in some cases the chests of drawers appeared to have been slammed against the back wall. Here and there were drops of blood on the floor. A couple of the rooms had bloodstains on the walls, but for the most part the ship was clean, just very banged up.

"This ship is in the same condition as that old hulk we were on last night," Les said. "Every door has been knocked off its hinges."

"But the doors were made of flimsy wood on that hulk," Mike said. "These doors are solid steel. Look at this place. It's as though any place of refuge, any safe area behind a lockable door has intentionally been compromised. What the hell are we up against?"

Les looked at Mike. "I think something came in here and took the crew man by man."

"Yeah," Mike said. "But took them where? The life rafts are in place and the gangplank hasn't been deployed. Somebody would have had to stay behind to pull the gangplank back in. No ladders or climbing ropes were left hanging over the rails. Hell, the anchor wasn't even dropped. The engines still work so there's no reason to have abandoned ship. Why is everybody gone? Where in the hell did they get taken?"

"I don't think they got taken anywhere," Les said with a solemn, calm voice. "I think whatever came and got the crew ate them right here."

Mike's eyes almost popped out of his head. "What?"

"I know it sounds crazy, but it's the only explanation. Something very strong smashed in these doors. And it must have had a good reason."

Mike bent down and inspected the smashed door on the floor of the cabin. It looked to have been hit with a wrecking ball.

"You don't see any bodies do you?" Les said.

"No," Mike said. "But what in the hell could have done this? There isn't a creature on this planet that could do something like this."

Les stepped back into the hallway and went to the end. There was a larger room that had been wrecked the same way. "This looks like the captain's quarters. See if you can find a log book of some kind."

In addition to the clothes and linens scattered about, there were maps and charts everywhere. Les picked up one of the wall-sized charts and studied it. There were markings all over it where notes had been written, scratched out and written over again. There were question marks written in several places. Finally, written in bold red pencil at the bottom was the word "LOST!" Les held it up for Mike to see.

"Look at all these question marks," Les said.

Mike studied the map. "Looks like they tried to determine where they were several times and finally gave up. I guess that means we're lost too."

"Yes, but we have a talisman." Les smiled. "Look, there's the logbook!"

Mike looked where Les was pointing and saw it lying under the bed. It was open and face-up. Les picked it up and sat on the bed. Luckily, the notes were in English and written very neatly. Les read it silently as Mike continued looking around the demolished room.

"Well, what does it say?" Mike said.

"Just a minute." Les didn't take his eyes off the page.

"The ship is of British registry," Les said. "Deployed out of Brighton in May of 1931. It says their destination was Boston to deliver products. They arrived in Boston harbor on June sixteenth, spent two days, then sailed for Savannah, Georgia on June eighteenth. They got there and loaded the hull with grain. It took two days to fill the hold and stock supplies. Then on June twentieth they sailed for home. That brings you up to date on what I've read."

Mike set a chair upright and sat down across the room.

Les then began reading the logbook aloud.

"June 22: Day started out foggy, so thick you couldn't see the bow from amidships. We've been traveling steadily day and night. The night crew reported that the fog first appeared around 0300 hours and was accompanied by a brief cold spell. Soon thereafter we noticed that the radio was silent, perhaps damaged by heavy salt in the air. When the sun rose, we could only see 200 yards in any direction. Fog appears as a wall encircling the ship, however the sky overhead is clear. The water here is very calm, almost like a lake. Fog remained until 1500 hours, then cleared. All navigation equipment has failed. We continued sailing northeast for British Isles using the sun as a compass.

"1900 hours: Sun has set and my attempt to use the stars as a compass is difficult. The constellations are not in their normal positions. Many stars are closer together than they should be. Off the starboard stern, which I believe is to the southeast, a constellation appears near the horizon, which I would almost swear is the Southern Cross. I saw the Southern Cross constellation in the night sky when I sailed around the horn of Africa several years ago and I believe this to be the same cluster of stars. I cannot explain how I am able to see a constellation that is only visible from the Southern Hemisphere in the waters off the coast of the United States mainland. To my knowledge we have not drifted south at all. Certainly not across the equator. I ordered the ship to stop and remain here until dawn. We will continue our journey in the morning."

"Man, that's weird," Mike said. Les continued reading.

"June 23: Two crewmen are unaccounted for this morning. Their posts were unmanned when the morning watch reported at 0600. I believe they must have fallen overboard during the night. We have been unable to locate their bodies in the water.

"Engines won't start. Control instruments are still useless as well. Crewmen are working on the problem.

"1800 hours: Maintenance crew chief reports that engine problems seem to be in the propellers. Something is clogging them making travel impossible. Will try to send divers down to free them tomorrow morning. Instruments continue to either not function at all or give bizarre readings. I believe we have entered the 'Devil's Triangle'. I have never believed the stories of such a place, yet there is no explanation for our situation. We get no response on the radio at all.

"Sunset: Crewman reports sighting another vessel from observation deck just before dusk. We will attempt to make contact with it in the morning.

"2000 hours: Night watchman reports unexplained sounds coming from distant ship. Gunfire could be heard. At first feared it was aimed at us but apparently not. Watchman also reported he thought he heard screams coming from other ship as well. I fear there may have been a mutiny over there. I plan to approach tomorrow and will exercise extreme caution when doing so.

"June 24, 0800 hours: Three more crewmen have vanished. Several men reported sounds of movement on deck during the night. An investigation was immediately initiated to determine if men from the other ship might have come aboard during dark hours. There is no evidence to support this theory. As a precaution however, I ordered the ladder removed from the side railing. Crewmen with blowtorches detached it so no one can come aboard the ship without assistance from men already on board. Other vessel is still a good distance away. Heavy rain during the night may have explained the sounds some crewmen reported hearing. Still, only twenty-two of my original twenty-seven crewmembers are accountable.

"1400 hours: Took launch alongside other vessel for a closer look. The name *Carrie On* is printed on the stern. Went aboard and found it void of life. There are many bullet holes in the floor and walls. Blood is visible in places but there are no bodies to be found. I believe there was a mutiny, which would explain the gunfire. However, there almost certainly would have to have been another vessel involved, as the lifeboats remain undisturbed. No other vessels can be seen in any direction.

"My second officer, Dr. Timothy Harwell recommends getting away from the other vessel as quickly as possible. He thinks it may be contaminated with some strain of virus that led the crewmembers to kill one another. I doubt his conclusions, however I'm following his advice as a safety precaution.

"2200 hours: I was awakened by the sounds of conflict on deck. Apparently, we are under attack. I will arm myself and confront our attackers. If all goes well, this will not be my final entry."

Les looked up from the logbook.

"That's it."

Mike glanced over at the smashed metal door. It looked like something only an elephant could have done. It gave him a frightening feeling. "Whatever did this appears to only come out at night. Maybe that's what we heard on deck when we woke up this morning. At first only a few come, then when they realize there are many men on board they come back in larger numbers. That might explain why the captain survived long enough to complete several entries."

"But what is it we're talking about?" Les looked around at the disheveled surroundings. "What type of creature could do this?"

"I shudder to think what would have happened to us if I hadn't awakened this morning when I did." Mike stared at the demolished door on the floor.

"I wonder what's going to happen when the sun goes down tonight," Les said.

Mike stared at him. There was no reason to believe that whatever had come aboard and destroyed the ship wouldn't be back. "We'd better get busy."

They hurried topside. The sky was partly cloudy and it appeared to be sometime around noon. Les headed to another stairway that led below decks. This door had also been ripped from the frame. "This must be the way to the hold."

"Think something might be down there?"

"I don't know. We'd better be alert."

Les spotted a switch and flicked on the lights. A full two stories below them the hold lit up. It was a huge room that appeared the size of a warehouse. Nothing seemed out of the ordinary and nothing moved. The two of them descended the metal stairs as quietly as possible.

Once at the bottom they looked around the deserted hold. Several tremendous storage bins were lined up along the floor.

"That must be where they've got the grain stored," Les said. Overhead they could see large, removable squares in the ceiling. "They take out those panels and load the cargo in with a crane."

"Wait a minute," Mike said.

"See something?" Les whispered.

"No, I just had a terrible thought. Remember studying about Christopher Columbus and all the things his men feared? What was it they feared most?"

"Well, if you exclude falling off the earth I guess it would be sea monsters."

"Exactly," Mike said. "Now let's suppose that fear came about because of real sightings."

"Come on," Les said. "That was just superstition."

"We've always just assumed it was," he said. "But then again we now know that the earth was once inhabited by monsters we call dinosaurs. Evolution took care of them millions of years before man appeared, yet a fish that was thought to have been extinct for millions of years was caught about fifty years ago off the coast of Africa. Evolution had somehow missed that dinosaur because it was in the sea."

Les stared at Mike.

"There was a Japanese fishing vessel in the 1970s that picked up a dead creature in its net one day that scientists believe was some kind of aquatic dinosaur. It may have been something like the Loch Ness Monster."

"Okay, I follow you," Les said. "I've heard all those stories too. But are you trying to say that there's some kind of dinosaur swimming around in these waters? Don't you think that's a little crazy? How could those things have gotten into this century?"

"I don't think they did get into our century. I think we got into theirs."

"How do you figure that?" Les said.

"Remember what the captain's log said about the stars? He said that the stars were too close together in the familiar constellations. Since all the stars, including our own sun, are zooming through space at millions of miles a year, then the constellations would have looked the way he described them many centuries ago. The giveaway is what he said about the Southern Cross constellation. Today, that is in 2001, it is only visible in the sky south of the equator. In fact, the Australians have it on their flag. As recently as the tenth century, it was visible as far north as

Greece. There are ancient written records in some of the Mediterranean cultures that support that."

"How do you know all this?" Les said.

"Studied it in astronomy in college," Mike said. "In the last thousand years the stars of the Southern Cross have gotten farther away and now can be seen only from the Southern Hemisphere. The fact that the captain saw the Southern Cross in the night sky means one of two things: either we have crossed the equator, which I seriously doubt, or we have traveled through time several centuries somehow to when the Southern Cross was still visible from the northern hemisphere."

"Do you have any idea how crazy that sounds?" Les said.

"Absolutely," Mike said. "But we already speculated that the island we just left was Atlantis and that place sank under the ocean many centuries ago. If there is some kind of time-warp in the Bermuda Triangle, it would explain a lot of the disappearances, including yours and mine."

Les sat on a wooden crate. "You know," he said. "That would also explain why the two ships we have encountered so far have been from so far apart in history. Maybe they vanished from their present day, whenever that was, traveled through time to get here, and then were boarded and taken by those creatures from the deep."

"Yes," Mike said. "It's also possible that abandoned ships sometimes float back through the time-warp to the present day and drift until somebody finds them. That would explain why some ships have been found in the Bermuda Triangle, drifting aimlessly with no people on board, operable engines and undeployed lifeboats."

Les sat quietly. "Well, regardless of how or why, we have to think about tonight and the likelihood of those creatures returning."

"Right. First of all I need to eat. If I don't there won't be anything of me left for those creatures."

"Let's see what's in these bins." Les walked over to one of the huge wooden crates and inspected it. Around the far side was a large hole. It was empty. "That's strange," he said. "Let's look at the others."

They checked several other bins and found them to have been emptied as well. Each had a large hole at the bottom and nothing inside. "Look at this," Les said. "It looks like somebody went through these things with a vacuum cleaner. There isn't even a scrap of grain on the floor. What in the world could have a voracious appetite like that?"

"There must have been dozens of them," Mike said. "It looks like they eat anything edible, alive or dead." He looked at Les and saw the same look of concern that he felt himself. "We've got problems."

"Let's go find the galley," Les said. "Maybe we can find something to eat there. Then we'll start planning for tonight."

Mike started up the steps with Les behind him. "Don't worry." He put his arm around Mike's shoulder. "We'll think of something."

They got back up to the deck and started searching the other parts of the ship. They came to a large doorway that led to a big room with several dining tables and about forty chairs. Unlike most of the rest of the ship, this area was neat and clean.

"There must not have been any people in here when the visitors came aboard," Mike said.

Les spotted a doorway leading to an adjoining room and walked in.

There he saw a large stove, two huge ovens and many cooking utensils hanging from a rack suspended from the ceiling. There was a doorway that led to a walk-in pantry. This door was also smashed. "They were here too."

"I guess they left nothing to chance," Mike said. He glanced up on a shelf and spotted dozens of large cans. "Food," he said.

Les rushed over and looked up. The shelf was filled with dozens of huge cans labeled with everything from applesauce to zucchini. There were canned potatoes, soups, tuna, fruit cocktail, lunch spreads, oysters and sliced peaches. Les checked the drawers for a can opener and found an industrial-sized one. He opened a gallon-sized can of sliced pears and fished one out with his fingers. It tasted so good he felt his knees go weak. Mike got a couple of bowls off the pantry shelf and poured some of the contents of the can into them. Les found a couple of forks and they stood at the counter and ate. They finished by turning up the bowls and drinking the juice. Both of them had it spill down their shirts. Mike pointed at Les' wet shirt and laughed. Les looked down at it and laughed too.

"I think we've struck gold," Les belched.

"Not only that," Mike said. "We learned something about those creatures too."

"Yeah," Les said. "They can't read."

They both broke up laughing.

"No idiot," Mike said. "They can't use tools. They're stupid. That's how we're going to defeat them. They're stupid."

Les spotted some canned fruit drinks and popped the tops on them. He handed one to Mike. "I'll drink to that." They clicked the drinks together and then turned them up.

"Hey," Mike said. Maybe there are some steaks in that freezer over there!"

"Oh yes," Les said.

They walked over to the big metal box against the back wall.

Mike pulled the big handle and opened the door with a smile. He looked inside and his smile quickly turned to horror. Sitting on the floor, frozen solid, was a man.

Mike jumped back. The drink slipped from his hand and fell to the floor.

Les reached in and pulled the stiff man out. He was sitting cross-legged with his elbows on his knees. The man, who appeared to be about forty, was wearing long-sleeves but no coat. His eyes were open and ice was caked in his hair. When Les moved him, a hand-written note fell from his lap to the floor. Mike picked it up and read it.

"They come at night," he read. "They eat anything and everything. Hopefully they won't eat frozen meat. Anything is better than being eaten alive. They won't eat me. They come at night."

"That's all it says?" Les said.

"That's it. He didn't crawl in there to hide, he crawled in there to die."

"I'll bet those creatures didn't smell him so they didn't bother to look in there," Les said.

"No," Mike said. "If they had, the door would be smashed."

Les gently set the frozen man back inside the freezer. "We'll decide what to do with him later." He looked at Mike. "We might have to thaw him out and use him for bait."

Mike glared at him. "You don't mean fish bait do you?"

"No, sea monster bait."

At first Mike thought Les was making a sick joke but he quickly realized that he was serious. It was a terrible thought but a realistic one just the same.

Les slid the guy back into the freezer and closed the door. "If there's any frozen food on the ship it's in another freezer somewhere. We can search for it later."

"Yeah," Mike said. "If we're still around."

Les looked at him but didn't reply.

"We need to try getting the propellers clear," Les said. "Let's finish lunch and then go out and get started."

When they walked back out on deck they checked the sun to estimate the time.

"Looks like we still have a few hours," Les said.

"What are we going to do?" Mike said. "We don't even know what we're dealing with."

"Remember that the ship was stopped when those things came aboard," Les said. "I don't think the creatures would have gone to the trouble of clogging the propellers if it wasn't necessary. If I can get us moving then maybe we won't have a problem."

"That sounds like a pretty good plan," Mike said. "But are you willing to swim down to the propellers to try to cut them free?"

"Guess I'll have to. Maybe it won't be too dangerous during the day."

"You know they'll just clog them up again," Mike said.

"Well, at least maybe this will buy us some time," Les said. He pulled out a knife he had found in the galley and got some rope and a life preserver. Then he carefully tied the rope to the preserver and lowered them into the swirling water behind the ship. He then tied the end of the rope to the back railing.

"Hey," Mike said. "Why don't we try running in reverse to loosen whatever is in the propellers. That might make it easier to cut them free."

"Great idea."

They rushed back up to the console. Les cranked the engines and threw the ship into reverse. Just as they started to move backwards he cut the engine. Rushing back to the stern he removed his shirt and put the blade of the knife, sharp side out, between his teeth and jumped in. Mike watched as Les fell to the water and disappeared under the surface.

"You are one brave soul," he muttered.

When Les hit the water he swam under the back end of the ship. The twin propellers were about six feet below the surface. He looked around. All he saw were a few large fish.

He swam to the propellers. Thick green seaweed was wrapped around both of them. The long trails of the hardy vines dangled a good fifteen feet from the shafts. He grabbed the first one and slid the knife into the narrow gap between shaft and choking weed. Backing up the ship had helped loosen the vines but it was still going to take some time to completely free them. He cut a little and then headed back to the surface.

"How does it look down there?" Mike said when he surfaced.

"Pretty bad." Les grabbed the life preserver. "This is going to take a few minutes."

"Any sign of our friends from below?"

"No. I think the sunlight wards them off for some reason. Hope so anyway." He took a big breath and dove back down again.

This time he went straight to the same propeller and quickly cut it completely free. He started on the second one before having to surface again. When he broke the surface he looked up at Mike. "Almost done."

Mike gave him a thumbs-up.

Les returned to the second propeller and cut as fast as he could. The seaweed was thick and stringy but the knife was sharp and effective. Les waited until almost the last moment before he had to breathe to finish the job and return to the surface. As the last of the seaweed broke loose from the propellers and fell free, Les turned and swam for the surface, knife still firmly in his right hand.

Something cold and strong wrapped around his leg and tightened its grip. Almost without breaking stride, he reached down with the knife and cut whatever it was that held him. A thick cloud of blood poured out of the stump as the end of it still held fast around his leg. He made it to the surface. "Mike!" He grabbed the life preserver. "Pull me up quick!"

Mike hurriedly untied the rope from the railing and began pulling. As Les slowly rose out of the water he looked down. Under the surface he could see some large

object emerging from under the ship. A large snout, similar to that of an alligator rose out of the water and lunged
at his dangling feet with a loud grunting noise. Les pulled
himself up just an instant before the snout, filled with
long sharp teeth, snapped shut a couple of inches from his
toes. He watched in horror, as the creature seemed to cry
out in pain from the bright sunlight and sank back into
the water.

Once he got Les completely out of the water Mike
found pulling him up more difficult. Les tried to stay calm
as he swung gently from side to side just three feet above
the water's surface. He reached down and pulled at the
detached tentacle, which was still tightly gripping his leg.
Using the knife again he cut it in half. Purple blood flowed
from it all over his foot as he shook it free and watched it
tumble back into the water. Another tentacle, this one as
big around as a grown man's thigh, suddenly rose from the
water and began feeling around in the air. It swung at him,
just missed and thumped hard against the side of the ship.
"Hurry Mike!" A moment later he was high enough to
grab the railing and pull himself over and onto the deck.

"Oh man, look at your ankle," Mike said.

Les wiped the slimy blood off, revealing several large
red welts where the suckers had attached themselves to his
skin. "That son-of-a-bitch almost got me!"

"Let's get moving before they clog the propellers again,"
Mike said.

They hurried back to the console and started the
engine. A moment later Les put it in gear and the mighty
ship began moving forward. He turned toward the north,
increased the speed to maximum and sat back in the captain's chair as the speedometer rose to twelve knots.

"Could you tell what was clogging the propellers?" Mike said. "Just what we suspected," Les said. "Seaweed. Those things had wrapped it on several inches thick."

"I'm glad you were able to cut through it," Mike said.

"Me too." Les looked out through the big window at the sea ahead. "Those things were smart enough to figure out how to stop the ship. I'm sure it won't be long before they stop it again. We're going to have to come up with a new strategy fast or this is going to be the last day of our lives."

Mike already knew what Les had just said but somehow hearing it made it really hit home.

CHAPTER 15

▼

TRIXIE

With Les piloting, the *San Mateo* was moving along nicely. Up ahead they spotted a small yacht sitting still in the water.

"Let's swing by and have a closer look at that vessel," Les said. "Maybe there's someone on board." He turned slightly to starboard and gradually closed the distance.

A few minutes later when they approached the yacht, Les lowered the speed to a slow crawl and Mike ran out to the starboard railing to get a better look. "She's heavily damaged," Mike said. "And listing to port. Looks like she's taking on water."

Les stayed at the helm and kept the *San Mateo* moving. "Is all the damage in the hull?"

"No," Mike said. "All the windows are smashed and there are pieces of upholstery scattered about on the deck. I see no signs of life so we might as well keep moving."

"Okay," Les said. He reached for the throttle to speed up when Mike saw a small dog run out on deck and begin barking.

"Hey, there's a dog on board."

"I'll get us along side and we'll tie off," Les said. "We can at least rescue him."

He piloted the big ship close to the yacht and put the engine in neutral. Mike got a gaff hook off the wall, attached the chain ladder to the railing and descended to the bottom step. He then reached over and hooked the yacht's railing. As he clung to the ladder with his left hand he pulled the smaller boat toward him using the gaff in his right hand. Once he had maneuvered the yacht up against the hull of the big ship he leapt on board.

The dog ran terrified back to its hiding place. From somewhere out of sight Mike heard growling. He looked around and spotted a dog bowl with the name "Trixie" printed on the side.

"Here Trixie," he said. He looked down and saw the dog's nose sticking out from under one of the damaged seats. "It's okay girl," he said in a soft voice. He reached down and put the back of his hand where the dog could sniff it. Once she demonstrated that she wasn't going to bite he gently petted her head. After a few pats he pulled his hand away and Trixie crawled out. "That's a good girl." He rubbed her head. The dog was trembling noticeably and still seemed unsure about this stranger. At the same time she was obviously glad to see a person.

"Man, that dog's terrified," Les said from behind him. He had descended to the yacht's deck with a rope and tied it to the railing. "I wish she could tell us what happened to her owners."

"I think we can guess," Mike said. He walked below to the cabin under the front deck of the boat. The first thing he saw was an unmade bed with a few drops of blood on the sheets. Obviously this was where the final showdown had taken place. He looked down at the floor and noticed several inches of water. As he had suspected, the boat was slowly sinking. It would only be a couple of days at the most before it went completely under.

The door to the cabin had been smashed. He walked back topside and looked around for anything they could use. There were some sunglasses, sunscreen and beach towels. He spotted a refrigerator and looked inside. There was some spoiled milk, spoiled fruit and meat, an unopened bottle of wine and four cans of beer. "Hey Les, there's some beer in here!"

"Grab it."

Mike began piling the useable items and the drinks along with Trixie's food and water dishes into a blue plastic basket he found on the floor. He also spotted a litter box that the dog had apparently been trained to use. Better take that along too, he thought.

He looked into the cabinets and found several cans of food, some of them dog food and put them into the basket as well. Les was combing the stern for anything else that might be useful.

"Let's take what we need and get back aboard the big ship," Les said. "Those creatures might be wrapping seaweed around the propellers as we speak."

"You're right." Mike climbed back up the ladder to the deck of the big ship and lowered a rope. Les tied the bag of food to it and Mike pulled it up. The litter box went next and proved to be more difficult. "Don't stand underneath." Mike smiled as he started pulling it up.

"Here Trixie," Les called out softly.

The dog hesitantly approached him and stood several feet away. He took a step toward her and she ran toward the front of the boat, attempting to hide under one of the seats behind the front windshield. "Come on Trixie," Les said. He knelt down in the captain's chair and looked underneath the seat. That's when he spotted a large wooden crate. He pulled out the crate and the dog sat behind it, trembling. "It's okay," he said. "I'm not going to hurt you." He reached forward and grabbed her. She snarled and wiggled but didn't bite. As he stood up holding the dog, he glanced at the contents of the crate he had moved to get to her. It was full of dynamite. "Oh my goodness, what have we here," he muttered. He looked up. Mike was still at the railing looking down at him.

"Want me to lower the basket for the dog?" Mike said.

"Yes," Les said.

Mike lowered the now empty basket and Les put Trixie inside it. Mike hoisted it up and let the dog out on the deck of the big ship. She immediately took off running, looking around everywhere, apparently for any sign of the creatures.

"Lower the basket back down," Les said. "There's a big box of dynamite down here."

"Did you say dynamite?"

"Yes. Plenty of it."

"The owners of the boat must have been on their way to some kind of salvage operation," Mike said. "Sometimes the

Army Corps of Engineers uses that stuff to destroy old docks and bridge supports that need to be cleared out for new construction."

"Do you know how to use it?" Les said.

"Oh sure," Mike said.

Les pulled the box out and set it on one of the torn seats.

"I've got another idea," Les said. "Suppose we bring that frozen guy down here and put him in the pilot's seat. When he thaws some of those creatures might come aboard to visit. Might buy us some time."

"Good idea," Mike said. "I can even rig up some dynamite so if they move him the whole boat will blow up."

"Great," Les said. "What do you need?"

"Blasting caps," Mike said. "They probably are somewhere well away from the rest of the explosives, maybe in a drawer or something. I'll go get Chilly Willie and we'll come help you."

Les smiled and looked up at the railing but Mike had already headed for the freezer. "Chilly Willie," he muttered. He looked in the top drawer in the galley and spotted a small box containing some blasting caps. He held up the box and inspected it. A moment later, a loud thud on the back deck startled him. He whirled around. Mike had tossed the dead man over the *San Mateo*'s railing and he had landed face-up on the yacht.

"Damn," Les said. "Scare the hell out of me next time!"

"Sorry." Mike started down the ladder. "Willie has this nasty habit of barging in on people. I've been meaning to talk to him about it."

"I found your blasting caps." Les handed him the box.

"Good," Mike said. "I'll start rigging up a trap."

Les went to the back deck and grabbed the frozen man by the collar. He then dragged him up front and set him in the captain's chair.

Mike disconnected the yacht's battery from the engine to use as a detonator and placed it under the seat. He taped six sticks of dynamite together, wound the fuses into one, and then taped the whole thing to the frozen man's stomach, carefully hiding it under his stiff shirt.

He gently connected the blasting caps and ran a wire around the chair and then to the battery. "There," he said. "If anything moves the body more than a few inches it'll pull the trip-wire, closing the circuit and 'kaboom'."

Mike turned the radio on and they heard a steady hum.

"How is the radio going to work if you disconnected the battery?" Les said.

"I was hoping there was a separate battery for the electrical system." Mike started turning the radio dial and still heard only a humming sound. "I believe it's on. There just aren't any radio stations to be heard anywhere on the dial." He spotted a cassette tape and popped it in. Loud music blared from the speakers. He turned the volume down and looked over at Les. "This tape deck is continuous. It'll keep playing the tape over and over. Maybe it'll attract some attention from below." He turned it back up loud and stood up. "Okay," he said over the music. "Let's get the hell out of here."

Les untied the yacht and climbed up the ladder to the big ship's deck.

Mike followed, pushing the yacht away with his foot before ascending.

Les went back to the controls of the big ship and got the *San Mateo* moving again.

Mike noticed that Trixie had pulled her water dish out of the basket and was licking the bottom of it. "Oh you poor thing," he said. He took it to the sink in the kitchen and filled it with water. When he set it down the dog drank it dry. He refilled it for her and then opened a can of dog food and put the contents into the other dish. He set the dish by the water bowl and walked over to one of the chairs on deck and sat down. The dog ate every bite of the food and then walked over to Mike wagging her tail. He patted her head and she sat down in the shade under his chair. "I sure wish you could talk. You're the only survivor we've encountered."

Les set a chair against the steering wheel to hold it steady, then walked back to where Mike was sitting and pulled up a chair of his own. The yacht was about half-a-mile behind them now and drifting farther. From the looks of the sky it appeared to be around four in the afternoon.

"What do you think we should do if those things start coming aboard tonight?" Mike said. "I searched everywhere for a gun but couldn't find one."

"I wonder if we could set some kind of trap," Les said. "I noticed that the hold of this ship is refrigerated. They weren't using it hauling grain of course but we could chill it if we needed to."

Mike thought a moment. "I'll bet those creatures can't stand cold," he said. "That might explain why they left the frozen guy alone. Maybe, hey, wait just a second."

Les looked at him.

"I've got it," Mike said. "We can chill the hold down and go bundle up inside it. It'll make for a long cold night but at least those things won't be able to get to us."

"Great idea," Les replied. "But how would we bundle up?"

"Let's go search the cabins. I'm sure there are some warm clothes somewhere."

They went back inside the crew's quarters and began searching. There were a few jackets and long sleeve clothes, but nothing designed for arctic weather.

"You keep looking," Les said. "I'm going down to the hold to see what's down there."

Mike continued going from cabin to cabin searching the drawers and closets while Les headed downstairs.

When Les reached the hold he spotted the thermostat and found it set for 60 degrees Fahrenheit. He turned it down to 30 degrees and a moment later cold air blew in from the vents in the walls and ceiling. He then began searching the hold and spotted a storage closet. Inside it he found equipment designed to be used when the hold was coated with ice. There were several snow shovels, helmets and pairs of gloves. There were also several pairs of heavy overalls hanging from a rack and a few pairs of boots lined up on the floor. "Alright," he said. "This is just what we need!"

When he returned to the deck he told Mike what he had found. "It's getting late," Les said. "Why don't we go to the galley for an early dinner. We might as well do whatever we're going to do on a full stomach."

As they moved about the ship, Trixie followed them everywhere they went. It was obvious that she was glad to have some human company again. They headed to the galley and cooked up a feast of beef stew, beans, corn and okra.

"I'm sure glad we found Trixie," Les said. "She'll let us know if we're being visited from below." He held up a piece of beef and the little dog sat up on her hind legs. He dropped it and she caught it in the air.

CHAPTER 16

▼

LURKING EYES

By the time they finished eating it had been a couple of hours since the yacht had been set adrift. It now was several miles in their wake.

Mike and Les returned to the deck. The late afternoon sun loomed just above the horizon, casting the *San Mateo*'s long shadow across the surface of the water off the starboard side. "It'll start getting dark in just a few minutes," Mike said.

Suddenly the engine began to sputter. Mike's heart jumped into his throat. A moment later the engines cut off.

"Oh no, they've clogged the propellers again."

"I can't believe they did it so soon," Les said. For several long seconds the two of them sat, unsure of what to do next. At that moment the sun dipped below the horizon. Both of them looked up into the darkening sky.

"Let's go check the controls," Les said. They ran to the console and Les looked at the gas tank indicator. It read empty.

"Maybe we're just out of gas," he said. He switched to another tank and started to turn the ignition. At that moment a large explosion could be heard from far off in the distance.

"Hey, I think we scored," Mike said. He rushed out to the railing and looked in the direction of the sound. Large pieces of the yacht could be seen falling into the sea. "Something set off the dynamite and destroyed the yacht."

"I hope there were several of them aboard," Les said.

"Well, however many there were," Mike said, "they won't be bothering us anymore."

"Not those particular ones anyway." Les turned the ignition switch on the big ship and the engine roared to life. He and Mike both sighed. "Do you think we should stop the ship for the night?"

"Might as well," Mike said. "At least that way we won't run into anything in the middle of the night."

Les let off the throttle and cut the engine. The *San Mateo* drifted to a gradual stop.

Mike led the way to the stairs. As they descended to the hold they could feel the cooler air. "The refrigeration unit is working," he said.

When they reached the bottom step Les checked the thermostat. "35 degrees. If only we had something to cover the doorway maybe we could get it colder in here." They looked around but didn't see anything that might work.

"Hey, I've got it," Mike said. "There's a tarp covering a lifeboat up on deck. Maybe we can use that."

"Good idea," Les said.

They headed back up the stairs and found the life raft. Together they untied the ropes and neatly folded the tarp. "Need anything else while we're up here?" Mike said.

"Not that I can think of," Les said. "I'm sure I'll probably get hungry in the middle of the night though."

"Go grab something from the galley."

"No, that's okay. Anything we get will just freeze. We could use some blankets and pillows though."

"I'll get them," Mike said. He hurried to some of the bunks and returned with what they would need. "Here Trixie."

"Don't worry about her," Les said. "If she managed to survive on that small yacht she'll do fine on this roomy ship. She'll be okay."

Mike handed Les one of the blankets and then took the rest below. Les tied the tarp to support beams on either side of the doorway.

"Wow, it's cold down here," Les said when he joined Mike at the bottom. "There are plenty of warm clothes in a storage closet over here."

Mike walked over and took a look inside. "Yes, these should do fine."

Once they were fully decked out in the warm clothes they got quite comfortable. "As long as we keep moving we'll be fine," Les said. "But we're still going to get plenty cold before the night is over."

Mike looked around. "Maybe we can make a cabin out of one of these huge crates. By staying inside we could get out of the cold draft. That would make it a little more tolerable in here."

"That's not a bad idea," Les said.

The crates were big enough for a person to get in and move around. Each one was about half the size of a railroad flatcar.

"Hey, we can use some of that pipe over there to make a chimney," Les said. "Then we can build a fire inside the crate."

"Great idea," Mike said. "This piping must be for pouring the grain into the hold." He walked over to the stack and lifted one of the heavy pipes.

Les looked up at the portholes just below the ceiling. "Let's connect several pipe sections together and ram the end out through one of those portholes. We can place the other end through the top of one of the crates. Then we could break up the other crates and burn them for heat."

"That should work," Mike said. "But the problem is we'd set the crate on fire too."

"Not if we used one of those metal tool cabinets as a fireplace." Les pointed to one of the rusting old boxes that stood a few feet away by the wall. "We could take all the shelves out and connect the pipe to it."

As they began fitting the pipe together to build the chimney they suddenly heard a noise on the other side of the tarp. Both of them stopped what they were doing and looked in the direction of the doorway.

"You don't think those creatures are here already do you?" Les said.

Suddenly they heard the dog bark. Mike went up to the tarp and untied one of the bottom corners. Trixie crawled through wagging her tail.

"Scared me," Les muttered.

Mike retied the tarp and they quickly returned to what they were doing.

Once they got about twenty-five feet of pipe screwed together, they lifted one end up. It was very heavy and cumbersome. They lifted, leaned the end against the wall, backed up and lifted some more. Finally they got the end of the pipe up against a porthole two stories above their heads.

"Don't let this thing fall on you," Mike said. "It would probably knock you through the floor."

"You hold it steady and I'll try to ram it through the porthole," Les said.

Mike got a few feet in front of Les, reached as high as he could above his head and tried to keep the high end of the pipe in front of the little window. Les struggled to pick up the other end of the pipe and thrust it forward. High above them the end of the pipe hit the glass but didn't break it. Les pulled back a few inches and then thrust forward again. Once again the pipe hit the mark but failed to break the glass.

"I need to rest a moment," Mike said. They leaned the pipe against the porthole and Les set his end down.

As they stood a moment with their hands on their hips, catching their breath, Les looked outside the porthole. "Looks like sea monster hour has arrived."

"Ready to try again?" Mike said.

"Yes," Les said. "Let's really smack it this time."

Mike got back into position and Les lifted up his end of the pipe. "Okay, on three."

Together they gently rocked back and forth a few times and then charged forward as hard as they could. From high overhead came the sound of breaking glass as the end of the pipe bashed through. Both men closed their eyes and turned their heads as splinters of glass fell to the floor all around them. Then they slid the pipe further through the now-open porthole and stood it upright. Together they pushed the bottom end as close to the wall as possible and set it firmly on the floor.

"That should hold it in place until we get the tool cabinet attached," Les said.

They had chosen that particular porthole because it was the closest to one of the big empty wooden crates.

"Now let's see if we can push this crate closer to the wall," Les said.

He and Mike got against the crate and began pushing. It was extremely heavy and only moved a little.

"Keep trying," Les said and they pushed again. It barely moved.

"I've got an idea," Mike said. "Let's both push this corner a little and then push the other corner a little. That should work."

Doing it this way, they gradually moved the massive crate.

"Perfect," Mike said when they finished. "Now let's cut a hole in the top of this crate and slide the chimney down into it."

Les found a ladder and leaned it against the side of the crate. "You know," he said. "I think this is actually going to work. How about handing me a crowbar when I get up there."

Mike found one and passed it up to him. Les found a good spot and removed several boards from the top of the crate. Mike then tied a rope onto the end of the pipe and passed the other end of the rope up to Les. He then climbed the ladder and helped Les pull the end of the pipe up to the top of the crate. Once they got the end of the pipe high enough to reach the top of the crate they felt its center of gravity shift. They quickly got the pipe over the hole and pushed it down. It slid through and hit the bottom of the crate with a bang.

"Why don't you pick out a cabinet while I start making a doorway in the crate," Mike said.

Les agreed and they both descended the ladder. When they got to the bottom Mike rested a moment. He was starting to sweat inside the warm clothes and could see his breath every time he exhaled. He estimated the air temperature to be around thirty degrees. A quick check of the porthole told him it was now totally dark outside. He looked at the tarp over the door and saw that it was undisturbed. Trixie was holed up somewhere no doubt trying to keep warm. He hoped she was paying attention. If any of those creatures came in he wanted her to tell them.

Mike took the crowbar and began prying a board loose from the side of the crate. There was already a gaping hole where the sea monsters had apparently broken in and removed the grain. He figured he could remove about six more boards and make a doorway wide enough to get through. They could then take several boards from another crate, nail them together and make a door to cover the opening.

"This looks like a good cabinet," Les said from a few feet away. He was squatting down in front of the open doors of the wrought iron cabinet and looking inside. "There's a hole rusted through the bottom of it."

"A hole in the bottom?"

"Yeah." Les got to his feet. "We'll turn it upside down and fit the pipe onto the hole. Come help me drag it over there."

Les opened the double doors on the cabinet and pushed it over, spilling all of the contents onto the floor. They then lifted it up and removed the shelves. It was a sturdy, heavy cabinet. They slid it over to the doorway Mike had made and together dragged it inside. Pulling it all the way to the back wall, they got it in place. Then they lifted the end of the pipe and set it onto the top of the cabinet. The hole was a little too small but Les hammered the edges a little to widen it and then the pipe fit right in.

Mike placed one of the shelves across the front opening inside the cabinet and hammered it down, creating an area in the bottom about four inches deep. "That'll hold the boards in when we light the fire. Once we get it going we can close the cabinet doors and that'll force the smoke up the pipe. When we get the smoke established in the chimney we can open the doors to let out the heat without the crate filling with smoke."

"This is turning out great," Les said.

Mike shivered momentarily and mentally noted his cold ears and toes.

They stepped out and went to one of the other crates to start breaking it apart. Les carefully removed some of the nails, selected some choice pieces of wood and started building a door. Mike started breaking up the rest of it to use as firewood. After getting a nice stack he took a hammer and some nails and went to the roof of their new home to close some of the open areas around the pipe. There was no way to seal it tight but the additional work would at least limit the amount of cold air that would seep in. By using the blankets they could then stay reasonably warm.

"I'll put the wood pile inside so we won't have to leave the safety of the crate during the night," Mike said. He made a number of trips back and forth until there was a large stack of burnable boards piled up inside. He then spotted an old cardboard box and took it inside to be used as a fire starter. Les finished making the door and fixed it so it could be slid snugly into the doorway. Mike called the dog and she followed him inside. The last thing Les did before sliding the door into place was to check the tarp over the doorway. It appeared undisturbed.

Mike took off his gloves and pulled out a box of kitchen matches he had found in the galley. He lit the cardboard he had placed in the bottom of the cabinet. Once it caught up he added several small pieces of wood and then closed the white metal doors. A small amount of smoke escaped the makeshift fireplace but for the most part it worked very well. A few minutes later he opened the doors and found the fire to be going nicely. They began adding firewood from time to time and the cabin soon warmed up. A short time later they were able to remove the jackets and hats without getting cold. Finally they divided up the blankets and lay down on opposite sides of the crate to sleep. Trixie got close to the fire and curled up as well.

Mike lay awake for a few minutes watching the firelight dance off the ceiling of the crate. He couldn't help but wonder if the sea creatures were boarding the ship at that very moment. As he lay there something cold and very alive touched the side of his face in the dark. He sat up and cried out. That's when he realized it was just the dog's nose.

"What's wrong?" Les said.

"Damn dog scared the hell out of me."

Les laughed.

Trixie found a warm place near Mike's feet and lay still. Mike could feel a slight draft from the gap around the pipe overhead. He then realized that it was probably a good thing. It would allow fresh air in, but not enough to make it cold inside the crate. He didn't really feel that tired and knew it would be some time before he'd manage to drift off to sleep. He tried to think relaxing thoughts and his mind began to once again take him to a place far away. As always he wondered about Jan. He hoped she missed him as well. Sometime later he fell asleep.

During the night there came the sudden loud crash of something heavy hitting the outside of the crate. Mike and Les woke up. The dog yelped and jumped up from the blanket at Mike's feet and ran to one of the crate's corners. The sound came again. The dog started barking in rapid spurts. From outside the door something started slamming against the wood very hard. With each bang the boards gave several inches and creaked ever so slightly before snapping back into place.

Les jumped up and stuck the ends of several three-foot boards into the fire. "We might have to burn the bastards."

Mike got to his feet. The two of them stood and looked back at the door to their makeshift cabin. Thirty seconds had passed since the last sound. "Think that door will hold?" Mike said.

"I don't know. Doesn't really matter though. There's no lock on it. All they have to do is pull and it'll pop right out."

Thirty more seconds passed and there was still no other sound. Les reached down and got a burning stick in each hand. "When I tell you, push the door out and then get back."

Mike went to the door and leaned into it. "Now," Les yelled and he charged the door. Mike shoved the door out and jumped aside. Light came pouring in. Les jumped to the freezer outside the crate door and saw nothing. Then he looked down.

"Damn," he muttered.

Mike stood motionless. Lying twitching on the floor was a creature that appeared to be eight feet tall and weighing at least three hundred pounds.

"Do you think it's dead?" Mike said.

Les stood with his eyes locked on it. "I think it will be in a few minutes," he said. "Looks like the cold is getting to it."

He reached down with the still-lit torch and poked it with the burning end. It twitched, but showed no other signs of movement.

"Look at its teeth," Mike said. "That thing's big enough to eat a man whole." He kicked the mouth and jumped back. The creature remained motionless.

"Yeah," Les said. "It's dead."

He reached around to the opposite end and carefully lifted one of the dozen-or-so tentacles. "From head to tip this thing is about fourteen feet long." The creature suddenly came alive and snapped at Les. He jumped away just before the powerful jaws got his arm.

Mike gave it another swift kick to the mouth, this time harder. The defeated creature attempted to rise up again, but appeared to lack the strength.

Les stood and stared at the horrible creature for a few long seconds. "Maybe you're developing a sixth sense," he said. "It looks like our little plan worked."

"From now on we'll keep a couple of buckets of water inside the crate," Mike said. "Then we can always douse them to speed up the deep freeze."

"Let's get back inside," Les said. "It's cold out here."

He looked up at the porthole. It was still dark outside. They went back in and he pulled the door back into place. "We'll bring a couple of cots down here tomorrow." Les added more wood to the fire. "If we have to be cold at least we don't have to get stiff backs too." Mike chuckled and crawled back under the blankets. Trixie got back in her spot at his feet and soon they were all asleep again.

A few hours later Les awoke, more because of the cold than anything else. He went over to the door and popped it out so he could check the porthole above. Seeing daylight, he went back in to wake Mike. "It's morning."

Mike sat up. "Let's eat," he said.

The dog barked and started running around the crate.

"I agree with both of you", Les said. "First though, I want to see what damage those things did." They bundled up and walked out into the hold, carefully stepping over the dead sea creature. The first thing Les checked was the tarp over the doorway. It had been pulled free on one side and was hanging loose. Mike headed on up the stairs and the dog followed. Les tied the tarp back into place to hold in the cold air, then headed upstairs himself.

When they exited the cargo hold and walked out on deck the warm tropical air felt wonderful. Mike's fingers and toes had started to get numb. They quickly removed the heavy clothes and took a moment to sit in one of the deck chairs.

"Why don't I go get us moving and you start on breakfast," Les said after a couple of minutes of warming up.

"Sounds like a good idea," Mike said. He headed to the galley and quickly discovered unopened cans of food on the floor and chairs lying on their sides.

He got some coffee brewing and then opened a can of dog food for Trixie. As he was turning the crank on the opener he heard the engines roar to life. A moment later he felt the big ship start to move. It was a very refreshing feeling.

Les pointed the bow northward and ran the speed up to about twelve knots. He reached up and turned on the ship's radio. Static came through the speaker but nothing else could be heard. He turned the dial around and got nothing but silence. There was a shelf above the windshield and he noticed the bag of gold trinkets lying there. Les pulled out the little gold ship, setting it on the shelf and watching for it to move. It sat motionless.

"Coffee?" Mike said.

"Yes, thank you," he replied.

Mike handed him a large mug and noticed the little ship.

"Oh, I meant to take this to the hold with us last night and forgot."

"Well we got lucky," Les said. "The sea creatures didn't want it."

"I'll be more careful from now on," Mike said. He picked it up and admired it. It could lead them home; at least he hoped it could.

"That's a fascinating little trinket," Les said. Mike nodded in agreement. "I'd sure like to know how many other men have held it in their hands."

"I'm sure there are plenty more that would have liked to", Mike said. He held it close to his heart for a moment and thought again about Jan. Get me home little ship, he thought. I want to ask the woman of my dreams to be my wife. He gently placed the gold ship back up on the shelf and felt a twinge of disappointment when it didn't move.

Les set the chair back into place to hold the wheel steady. "Let's go find something to eat."

They went to the galley and found some flour to make pancakes. "I found some binoculars in one of the cabins," Les said. "After breakfast I think I'll go up to the observation deck and see if I can spot anything."

After eating, Les stepped out onto the deck and looked around. He grabbed the binoculars, climbed the stairs to the roof and walked over to the center of the ship. There was a support beam that ran about twenty feet or so straight up. Near the top was a small crow's nest big enough for one person. Just above that was a flagpole sporting a well-worn V-shaped, blue and white flag. Guy wires ran from the top of the pole to the four outer corners of the cabin. Les climbed up the metal steps in the pole to the crow's nest. The mesh steel floor provided just enough room to stand and a rail ran the circumference about waist-high. He leaned against the rail and looked all around with the binoculars.

"See anything?" Mike said from the deck below.

"No," Les said. "Not a damn thing." Mike couldn't tell if Les was disappointed or relieved.

"Maybe later." Mike took his shirt off and applied some of the sun tan lotion.

Since the ship was virtually driving itself they decided to wander about, partly to kill time and partly to look for anything else that might be useful to them. From time to time one of them would play with the radio for a few minutes and get only static. Mike spent a few minutes in the crow's nest with the binoculars as well.

"Hey Mike," Les called up to him from the deck. "Why don't we pick out a couple of cots and haul them down to the cabin?"

"Okay." Mike started down.

Les led them to a storage room where he had found several folded cots leaning against the wall. They selected the ones they wanted and took them down to the hold. Pausing on the stairs to put on the heavy clothes, they took the cots inside the hold and inserted them in the cabin. They also took a few minutes to bust-up another crate to be used as firewood and put the wood in a neat pile next to the fireplace.

"Let's haul our ugly little frozen friend up and throw him to the fish," Les said.

"Good idea," Mike said. "I definitely don't want to look at him anymore."

They put on gloves and pulled the frozen sea monster loose from the floor and dragged him upstairs. "This thing is all muscle," Mike said.

"And a little stiff from the cold," Les said.

Once they got the corpse topside, they pulled it to the railing and rolled it overboard. They then watched for several minutes as it floated slowly away. There didn't appear to be anything coming up from below to check it out.

"I imagine it'll attract hungry neighbors once it starts to thaw out," Les said.

The ship continued its steady progress northward and the little gold ship remained motionless on the shelf. The fuel gauge on the third of the four tanks slowly moved past the half-full marker and the sky overhead clouded up a bit.

Some thirty feet behind the ship the *Spear* followed along, pulled by its towrope tied to the back railing.

Late in the afternoon they cooked a big meal and enjoyed the four beers they had found on Trixie's yacht. It had been a long time since Mike had tasted beer and it really went down good with the canned ham and turnip greens. About half-an-hour before the sun hit the horizon Les shut off the engine for the night and they went below to the cabin in the refrigerated hold. Mike took another cot down with them to make a bed for Trixie. They also took a big bucket of water to be used as a weapon on any sea creatures that dared to venture to their doorstep. Mike set it a few feet from the fireplace so it wouldn't freeze. A short time later darkness fell and the creatures from the depths began coming aboard for their nightly food trek.

"I guess we're somewhat southeast of Florida." Les lit a piece of cardboard and placed it in the bottom of the fireplace.

Mike started adding small chips of wood and the fire started to catch.

"It's hard to tell though with the navigational instruments all messed up," Les said. "I figure it would be best to be too far north than not far north enough before we swing west. That way we won't miss Florida and wind up in the Gulf of Mexico accidentally."

"Sounds like a good plan to me," Mike said. He watched Les reach into his pocket and pull out the talisman.

"I remembered to bring this with me this time," he said. He placed it on the floor and they both watched it sit motionless. A few minutes later it got fairly warm inside the crate and they got out of the heavy clothes and crawled into their respective cots.

Chapter 17

▼

Pirates

Somewhere over the northeastern horizon, a wooden pirate ship with five tall masts, a greedy captain and sixty-six other cutthroats on board sailed into the Bermuda Triangle some 600 nautical miles east of the North American coastline. It was the eleventh of January 1739, 11:30 p.m. Most of his shipmates were asleep, but Mr. Creed, the night watch of the foredeck, was wide-awake and shivering in the brisk wind.

A large sand timer that measured approximately one hour was used by the crew as a time clock. Mr. Creed had stood watch through three cycles and was just past the halfway point in the last one. After four hours he would go below and wake his replacement, Maxwell "Mad Dog" Doberman.

Mad Dog always woke up angry, it was his nature. He'd call Creed every name in the book for waking him, then stagger up on deck for his assigned duty. Creed hated waking him but preferred it to the alternative. Even one extra minute on the cold deck was one too many, and especially on this cold night Creed looked forward to waking the skuzzy bastard and getting into his own warm bunk. But that moment was still an hour-and-a-half away, and Creed doubted his toes were going to make it. He already knew his fingers and nose wouldn't.

He stood at the bow railing, looking out into the dark empty sea. The sails were tied tightly around their masts and the ship's movement was limited to a slow, gradual drift to the southeast in a weak but steady current. The big hulk of a ship, appropriately named the *Scamp*, gently bobbed up and down in the mild waves. Now and then a gust of wind would hit one side of the ship and it would list slightly. The big ship handled moderate seas quite well, especially now when it was loaded with supplies. There were tons of equipment, cannons and cannon balls, barrels of water, food and rum.

There was however one commodity conspicuously absent: gold. The current voyage had left the Dutch harbor of Amsterdam more than a year ago and still not one piece of gold had been located. The only close call came six months ago when a Spanish galleon had been encountered on its way back from North America to Spain. The *Scamp* spotted the Spaniards and approached. The Spanish, not anxious for a fight but ready to defend their cargo if necessary, saw them coming and immediately prepared their cannons. The *Scamp*'s captain, Douglas McGriff, chose to back off and the Spanish ship sailed away. Captain McGriff told the crew that in the future they would attempt to take such a ship, but on this occasion the Spaniards had been

ready for them and it would have been too risky. There was
no reason to commit suicide with no chance of winning, so
McGriff let the opportunity pass by.

Since that time the *Scamp* had barely managed to survive, raiding fishing vessels and storming ocean-side
farms. They had managed to keep from starving but that
was about all. After sixteen months of waiting for a big
payoff, or even a not-so-big one, the captain and crew
were growing anxious.

Everyone seemed to be getting more and more vicious
as the long days passed, and the captain had ordered his
share of floggings accordingly. "The Cat" as he called the
Cat of Nine Tails, had wailed several times in the last few
weeks, keeping a lid on an ever-increasing uneasiness per-
meating throughout the ship. Creed had been lucky
enough to avoid the sting of the cat thus far, but he had
seen its effects on his unlucky fellow crewmen.

Creed looked at the sand timer and watched the last
few grains of sand drip through. He tapped it with his
frozen hand to be sure all of the sand was in the bottom
chamber before turning it over. The cat dealt with sand
timer cheats too, although he didn't see anyone around
that might rat on him. He inverted the big timer for the
last time on his watch and quickly put his hands back into
his pockets.

The cold was agonizing. The last hour was always the
worst. It was the one that made him consider the benefits of
drowning. His bunk was no vacation spot, but compared to
the deck it was heaven.

Every night watch was exactly the same. One sailor stood
at the stern and one at the bow, both looking endlessly into
the dark sea in hopes of spotting a ship. Merchant vessels

were the best. They often offered vast wealth and little resistance. At the same time, certain other vessels were to be avoided. Any ships belonging to a European navy posed serious danger.

Life on the seas was rough, but times were hard back in England and, since many on board were wanted criminals, the options were limited. Creed felt he had gotten lucky the day he joined the crew. He had robbed people at knife-point in downtown London and made a pretty good living on the run for several years. But when one elderly rich man finally called his bluff, Creed had been forced to kill him. It was messy and noisy, and he had almost been caught. Creed went straight to the wharf and hurriedly enlisted with the ship that would sail less than three hours later. He got away with his first and only murder.

Years earlier, while Creed sat out a three-day sentence in a London jail for his involvement in a bar fight, an older, wiser thief told him some of the facts of life the criminal needs to know if he's going to survive. "Make your money and disappear," the scummy old man told him. Creed had partially fulfilled the plan. He hadn't made his money yet but it was certainly time to get out. He left England aboard the *Scamp* with no promises and no questions asked. The captain had told the entire crew in the beginning that a big payoff, should they find it, would be divided fairly among the crew and each man could then go on his way. He'd made it sound good, but as the days became weeks and the weeks became months, the reality told a different story. Creed often dreamt of getting a small piece of a huge pie and vanishing under a new identity somewhere in the English colonies.

A man could make a fresh start there, he thought. As the thought passed across his mind, he stood watch at the bow of the rickety old ship and shivered as the sand crept through the hourglass.

Through almost frozen eyeballs Creed glanced around the dark horizon. There was nothing to be seen. All he was doing was following orders and making sure nobody caught him snoozing. The captain was strict and firm, and Creed remembered all too well the other sailor that was caught sleeping on his watch. He had overdone it with the ale at dinner and was ill prepared when his watch began at 0400 the next morning. The morning watch crewman caught him snoring and woke him up with the cat. When the same thing happened three days later, the captain ordered him hanged. The rest of the crew watched in horror as the fellow was hoisted up the yardarm with a noose around his neck and his feet kicking. If ever there had been any doubt among the crew about discipline being carried out on this vessel, that squashed it. Creed then knew why no questions about his past had been asked when he signed on. From the Captain right down to the cabin boy, they all were nothing but cheap, lowlife pirates.

Creed looked around behind him. There was one lantern near the stern and just behind it stood Mr. Larsen, the stern watch. Creed could see Larsen pretty well in the faint light of the lantern. Like himself, he appeared to be quite cold. Talking was prohibited except in the event of an emergency. The captain often reminded them that they had many enemies and only each other as trusted comrades. There were no friends out here on the sea with them. They must never let their guard down for even a minute, and never feel sympathy or pity for anyone. Creed slowly paced around the front of the ship and gritted his teeth every time the wind gusted.

Creed and Larsen had an agreement to periodically check on each other and make sure they were staying awake. Larsen glanced over and waved briefly with his hand. Creed hated to take his hand out of his pocket even for a second but did so and waved back. He didn't trust Larsen. The guy had killed his own brother during a dispute over their father's possessions two days after the old man died. Creed didn't trust anybody on this ship, especially Larsen. Still, they had an agreement and he would honor it.

Creed walked over to the front-most mast and leaned against it. The tall, wide beam provided a minute amount of wind protection but not nearly enough. The mast, along with the rest of the ship, listed ever so slightly to port in a steady gust of wind. All of a sudden the wind changed direction and started coming from in front of the ship. It increased in velocity and got much colder, more so than at any other time the whole night. It was as if this one gust of wind had come directly from the Arctic Ocean. Creed felt it cut straight through him. In a desperate attempt to keep warm he started hopping up and down.

Suddenly the whole vessel jolted and the bow lifted abruptly. It was as if the ocean underneath the ship rose several feet. For an instant, Creed lost his balance and had to grab hold of the mast to keep from falling to the deck. A moment later the wind became still and the air temperature plunged even lower. His breath formed large billows in the air and he heard faint splintering in the boards beneath his feet as the wood contracted from the bitter temperature.

"What's going on?" he muttered. He looked around at Larsen. The back half of the ship, including Larsen and the lantern between them, couldn't be seen. All was dark. In the faint light of a suddenly visible third-quarter moon, Creed looked down the deck to a point where the ship vanished into oblivion. He rubbed his eyes and stared again. Suddenly the lantern popped into view and illuminated the deck beside it. Beyond that, an invisible wall seemed to be obscuring the rest of the ship. He walked back toward the edge of the darkness and watched the planks of the deck emerge as he walked along. Then, just as mysteriously as the shroud had appeared, it vanished off the back of the ship. Creed looked up to see Larsen standing at his post looking confused. "Did we just pass through a fog bank or something?"

"I guess that's what it was," Larsen said. "I couldn't see you for a moment there."

Then, almost as suddenly as it had begun, the cold started to abate. Like a large cloud it seemed to lift and fade away. The air temperature rose steadily and within two minutes got warmer than it had been in a week. Creed was somewhat dazed by the vast and sudden variation in temperature. There were many strange things about being out in the middle of the Atlantic Ocean but this was the strangest thing he had ever experienced.

Creed continued to stand some three yards from Mr. Larsen as the two men silently adjusted to the bizarre experience.

"I guess we should tell the captain about the fog when he wakes up," Creed said.

Larsen glared at him. "You tell him. I didn't notice anything."

"Well something just happened," Creed said.

"Yeah, well you report it. My hourglass says about ten more minutes, then I'm going to bed."

Without seeming to notice what he was doing, Larsen unbuttoned his coat. Creed did the same.

"Didn't you notice that it got warm all of a sudden?" Creed said. "And what about the moon suddenly appearing?"

"Nine more minutes Mr. Creed," Larsen said unemotionally. "If I were you I'd get back to my post until the sand in the hourglass runs out."

Creed realized this was a healthy suggestion and walked quickly back to his post at the opposite end of the ship. Several minutes later the sand ran out and Creed went below decks to wake Doberman. He roused slowly as usual and sat up in his bunk. Creed waited for the usual tirade of obscenities. "Finally warmed up." Doberman stood up and headed for his post.

"Hey, Mad Dog," Creed said.

"What?"

"I think something happened out there."

"I don't give a damn." He walked away.

Creed paused to watch him go. "Me neither."

Once Creed got his shoes, stockings and coat off and got into his bunk, he put his still cold hands against his stomach to warm them. Moments later he drifted off to sleep.

An hour or so after that the first mate came through and started yelling for everyone to get up. He carried the cat with him. The men had long since learned to get up after being invited to do so only once. "Night watch," Creed muttered as the first mate walked by.

"Lazy son-of-a-whore," the first mate replied without breaking stride.

Creed drifted back off to sleep despite the noises from overhead. Above him, the crew shared a breakfast of gruel and hardtack as they hurried to raise the sails to catch the early morning wind. Nobody on board noticed anything out of the ordinary.

The captain took his position on the deck and used the rising sun to get their bearings. They were headed south by southwest for the Caribbean. Another routine day in the life of the pirate profession was underway.

CHAPTER 18

▼

OLD WORLD MEETS NEW

Trixie's tail wagging across Mike's nose woke him up. He got up and looked out the crate door to see sunlight through the broken-out porthole. Les heard him and got up too. They quickly went to the stairs and out of the refrigerated cargo hold. No sooner had they reached the top of the stairs than signs of the previous night's visits became obvious. Deck chairs were again scattered around and more unopened cans of food lay on the deck in front of the galley doorway. It looked like the creatures had spent the night trying to figure out how to get the cans open and simply couldn't do it. "I tell you what," Mike said. "I can never keep anything nice on this ship."

Les chuckled. They both had slept well on the cots and were very refreshed. "I'll go start the engine," Les said.

Mike began straightening up in the galley while the dog walked around his feet waiting for her breakfast. Just as

Mike began turning the can opener crank to open a can of dog food, he heard the sound of the starter kicking on. The sound ground in a long, steady hum but the engine wouldn't turn over. Les turned it off, waited a moment, then tried again. Nothing. He tried again. After five futile minutes it became obvious that the sea creatures had clogged the propellers. The sinking feeling Mike started to get at the first sign of the problem had now hit bottom.

A moment later Les stepped into the galley. "I guess you heard."

"Yeah," Mike said. "Here we go again."

"At least we still have power. Let's go ahead and eat breakfast while we decide what to do next."

After preparing the usual fare, they took their plates and coffee mugs and stepped out onto the deck. Behind the ship's deck building was a table bolted to the floor. They sat and ate, enjoying the morning sun and warm air.

"Looks like we might get some rain today." Mike gazed out to sea. Les looked in the direction he was indicating and saw thick cloud cover. Rain could be seen falling into the sea a few miles away.

After eating, Mike walked up the metal stairs to the top deck and looked around. "Hey Les," he called out. "Land ho."

Les hustled up the steps and looked where Mike was pointing.

"Why don't we fuel up the *Spear* and go check it out," Les said. Mike agreed and they found themselves running down the steps. The dog barked and jumped around excitedly. Mike ran to the stern and reeled in the rope with the *Spear* at the end and it coasted up alongside the ship. Les had found some life preservers and tied them to the

Spear's railing to buffer any contact it might have with the big ship. The *Spear* bumped the ship quite hard, then bounded back away from it as the life preservers padded the contact.

Les came out with a gas can and the plastic bag with the gold, the binoculars and some food in it. "I found some gas and motor oil in the storage room. Now we've got enough for a full tank. I thought we'd better take along something to eat too."

"Good thinking," Mike said. "There's no telling how long we'll be gone." He grabbed the two wineskins of water and then lowered the ladder over the side of the ship. Les climbed down to the *Spear* and Mike lowered everything else down to him with the rope.

Les filled the *Spear*'s gas tank and then sent the empty can back up. "We'll have plenty of gas now."

Mike picked up the dog and climbed down.

Les ran some gas into the motor with the hand pump. After a few pulls the engine sputtered and came to life. He let it run a minute while Mike pushed them away from the ship. A moment later they were on their way.

Mike took a moment to check the contents of the burlap bag that Les had put inside the big blue plastic bag. The gold coins were shiny and the gold ship just as mystifying as ever. He again held the little ship up and admired it.

Les smiled. "We can never let that thing out of our sight."

Mike nodded. He placed it back in the burlap bag and decided to stuff it into the *Spear*'s glove compartment. The binoculars and food were fine in the plastic bag, which he left on the floor under one of the seats.

The landmass they were approaching was an island, a much smaller one than the one they had left behind.

"I hope there's some fresh water here," Mike said over the roar of the motor. "That stuff on the ship is getting stale."

"Yeah," Les said. "That's one thing about our old island that I miss, fresh spring water."

Mike took a deep breath and smelled the fresh morning air. "It sure is nice to have transportation again."

Les smiled. "Yes it is."

Les steered a little to one side then the other. "See, runs good."

"Sure does, man." Mike smiled. He turned and looked toward the approaching island and the smile slowly faded. Getting home, to his old life and Jan was still far away.

When they got to the outer edges of the breaking waves about sixty feet or so from the shore, Les steered right and started around the side of the island. "Let's look around a little before going ashore. Maybe the waves are a little smaller around on the other side."

They went the short distance to the opposite side of the island and saw how small it was. Les slowed down a little more and they finished cruising around the heavily forested outcropping in about ten minutes. The island was oval-shaped and appeared completely void of human existence. Les got to the leeward side and started ashore. The waves were moderate and one gave them a boost from behind, then carried them up onto the beach.

Mike jumped out and pulled the *Spear* in further with the rope. Trixie jumped out right behind him and splashed up onto the hot, white sand. Les cut the motor and got out.

"The place seems oddly familiar." Mike chuckled.

"Too much so," Les said. They walked around in the shade for a few minutes and soon discovered a number of fruit trees and a small, fresh water stream. Trixie wasted no time jumping in and drinking her fill.

There was a hill in the middle of the island that rose some thirty-five or forty feet. It ended abruptly as a short cliff at the south end of the island.

The three of them got comfortable in the shade beside the stream and relaxed for a while. A short time later a light rain began to fall. It had been mostly cloudy and now was rather dark for so early in the day. Within a few minutes it was pouring hard.

"Maybe those sea creatures can't come up on land," Mike said. "That must be why the one Roscoe found on the beach was dead."

"Yes," Les said. "And we never saw one on Atlantis. The way Roscoe described it I think it was the same thing that we found frozen in the hold."

Mike nodded. He noticed a big banana tree and headed for it. They spent the next hour snacking and relaxing under the canopy of trees. Once it stopped raining, they headed for the *Spear*.

Rainwater had accumulated in the bottom and added to what had already seeped in. They got in and cranked it, then headed for the big ship. Once they got going fast, Les removed the plug from the well in the back floor and let all the water run out. Once the water was out he put the plug back in and slowed down for the approach to the ship. They pulled up alongside and Les cut the motor. Mike took hold of the rope they had left dangling from the *San Mateo*'s railing and tied off the *Spear*.

"I'll go get dinner started." Mike took the dog in his arm and started to climb up. "I'll lower the rope for you to tie the basket to. Can you get the gold when you come up?"

"Sure," Les said. "How about lowering the life preserver for me. I want to try cutting the propellers free if I can."

Mike lowered the life preserver and stood at the rail.

Les dove in. Thick seaweed again entangled the propellers. When he surfaced he got straight into the *Spear*.

"No luck?" Mike hollered down from the railing of the big ship.

"Afraid not. The creatures have stopped us again. I'll wait until tomorrow to go down and try to cut them free."

Mike looked up at the late afternoon sky. "Might as well. It's too late to risk it today." He turned and headed for the galley.

Les sat in the *Spear* and started securing it. After making sure it was well tied to the bigger ship he concentrated on the motor, disconnecting the gas line and doing a few other minor tasks to prepare it for the night. Once he was done securing, he placed the various items into the basket. When he grabbed the burlap sack the little gold ship fell out of it and onto the floor. "I've got to be more careful." He picked it up and prepared to put it back into the bag.

The *Scamp* came silently from the other side of the *San Mateo*, passed in front of it and threw a large shadow across Les' back. It took several seconds for Les to realize that he was in the shade and he whirled around to see the big pirate ship with a number of sailors on the deck. The sight startled him so much he almost tumbled overboard. Les sat in the *Spear* with his mouth hanging open as the pirate captain walked casually up to the railing and smiled at him.

"Good afternoon my good man." The captain wore a three-cornered, black hat, a dirty, white shirt and black pants. He held a large sword in his right hand and smiled broadly, revealing a big gold front tooth. There was a long scar down his left cheek and his long black hair fluttered in the light wind.

Although the other sailors had beards and were rather skuzzy-looking, the captain was clean-shaven and neat. There were about fifteen other sailors at the railing looking down at him and smiling. All appeared to be admiring the little gold ship in his hand. "You, sir, are my prisoner," the captain said. "And I believe that little ship you are holding now belongs to me."

Les forced a smile. "This is some kind of joke isn't it?"

The captain's smile quickly faded. "Oh, I assure you this is no joke. There are plenty of dead men who found out first-hand that I don't joke."

Several of the other pirates began to display their swords. "That object in your hand," the captain said. "Throw it up to me now."

Les sat motionless, staring up at the captain.

"Give me the gold now, or my friends here will come down there and remove it from your hand at the elbow."

"I do not think so, old chap," Les said in his best British accent. "I am nobody's prisoner and this gold does not belong to you. So why don't you and your friends turn your ship around and go play polo somewhere."

Rage covered the captain's face for an instant. "You have a mighty courageous mouth, sir. Mr. Walters." The Captain didn't take his eyes off Les. "Show this bloody scum that we are not joking."

"Aye Cap'm," a toothless fellow a few feet away said and he and another sailor quickly rolled a large cannon up to the edge of the *Scamp*'s deck and aimed it at the side of the *San Mateo*. He then produced a burning torch and touched it to the fuse. A moment later the cannon went off with a deafening bang and blew a hole in the side of the big ship about five feet above the water line. An instant later Trixie came running out on deck barking and snarling, followed closely by a stunned Mike.

"What in the fu…" He spotted the pirates. "Who the hell are you?"

"Captain Douglas McGriff. As I was just telling your friend here, your vessel is now under my command."

"Like hell it is," Mike said. He looked down at Les and saw from his facial expression that the situation was serious. The man at the cannon, assisted by several others, reloaded and then pointed the big gun at Les.

"You watch how you talk to me, you son-of-a-whore," McGriff said. "Are there any other people aboard?"

Mike paused a moment, mentally noting that the entire pirate crew appeared to be male.

"Yes," Mike said. "Six women. We will surrender to you if you'll give me a moment to inform them of the situation."

"Winches, eh," McGriff said. "Very good. Go quickly."

"Alright." Mike winked at Les. "I'll be right back."

"See that you are." McGriff again turned his attention to Les. "I'd hate to kill your friend before his time is due."

The cannon was pointed right at Les and the burning torch was being wavered dangerously close to its fuse. "Now give me that gold," McGriff said.

Les held up the gold ship. "Oh, you mean this?"

"Precisely." McGriff smiled with about nine or ten teeth, including the gold one. "Throw it up to me now."

Les held the ship out over the water and all the pirates gasped. "Get that cannon off of me or I'll drop it in."

The pirates all stood silent, looking at McGriff.

"You do not want to do that, sir," McGriff said. "You drop that gold into the water and I'll personally beat you to death with a cat-of-nine-tails."

"Oh, I can make another one." Les smiled. "In fact, I could make hundreds more with all the gold stored in my secret hiding place."

An object making a sizzling sound came flying from the *San Mateo*'s deck and sailed over to the deck of the *Scamp*. It was several sticks of dynamite Mike had tied together and lit.

Nobody on the pirate ship seemed to know what it was as the sticks hit the deck and scattered all around.

"Get it overboard!" McGriff screamed. Nobody moved.

Les pocketed the gold ship, untied the *Spear* and grabbed the starter cord.

"Move, you cowards," McGriff screamed. A moment later explosions rocked the *Scamp*. Several pirates were thrown overboard and one of the masts tumbled over.

Les pulled the cord and the *Spear*'s motor sprang to life. He threw it into gear and took off around the stern.

"Stop him," McGriff screamed. The cannon fired and the shot landed in the water just behind Les.

Les drove around to the other side of the *San Mateo* and slowed down.

Mike rushed through the cabin and grabbed a flashlight and a few more sticks of dynamite. The dog followed close on his heels and when he got back on deck he tossed her into the water. Trixie swam to the *Spear* and Les pulled her in.

"Don't drop this dynamite." Mike tossed a burlap bag down to Les. He caught it and quickly stuffed it under one of the seats.

Mike heard someone yell: "There he is!" He turned to see that two of the pirates had climbed aboard the *San Mateo* and were coming at him with swords drawn.

"Jump," Les said.

Mike climbed over the railing, jumped into the water and swam for the *Spear*. Les helped him in just as the *Scamp*, thick smoke bellowing up from its deck, came around the stern of the *San Mateo*.

"Hit it," Mike said as he watched the gunner prepare to take a shot at them.

Les punched it and the *Spear* sped away. Mike sat in the back next to him and watched the *Scamp*, its deck filled with bewildered pirates, fade away behind them. The sudden blast of late afternoon wind chilled him.

"I guess we'd better head back to that little island," Les said. "At least we'll have fruit to eat and fresh water to drink." He looked over at Mike with a concerned expression. "I guess we're going to find out first-hand if those creatures can come up on shore."

"Those sons-of-bitches," Mike said. "I had just pulled out the cork on that bottle of wine when they fired the cannon. Now we don't get a hot meal, the wine or a good night's sleep."

"Maybe the sea creatures will go aboard and clear all those pirates out tonight," Les said. "That is if their ship doesn't sink first. That dynamite really did some damage."

"Yeah." Mike smiled. "I hit the bulls eye. Did it look to you like they did a lot of damage to the *San Mateo*?"

"Yeah, they popped it pretty good. Blew a hole about three feet wide in it. If a few good-sized waves come along it'll start to take on water."

"Damn." Mike looked back at the two vessels, now about a mile away. There was no more smoke to be seen; just the two ships side by side with the sinking sun behind them. Up ahead, the island where they had spent the afternoon awaited.

Les steered around to the far side and beached them. "How about we drag the boat all the way up into the jungle to hide it."

"Sounds like a good idea," Mike said. The beach wasn't very wide and they didn't have to drag the heavy *Spear* more than about twenty feet. They put palm branches around it and headed inland.

"I don't suppose you thought to grab a cigarette lighter," Les said.

Mike pulled one out of his pocket and held it up with a smile. "I had to light the dynamite with something."

They picked out a level place near the stream and gathered firewood and some palm branches on which they could sleep. They used the last of the daylight to gather bananas and other fruit.

Les got the fire going while Mike went to the stream. "I hope this fire won't attract attention tonight," Les said.

"We're surrounded by thick vegetation here," Mike said. "Besides, if any of those creatures do come ashore we'll need something to fight with. I imagine fire will do."

"Yeah, I guess it will." Les threw a few more sticks on and soon they had a nice fire going. They then got comfortable and rested.

They didn't have any dog food and had to give Trixie fruit scraps. "Sorry girl," Mike told her as he handed her a piece of banana. She whimpered a little but eventually ate it.

They relaxed for a while, eating fruit and drinking lots of fresh water. Mike lay down on the palm branches and tried to get as comfortable as possible. "I didn't realize how good we had it on the *San Mateo*."

"I hear you." Les tried to get his palm branches on as level a spot as possible. "We might not get to spend any more nights on that ship since it's at risk of sinking now. Hopefully we can at least go back and get supplies off of it."

Mike sprawled out on his back and looked at the stars through the thick canopy of trees overhead.

"Les," Mike said. "Let me ask you something."

"Fire away."

"What are we going to do if we get home and find ourselves in the next century, or even the last one for that matter? How are we going to make a living?"

"We'll figure something out," Les said. "No matter what, we've still got our intelligence and our talents. This triangle isn't going to take those away from us. And if nothing else, we've got the bag of gold we can sell. That'll at least set us up financially for a little while. Don't worry, the Lord will provide."

"Well, think about all the things we've probably already lost," Mike said. "Our careers, our bank accounts, our homes. We'd literally be starting over from scratch. I'm not so sure I can do that."

"Well," Les chuckled. "What are our alternatives. Do you just want to stay here?"

"No, I don't want to do that."

"Neither do I. So we have no choice but to move forward the best we can."

The two of them lay silently on opposite sides of the campfire.

Mike silently said his prayers as he had done every night his whole life. "Please God," he whispered. "We need a miracle."

CHAPTER 19

▼

TERRORS ON DECK: THE *SCAMP* GETS VISITED

Back on the *Scamp*, the pirates had spent the afternoon attempting to repair the damage to their ship. The mast that was knocked down had to be removed completely and jettisoned. Once the smoke cleared they found that they had a gaping hole in the deck but the hull below was still intact. No sailors had been killed but several had suffered minor scrapes and bruises.

Captain McGriff was livid at the two strangers that had outwitted him, damaged his ship and escaped in a remarkably fast boat. He knew he wasn't dealing with anything he had encountered before but was too intent on revenge to be afraid. "Mr. Townley," he called to his first mate. Townley hurried over to him.

"Sir."

"How bad is the damage?"

Darkness had fallen and they had lit the lanterns. The captain had been trying to follow the progress of the fast little boat and it appeared to have gone to the small island. Townley had been assigned to assess the damage and it had taken him until well after dark to complete the task and report back to the deck.

"No serious injuries Captain and all men are accounted for."

"I meant the ship Townley," McGriff said.

"Oh," Townley said. "She'll stay afloat but we'll never get the speed we're used to with the mainsail missing. A return to England would take months."

"We won't be returning to England. Tomorrow morning we're going to visit that little island. And when we leave there will be two funny dressed men and a dog hanging from nooses made just for them."

McGriff walked around the deck, then gave the order for lights out. Shortly after that, all hands were in their bunks except the four on watch. The guard was doubled in case the strangers decided to come back.

During the night watch two men paced the sides of the ship while one was stationed at the stern and another at the bow. Each had to be careful to avoid the hole in the middle of the deck. What was left of the broken mast stood in the center of the hole a few feet below the level of the top deck, waiting to impale anyone that should fall in.

Creed woke up and looked around. He was scheduled for the stern watch at 0200 and it seemed much later than that. The stern watchman never forgot to wake him. He lay in the silent darkness with his eyes open and listened. Overhead he could hear light movement but nothing distinctive. After several minutes he decided to go up top.

He quietly got dressed and shuffled down the aisle between bunks. The snoring that he somehow tuned out during sleep wailed from all around. Creed ascended the steps and exited the doorway onto the deck. The sky overhead was cloudy and quite bright. He guessed it was much closer to sunup than it was to 0200.

A quick scan to the left side of the ship told Creed there was a post that was unmanned. He looked over to starboard; there was nobody on that watch either. The wind blew hard for a brief moment and the lanterns jingled softly, other than that there was no sound except the lapping of the waves against the hull. Creed walked toward the stern and found it abandoned. For the first time since he first came aboard the *Scamp* he began to fear something that wasn't aboard the ship. Captain McGriff was a cold, cruel man. Creed had once seen him swipe at a sailor with a sword and almost cut his head off simply because he had called him by his first name. He figured the captain would kill anyone that dared to call him "Dougie." That cruel nature of McGriff's made anything else pale by comparison. McGriff drove them so hard that nothing they would ever encounter could be worse. Yet, something had to be very wrong on the deck this early morning. No crewman in his right mind would dare abandon his post on McGriff's ship. He decided to go up front and see if that one was gone too. The term "desertion" came to mind. It appeared to be the only explanation.

After exploring the deck and finding no trace of the watch, Creed decided to cover his own hide. It would be daylight in a few minutes and it would be better if he went and woke the first mate to report the desertion than it would to let him find out on his own. He went below decks and found Mr. Townley just getting up.

"Sir, it appears that the four men on night watch have deserted," Creed said.

Townley stared at Creed for several seconds. "What are you talking about?" He reached for the cat without even looking around for it.

"I reported to the deck for my watch and found it deserted," Creed said. "My guess is that they swam to that little island we spotted yesterday."

Townley got up and started for the deck. "Well they had better have the explanation of a lifetime when I find them. Come with me."

They went to the back-most compartment of the lower deck and Townley knocked on the captain's door. It opened a moment later and Creed immediately stood at attention. McGriff ignored him.

"What is it Townley?" McGriff said.

"Begging the Captain's pardon sir," Townley said. "But we seem to have a desertion of four men."

The captain's eyes darted to Creed. "That's right Captain," Creed said. "Nobody woke me for my shift this morning so I got up and investigated. That's when I discovered that the whole deck was vacant."

McGriff turned and reached for his shirt. "Well who's up there now?"

Townley turned and looked at Creed.

"Why, nobody," Creed said.

"You went off and left the deck unguarded?" McGriff said. He snatched the cat from Townley and cracked it at

Creed's face. Creed turned his head aside and felt the whip cut across his left arm. "Get up there now."

"Yes sir." Creed turned and ran for the deck hoping he could get away before McGriff took another swipe at him. When he got topside, he grabbed a shirt he found lying on the deck and used it to dry off the blood on his arm. Then he decided to walk the whole deck until told to do otherwise. He started toward the stern, noticing that the sun was now just under the eastern horizon. The first signs of a red morning sky could be seen.

As Creed approached the back railing, he suddenly became aware of a very large man standing silently in the dark. As he neared him, Creed began to realize that this person wasn't a member of the crew, there wasn't anybody on board that size. He froze in his tracks when he realized that it wasn't even a man.

Creed felt his blood run cold as the thing in the dark that looked to be twice the size of a man, stared at him through red eyes. "Who are you?" he said in a voice that tried to sound demanding. There was no reply. Creed took a step forward and the thing snarled and bared a very large set of teeth. It had a snout like a crocodile but stood upright on several legs, or something that worked like legs. Creed froze again, suddenly fearing for his life. The creature began to move and in the dim light Creed could see several tentacles writhing about. It hissed and began to slither toward him. The sound of footsteps approached from behind Creed and the creature started backing away. Creed didn't dare take his eyes off the creature but saw that its attention was diverted. A moment later it turned to the railing and wriggled over the side, followed by a loud splash as it hit the water below.

Creed tried to justify what he had just seen but nothing in his mental directory of known creatures matched this. Townley walked up to him and began asking for more details of his discovery of the missing men. It took a few seconds for Creed to even notice. "Did you just see something?"

"Where?" Townley said.

"At the back railing. Just now."

"No," Townley said. "Was it one of the missing men?"

"No," Creed said. He looked at Townley and realized he might be better off keeping his mouth shut. "Must have been my imagination."

He recanted the details of his discovery of the vacant deck to Townley, keeping his eyes on the back railing the whole time. Secretly, he hoped that whatever it was would return so Townley could see it for himself. Creed knew better than to tell Townley what he had just seen. He'd be accused of being drunk on his watch.

McGriff walked out on deck and began looking around. He walked over to the railing and looked down. "Looks like the lifeboats are still secure."

Creed continued to stare at the back railing. He would stick to his story that he thought the men had left for the little island. But deep down inside he knew differently. The only detail he couldn't figure out was why none of them could have been heard screaming. Whatever this thing was that got them, it somehow managed to get all four without even one of them crying out for help, at least loudly enough to be heard by anyone.

It wasn't long before the bright daylight filled the air. Shortly thereafter, the captain ordered two rowboats deployed with six men in each to go to the island. Within ten minutes of the giving of the order, the rowboats were on their way. Two oarsmen in each boat rowed as the other four prepared to storm ashore.

Townley was the leader in one boat while McGriff personally led the expedition from the other. McGriff carried fifty feet of rope in one hand and his pistol in the other. His sword was sheathed in his belt. "I hope we brought enough rope," he said with a seedy grin. "We're going to have a hanging."

Mike's eyes opened when he heard Trixie barking somewhere toward the beach. He sat up and looked around, quickly realizing that whatever had the dog stirred up wasn't a sea creature. He got up and followed the sound. Looking out at the water he spotted the two rowboats, now less than a hundred yards away.

"Les, wake up!" Mike ran back to the campsite.

Les opened his eyes and sat up.

"Two boat loads of pirates are headed this way," Mike said.

"Oh great." Les stood up and brushed sand off himself. "Well, I guess we'll just have to go kick some ass."

Mike reached into the burlap bag and took out several sticks of dynamite and the lighter. "Let's try to get them before they get ashore. Otherwise we'll have to fight them hand to hand."

"Good idea," Les said.

They ran to the beach that the pirates were approaching and stepped out of the jungle.

"Hey guys, over here," Les shouted, waving at the pirates like they were old friends.

"What the hell are you doing?" Mike said.

"Bringing them in closer," Les said. "Let's wave and act friendly. Maybe we'll catch them off guard." Mike stuck the dynamite in his back pocket and started waving too. McGriff fired his pistol and the slug hit the sand about three feet from Mike's feet. He turned and stared at the spot.

"Keep waving and acting friendly," Les said.

"Screw that." Mike reached into his pocket and pulled out a stick of dynamite. Once he got the fuse lit he reached back and threw it at the approaching pirates. It sizzled through the air and fell about ten feet short. "Damn, I missed." He watched it float on the waves. A moment later it exploded and spewed water all over the pirates.

"Keep charging," they heard the captain shout.

"Yeah," Mike screamed at them. "Come and get us you losers."

They pointed right for him and continued rowing hard.

"Look at those idiots," Les said. "They're actually still coming for us. Give me a dynamite stick."

Mike handed him the lighter and then pulled out a stick. Les walked out knee-deep into the water and lit the fuse. He reared back and threw it at the captain's boat but threw too hard. The dynamite sailed past them and blew up in the water a few feet away. McGriff had been reloading his pistol and was now taking aim at Les. As he started to fire, Les dropped into the water and the shot missed wildly. "Missed me," he yelled at McGriff in a taunting voice. McGriff yelled out in anger.

Mike lit a third stick and held it a moment as he lined up a throw. He was an outfielder on the department softball team and had a good arm. Hit the cut-off man with this one, he thought as he wound up and threw. He stood and watched the dynamite sizzle as it flew through the air. All the pirates on Townley's boat watched it. Two of the men jumped overboard an instant before the dynamite landed in the front of the boat and rolled under one of the seats. An instant later it blew the boat apart. Mike and Les watched from shore as pieces of splintered wood flew into the air. After the smoke cleared, only one of the two that had jumped out appeared to still be alive. It was Townley. He was swimming frantically toward McGriff's boat.

"Help me, I can't see," Townley screamed.

"What good are you to me if you can't see," McGriff said.

Townley managed to get a hand on the side of the boat and McGriff whacked it with his sword. Townley screamed and fell back into the water.

"What did you do that for?" he cried out.

"I call it 'thinning the herd'." McGriff ordered the oarsmen in his boat to keep rowing toward shore. He paid no attention as Townley struggled briefly before drowning.

Back on the *Scamp*, the remaining sailors were all gathered at the rail, watching the drama unfold. Some of them applauded and cheered softly when they saw that Mr. Townley wouldn't be coming back.

Les ran to the campsite and grabbed a few more sticks of dynamite. He got back to the beach with it just before McGriff's boat got ashore. Mike had run back to the trees and was hiding behind a large palm. Les ran out with the dynamite and approached the boat, which was now in water shallow enough for them to walk ashore.

McGriff saw him and tried to steady his hand in the rocking boat to take another shot. Les hit the ground and the slug sailed overhead. He then got up and lit the fuse and threw. McGriff saw it coming and ordered his men to retreat. The dynamite landed in the water a few feet away and exploded, sending sand and water into the air and all over McGriff's party.

The captain saw that Les had plenty of dynamite handy.

"Get us out of here," McGriff shouted.

The struggling sailors turned the boat around and headed back for the *Scamp* as Les stood on the beach, dynamite in hand. Mike walked out and stood beside Les as they watched the pirates row away.

"You got lucky today you bastards," McGriff yelled as he sat in the back of the boat and shook his fist at them. "I'll kill you, I swear I will."

"Nice to see you again too Captain McShit," Mike yelled back.

"If you're hiding my men then tell them they're dead too." McGriff yelled. "I'll be back."

"And we'll be waiting for you," Les said. He looked over at Mike and laughed.

"What do you suppose he meant about hiding his men?" Mike said.

"I don't know. Maybe the sea creatures ate some of them last night and he thinks they came here. I guess if we can wait a few days then they'll get all of them." Les looked over at the *San Mateo* a mile or so away. It appeared to be in pretty good shape. Several of the pirates could be seen moving about its deck. "I hope we can get back aboard for supplies before the seas get rough again."

Mike nodded. "A little help from the sea creatures would be nice."

They walked back into the shade of the trees. Off in the distance, Captain McGriff and his group reached the *Scamp* and went back aboard.

"I'm ready to eat," Mike said as they returned to the campsite. They found Trixie lying on Les' blanket, anxiously awaiting their return. Mike took a moment to look in the burlap bag for the little ship. It wouldn't hurt to see if it would spin. He pulled it out and set it on a flat surface. It didn't move.

"We'll need to keep checking it several times a day," Les said. "When it starts moving again then we'll take to the water. Meanwhile, I guess we wait until the pirates either leave or die off, then we'll go back aboard the *San Mateo* for some real food."

Mike took the binoculars out of the bag and walked down to the edge of the woods. "I guess it wouldn't hurt to check on them every now and then too."

"You're right. We never know when they might try coming back again."

"Oh no." Mike peered through the binoculars.

"What?" Les said.

"Bad news. They found the wine."

"Oh. Hopefully they won't figure out how to open the canned food." Les walked over to the banana tree and started picking. For the rest of the day the two of them took it easy and ate fruit, periodically checking the binoculars to see what the pirates were doing. For the most part they appeared to be pillaging the ship and relaxing themselves. They seemed to be waiting for Captain McGriff to give the next order. Mike and Les had little else to do but await the same thing.

Back on the *Scamp*, Mr. Creed decided to turn in shortly before it got dark. The captain had doubled the guard to eight men and Creed's assignment was to start at midnight. He awoke sometime before that and decided to go topside. When he got up there he found all eight watchmen pacing around the hole in the deck and talking amongst themselves. They were more lax than usual, probably due in part to the permanent retirement of Mr. Townley. Apparently they figured the cat was on the shelf to stay now and they didn't have to worry about protocol, at least not until the captain chose someone else to do his enforcing.

"Have any of you men seen anything come up from the sea tonight?" Creed said. They all looked at him like he was crazy.

"No," one said. "But if a mermaid shows up I get her first." The others all broke up laughing.

"I mean one of those strangers," Creed said.

"No," said another. "But if they do we'll be ready for them" They all fondled their swords and knives.

Creed realized he'd better keep his questions to himself. There was no explanation for what he had seen on the deck the morning before, nor was there any for the men in the fast little boat that had no sails and no oars, yet went faster than any boat he had ever seen. Since that strange experience with the cloudbank two nights earlier a number of unexplainable things had taken place. What made it even stranger was the level of acceptance. There was hardly any talk at all about the big ship they had taken from the strangers. It seemed to be made of iron. Creed had encountered a lot of ships, but never one like it before. Like the little boat, it had no sails and no oarlocks.

Creed walked around the deck a few more minutes before sitting against a wall facing the stern. There were so many others on deck that he felt they were reasonably safe.

As he sat and thought about England, his home that he would probably never see again, his eyelids grew heavy and he began to drift into and out of sleep.

A few feet away one of the sailors walked past and went to the railing. He stood with his elbows on the rail, looking off into the distance. A large tentacle rose up from below and wrapped itself around his neck and head. Unable to make a sound, he was yanked silently over the railing and into the water.

Creed awoke when he heard the splash and glanced around. Everything seemed to be unchanged from the last time he looked around and he dismissed the sound. A moment later he set his head back against the wall and drifted back to sleep.

Sometime later he awakened. The men that had been around him earlier were nowhere to be seen. The whole deck was quiet and deserted. That alarmed him. Suddenly he became aware of movement near the back rail and awoke. In the dim light, he saw the same thing he had seen there twenty-four hours earlier. It looked like a huge octopus but stood upright and shuffled slowly around on several tentacles like a caterpillar. Creed rubbed his eyes and stared. There was a barrel a few feet from where he sat and he realized it had kept him from being spotted. He crawled over and got right behind it.

Looking over the top of the barrel, he could see two more of the things slithering aboard. He stared in horror as the three of them began moving about the deck. He had not armed himself. He looked up above him and saw the alarm bell that hung from the mast ten feet away. He debated whether to ring it. It might wake the crew like he hoped or it might accomplish nothing more than alerting the creatures to his whereabouts. Then again, he thought, they'd find him eventually. He grabbed the string and rang as hard as he could. It was only a moment before he felt a thick rope around his ankle. It was one of the creatures, pulling him toward the deck below. He started to scream, drowning out the sound of shouting men as they charged up the stairs.

"Look there," one man shouted as he and three others ran out onto the deck.

Creed was holding the railing with both hands screaming. One man ran at the creature with a sword and cut off the tentacle that was holding Creed's leg. Warm blood spewed into his face and the creature wailed. Another sailor charged with his sword and stuck the creature in its neck. He pulled back and stabbed again. The sword sank in up to his fist. The creature fell to the deck and flopped around for a few seconds before dying.

A few feet away, Creed was trying to get the end of the tentacle off his ankle. Once the other sailor cut it free the end of it tightened and began cutting off the circulation. It felt to be still alive. Creed got up and limped down the deck to find a sword.

Less than twenty feet away one of the creatures was staring face to face with a sailor ready with his sword. Creed found a sword in a rack by the door and turned to watch his shipmate take on the creature. "Come on ye slimy bastard," the bearded man said with a thick Irish accent. He lunged forward and stabbed at the creature. It jumped away momentarily and hissed. The man lunged again and the creature again avoided him. Then a tentacle seemingly from nowhere swung around and hit the sailor across the face. He sailed into the wall behind him. Another tentacle flew and wrapped around his arm just below the shoulder. Another came out and pulled the arm off. The terrified sailor lay helplessly on his back and watched in horror as the creature ate his arm. The sword dropped from the fingers and onto the deck where another tentacle kicked it overboard. The creature approached the pirate and picked him up. The one-armed man screamed as the creature reeled him in. Then it quickly crammed him into its massive mouth, which was suddenly wide.

Creed couldn't stand to watch yet was unable to draw his eyes away. The sailor's screams could be heard for just a moment from inside the creature's throat. He finally went quiet about the time his feet dropped out of sight in its mouth, one of his shoes dropping to the deck with a thud.

The creature then turned toward another sailor a few feet away. Like Creed, he had seen the whole thing and wore a look of sheer terror. Creed pointed his sword and charged toward the creature. The other sailor's eyes glanced over at him and the creature noticed the movement. It turned on Creed and hissed. Creed kept charging. The creature flinched away, narrowly avoiding the sword. Creed fell and his sword tumbled harmlessly away, landing at the other sailor's feet.

An instant later Creed felt several massive tentacles wrap around him. He could feel one around his waist, another around his feet. He reached around it with his arms and noticed how rough it was when he rubbed against the grain. It was like trying to pet a large fish from the tail up.

He pounded the tentacle with his fist as hard as he could but made no progress freeing himself. His breathing was halted and he could feel his stomach being squeezed into his throat. He saw the other sailor approach with a sword in each hand, holding them at arm's length. Creed gritted his teeth and closed his eyes. An instant later he heard a scream.

Warm, gooey liquid poured all over his head and the tentacles loosened just enough for him to free his arms. He gasped, thinking he was going to suffocate. For just a moment he was a little boy again, playing in his mother's garden. Then his senses came back.

Several of the other sailors were pulling the wiggling tentacles off of him. They had taken their swords and diced the creature into pieces. The largest of the tentacles rolled and squirmed around a moment. Then, almost as if it could see the ocean, it made its way to the edge and over the side. Several other smaller ones followed. A few feet away, the creature lay in a pool of foul-smelling blood. Its head lay several feet away, its three-foot snout pointed toward the sea. It grinned as if it had died happy and all of its teeth, some of them the size of a man's foot, lay idle.

"I guess it's true," one sailor said in a shaky voice. "Sea monsters really do exist." Another sailor crossed his chest with his right hand. There were no more creatures to be seen at the moment.

The captain walked over to the corpse of the creature and kicked it lightly. Nobody spoke. Creed watched the captain's face and was unable to tell if it was the look of anger or fear. Either way, he thought the captain was going to vomit. Creed chuckled to himself. The crazy son-of-a-bitch actually looked scared.

Nobody left the deck until the sun could clearly be seen making its appearance an hour-and-a-half later. A head-count revealed that only thirty-two men were left aboard.

Back on the nearby island, the horrible sounds from the pirate vessel had awakened the dog, causing her to bark an alarm. Mike and Les sat up, ready to fight, but soon noticed all the noise themselves. They took turns watching with the binoculars. It was quite dark and only a little could be seen in the faint moonlight and even fainter light of the pirate's lanterns. The big electric light on the back of the merchant vessel had been turned on. In the light they could see several of the creatures dropping overboard. They were two miles away and in very dim light, but their horrible presence was unmistakable.

Now, just past sunrise, Les and Mike opted for a little more sleep. Trixie stood ready to sound the alarm if anything moved.

Les awakened sometime mid-morning. He stood up and looked through the binoculars at the pirate vessel. Flying boldly from the highest mast was a snow-white flag. "Hey Mike."

Mike mumbled to let Les know he was awake and listening.

"I think those pirates are surrendering," Les said. "They're flying a white flag."

"What do they expect us to do," Mike said. "Come out and take them prisoner one at a time?"

Les chuckled. "Always the funny man. I think they want conversation." He sat looking through the binoculars. "Those creatures had a heyday last night. I guess the pirates realize now that it'll only be a matter of time before they get them all."

"Good." Mike sat up. "Those lousy dirt-bags drank our wine and ate our food. Next thing you know the *San Mateo*'s going to sink." He stood up and arched his back.

"Ouch, I'm tired of sleeping on the ground, I'm tired of eating fruit and I miss my girl."

"Are you finished?" Les looked away from the binoculars with a mild grin.

"No," Mike said. "I'm just pissed off." He turned and looked out at the pirates a mile or so away. "Hey you assholes," he yelled. "Don't mess with the engine."

"Will you stop fooling around?" Les said.

"Who's fooling? Mind if I see the glasses?"

Les handed them over. "I don't think they're in much condition to mess with us today."

"To hell with them," Mike said. "I've had enough of them messing up our plans. I'd go over there and sprinkle barbecue sauce on each pirate personally if I thought it would make those sea creatures hurry up and finish them."

"Will you calm down and listen to me for just a minute?" Les said.

"Okay, I feel a little better now."

Les took back the binoculars and looked again. "I think we might be able to talk to them now that they realize they're in trouble."

"Why on earth would we want to talk to them?"

"To try to find out where they were when they went through the eye of the needle. They're as out of place here as we are and they had to have come from somewhere. Maybe they can shed some light on which way we should sail to find the eye of the needle, or maybe which way not to sail."

"I see your point. If they just came from the days of the American Revolution then we know where we don't want to be when that little ship starts spinning."

"Right," Les said. "We don't want to be wherever they were when they came through. If we're nice to them then maybe they'll tell us what it was like for them going through the eye and how far they've come since then."

"Yeah," Mike said. "And maybe they'll turn that cannon on us again and maybe this time they won't miss."

"I don't think they'll do that," Les said. "They're scared. I think they'll negotiate. Besides, I might be able to talk them into giving us back the *San Mateo*."

"They'll want the talisman in return," Mike said. "Let's just steal it back."

"Let's take a ride out there and see what we can accomplish. Then we'll play it by ear."

Mike looked again through the glasses. "Well, let's go."

A few minutes later the two of them were in the *Spear* headed for the *Scamp*.

Trixie stood on the beach whining and whimpering as they sped away. "Poor little thing thinks we're going to leave her," Mike said.

"She'll get over it," Les said. He steered toward the *Scamp* while Mike observed them through the glasses.

"They see us coming," Mike said. "We still have a few sticks of dynamite if we need it. It's under my seat."

"I don't think we'll need it. Still, it will be easier to talk peace if we're prepared to back it up with war."

As the small craft approached, the captain emerged in his dress uniform, what there was of it. He had met with all the men earlier, told them he needed a new first mate and prepared to name one. Everyone was shocked when it ended up being Creed, who figured the captain had been impressed by the way he handled himself in the early morning hours the day before.

"Mr. Creed," McGriff said. "You stay close when they get here. I might need your advice."

"Aye, Captain", Creed said. He still wasn't sure if his new title as first mate was an honor or a curse.

Every man on the **Scamp** was at the railing when the **Spear** approached.

"Greetings gentlemen," McGriff said when they got close enough to hear him.

Les kept his hand on the throttle and had the **Spear** turned sideways, parallel to the bigger ship. He was prepared to speed away if they made any false moves. Mike sat ready with dynamite sticks and the lighter.

"Morning Captain," Les said. "We noticed your white flag and decided to come out and chat."

"Yes, my good man," McGriff said. "I feel that we should stop being enemies."

Les and Mike looked at each other. Mike looked over at the cannon that had just missed them before. There was nobody standing next to it but there was a small amount of smoke rising from somewhere near it.

"Let's be sure we understand each other." Mike stood and revealed three sticks of dynamite. "I'm ready to attack at a moment's notice and you already know that I am a very good shot."

The men on deck began backing away from the railing.

"Let's keep this peaceful shall we?" Mike said. "You stay away from your cannon and I'll keep these unlit. Agreed?"

"Absolutely," McGriff said. "We don't want a fight with you."

"Good," Les said. "Now, why the white flag?"

"We seem to be encountering some sort of sea creatures at night that are slowly eliminating my men," McGriff

said. "I've noticed that they have demolished that merchant vessel as well. Yet, despite the fact that there are only
two of you the creatures don't seem to be giving you problems. I just want to know how you've managed to survive
when so many others have perished."

Les looked over at Mike. "I don't know where to start,"
Les said.

"Allow me," Mike said. "Let me ask you this captain, do
you know what month and year it is right now?"

"Of course I do." McGriff sounded a bit miffed. "It's
January, 1739."

Mike and Les both tried not to appear stunned.

"Not here it's not," Mike said. "Here, it is sometime
well before the birth of Christ, I'd say roughly 10,000 BC"

The pirates looked at each other and began muttering.
McGriff was not happy.

"We're from the twenty-first century ourselves," Mike said.

"I am in no mood to jest," McGriff said.

Mike noticed one of the pirates shuffling slowly toward
the cannon.

"I wouldn't do that if I were you." Mike showed the
dynamite again. The fellow froze in his tracks and held up
his hands.

Mike turned to the captain. "The creatures you are
encountering are some kind of ancient animal that lived in
the seas many centuries before man first appeared. Your
vessel has been pulled into an area in the ocean we call the
'Devil's Triangle'. Ours was as well. Somehow, we have
spanned a great deal of time into the past to arrive here."

The captain seemed to study Mike's face and was obviously not accepting what he was being told.

"Look at that ship over there." Mike pointed at the *San Mateo*. "Have you ever before seen a merchant vessel with a steel hull like that? What about this outboard motor that drives this boat with no sails or oars. Do these things come from your time?"

The captain was silent and the other men started muttering again. "There's some kind of a doorway out here in these waters," Les said. "A passageway to a different dimension or something. Whatever it is, it has an invisible opening that allows vessels to sail through to another time. We've been trying for months to find our way out and haven't managed to do it."

"What you are saying is preposterous," McGriff said. "However, I have seen much in the last several days that I cannot explain, so I must at least consider what you are saying as having some validity. This doorway you speak about, where is it?"

"We don't know," Mike said. "You can't see it or know when you are approaching it. The only thing we do know is that you notice changes when you pass through, changes in time of day and weather, stuff like that. It's kind of like going through a tunnel."

"We have not been through any 'tunnel'," McGriff said angrily. He glanced over at the pirate near the cannon.

"Hey," Mike yelled, showing the dynamite again. "I'm a real good shot. I could throw this down your throat from here."

The gunner backed away.

"Why don't you stop this joke," McGriff said. "My vessel has not experienced any of the things you speak of."

"Yes we have, sir," Creed said.

McGriff looked over at his new first mate.

"I remember going over some kind of bump during my watch a few nights ago," Creed said.

"You never reported this to me." McGriff snarled.

"I didn't know there was anything to report," Creed said. "We went through a fog bank that blocked my view of the back of the ship for a moment, that's all. I did not know we had traveled back in time. The only thing I noticed was the change in the cold weather."

McGriff looked stunned.

"How do we get back through this doorway?" McGriff said.

"You'll just have to get lucky," Les said.

The entire pirate crew seemed to be let down by the response.

"Look," Mike said. "Your latitude seems to have some bearing on the situation. Have you traveled north or south in the last several days?"

"A little south," Creed replied.

McGriff glared at him. "Shut-up."

"How far south?" Les said.

Creed looked at the captain for his okay to reply. After a few seconds the Captain nodded.

"Two days' full sail," Creed said.

"Okay, thanks." Les gunned the engine. "See ya."

"Hey, wait," McGriff said. "What about those creatures?"

"Stay awake all night and fight them with your swords," Les said over the roar of the motor.

"Yeah," Mike said. "They taste great with carrots and potatoes." He looked at Les and they both laughed. They sped away quickly. Mike looked back and saw that the pirates weren't even attempting to fire at them. All McGriff was doing was shaking his fist and yelling.

They returned to the island and pulled the boat ashore to the same spot. Trixie had been watching them approach and was wagging her tail vigorously when they arrived.

"Why don't we catch some fish for dinner?" Mike said.

"I'm for that." Les pulled out the fishing poles from the long compartment that ran the length of the inside of the *Spear*.

Mike fished out a few minnows using the net in the calm water near where they beached the boat and they soon were baiting the hooks. As they fished they watched the pirates off in the distance.

"Maybe we'll go back out and visit with them tomorrow," Les said. "Maybe find out how many of them survived the night."

"Hopefully none of them," Mike said. "We need to get our ship back and soon." He stared at the rusty merchant vessel.

"Try not to think about it," Les said. They caught what they thought they'd need and then headed inland to start the fire.

CHAPTER 20

▼

QUASARS IN THE BERMUDA TRIANGLE

Sometime around three in the morning, the dog's growling awakened Mike. There was a humming sound coming from the water and he snapped alert fearing there was someone coming toward them in a boat. He sat up and listened. The fire had burned down to just embers and there was virtually no light except for the fading moon.

"Les, wake up," he whispered. He heard Les stir but wasn't sure if he was awake or not. "Do you hear that sound?"

"What sound?" Les said groggily.

"That loud hum," Mike said. "It sounds like it's coming from out toward the merchant vessel."

"Maybe those idiots are fooling with the engine," he said. "Don't worry about it."

Mike sat listening a moment longer. "It doesn't sound like the *San Mateo*'s engine to me." He thought again of the eerie sound that he heard while out on the water so long ago in the *Dream*, that sound of the third voice one heard when two people scream simultaneously. "I think I'll go have a look."

Les remained motionless.

Mike felt around in the dark for the burlap bag and located the binoculars. Walking down to the spot where the trees met the small beach, he trained the glasses on the pirates. The two ships, the *San Mateo* and the *Scamp*, sat in their usual places. Both were still and dark except for a couple of lanterns visible on both decks. Nothing seemed out of the ordinary except the strange sound. The humming noise Mike was hearing had gotten louder. From what he could tell it wasn't coming from the *San Mateo* at all.

"Les," he said. "Come here, quick! There's something going on out there."

Mike took another look in the binoculars. "I see something." Les walked slowly over to Mike and stood next to him.

"I hear something too," Les said. "But I don't see anything."

Mike handed him the glasses. "Look right over there. I see a dark object cutting through the water. It looks like a big shadow."

Les looked where Mike was pointing. "I do see something," he whispered. "It's heading toward the pirate vessel. You're right about it looking like a shadow. I think it's a black ship of some kind, with no running lights whatsoever."

"Apparently the pirates hear it too," Mike whispered. "They're all out on deck looking in that direction."

"I can't figure out what that is," Les said. "It looks like a ship of some kind but it's darker than the night itself."

"Maybe it's another hidden secret of the Bermuda Triangle," Mike said. "Let me have a look."

Les handed back the glasses. The dark object was getting close to the pirates now. All of a sudden an extremely bright searchlight came on and illuminated the deck of the pirate ship. A moment later, the dark vessel's lights came on, illuminating its deck, cabin and large antennae.

"It's another ship all right," Mike said. "A really fancy one."

"Let me see the binoculars," Les said. Mike handed them back and they watched silently for several seconds.

"That is one advanced watercraft," Les said. "Whoever they are, they certainly aren't from the eighteenth century."

"Judging by the humming sound it must be all electric," Mike said. "I can't imagine an electric engine that powerful."

"I can see several people on board it now." Les continued to watch through the binoculars. "They've pulled alongside the *Scamp* and are boarding it. Looks like they're carrying rifles too.

"Wait a minute. I can see one of those sea creatures on the deck." A weapon fired with a trail of red light and the sea creature collapsed to the deck emitting smoke from its wounds. "Wow, those are laser weapons they're carrying. These guys must have come from farther into the future than we did."

"A lot farther," Mike said. "Let me see."

Les handed the glasses back.

"A couple of the new guys have gone aboard the merchant vessel," Mike said. "They're leading the pirates at gunpoint back aboard the *Scamp*." Mike caught a faint whiff of smoke from the campfire and took his eyes away from the binoculars. "We'd better make sure the fire doesn't advertise our presence. We sure don't need to let these guys know we're over here watching them."

"It's out," Les whispered. "I tossed some sand on the remaining embers right after you woke me."

Mike resumed watching through the binoculars. "That's odd. Once the last of the men from the merchant vessel was aboard the *Scamp*, they cut down the rope bridge between the two vessels."

Mike took a closer look at the new vessel. It was smaller than the *Scamp* and sat lower in the water. The men from it had deployed a gangplank that rose sharply uphill to the pirate's ship. A man just walking up the gangplank caught his attention. He appeared to be studying the readout on some kind of device he was holding in his hand. Mike could clearly see that all of the pirates, including McGriff, were now standing fast with their hands up.

"One guy is walking from pirate to pirate with some kind of detection device," Mike said. "He's scanning each man one at a time."

A pirate jumped from the shadows and ran at one of the intruders. Another one of them saw him and fired with his laser weapon. The pirate fell in a smoky heap onto the deck. Faint shouting could then be heard. As Mike watched there was more laser fire on the deck. More shouting followed. "I hope none of those pirates thinks to mention us to those new guys," Mike said.

"Let me look," Les said.

Mike handed the binoculars back. "I wonder what it is they're looking for," Les said.

"Whatever it is, it's obviously small enough to be carried on a person," Mike whispered. "Do you suppose it's gold they're after?"

"Maybe," Les said. "But they sure are looking for small pieces if they are searching the sailors individually." The strangers continued to hold the pirates at gunpoint while the man with the hand-held device began moving about the deck. "Looks like he's searching the rest of the ship now. Those guys sure are high-tech. I'll bet they're from at least one-hundred years farther into the future than we are."

"I can't figure out what they want with those pirates," Mike said. "If it's gold they want, then it would seem that there are plenty of other places they'd check before messing with them. It must be something else."

"It's real strange," Les said. "Whatever it is, they sure want it badly." He handed the glasses back to Mike.

There was more laser fire on the deck but Mike couldn't tell what was hit. The strangers walked around the deck a moment more, each of them apparently very interested in what the one with the hand-held device was doing. He walked back down the gangplank and the others followed. Mike kept his eyes on the one with the device. He appeared to turn it off and then snapped it onto his belt. A moment later the gangplank lowered from the edge of the *Scamp*'s deck and disappeared into the side of the newer vessel. The humming sound grew louder and the small ship began to back slowly away, keeping the pirates in the spotlight the whole time.

"Looks like they're leaving," Mike said. "I wonder where they're headed next. Want to look?"

"Yeah."

Mike handed the glasses back to him and Les tried to see as much as he could of the dark vessel. As he watched, a harpoon of some kind was fired from the smaller vessel and hit the *Scamp* with a loud thud. "They're tying some kind of line to the pirate ship," Les said. "I think they're going to tow it somewhere."

"Why in the hell would they do that?" Mike said. "This just doesn't make sense."

Mike and Les watched as the mysterious vessel began backing up, pulling the *Scamp* away from the merchant vessel. After they dragged it about three hundred yards, the towline was pulled loose and retrieved. "They've cut it loose now," Les said. He looked over at Mike and shook his head.

Suddenly the humming sound could be heard again. The sound grew louder and louder, gradually approaching a crescendo. Then a large, wide beam of bright red light blasted from the front of the dark ship. The *Scamp* glowed red for a moment, then exploded. For about ten seconds the resulting fireball flashed as bright as day before fading into darkness again. The *Scamp* was reduced to a few chunks of smoldering wood, floating in the water over an area the size of a football field. "Damn," Les said. "They destroyed the whole ship."

"Those guys don't fool around," Mike said. "They got what they wanted and then destroyed everything." He looked at Les. "Are you thinking what I'm thinking?" he asked.

"I believe I am." Les whispered. "If they spot us over here then they'll come kill us too."

"What about that hand-held detection device?" Mike said. "If they've got something that detects gold then it'll only be a matter of minutes before they realize we're here."

"You're right," Les said. "In fact, it may be our gold that attracted them in the first place. We know the pirates did-n't have any. They may have been drawn in this direction because they detected our gold. Then followed the logical order of things by boarding the first vessel they saw."

"And with the pirates out of the way they'll keep searching the area until they find the source of the signal," Mike said. He looked out at the dark vessel and saw it approaching the *San Mateo*. "It looks like they've turned their attention to the merchant vessel now."

From their place under the trees on the small island, Mike and Les watched as the mysterious boat pulled up alongside the large ship. The man with the hand-held device appeared on deck again and began taking a reading. He then gave a hand signal and the gangplank was deployed. It fed out from the side of the ship and then raised steadily upward until it attached itself to the deck of the larger vessel high overhead. "Look," Les said. "That gang plank's adjustable. It's now extended farther out and up to adjust to the size of the ship they want to board. Pretty fancy."

"I guess they're going to search it and then destroy it just like they did the *Scamp*," Mike said. He looked over at Les. "I don't think it takes a sixth sense to figure out what they'll do next."

Les was watching intently with the binoculars. "That guy with the device has a second tool out now. He has one in each hand. I guess he's doing two different kinds of readings."

"Obviously, one of them detects gold or whatever they were searching for on the pirates," Mike said. "My guess is that the other one detects living things or movement. Something humans do."

"I'll bet you're right," Les said. "I'm convinced they're going to come over here as soon as they're done with the *San Mateo*."

"If they do then we're dead," Mike said. "We don't have anything to fight back with but a few pieces of dynamite, which won't do much against those laser weapons. We've got to do something fast."

Les watched as the man with the devices led the others aboard the *San Mateo*. "I count six people going up the gang-plank," Les said. "From what I can see there's nobody left aboard the smaller vessel. It won't take them long to determine that there's no gold on that ship."

"I figure we've got about a ten minute head start," Mike said. "If we jump in the *Spear* and head the other way then maybe we can get out of detection range before they continue the search. That's our only hope."

"That won't work," Les said. "It would only take them a few minutes to get us."

"Then what the hell are we going to do?"

Les looked over at him and grinned. "I've got a better idea. You're experienced at driving powerful boats. Do you think you could drive that thing?"

Mike's eyes got wide. "You mean that fancy ship? Are you suggesting we try stealing it?"

"I don't consider self-preservation to be stealing," Les said. "Besides, have you got any better ideas?" He took another look through the glasses. The six men had disappeared inside the *San Mateo*. "We're down to nine minutes."

"Well, it beats the hell out of waiting for them to come get us," Mike said. "You think we can sneak aboard in the *Spear?*"

"We won't know until we try," Les said. "It's now or never."

"Hell," Mike said. "Let's do it." He grabbed the dog while Les grabbed the little gold ship and the burlap bag of gold. They ran to the *Spear*. A moment later they were racing for the fancy boat and praying that nobody would hear them coming.

As they approached, Mike sat up front and watched the deck of the merchant vessel closely. Les steered the *Spear* in a direct line; going full-throttle at first and then slowing down to cut the noise as they got closer. When they were only ten yards or so away Les cut the speed to a crawl.

"Just one of those guys walks out on deck and it's over," Mike said.

The sputtering motor seemed awfully loud as they approached the mysterious vessel. Mike stared at it as they got closer. It seemed smaller than it looked from far away. The hull was now brightly illuminated by deck lights from bow to stern. The name *Quasar I* was printed on the hull in fancy lettering. It was sleek, dynamic and very high-tech. There were many similarities to the boats of Les and Mike's day, but this one somehow looked even more extraordinary.

They were getting close now, only a few more feet, and there was still nobody to be seen either on the *Quasar* or on the deck of the *San Mateo*. Mike began to assess what he saw as they got near. She was an inboard, a cabin up front with a flat deck taking up the back half. She appeared to be a twenty-four footer with long narrow portholes just below the deck in the front that provided windows for the lower deck. She also emitted a low humming sound as the electric engine idled.

When they got up alongside, Les put the *Spear* into neutral and Mike raised up and peered over the side of the *Quasar*. There was nobody aboard, at least not that he could see. He reached up and grabbed the railing that ran around the perimeter of the deck. The first thing that caught his attention was the large gun mounted to the deck in front of the cabin windows. It looked like a big satellite dish of some kind, aimed straight ahead. He glanced up and saw several large antennae and other types of communication apparatus mounted on the roof.

"Go ahead and crawl aboard," Les whispered.

Mike pulled himself up and quietly slipped onto the *Quasar's* deck. The hull was amazingly slick, even more so than fiberglass. He slowly stood up and looked in the windows and through the open doorway. He saw no one.

"It's all clear," he whispered.

"Good," Les said. "See if you can find a weapon of some kind. We need to arm ourselves fast so we'll be ready if those guys come back out." Les picked up the dog and set her onto the deck. She immediately ran into the open door of the cabin and disappeared inside. "Hopefully she'll growl if she finds anybody." He grabbed the bag of gold and the binoculars and set them on the *Quasar's* deck. He then reached down and put the *Spear* back in gear. Setting the throttle on low, he aimed it back out to sea and pushed it off. The unmanned boat began to slowly sputter away.

Once Les got inside the cabin Mike handed him a laser rifle. "Here you go," Mike said. "Now, let me see if I can get this thing running." Les found a seat at the back of the sleek boat while Mike rushed to the controls and sat down at the wheel.

Mike found the *Quasar*'s controls to be similar to ships he had driven. Most yachts were basically the same and it only took a moment for him to figure out how to drive it. He pushed a button marked "Gang Plank" and the platform dislodged itself from the *San Mateo*'s deck and retracted into the side of the *Quasar*'s hull. He then put the throttle in gear and the ship began to pull quietly away.

Les took aim with the laser rifle at the *San Mateo*'s deck. As the *Quasar* started pulling away, one of the men on the *San Mateo* walked out on deck and spotted the *Spear*. "Hey," he shouted. "There's another boat out here." An instant later he noticed the *Quasar* being piloted in the opposite direction. He grabbed his gun to fire.

Les pulled the trigger and a red beam of light emitted from the barrel of the rifle. The stream of laser fire went just over the man's head and threw sparks everywhere as it struck the wall behind him. The other five men had run out onto the deck and all six of them dove for cover as Les kept firing, sending sparks everywhere and lighting up the *San Mateo*'s deck.

Mike hit the throttle and the boat accelerated away. The men on the *San Mateo*'s deck fired back at them but none of the shots hit. A moment later they were well out of range.

Les made his way up to the cabin and sat in the seat across the aisle from Mike. Once Mike saw that he was seated safely, he pushed the throttle even more. Within a few seconds they were cruising at over a hundred knots.

"Wow," Mike said. "This is the most incredible boat I've ever seen." He sat back and laughed. The wonderful sensation of driving a fast boat overcame him again. It gave him a warm feeling all over. It felt like the first time.

"Take a look at that console," Les said. "It has indicators for everything."

"I really haven't had a chance to study it," Mike said. "I don't want to take my eyes away from the water at this speed."

"Good thinking," Les said. "Why don't we go due east and get over the horizon from those other guys. Once we're safely away from them we can shut down for a while and decide what to do next." Mike turned slightly to the left toward the east.

After a few minutes, the *San Mateo* had disappeared over the horizon behind them. Mike decided they had gone far enough and cut the speed, bringing the boat to a smooth halt.

As they came to drift in the empty sea, they decided to spend a little time getting to know the vessel.

Mike looked over at Les and smiled. "I think our chances of getting back to present-day Florida just increased ten-fold."

He peered at the controls in front of the steering wheel where he sat. The quartz digital speedometer had peaked at around one-hundred-thirty knots during their high-speed getaway and now read zero.

"Let's see if we can get anything on the radio," Les said. He flipped on the switch and they immediately heard voices. "Hey," Les said. "Sounds like we've got something."

He pointed to a light next to the microphone with fine print beside it that read "MIC ON". The light was off. "As long as that light's off then we can't be overheard." For the next several minutes they chose to only listen.

"*Quasar Two*, this is *Starrider*," said the voice on the radio. "We've just learned that *Quasar One* has been hijacked by two unidentified men. Their current location is sector 7718, northeast quadrant. How long will it take you to get there?"

Mike looked over at Les with a surprised expression on his face.

"We're currently about six minutes away from *Quasar One*'s present location, *Starrider*," came the reply. There was a brief pause. Les figured the crew was deploying their vessel at that moment. "We have it on radar," the voice said. "We're en route now. As soon as we can lock-on we'll take control of her."

"Excellent," the first voice said. "Don't hesitate to destroy it if necessary. Repeat, green light to destroy vessel."

"Acknowledged," the second voice said. The radio went silent. A few moments later someone gave the order to switch to a back-up channel and nothing more was heard.

"I think they just realized we might be listening," Les said. "I doubt they wanted us to know their intentions."

"A lucky break for us. At least we know they'll be here pretty soon." Mike glanced around at the dark ocean surrounding them. He reached for the throttle and got them moving again.

Les went back to studying the controls. "I've got to figure out how to operate the laser cannon on the deck. Looks like we're going to need it."

"Wait a minute," Mike said. "What's this thing marked 'STEALTH'?" Les looked where Mike was pointing. "It must be some kind of masking device. Don't go any faster. I'm going out on deck. When I give you the signal I want you to flip that switch and we'll see if anything happens."

Careful to keep his balance in the speeding boat, Les walked to the back deck, holding the railing firmly as he went. He then hollered to Mike to turn on the "Stealth" function. Mike hit the switch and two round metal bars, each roughly the size of a baseball bat, lifted up from the roof of the *Quasar*. Each bar then opened up into a "T" shape and started to spin slowly around. A moment later the ship slowed just a bit.

"I'm getting a reading that it's deployed," Mike said.

"Good." Les returned to the cabin.

"There's another function here called 'Chameleon'," Mike said. "You want to try it too?"

"Wouldn't hurt. Let me get back out there first." Les walked back out to the deck and gave Mike the go ahead. Mike hit the switch and the entire exterior of the *Quasar* began to change color. The sea and sky were both a dark grayish color. It was still night, although the first signs of dawn could be seen in the east. Over the span of one minute, the *Quasar* became the same color as the sea and all exterior lights went out.

"Hey." Mike looked out the windshield. "I can actually see where we're going."

Les walked into the cabin and looked out the front windshield. Although everything was a greenish color, they could see the tops of the waves in the water and a line that formed the horizon ahead. They could even see stars in the sky, marked by little green dots on the windshield.

"This vessel has 'Night Vision'," Les said.

"I can't believe it," Mike said. He glanced over at the radar screen and noticed that it had gone dark. "Look, the radar has gone out."

"The ship's computers must have shut it down automatically when we activated the concealing devices," Les said. "Any radar signals we emit could be traced to their source."

"Oh, I see," Mike said. There was another screen right next to the radar screen labeled "Listen". It had a grid on it similar to the one on the radar screen and indicated the presence of something about thirty nautical miles away.

"That 'Listen' screen must replace the radar when we're concealed," Les said. "I guess it detects sounds and vibrations."

"You want to see if there's an owner's manual lying around here someplace?" Mike said. "I'll bet this thing can do lots of other amazing things."

"Okay," Les agreed. "But meanwhile, speed-up and get us out of here before those creeps get any closer."

Les started searching the cabin drawers and soon was below decks looking in cabinets as well. The cabins below were luxurious but inspecting them in detail would have to wait. He finished his brief search and returned topside. "No sign of any written instructions."

"Doesn't surprise me," Mike said. "The information is probably buried somewhere in the computers. I'll have to find it later."

Les turned his attention back to the radio. It had been totally silent now for about fifteen minutes. "I guess we're in a quiet game of cat and mouse," he said.

"What do you suppose that guy meant when he said they'd take over the vessel once they could 'lock-on'?" Mike said. "Do you think they've got some kind of override capabilities, something that allows them to control this vessel from theirs?"

"Yes," Les said. "They probably have to get close, maybe within line-of-sight of us to do it. But I'll bet that's exactly what he meant." He looked at Mike. "If they pull that off then we're finished."

"Well, we'll just have to make sure they don't." Mike continued to drive as the two of them sat thinking.

"Hey," Mike said. "It seems to me, that logically, there would be a security device to defend against that override feature. That way they could keep themselves from being taken over by someone else in another vessel with the same technology."

"Of course," Les said. "There has to be a security device of some kind. The only question is, can we find it before it's too late?"

"We don't have much choice," Mike said. "Where do you think it'll be?"

"It could be anywhere," Les said. "It may be a device that's built into the engine or it could be a chip in the ship's computer."

"Ouch," Mike said. "Finding it could take a while." He took a moment to stretch. "I'm about ready to stop driving. There's nothing showing on the 'Listen' screen. We've gone about fifty miles since we activated the Chameleon and Stealth functions. If they're working properly then we should be invisible to any long-range detection devices. Why don't we park and start searching."

"Sounds okay," Les said. "I'll start trying to get into the computers. Why don't you try searching inside the console."

"Okay." Mike pulled the throttle to neutral and the *Quasar* came to a halt. The ignition was push-button and he decided to turn it off.

When Mike had completed shutting down the *Quasar*, a small alarm on the console began flashing. "What's this?" Something labeled "DECK GUARD" was flashing and buzzing. "Hey Les, come see what you make of this."

Les appeared in the cabin a moment later. "Deck Guard? What do you suppose that is?"

"Burglar alarm?"

"Must be." Les reached over and pushed the button to turn it on. A moment later they could hear the doors on either side of the cabin that led to the exterior deck lock automatically. The buzzer stopped and a green light came on.

"I think I know what that thing is for," Mike said. "The people that designed this vessel must know about the sea creatures in these waters. They built the decks with some kind of barrier, probably an electric one, to keep them at bay. The doors lock automatically to keep a forgetful passenger from wandering out on the deck and getting fried."

"Very ingenious," Les said. "There must be a photo-electric cell on the roof to detect darkness. That sets off the alarm to remind the pilot that the Deck Guard needs to be turned on. Otherwise some unwanted visitors may be showing up soon."

"I'm just glad it wasn't activated when we first came aboard," Mike said. "If it had been it would have fried me."

"I guess they figured they'd only be aboard the big merchant vessel for a few minutes and it wouldn't be a problem." Les gently tried the door to confirm that it was indeed secure.

"You know what's really scary about the whole thing?" Mike said. "This Deck Guard system, by its very existence, tells me that they already knew about the sea creatures when they first built the ship. They knew what they were getting into when they first came here."

"You're right," Les said. "they came here from the same way we did. But this means they're here by choice."

"It also means they must have done a lot of research," Mike said. "And I mean the field variety, not just in the drawing room. They may have been sending vessels back and forth through the eye of the needle for years."

Les looked out the window at the dark ocean. "That's unbelievable. How in the world have they been doing it?"

"The main thing I want to know is why have they been doing it?" Mike said.

"Maybe the ship's computers will tell us something," Les said. "I'll be down below if you need me."

Now that the boat had stopped, Trixie came out from her hiding place somewhere below decks and began running around.

"Let me get you some water," Mike said. They had left her things on the *San Mateo* but he found a bowl in one of the cabinets in the small galley and got some water from the sink.

Les went to the den and started fooling with one of the computers. General information was accessible and plentiful. When he went after technical information like the plans for the *Quasar* engine and its manufacturer, somebody called Starrider Corporation, the computer politely told him that he would have to produce a password for clearance to delve into that area.

"It looks like I've hit a dead-end down here," he called out. "This computer wants a password."

"No problem." Mike walked down the stairs. "I'll get in there later and give it one."

Les looked over at him with an amused expression. "Just like that, huh?"

Mike smiled broadly. "Yeah, just like that. First I want to look inside the console but I need some tools." He looked around and spotted a small closet in the middle of the lower deck that had a label on the door that read: "Utility Room." "That looks like a good place to start." Inside were several shelves. He chose a screwdriver and noticed that it had a small button. "Cool," he said as he hit the button and the point started to spin slowly. There was also a small switch on it to reverse the spin.

Les grabbed a screwdriver himself and began looking for removable tiles in the floor.

When Mike got on the floor under the *Quasar*'s steering column he spotted several screws that held the outer cover to the wall. Within a couple of minutes he had the front casing of the base of the console completely off. It was dark inside but he spotted a small switch and flicked it on. A light came on, completely illuminating a six-by-eight inch circuit board. On the inside wall to the left was a metal plate that was about two inches high and six inches long. The plate was held into place by a screw in each corner. "I wonder what's in here," he muttered.

A few seconds of applying the screwdriver had the plate off. He smiled. "Hey, Les. I think I've got something."

Les came rushing up.

"Come down here and take a peek." Mike backed out of the small area. "Look inside this doorway and to the left."

Les got down on his hands and knees and stuck his head in. There were six little dials imbedded in the wall that read the number 107239.

"That looks like some kind of serial number to me," Mike said. "The numbers can be changed by turning those little dials underneath each digit. I'll just bet that's some kind of combination. That's the code they'll use to take over this vessel."

"I'll bet you're right," Les said. "I'm going to change it." He reached over and started turning the dials to different numbers. "I guess it wouldn't hurt to make it a number we can remember. Got one handy?"

"How about my birth date," Mike said. "061569".

Les input the new numbers. "I'll leave the metal plate off in case we want to change it later." He crawled back out.

Mike took a quick glance around the circuits before replacing the front panel. "I wonder how long the batteries last in this boat."

"With so much more technology than we have going into it," Les said, "probably months or even a year. How about something to eat?"

Mike smiled. "I thought you'd never ask."

They headed below to the small galley and looked inside the freezer that was built into the floor. There were all kinds of frozen foods that could be heated by microwave. They each made a breakfast selection with another for the dog and put them into the oven.

The food was delicious. They ate, then Mike fed Trixie while Les took a shower in the small bathroom. Mike then enjoyed a shower himself. When he got out he found Les asleep in the pilot's chair up at the console. The sun was up and the sea all around was empty. It appeared to be a good time to finish the night's sleep they had started on the island the evening before. Mike plopped into the co-pilot's seat and soon was asleep himself.

CHAPTER 21

▼

GETTING ACQUAINTED

A short time later, the *Quasar*'s radio came on and woke them both. "This is *Starrider* calling *Quasar One*, come in please, over," a voice said.

"I guess that's us," Les said. He reached for the "MIC ON" button.

"Hey," Mike said. "You're not going to respond are you?"

"Sure, why not?"

"They might be able to trace the signal and find us," Mike said.

"We're still concealed," Les said. "Besides, they might have something interesting to say." He opened the channel and responded. "This is *Quasar One*. We read you."

"To whom am I speaking?" the voice said.

"My name is Les and with me is my friend Mike," Les said.

"You have stolen my ship," the man said. "I want it back right now. Surrender and we'll let you live."

That last comment left Les a bit surprised and he took a moment before responding. "Well, good morning to you, too," he said at last. "I'm glad to hear you are in such a generous mood this fine morning." He looked over at Mike and winked.

"Turn off the concealing devices and we'll come meet with you," the voice said. "I promise we won't kill you if you cooperate."

"Well, that's mighty neighborly of you," Les said. "I especially find that encouraging considering how nice you were to that ship full of pirates you killed last night. Too bad you didn't notice that we were on the little island watching the whole ordeal. You didn't even give those poor guys a chance. Do you think I'm stupid enough to believe you wouldn't do the same thing to me? You're not getting your ship back so you can just forget it."

"Now you listen to me, you brainless bastard," the voice said. "It'll only be a matter of time before we find you and when we do I'm going to enjoy stringing you up."

Mike reached over and took the microphone from Les. "What's your name, bucket mouth?"

"Greg Fannin," the voice said. "President and CEO of the Starrider Corporation. I happen to own the ship you are sitting in right now."

"Correction," Mike said, "you used to own it. The *Quasar* has been confiscated. Consider it payback for the lives of all those pirates that you saw fit to take last night."

"Mike and Les," Fannin said sarcastically. "Do you fools have last names? I just want to know so we can put them on your headstones."

"We do," Mike said. "But you won't be needing them. As for you and your belligerent attitude I think there is something you might be interested in knowing. We've taken the liberty of changing the secret code of this vessel so you won't be liberating it from us. You are no longer in control of the situation. Instead, it is I who am in control here. You will not give orders; you will only take them. You get me dickhead?" He closed the microphone and looked over at Les and laughed.

"Jeez," Les said. "Lay it on thick." They waited for Fannin's reply but were getting only silence at the moment.

"This is Dr. Henry Spellman," another voice said over the radio. "Do you mind telling me where you are from?"

"I don't see any harm in answering that one," Mike said. "Florida."

"Well," Spellman said. "I was referring to the place in history. I guess I should have said 'when' instead of 'where'."

"I'm sorry Dr. Spellman," Mike said. "I can't answer that one." A flashing indicator on the dashboard caught his attention.

"Say, Spellman," Mike said. "What does it mean when this indicator on the console lights up?"

"What indicator is that?" Spellman said.

"This one that says 'ATMOSPHERIC DISRUP-TION'," Mike said. "It's flashing like crazy."

"It means you're in trouble," Spellman said. "Look outside. What do you see?"

Mike looked out. It was starting to rain and a thick fog was rolling in. "It doesn't look good," Mike said. "The outside thermometer indicates that the temperature is dropping fast."

"That's enough," Les said. "Don't tell them anything more. I think that 'ATMOSPHERIC DISRUPTION' indicator is some kind of invention they came up with to spot the eye of the needle."

Mike froze and stared at him. "Think so?"

Les pulled out the burlap bag and reached inside for the little gold ship. When he set it on the deck it didn't spin at all. The only thing it did was tip over on its side and slide across the deck when the boat shifted in the surf. "I don't understand. For some reason the indicator on the dashboard is giving a readout and the talisman isn't moving at all."

"Maybe there are two different kinds of openings in the vortex," Mike said. "I don't know how that could be, though."

"Me neither," Les said. He stepped out on the deck and walked to the railing. The air temperature had plunged about forty degrees and the wind was really kicking up. When he put his hand on the railing it burned him with cold. A moment later a thick fog began surrounding them.

Les stepped back inside the cabin and closed the door with a shiver. "The radio's gone dead," Mike said. "And according to the console, the masking devices are off-line as well.

"Oh hell," Les said. "I have a feeling they know exactly where we are."

CHAPTER 22

THE WRATH OF THE TRIANGLE

The wall of fog reached the *Quasar* and immediately enveloped it. Along with the fog came large, rough waves and pelting rain. The ATMOSPHERIC DISRUPTION" indicator on the console started emitting a buzzing sound that went on and off with a flashing red light. Mike found himself struggling to control the ship and he and Les both fought to stay in their seats. After several minutes, the *Quasar's* engine died suddenly and left them totally without power. Any attempts to restart it proved useless. "Oh no," Mike said, "we're dead in the water."

Les started fooling with the controls. "There's no apparent reason for engine failure. It's almost as if the atmosphere is sucking the power right out. The only thing I can figure is that heavy static electricity in the air is somehow rendering the electric engine useless."

"Hopefully it's having the same effect on their vessels too." Mike looked outside. "If not and they find us, then we're defenseless."

"I wish I knew how large a fleet they have," Les said.

"We may be about to find out if we can't do something fast," Mike said. He looked down and saw the talisman slide past him along the floor when the boat shifted and he reached down to grab it. The two of them then got belted into their seats to try to ride out the storm. At that moment hail started falling and the sea got even rougher. The giant waves tried to capsize the *Quasar* but the well designed boat remained upright. Mike looked at the console and noticed that the gyroscope that sat atop it was spinning around. Outside, bright flashes of lightning immediately preceded deafening crashes of thunder.

"The wrath of the Bermuda Triangle strikes again," Les said.

"This is exactly what the weather was like when I first got tossed from my boat into this awful place," Mike said.

"Same here," Les said. "I'm not letting the boat throw me out this time!"

"I heard that," Mike said.

The violent weather kept getting worse and the fog got so thick that it was difficult to even see the front railing only ten feet in front of them. At times the entire boat went completely airborne before splashing back into the sea. Mike decided not to mention to Les that if they had been in *One Summer Dream* they'd be dead by now. "I've got to give that Greg Fannin credit," he said. "He's built the toughest boat I've ever seen."

The pounding hail eventually turned to rain, but the storm went on for almost an hour before it finally began to abate. Mike and Les spent the entire time looking outside and hoping not to see any other ships. Finally the rain tapered off and the wind started to calm. A few minutes later the surf backed off. It was only about another fifteen minutes before the sky cleared up and the warm sunshine started burning off the dense fog. The sea continued to be rougher than usual but was considerably calmer than it had been during the height of the storm.

Mike kept trying the ignition periodically to no avail. At first, the *Quasar* only made a clicking sound when he tried starting her. Once the last of the fog cleared, the engine started turning over just a little. After the sun came back out and juiced-up the solar collectors on the roof, he was finally able to crank her up.

"Excellent," Les said when the instruments suddenly came to life. "Let's get the hell out of here." He had been holding a laser rifle and looking around, expecting to have another *Quasar* appear and start pounding them just any minute. They were both relieved to see no other vessels around when the fog cleared. Once the engine was running again they could at least run for it. Mike activated the concealing devices and hit the throttle.

"The first opportunity we get I think we should try using that solar sail," Mike said as the *Quasar* slowly picked up speed. "She's just not responding like she was before." He checked the power indicator and saw that the batteries had about a quarter of their normal energy supply. The switch on the console marked "Solar Sail" also included the phrase: "Maximum velocity 50 knots when deployed." "I just hope we get the chance before the batteries run completely dry."

"Looks like we weren't the only ones inconvenienced," Les said. The laser rifle still lay in his lap as he continued to scan the horizon. "Knock on wood."

About an hour later Mike slowed them down. "You want to drive a while? I'm getting tired."

"Sure," Les said.

Mike removed the seat belt and stood up. "Now that the surf has calmed, I thought I'd go below and see if I can do anything with the ship's computers. Since they're from so far in the future I'm afraid they may be over my head."

"They're certainly over mine," Les said. "I tried my luck with them this morning and couldn't get past the passwords."

"I'm good at beating those," Mike said. "At least I used to be."

"Just be careful not to emit a signal that they can trace," Les said. "Or the next thing we know they may be breathing down our necks."

"I'll be careful." Mike stood a moment studying the ocean around them. "The first question I'd like answered is 'why'."

"Why what?" Les said.

"Why are those jokers going around killing everybody they see? There's no profit in it for them. Those pirates certainly weren't a threat. I just can't figure out their motivation."

"Maybe the computers will shed some light." Les continued steering the *Quasar* around, careful not to form a pattern.

"Or, if not, maybe the database of the mother ship will," Mike said. "I bet I could learn a lot in a very short time."

"Now how do you think you're going to get to do that?"

Mike studied the instrument panel a moment. "I used to do some computer hacking as part of my job with the Department of Natural Resources. We found out a lot about drug dealers that way. Whenever we confiscated computer equipment I was the one in the department assigned to get in and derive information that could be used in court. I got pretty good at beating security systems and bypassing passwords. Many times I found information that caused some of those drug runners to hang themselves during the trial. We caught a lot of co-conspirators that way too."

He glanced over at the "Listen" screen. It revealed nothing. "They're probably a good distance away from us at the moment," he said. "If we let them know where we are then they'll have to let down their concealing devices to get here as fast as they can. Once they do that I might be able to link-up with their database."

"Only one problem," Les said. "How are you going to get them to drop their cover?"

Mike pointed at the gun turret. "Suppose we start firing shots with this thing. They're bound to hear it and start probing us. Even if they stay concealed I still might be able to trace the signal. If so, then maybe I can hack into their database. I could get a lot of information before they realize what I'm doing and lock me out."

"Hey, that might work," Les said. "But first, you need to hack your way into the computers on this boat. Once you've mastered that then we can try virtually boarding the *Starrider*."

"The needle on the battery indicator is getting close to the bottom," Mike said. "We'd better charge-up now while the sun is out and things are calm."

"Good idea," Les said. "I'll get us charged. You go start hacking." He hit the button marked "Solar Sail" and a soft hydraulic noise came from underneath the deck.

Mike looked outside and watched as two large poles, each pulling a thick wire mesh, appeared from either side of the boat up near the bow. Once fully extended, the poles swung out and back like two huge arms, locking into place at the stern and forming wings on either side of the vessel.

When the process was completed, the *Quasar* looked like a big round disk, with wings on each side that extended about thirty feet out and about five feet above the surface of the water. The wings, which were made of some kind of light, flexible material, were covered with solar panels.

A green light on the console came on and indicated to Les that the vessel was charging. "It's working," he said. "The Chameleon device deactivated itself, but the Stealth function is still operational. I'm pretty sure we're invisible to their radar. That should buy you some time."

"Sounds good," Mike said.

"But we're not completely safe," Les said. "If they've got aircraft, these solar sails will be visible from miles away."

"I'll work as fast as I can." Mike booted-up and started typing. The computer demanded a password. "Oh, I'll give you a password," he said.

He found a screwdriver and removed the cover from one of the two desktop computers that sat side by side on the workstation. The hard drive was vastly different from any computer he had ever seen before. "This is going to take some time to figure out," he said.

"That's a luxury we don't have," Les said. He looked around and didn't see any other ships. "I'll call you if anything starts happening."

Mike began trying to familiarize himself with the internal circuitry of the computer. One aspect of it caught his attention right away. "This thing doesn't have any transistors," he said.

"Is that bad?"

"Maybe," Mike said. "Let me try something." He worked silently for several minutes and then cried out in amazement. "Wow, this is so unbelievable."

"What?" Les said.

"The technology of the future," Mike said. "The innovation is just incredible."

Les continued to scan the sea around them. "Can you do anything with it?"

"I don't know. I've got an idea though."

"Hurry up," Les said. "They could be on top of us any minute."

Mike disconnected several wires, switched some components and reconnected some of the wires into different ports. He found a soldering iron in the toolbox and plugged it into a wall socket. "I need more parts," he said.

"Why don't you try the other computer," Les said.

Mike glanced two feet to his right at the other desktop computer. "What would I do without you, Les," he said. He grabbed the screwdriver and opened the casing.

Les continued driving them around the whole time, keeping an eye out for any other vessels and monitoring the "Listen" screen. It was also a great opportunity to further familiarize himself with more of the *Quasar*'s many features.

"This boat's equipped with infrared vision," Les said. "It'll help us navigate in darkness and fog."

"Try getting comfortable using it. Then you'll know how to deploy it when we need it."

"I'm already doing just that," Les said. "Any chance of you getting that computer working today? We're sitting ducks out here."

"Patience," Mike said. "Just keep watching our backs." He continued soldering while steadying himself against the rocking boat. Using a small oscilloscope, he was able to run tests on individual parts of the computer. This enabled him to identify and bypass security circuits. He then began adding new connections and reworking the entire interior. Each time he finished a part of the function, he ran an internal test to make sure he had done it right.

"You haven't fallen asleep down there have you?" Les said.

"No," Mike said. "In fact, I'm going to turn this mean computer into my friendly little pet."

"What's taking so long?"

Mike stared into the monitor. "There are dozens of built-in security levels. I'm trying to override them in the software when I can. If that doesn't work, then I have to go inside with the soldering iron and bypass them manually. It's a very time-consuming process."

"You're telling me."

"Any sign of trouble?" Mike said.

Les took another look around. "Not yet."

"Finished," Mike said a few minutes later. It had been almost two hours. "I've just completed the greatest computer achievement of all time." He replaced the casing on the computer and tightened the screws. "Thank heaven!" Les said.

"The batteries are completely charged and there's still no sign of the *Starrider*. I'm going to retract the solar sails."

Before disarming the masking devices, he hit one of the firing buttons mounted on the steering wheel. A message on the console told him firing couldn't be done while either the Chameleon or Stealth functions were deployed.

"Just as I suspected," he said. "We can't fire while concealed." He then deactivated the concealing devices and tried firing again. This time laser fire blasted out of the big turret on the deck and from the smaller ones mounted on the roof.

"See them on radar yet?" Mike said.

Les watched the screen. A moment later two blips, one large and one small, appeared and started moving toward them. "Yes," he called out. "They're on their way."

CHAPTER 23

▼

STARRIDER TAKES THE BAIT

"I'm going to go slow for a while to make them think they have a chance of catching us," Les called out. "Once they get within a hundred nautical miles I'll speed up."

"Good," Mike said from his seat in front of the computer screen. Now let's see what we can learn from that computer database." He immediately started hacking into the *Starrider*'s computer network and bypassed the initial security levels in a matter of seconds.

"Hey," Mike said. "The *Starrider* is a large merchant, heavily armed and designed to carry tons of equipment and cargo. Apparently it's also some kind of mining vessel."

"A mining vessel?" Les said. "What are they hauling?"

Mike continued typing away. A moment later he got a surprising answer. "Crystals."

"Crystals?" Les said. "You mean to tell me they're in here for a bunch of rocks?"

"Looks that way," Mike said. "Not only that, they're here in the Bermuda Triangle on purpose just like we suspected." He kept typing, downloading files as he surfed. "Boy they are going to freak when they find out what I'm doing." He smiled.

Access to the *Starrider's* computers lasted about ten more minutes before the transmissions abruptly stopped and the words "Access Denied" suddenly appeared on the screen. "Show's over," Mike said. "Might as well turn the concealing devices back on. They're onto us."

Les quickly reactivated the concealing devices, changed course ninety degrees and sped up. Mike saved all the new information, shut down the computer and walked up to the main cabin.

"How did we do?" Les said as Mike sat down.

"It'll take some time to analyze the data," Mike said. "But I grabbed files right and left while I was in there. My guess is we made out like bandits."

"Or perhaps, pirates." Les smiled. "They've reactivated their concealing devices and are probably heading toward our last known coordinates. I have the sneaking suspicion that they might be a little mad."

"Glad to see that sixth sense is working good again." Mike chuckled.

"It doesn't take a sixth sense to know we're in serious danger if they find us now," Les said with a serious expression. "They know we tricked them into letting down their defenses and burned them badly. They want us worse than ever now."

"Yeah, I guess you're right." Mike looked out the windows at the empty sea around them. "We've stolen too much information for them to risk letting us get away. I guess for them, destroying this boat is the only option left."

"At least we have a little more fire power than I originally thought," Les said with a grin.

"Oh," Mike said.

"Look right here." Les reached to the far right end of the controls and lifted the plastic cover that shielded a switch. "This boat is armed with some kind of a missile. The lever goes to 'ready' and then to 'fire'. For all I know it may be nuclear-tipped." He re-closed the plastic shield.

"How many missiles do you suppose we have?"

Les thought a moment. "Judging by the size of the boat I'd say not many. Maybe only one."

"Then we'd better save it until we really need it," Mike said. "As it stands right now we need two of them." He glanced all around. "Let's travel a little longer. It'll be dark soon and we can shut down for the night. I'll activate the deck guard and set the alarm on the Listen screen to go off if anything gets within fifty miles. Then we can eat, analyze some of the data we retrieved and get a good night's sleep."

After enjoying dinner, Mike sat down at the computer and began analyzing the new data while Les began going through all the closets and drawers. They had already found some nice clothes to wear and Les was taking inventory of everything the *Quasar* had to offer.

"Wow," Mike said as he gazed at the computer screen. "This boat is from at least a hundred years farther into the future than we are. Starrider is a large shipbuilding company that didn't even exist until the year 2100."

"What do they need crystals for?" Les said. "That's been bugging me all day."

Mike typed a few keys. "It seems that the Earth's fossil fuel supplies have dwindled and the Starrider Corporation has become the world's leader in solar energy research."

"Solar energy." Les was admiring some of the shirts he had found. Each was emblazoned with the *Starrider* logo. "As I recall, back in the 1980s, the United States government tried to inspire corporations to invest in research in solar energy. The only people who made any money at it were scam-artists."

"Yes," Mike said. "It wasn't practical economically. Collection of energy from the sun is a process called photovoltaics. Solar cells that convert sunlight into electricity are made of silicon. They have to be baked in a furnace for almost a whole day, a process that uses a lot of energy. In the late 1990s, researchers found ways to cut the baking time down to about nine hours, but the process still used up a lot of fossil fuel. What's worse, the final product only offered about an eighteen-percent efficiency rating. That meant having to have photovoltaic cells spread out over acres of land just to produce enough electricity for an average-sized office building."

"So, these Starrider characters are here collecting crystals for use in making solar collectors," Les said.

Mike continued typing into the computer. "Yes. Evidently, they lead the world in photovoltaic research." He looked over at Les. "I guess they've exhausted the world's supply of crystals in their own time and have figured out a way to go back in time to get more."

"Time travel through the Bermuda Triangle for profit," Les said. "Now I've heard of everything."

Mike continued examining the information that was pouring out of the screen in front of him. "Well, they're still using silicon solar cells in the future," he said. "It looks like they need the crystals to make filters that magnify the sunlight."

Les had stopped folding clothes and stood looking over Mike's shoulder. "Thereby making the collectors work more efficiently."

"Yes," Mike said. "A lot more. Here's a model comparing the power generated by solar collectors with and without crystal filters."

Les studied the monitor. "Wow. The difference is staggering."

"Natural crystals magnify the sun's rays without significantly increasing the temperature on the surface of the silicon cell," Mike said. "That makes the cells last longer and raises their efficiency rating twenty to thirty times." He looked up at Les. "That means the amount of area that has to be covered with solar collection panels to generate enough electricity for a town can be reduced to only a few dozen square feet. With the solar technology of our time, it would have to be several square miles."

"But what I don't understand is why they have to have natural crystals," Les said. "Why can't they just manufacture them?"

Mike typed some more on the keyboard. "Synthetic crystals aren't nearly as efficient as natural ones. Plus, the synthetic ones begin to break down after only a few months of use. Natural crystals last for years. It looks like the entire Starrider corporation is built on their ability to manufacture solar powered boats and ships."

"Wow," Les said. "It looks like these Starrider people are pioneers in the field."

"I think they're more than pioneers," Mike said. "Judging by the way all this information is written, I'd say they have a big edge over everybody else and they're keeping it all to themselves."

"What makes you think so?"

"Look at this list of their customers. The U.S. Navy, the Coast Guard, even most of the cruise lines. These guys are rich."

"But why did they have to come all the way here?" Les said. "Crystals are everywhere in our time, and they can even be grown at home with a kit you can pick up for ten dollars at the toy store."

Mike typed more. "The crystals Starrider uses are boulders that have to be pulled out of the ground by cranes. It appears that, in the future where they come from, virtually all of the large deposits of crystals have been used up, sort of like dried-up oil fields. The nations of the world are all desperate for whatever crystals they can get their hands on, and are even willing to go to war over supplies."

"But why here in the Caribbean?" Les said. "I'd think they would find more of what they need in mountainous places."

"Well, if they've traveled back in time, then it wouldn't make sense to mine the same areas they've already mined back in their future," Mike said. "That would mean that there must be virgin territory somewhere here that doesn't exist a few thousand years in the future."

"Virgin territory," Les said. "Where?"

"Let me see if I can find out." Mike typed more. "There's your answer."

Les looked at the monitor. "Atlantis. They've been mining on Atlantis!"

"The same island we just left a week ago," Mike said. "And it looks like they've been there for the last couple of years. That's why they had to come into the Bermuda Triangle. They had to go back in time to tap the vast crystal deposits on the lost continent before it sank into the ocean forever."

"Well, why didn't Roscoe see or hear them?" Les said.

"They must have been on the other side of the island. Remember that Roscoe told us he never actually went over there. For all we know, that island may be the size of the state of Connecticut. They could have been over there the whole time we were on the island and we'd have never known it." He looked around the *Quasar*. "And judging by their weaponry and dislike of strangers, maybe that's not such a bad thing."

Les had finished his inventory of the clothes and set them down on the table next to Mike. Now he was staring at the computer screen with a blank expression on his face. "But why the violence? Why are they going around killing everybody?"

"I don't know," Mike said. "They want something but I can't figure out what it is." He resumed typing.

"From what I gather, the mining operation was completed a couple of months ago," Mike said. "The mother ship's hull is full of crystals. Why don't they just sail for home and get rich?"

"That's it," Les said. "They can't get back. They're stuck here just like we are."

"Well, they've gotten back and forth before," Mike said. "We know they have because this vessel is equipped with an Atmospheric Disruption device. This boat was made specifically to travel through the eye of the needle."

"I'll bet you're right," Les said. "This Greg Fannin must have somehow accidentally discovered the eye of the needle and has been traveling through it for some time. Dig some more and find out why they can't get back to their present day."

Mike began typing again. "Look at this. The *Starrider* vessel came through the eye of the needle during a hurricane. About a month ago they tried to take it back through the eye using the Atmospheric Disruption detector as a guide. The two *Quasar* vessels made it through with no problem but the big ship couldn't follow."

"So they're stuck with a multi-million dollar cargo they can't get home," Les said. "But what do they want with people like those pirates?"

"I don't know." Mike stared at the computer screen. "This might help. There's some video footage the *Starrider*'s cameras picked up that may tell us something."

"Well, pull it up," Les said.

"I don't know if I can. This is the file that was being downloaded when they got wise to us and cut off the transmission. Only part of the file appears to be here."

"Show what you've got," Les said.

"Here goes," Mike told the computer to run the video footage and the image of what appeared to be a pirate vessel appeared on the television monitor mounted to the wall above them. He and Les watched as the pirate vessel, apparently being pursued by one of the *Quasars*, was raising its sails and trying to flee.

"That doesn't look like the crew of the *Scamp*," Mike said. "These must be some other poor bastards they killed."

The *Quasar* quickly closed the distance and the pirate crew could now be seen on the video scurrying to get the big ship sailing as fast as possible. "I guess this is the part where the *Quasar* blows them out of the water," Les said. He and Mike kept watching.

"Look at that guy in the middle of the pirate ship's deck," Mike observed. "He's just sitting there cross-legged like he's doing some kind of special prayer."

"I hope for his sake it gets answered," Les said.

"Hey, what's that thing on the deck in front of him?" Mike asked. On the monitor they could see some kind of blurry object on the ship's deck in front of the sitting pirate. While two dozen other pirates rushed around, raising sails and scrambling to get the big ship moving, this one pirate sat oblivious to everything going on around him, watching the blurry, spinning object and pointing straight ahead. All of a sudden the pirate ship vanished.

"What the hell just happened," Les said. On the monitor was now nothing but empty ocean. The *Quasar's* cameras began panning around the area where the pirate vessel was last seen. The last image Mike and Les saw was the pirate vessel's wake, which led up to a point in the water and ended abruptly. The television screen then turned to snow.

"That's it for the video," Mike said. "In fact, that's everything I downloaded before they cut us off." He looked over at Les. "Let's take a look again at the pirate ship right before it vanished."

"Yeah. Evidently, it had something to do with what that guy sitting on the deck was doing."

Mike told the computer to run the video again and slowed it down when the strange man sitting on the deck came clearly into view. "Look at that guy. He's dressed in all black clothes with black boots and a three-cornered black hat. He looks like some kind of wizard."

"You can see the object on the deck in front of him now," Les said. "Tell the computer to slow it down to frame by frame."

"I'll see if I can zoom in on it," Mike said. He stopped the video completely, used the graphic controls to isolate the blurry object, enlarged the image to the full size of the computer screen and then enhanced the image.

"I don't believe it," Les said. "They've got a little gold ship exactly like the one we've got."

"And look at it," Mike said. "It's spinning around so fast you can't even see it." He looked over at Les. "The little gold ship is not only a talisman, but one that takes its user somewhere that nobody else can follow."

"So that's what the *Starrider* crewmen were doing with those hand held devices aboard the *Scamp*," Les said. "If it was just plain gold they could detect then they would have surely found the huge horde in the cave back on Atlantis. They were looking for a talisman. They must have some kind of detection device that specifically isolates it."

"But how could they distinguish it?"

"Maybe the talisman isn't made of pure gold. Perhaps there is another element blended in like uranium or something."

"Uranium," Mike said. "That would mean it's radioactive. Of course. They could find it with a Geiger counter."

"That's just one possibility," Les said. "But it might not be a good idea to keep it in your pocket. No reason to risk getting cancer because of it."

Mike turned off the monitor and the two of them sat silently for a long moment. "Do you suppose it was our talisman that drew them to the area the night they attacked the *Scamp*?" Mike said.

"I don't suppose," Les said. "I'm sure of it. That's what this whole thing is all about. The *Starrider* is loaded down with precious cargo and they can't get it home without a talisman. Our Talisman."

"Maybe we can find the vortex and leave them behind," Mike said. He glanced over at the motionless talisman. "If that thing will just start spinning then we're on our way." He looked over at Les and smiled. A moment later they were laughing.

CHAPTER 24

▼

THE SEA OF THE DEAD

The following morning, Mike woke up to the smell of fresh coffee. He went to the galley and poured himself a cup when he heard the faint sound of the engine being started. A moment later he felt the boat start to move.

"Getting an early start?" He walked into the front cabin.

"There's something a few miles to the northwest," Les said. "The 'Atmospheric Disruption' indicator alerted me to it. That's the direction we're headed anyway. Might as well take a look."

Mike looked at the indicator and saw the pulsating flash of its red arrow. It was pointing in the direction Les was taking them. He looked over at the talisman on the shelf and saw that it was motionless.

"This indicator they invented seems to pick up on something that the talisman misses," Les said. "I don't know if that's good or bad."

"Strange that the two don't agree," Mike said.

"I know," Les said. "It's got my curiosity up. My sixth sense is tingling a little too. I figured it wouldn't hurt to go check it out."

As they made their way in the direction indicated, the sound and flashing increased in frequency, both finally becoming constant. "We must be getting close," Mike said. He looked out ahead of them and saw dark clouds. "It looks stormy over there."

"Keep your eyes open for the *Starrider* and the other *Quasar*," Les said. "No doubt their indicators are picking up this disturbance too."

Mike picked up the laser rifle and started looking around. "You ready with the laser cannon?"

"Oh yeah," Les said. He gently brushed his thumbs over the firing buttons on the steering wheel.

At that moment the concealing devices began to fade. A warning alarm came on indicating that some kind of atmospheric force was rendering them inoperable. "Looks like the masking devices won't work around the vortex," Les said. "You want to back off?"

"No, let's go on in. If those other guys detect us and follow then their masking devices won't work either. At least we'll know where they are."

"They still have us outnumbered and out-gunned."

"I know, but I don't feel like running from those guys forever. I say we go on through and see where it leads us."

"You're right. We really have nothing to lose." Les sped up and charged straight for the atmospheric disturbance ahead of them. Once they got to within a hundred yards or so of the wall of rain and fog, the masking devices shut down completely and the sea got rougher. A moment later, Les and Mike felt the *Quasar* accelerate.

"Whoa," Les said. "She's speeding up on her own."

A moment later the engine died, the lights went out and the *Quasar* listed slightly to port. "We're being dragged in," Les said. "I think it's a whirlpool."

"Try steering into it," Mike said. "Otherwise, we may capsize." He quickly got seated and belted in just seconds before the *Quasar* entered the wall of fog. The vessel began bounding up and down. Heavy rain, some of it in the form of sleet, began pounding the windshield.

"Temperature's plunging," Les said. "Here we go again."

Large waves began crashing across the bow, throwing water against the windows and even across the roof. Les and Mike could see their breath now as the temperature plunged below freezing and continued downward. Ice began coating the railings and every burst of spray from the sea formed an icy puddle when it hit the deck.

The two of them were now nothing more than spectators. This continued for several minutes before the vessel passed through the vortex into the next corridor and the elements began to let up. Almost as abruptly as it had all begun, the storm subsided. The pounding sleet stopped and the surf calmed a good bit, leaving them powerless in a cold, blinding fog, waiting for whatever was going to happen next.

Les tried to start the engine. It gave no response. "Those jokers could be on us any second. We're dead for sure if we can't get moving real quick." He looked out the window at the thick fog. "I think it's the static electricity in the atmosphere again."

"Great," Mike said. "You'd think if those Bozos built this vessel specifically for a place like this then they'd have planned ahead enough to have some kind of back-up power supply."

Les looked over at him with a startled expression. "You may have something there. Look around the boat for another power source. Maybe there's a plain old gasoline powered motor in a storage closet somewhere." He hit the starter button one more time and didn't hear a sound.

"I think we'd better try finding some warm clothes first," Mike said. "I'm freezing." They rushed to the closets in the bedrooms and found some heavy clothing and bundled up. Then they began frantically searching for something that might get the *Quasar* moving again.

"Look around down here," Les said. "I'll go crawl around under the console. There's got to be some way to get the power back up."

"And maybe a little heat too." Mike started looking around the cabin and heard the dog whimper from somewhere. "Here Trixie." He looked around. "Where are you girl?"

A moment later he heard her whimper again. The sound seemed to be coming from under the couch that was built into the center of the back wall. Mike got down on all fours, looked at the small space beneath the seat and spotted Trixie curled up under there. "So there you are."

He carefully reached under the seat, half-expecting to get bitten, and gently petted the dog's head. She didn't bite and he could hear her tail hitting the floor as she wagged it. "Come on out, it's okay."

The dog slowly crawled out. When Mike petted her he noticed that the side she had been lying on was very warm.

He bent back down and put his hand back where the dog had just been lying. The floor was warm on the spot. He got up and found a flashlight and returned for a closer look. There was a yellow fan blade painted on the wall. "A nuclear symbol. Hey Les, come quick."

"Find something?" Les ran down the steps.

"Yes," Mike said. "Help me remove this couch."

They found small levers on each side of the seat cushion and pulled them forward. The seat released and came loose. They then slid the couch forward, revealing a square panel in the back wall.

"Bingo," Les said. "There's a back-up power source after all.

They quickly got screwdrivers and started removing the panel from the wall. Once the panel was off Les stuck his head in and looked around. "There are some levers on a control panel in here. They're marked one through eight. I'll bet they gradually remove the rods from the core."

"Perfect," Mike said. "We'll start with the first one and slowly work our way up to eight."

Les reached in and took hold of the lever marked "one". He pulled on it. "It won't budge," he said.

"Try turning it to one side," Mike said. "It probably has to be unlocked."

Les gently twisted the lever to the right. He then pulled it and felt it slide forward. Once he got it out as far as it would go he twisted it back to the left and it snapped into place. "It worked," he said. He then did the same with lever two. Soon, all eight levers were pulled out.

"Look," Mike said. A red light had come on at the bottom of the unit and a small screen revealed the word "Wait" in blue letters. A faint humming sound could be heard, gradually growing louder. When the sound reached a steady level the "Wait" sign went out and the word "Ready" appeared in green. "I think we've got it!" he exclaimed.

Les ran back to the controls and saw that all of the dashboard indicators were on. He hit the ignition button and the *Quasar's* engine came to life. He then activated the masking devices and the console indicated that the boat was concealed. "We're safe now."

Les turned on the heat and the cabin started warming up.

"I think I'll step out on deck while I'm still dressed for it," Mike said. "Maybe I can see something through this fog."

He walked outside and immediately shivered as the Arctic wind hit him. Careful not to slip on the icy deck, he made his way to the front railing and looked straight ahead. He could see maybe fifteen feet through the mist and no more. The waves had calmed a great deal and the swells were now only about three feet.

"There's an infrared camera mounted on the roof," Les said through the loud speaker. "I'll try turning it on." He hit the switch and a blurry image appeared on the screen. After a moment, he could tell it wouldn't help them much.

"Any luck?" Mike said.

"No, I think it's designed more for night usage. Either that or this salty, cold fog is just too thick for it to do us any good. Can you see anything at all?" Les said.

"No." Mike looked down. "Only icy water. Try going forward slowly."

Les pushed the throttle out of neutral and started them inching forward. Mike strained to make out shapes in the thick fog but it was impossible. He heard a soft crunching sound and looked down. There were many chunks of ice floating in the water. Some were hitting the boat's hull and sliding out of the way. Some of the ice chunks were rather large and made a soft squeaking noise as they scraped against the smooth hull. "Don't go any faster," he said. "We don't want to turn this thing into another Titanic."

"Got you," Les said over the speaker. He glanced down at the controls. The "Listen" device was active and gave no readout of any kind. As he studied the still-unfamiliar instruments he noticed a button labeled "Sonar Pulse". "Time to find out what this does," he muttered. He pushed the button and for a few seconds several objects appeared on the "Listen" screen. After a moment they faded away. He pushed the button again and the same thing happened again. "Hey Mike, can you come in here a minute?"

Mike entered the cabin and closed the door behind him. "Man it's cold out there."

"Tell me what you think of this," Les said. "Watch the 'Listen' screen." He pushed the button again and they both saw several objects appear briefly before fading again.

"You've got us concealed right?"

"Yes."

"This 'Sonar Pulse' must be detectable," Mike said. "If we activated the radar then it would give a steady signal that could be traced. The pulse of sonar isn't traceable as long as it isn't run continuously. I guess it's designed to give us some idea of what's around us without giving away our position."

"Oh, I get it," Les said. "It's kind of like trying to stay hidden in dark woods when you have to be able to see where you're going. If you shined a flashlight around then anybody could find you. But if you used an occasional flash from a strobe light then you could get a quick idea of your surroundings and still remain in the dark most of the time."

"Exactly," Mike said. "This device was designed specifically for use in a situation like this. We can't see where we're going without some kind of detecting device but we know someone is looking for us. *Starrider* might detect an occasional pulse of sonar but it won't be enough for them to track us and pinpoint our location."

"Why don't you get back out on deck and keep an eye out," Les said. "I'll see if I can spot a likely place to hide on the pulse. It's too dangerous to be sailing around without radar in this pea soup."

"Okay," Mike said. "But let's find a parking place quick. I don't need a case of frost-bite." He stepped back outside and slid the door closed behind him.

Les gave another push on the "Pulse" button. A very large object was sitting about half-a-mile to starboard. He waited about a minute and pulsed again. They had moved a little closer in the short span of time between pulses but the object itself had moved slightly as well. "I think I've found something," he said through the speaker.

"Which way?" Mike said.

"Directly to the right. About half-a-mile. A large object. It's drifting very slowly and not emitting any radar or radio signals. I think it's an iceberg."

"It could be a ship," Mike said. "Let me run inside and get one of those life-detectors I found in the closet. That way we'll know if there are living creatures on it before we approach."

"Good idea, scan it with a metal detector too." He waited for Mike to get the hand-held devices and get back outside before turning the *Quasar* to starboard and approaching the large object.

The fog had thinned a little and Mike could now see the waterline better and was able to tell that all was clear about ten feet ahead.

"You can speed-up just a little," Mike said. "Watch me though. If I point to one side then veer that way. If I don't point then keep it straight ahead."

"Ten-four," Les said.

By zigzagging back and forth they were able to avoid some of the larger pieces of ice in the water.

Mike continued to monitor, getting no readings indicating that anything alive was nearby. "So far so good," he said.

"Okay, the object is about two hundred feet dead ahead." Les slowed down almost to a standstill.

Mike checked the hand-held devices. "It's all clear. No life forms and no metals. Go ahead and approach slowly."

Les pushed the throttle forward and the *Quasar* crept toward the large object hidden in the dense fog. Mike stood at the front railing, trying to see through the gray-colored mist. Les gave another pulse and saw that they were heading right for the object. They were now less than fifty feet away.

"I'm getting a slight twinge on the sixth sense," Les whispered through the speaker.

Mike turned and looked at him.

"It's just a little twinge, nothing more," Les said. He pulled the throttle to neutral and the boat drifted slowly.

Mike continued looking through the mist for a massive wall of ice to appear. Finally, he saw a large object starting to take shape. It was big and dark, and appeared to tower over the small *Quasar*. The sound of creaking boards came to his ears and he realized this wasn't an iceberg at all, it was a ship. It emerged from the fog and Mike looked up to see three skeletons at the railing of an old wooden hulk. The three eerie characters were looking down at him and smiling, almost like they had been expecting him and were happy Mike could join them. Mike stumbled backward and almost lost his balance. He hit the rail behind him with the middle of his back.

"Whoa." Les pulled the throttle back. The *Quasar* pulled away from the old ship and he had to catch himself before he sent them blindly backwards. He regained control and put it in neutral. The abrupt movement of the *Quasar* caused Mike to lose his balance and he almost fell overboard. After a moment he regained his grip on the railing. The dense fog was clearing slowly and they could see the entire deck of the old ship. The three skeletons were slumped over the railing, a thick coating of ice holding them firmly in place. Mike looked up at the crow's nest and saw another skeleton slumped over, this one had a spyglass frozen into one of his hands. There were several others standing at the rails as well, each looking blankly out at the sea around them.

Les walked out on the *Quasar's* deck, keeping his eyes on the other ship, and strolled up to where Mike was standing. He put his hand on Mike's shoulder, causing him to jump.

"Damn," he said. "Scare the hell out of me next time."

"Sorry," Les said. He looked toward the skeletons on the deck a few feet above them. The dead sailors seemed to be laughing at them. "Whatever killed them must have hit so fast they died right in their tracks."

Mike walked back inside and Les came in right behind him. Outside, the fog continued to thin as Mike began steering them clear of the old hulk.

"Well, that was a rush," Mike said.

"I really didn't mean to startle you," Les said.

"Don't worry about it."

They drove silently for several minutes.

The sun pierced the clouds above them and the fog began to burn off. They looked around them and saw huge chunks of ice floating nearby. The ship they had just found was now about a half-mile behind them. Two other ships, also apparently with frozen dead crews on deck, could be seen in the distance.

"Look, a merchant vessel." Les pointed. Mike looked to see a large iron-hulled ship about a mile to port. Les picked up the binoculars. "There appear to be several dead sailors at its deck railing as well."

"It's the sea of the dead," Mike said. "Christopher Columbus wrote in his log book about it."

"I remember that," Les said. "But I don't remember anything about it being cold and icy."

"Maybe we've ended up in one of the ice ages," Mike said.

The gold ship on the console in front of them started to rock gently from side to side. They stood motionless, waiting to see what it would do next. The little ship slowly turned toward the port bow and stopped. Les reached over and turned it back toward them. When he let it go it once again turned slowly around and pointed toward the port bow. Les looked at Mike and smiled. "Let's go."

"You want to drive?" Mike said. "My nerves are still a little shot."

"No problem."

They switched places and Les started them in the direction the talisman was pointing.

The sky was overcast but by now the fog had cleared completely and visibility was pretty good.

"See any sign of the *Starrider* or *Quasar Two*?" Les said.

"Just icebergs and ghost ships," Mike said. "I don't see anything moving."

A large ice shelf about the size of a town lay in their path. "I'll see if I can find a way around that chunk of ice without getting off course." Les veered to the left.

"That shouldn't be a problem," Mike said. "We'll just keep going in the direction the talisman indicates and we should be fine. Let's just make sure we don't run aground on any of that ice."

Les kept the speed way down. The *Quasar* had indicators that detected objects in its path and he made sure to pay attention to them. As long as they didn't go over 20 knots they wouldn't have a problem.

Mike put his coat back on and grabbed his hat and gloves. "I'm going up top to look around. Since we're going slow to avoid the ice then the wind-chill should only be around zero."

Les smiled and handed him some amber-tinted goggles he had found. "These will protect your eyes," he said. "Let me know if you see anything."

"Will do," Mike replied. He went outside and climbed up the steps to the platform above the cabin. Up here he was about twelve feet above the level of the water and could see a little farther. He picked up the microphone and established contact with Les through the ship's intercom system.

As Les steered them in and out of narrow passageways, around large icebergs and in between small ones, Mike looked for any signs of other ships. They were nearing the northern end of the large island of ice that they were circumventing and it was getting smaller and thinner. The spot where it ended was only a few hundred yards farther ahead. Mike looked over the top of the ice. "I see something," he whispered into the microphone. "It could be another vessel. It's on the far side of the ice directly to starboard."

Les slowed them down to a crawl and Mike struggled to see over the small icy hillside. There were several support beams and masts sticking up into view. "There's definitely something over there," Mike said. "I don't think it's them but I can't really be sure."

"I'll activate the laser cannon," Les said. "Why don't you come back in and sit in the wizo."

"The what?"

"Wizo," Les said. "The weapon systems operator's chair or WSO." He hit the button to power up the cannon and its green indicator on the console said: "Ready". Mike climbed back down, entered the cabin and sat down in the WSO's seat a few feet from Les. He then turned on the targeting computer and immediately began searching for the other vessel. "Wizo," Mike said. "I feel more important already."

"We're going to be clear of the ice in just a few seconds," Les told him. "Try to get whatever it is in the cross-hairs and if it's them then fire away."

"Okay." Mike aimed the cannon to starboard and saw the wall of ice as it drifted from left to right on the green-tinted screen. Slowly, the ice faded behind them and revealed a large clear area. Les turned into the inlet and the targeting computer found the other vessel. Immediately the ship's computer told Mike the cannon was locked on and ready to fire.

"It's a fishing vessel," Mike said when he got a look at it. "And there's somebody out on deck." He zoomed-in with the targeting viewer which was linked into the camera on the front of the boat. Les looked at the monitor and saw exactly what Mike was seeing on his viewer, only in color. The person on the deck was a frozen man. He was wearing a short-sleeved shirt under a clear coating of ice. It appeared that he had been quick-frozen. The targeting computer placed the cross-hairs right on the man's nose.

"I see two other bodies in the cabin behind him," Les said. "I guess those poor dudes were out trolling with their nets when they got yanked in here."

"Talk about the fishing trip from hell," Mike said. He quickly scanned all around the icy cove and found it empty. They apparently were in some kind of frozen graveyard, where victims were encased in ice and destined to float around for all eternity.

Mike scanned around back to the frozen fisherman and looked at him one more time before they moved on. "I wonder how long that poor guy has been standing there."

"Who knows. Could be a week, could be years." Les reached over to the talisman and turned it back toward himself. The little ship remained in the position and didn't spin back around. "Oh no. We've lost the direction again."

Mike looked over at it and moved it ninety degrees. It stayed exactly the way he left it. "Oh great." He was trying to get used to the disappointments but just couldn't do it. He missed Jan so much that it was killing him. "I don't know how many more let-downs I can take."

"Try to hang in there." Les sped up a little. "We'll make it home. Don't worry."

CHAPTER 25

▼

THE SHOOTOUT ON THE ICEBERG

Les and Mike continued to check the talisman frequently. It seemed to be their one link to home. The *Quasar* would crest a wave and list to one side, tilting the talisman with it and sending Mike's adrenaline level soaring. A moment later he'd realize that it was just a false alarm and he'd go back to the agonizing waiting. He and Les both knew that the *Starrider* could be around any curve, behind any large iceberg, anxiously awaiting its chance to blast them out of the water. They cruised slowly, watching, waiting and wondering.

Les veered to the left and the gyroscope spun slowly as it seemed to respond in kind. When he straightened out, the gyroscope kept spinning. It spun completely around and kept going.

Mike was also watching the ship's directional compass.

"It's been doing that ever since we entered this sea of ice," Les said. The two of them watched a moment longer as the gyroscope tried to normalize.

"I've been getting the feeling for the last hour that the gyroscope is unreliable. It seems as though the Earth's magnetic field is unstable here, like it's not fully developed or something."

"The sixth sense?" Mike said.

"Yeah, I guess so. It's getting close to sunset. I don't think it's a good idea to travel around after dark. Why don't we scout around for a good place to moor for the night."

"Good idea." Mike put his hat and gloves back on and went out on the front deck to scan the icy surroundings as Les continued to cruise slowly. Several minutes later Mike spotted a place a few hundred yards away that looked ideal.

"There's an opening in the side of an iceberg over there." He pointed. "Let's go over for a closer look."

Les turned ninety degrees to starboard.

The iceberg was massive, big enough to accommodate several city blocks. The wall facing them was several stories high. The wind and movement of the water had created a small tunnel in the side of the wall at the water's edge, but the hole was way too small for the *Quasar* to fit into.

Les brought the *Quasar* to a full stop and walked out onto the deck. Bracing himself against the cold wind, he stepped up to the railing next to Mike.

"We can enlarge that hole with the small lasers and create exactly what we need," Mike said pointing. "Then we can back the *Quasar* in and disappear."

"Okay," Les said. "But be careful with that laser cannon or you'll bring the whole wall down on top of us." He returned to the console and turned off the concealing devices. He then steered the boat around until he had it positioned some fifty feet in front of the wall of ice.

Mike walked inside and turned on the small lasers and deactivated the larger one. "The roof-mounted lasers have several different settings," he told Les. "Obviously, they were designed to be used in a situation just like this. I guess it wouldn't hurt to practice a little first."

Les watched as Mike pointed the aiming device toward a nearby iceberg and pushed the firing pin. A long, steady stream of light emitted from the laser cannon and began boring a hole into the ice.

"Perfect," Les said.

Turning back to the small opening that would become the *Quasar*'s berth; Mike aimed into the ice wall and began cutting the shape of a tunnel. Over the span of five minutes, he was able to cut a hole fifteen feet high and twenty feet wide. He swung the laser beam from side to side and top to bottom, creating a hole that was a good thirty-five feet deep. Finally he cut under the water to make it deep enough for the boat to float into. "There, a tailor-made berth."

"Let's take her in," Les said. He slowly turned the boat around and began backing into the tunnel. Mike went to the stern rail and helped steer them inside.

The *Quasar* disappeared into the wall of the iceberg. There was plenty of room inside.

"Keep coming," Mike said. "Let's get a good way's back from the entrance."

The opening was ten feet in front of the bow when Les heard Mike tell him to stop. "Now I need to find a nail or something that I can pound into the wall so we'll have a place to tie-off."

"I've got a better idea," Les said. "I saw an ice screw on one of the storage shelves earlier. I'll be a lot safer than a nail."

"An ice screw?" Mike said. "What's that?"

"Mountain climbers use them," Les said as he led the way to the storage closet. "It's a ten-inch hollow tube with rifling on the inside and screw threads on the outside. As the screw is inserted, a long tube of ice cranks out and drops off. You use an ice ax to insert it. It's really the only safe way to drive a bolt or nail into an ice wall without cracking it."

Les found the device and walked to the stern. "Kind of dark in here."

"I'll turn on the exterior lights," Mike said and he walked back up to the console.

Les bore holes in the ice wall on either side of the *Quasar* and tied them off. "Now we won't drift out into the open tonight while we're asleep."

"Good," Mike said. "Now let's cook dinner and then get a good night's sleep."

The *Quasar* had been well stocked with food when Mike and Les got hold of it. The freezer had been stocked with fresh vegetables and meats and even some ice cream and pastries. Mike selected a T-bone that looked to be two inches thick and Les chose a lobster.

The boat automatically took on seawater and distilled it through reverse-osmosis and ultraviolet filters, providing plenty for drinking and other uses. Les got into the shower and felt like he was in a luxury hotel. The nuclear-heated water thawed his cold fingers and toes wonderfully.

When he got out of the shower, Les saw the door to Mike's room closed and figured he was already asleep. Only the dog remained awake, sitting up from her place on the floor of his room and wagging her tail. "Good night Trixie," he told her as he crawled in bed.

He wondered briefly where the *Starrider* was at the moment. Probably still looking for us, he thought. About three minutes later he was sound asleep.

Late the next morning Les awoke to the wonderful smell of fresh coffee and cooking bacon. That got him out of bed and into the galley in a hurry.

Mike was using some of the bacon to teach Trixie to sit. "You're going to spoil that dog," Les laughed.

Mike looked up and smiled. "I think I could live very comfortably aboard this boat."

"Me too," Les said. "It was nice of those jerks from the future to build it for us."

Mike laughed and poured them both a cup of coffee.

"Just imagine what we can do with this boat," Les said. "When we get home we'll have the most technically advanced boat in the world."

"All we'd need are spare parts," Mike said.

"Oh, I can make those in my machine shop," Les said. "When we get back I'll go through every piece of this boat and learn every part and how it works. I'll keep it in fine running condition, don't worry."

"I doubt I'll be able to get my old job back," Mike said. "So I hope you can use some help at your shop."

Les chuckled. "No problem. We make a good team you and I. Part-time boat repair, part-time bounty hunters. We'll be great at both."

"You've got a deal," Mike said. He held up his coffee cup and Les clanged his against it.

"I want to see if I can pick up anything on the radio." Les got to his feet. "Who knows, maybe those idiots are sharing valuable information over the airwaves."

"That's not a bad idea," Mike said. "Let's go out and untie."

They walked up front and started putting on the heavy clothes. "Let's let her drift just outside the opening," Les said. "Once the roof is clear we can raise the antenna and start listening."

The very moment the antenna was up and the radio on, an urgent message could be heard. "Mayday, mayday," someone said. "Mayday, can anyone hear me?"

"Mike, come here quick," Les said.

Mike had just driven a long screw into the ice outside the opening and was tying off the *Quasar*. He rushed in and sat down to listen.

"That doesn't sound like *Starrider*," Les said. They sat and listened. A moment later they heard someone else respond.

"We read you," came a voice that sounded a lot like that of Greg Fannin. "Please identify yourself."

"Whoever it is, they're very close-by," Les said.

"Oh thank God," the first voice on the radio said. "This is the *Prism*, we're a fishing vessel from the Bahamas. We're totally lost. Can you help us? Over."

"Sure," Greg said. "Keep transmitting and we'll find you."

"I wouldn't do that if I were you," Mike muttered.

"We were fishing near the Bahama Banks when we got caught in some kind of storm," the pilot of the *Prism* said. "The next thing we knew we were in this winter wonderland."

"Happens to a lot of people," Fannin replied in a pleasant, friendly voice. "Don't worry, we'll be there soon." The way he said it gave Mike the creeps. In his mind he pictured Greg Fannin as some kind of sick dog-catcher, smiling broadly while sneaking up slowly on an innocent puppy with a noose and saying things like: "nice doggy".

"What do you think Fannin is planning to do?" Les said.

Mike gazed outside the front windshield. "No telling."

They sat and listened for several minutes as the *Prism* and *Starrider* sought each other.

"I think I'll go outside and climb up onto the iceberg," Les said. "From up high I can probably spot them."

"Do you think that's a good idea?" Mike said.

"I'll stay out of sight. I'm curious about that *Starrider*. This may be our only chance to actually see what we're up against."

"Okay," Mike said. "Whatever you do, don't slip on the ice and fall into the water. You do that and you're dead for sure."

"I'll be careful. There are a couple of radios in the utility room. I'll take one with me so I can listen."

Les got bundled up in a white nylon jump suit, boots, hat and gloves. He then stepped into the utility room and found an ice axe and crampons, the binoculars and a radio. Once he got out on deck he stood on the rail and began using the ice axe to get himself up onto the iceberg.

After climbing several feet, Les reached a narrow plateau where he could stand. He then took a moment to assess the area, spotting a flat area along the ridge that he could use to ascend. The sky was still cloudy and light snow was falling. Now and then the wind gusted, sending the paralyzing cold right through him. Using the ice axe to steady himself, he started up the frozen hillside.

About twenty minutes later, very winded, Les reached the summit. He had come the last one-hundred feet on his stomach, digging in with the ice axe to get stable, then chipping out a foot-hold with his toes to hold the spot while he pulled out the axe and reached for a new hold further up the hill. When he finally got to the summit he found a flat place to sit and catch his breath.

The view from the top was striking; eerily beautiful and at the same time frighteningly dangerous. He could see at least twenty or thirty icebergs. It didn't take him long to spot the *Starrider*. It was large, about twice the size of a Coast Guard cutter.

Taking the binoculars for a better look, Les got the first glimpse of the ship that had been pursuing them for the last few days. It was cruising along about three miles from where he sat; pushing large and small chunks of ice out of its way like an icebreaker. The stark black hull stood out boldly from the white surroundings.

With a brisk Arctic wind at his back, Les pulled out the radio, set it down beside him, and listened as he watched through the binoculars. "Do you still hear me?" Greg Fannin asked the *Prism*'s pilot.

"Yes," the first voice said. The other vessel sounded much closer now. Les looked around with the binoculars. The *Prism* was less than a mile away. She was a medium-sized fishing vessel with a bright red hull. The *Starrider* had it in sight now and was approaching fast.

"Listen," Fannin said. "Most ships that travel through here have a talisman, a small gold ship that spins around on its own when it gets near the vortex opening of the Bermuda Triangle. Do you happen to have such an object?"

"No," came a confused reply from the *Prism*. "A talisman? What are you talking about?"

"Oh, never mind," Fannin said in a friendly voice. "It's not important." The *Starrider* had made a turn around a large iceberg and was now only a few hundred yards from the cove where the *Prism* sat. A loud humming sound grew from underneath the *Starrider's* decks.

The *Starrider* rounded the last corner and popped into the view of the men on the *Prism's* deck. They began waving and smiling. A moment later the smiles turned to terror as the large laser cannon on the *Starrider's* deck fired at them. The center of the *Prism* started to melt like it was made of wax. The rest of the ship started to glow red as its metal deck soared in temperature. Moments later the gas tanks under the stern ignited and the ship exploded. Les watched in horror as hundreds of pieces of the *Prism* fell into the water. One large burning chunk landed on a nearby iceberg with a loud clang and melted itself into a deep hole. It made a loud sizzling sound and left a black spot fifty feet across.

"Les, are you alright?" Mike's voice came over the radio. Les sat, binoculars still half-poised to his eyes, staring down at the radio a few feet away.

"Les, Les, what the hell just happened? Answer me."

"I'm fine," Les said. "Start the engine and sign-off immediately. I'll be there shortly. Out." He looked over at the *Starrider*. Several men rushed out onto the decks. They appeared to be scanning the surroundings with binoculars. A moment later they were all pointing in his direction. His heart jumped into his throat as the big ship turned toward the iceberg on which he sat.

"Show time," Les said. He got up carefully and retraced his steps to the top of the steepest part of the embankment. A quick glance around told him there was no sign of the other *Quasar* but he figured it wasn't far from the *Starrider.* Any moment now, both ships could be sitting in the cove ahead, shooting at him.

He rushed over to the spot where the hillside got steep. From here it was maybe two hundred feet to the water. Digging in his heels with each step, he slowly began making the descent. A voice in his head screamed at him to move faster. At the same time, one false move would be his last.

He had almost reached the halfway point when he suddenly lost his footing and started sliding on his backside down the slope. The velocity of the slide increased quickly. Down the embankment of solid ice he slid, out of control and fighting to stop himself with his feet and outstretched hands. The binoculars and radio flew from his grip. A scream tried to rise up from his throat as he looked ahead to the drop-off that lay at the bottom of the hill. Only about thirty more feet to go before he would plunge into the icy water.

The ice axe trailed along behind his left arm at the end of the strap, several inches out of reach. He grabbed for it several times, realizing with horror that he couldn't get a hold of it.

He slowly turned himself over onto his stomach. With one quick yank of his wrist, the ice axe flew toward his hand and he grabbed it. He then lay on top of it, driving it into the ice. It dug in but did little to slow him down, the blade skating on the frozen surface.

He was screaming. Pushing down as hard as he could, the steel point dug-in and began to slow him down. The ice axe finally found a hold and brought him to a halt. Les looked behind him and saw that his right foot was dangling over a small cliff about six feet above the water.

"Thank you God," he said. He took a quick glance around. There was no sign of the *Starrider* or Mike and *Quasar One*.

Having just the one ice axe to work with, Les had to dig a hole with his left foot to hold him steady while he pulled out the tool and then dug-in with it a couple of feet further up the embankment.

This went on for several minutes until he was finally able to reach a narrow level area where he could stand. "Got to hurry," he told himself. He was out of breath and shaking.

When he got moving there was a loud rumbling sound. He turned to look back, just in time to see the *Starrider* round a nearby iceberg and turn toward him.

"There he is," someone shouted from the deck of the ship. That was followed by the sound of a deck-mounted laser cannon powering up. As he tried to run and not lose his footing, Les screamed out Mike's name.

He ran several steps and then dove to the ground, sliding on his stomach. An instant later, the *Starrider* let loose a deafening blast of laser-fire that sailed about two feet above him. The blast struck a wall of ice some twenty feet away, sending steam and ice in all directions.

Les put his head down in his arms as large chunks of ice landed on his back and on the top of his head. The ice wall then collapsed, sending an avalanche toward him.

Les sprang to his knees, avoided the wave of ice, and then turned to see what the *Starrider* was going to do next. Its momentum had carried it past him and it would have to turn around to shoot again. There was no sign of the more maneuverable *Quasar Two* at the moment.

Les stood his ground for a few long seconds. As the ship made a cumbersome turn-around, he could see a smaller cannon that had just fired lowering into its port. Rising up to replace it was a much larger cannon.

"Oh hell," Les said. "They're going to blast the iceberg right out from under me. They won't have to kill me, the icy water will do that for them." As he stood helplessly watching, the *Starrider* passed the halfway point of its turn-around.

"Where are you, Mike," he screamed out.

"Right over here, buddy." Mike approached in the *Quasar* from about thirty feet away.

"Hurry before the *Starrider* completes its turn," Les said. "This iceberg is scheduled for demolition in about ten seconds."

Mike steered the maneuverable *Quasar* up to the ice cliff and Les jumped aboard. He raced to the open companionway, yanked it closed, jumped into a seat and belted in. Mike hit the throttle.

An instant later the *Starrider* let out a massive roar, and the iceberg exploded. A blinding cloud of steam turned day into night, and pieces of ice pounded the roof and sides of the *Quasar*. Mike and Les held on as a tidal wave threw the ship onto its port side. A moment later, the *Quasar* righted itself, and quickly accelerated. It took several moments of racing in zero visibility before they emerged from the cloud of smoke and into the open daylight.

"That was too close," Mike said. "Where are they?"

"Over there." Les pointed.

Mike looked to his left and spotted the *Starrider*, now in the middle of another turn. "Oh yes." He cut the wheel a sharp left and hit the throttle. A few seconds later, *Quasar One* was pointed directly at the broadside of the big ship.

"Most vessels are vulnerable from the side," Mike said as he placed his thumbs on the firing buttons. A quick glance at the controls told him the laser cannon on the deck was ready to fire. "Let's find out just how tough they really are."

Charging at some seventy miles-per-hour, Mike got the *Starrider* in the cross hairs and punched the buttons on the steering wheel so hard that he almost broke his thumbs. A long, steady stream of laser fire burst forth from the *Quasar's* gun turret and roared across the big ship's deck. Men scrambled for cover as sparks and chunks of steel flew in all directions. His thoughts quickly turned from offense to defense as he rushed to steer them out of the *Starrider's* path.

The huge ship completed its turn and began to lock its lasers on the *Quasar*. The *Starrider* roared and fired, sending a blast that just missed. From a scant few feet behind the *Quasar* came a huge explosion in the water that sent chunks of ice and spraying water fifty feet into the air.

Mike began a zigzag course through the channel, veering around the large chunks of ice and trying to keep the

Starrider from getting a good shot. The big ship roared in pursuit, firing at them constantly. The errant shots blew holes in nearby icebergs and caused loud explosions all around.

"I still can't figure out where the other *Quasar* is," Les said.

"They were probably searching for us a hundred miles from here when all this started," Mike said. "I'm sure they headed this way as soon as our cover was blown."

For the next several minutes Mike whipped *Quasar One* in and out of coves and around icebergs, constantly veering from side to side. "I can't believe how fast and maneuverable that big ship is, I just can't shake them."

Les continued looking all around. "We should be okay as long as it's just us and the *Starrider*. Try to lose it before the others get here. If you can't then it'll be two against one."

"If that happens then I'll try to stay between them," Mike said. "Maybe I can get one of them to shoot the other. Anyway, keep your eyes peeled. I'll try to make sure we stay out of the *Starrider*'s cross-hairs."

There was another loud blast and Mike caught a glimpse of a beam of laser fire across the back deck of the *Quasar*. The beam struck a nearby iceberg, creating a large explosion. The wall collapsed and sent ice tumbling into the water. "That could have been us."

"Look up there." Les pointed. "There's a hole in that big iceberg and the ceiling is too low for the *Starrider* to fit through. It looks like a good escape route."

"Good idea." Mike banked a sharp left. They raced toward the tunnel-like opening in the ice wall and went through.

Les looked back and watched the *Starrider* turn and charge at the same narrow opening. Just before getting there it fired a blast and blew the entire iceberg out of its way. As the mighty ship plowed through, huge chunks of ice were still in the air. They hit the windshield and sides of the ship and fell harmlessly away. The big ship looked like a circus tiger jumping through a ring of fire.

"So much for that idea," Les said. The *Starrider* turned toward them again and accelerated.

Mike veered from side to side again and a moment later the laser blasts resumed.

"It's still on our tail," Les said.

Mike actually thought he heard fear in Les' voice.

"Not for long." Mike had pursued drunken fools through the narrow waterways of Miami's coastline many times, crazed idiots that thought they could actually escape him and *One Summer Dream*. He had run down numerous drug runners as well, hotshots in fancy power-boats more powerful than his own.

He veered sharply to the left and cut the speed to zero, sending the *Quasar* to a sliding, sideways halt. Then he gunned it and ran away at a ninety-degree angle from the oncoming *Starrider*. By the time the big ship aimed and fired, the *Quasar* had been gone from the spot a full five seconds.

"That move worked perfectly," Mike said. "I'm going to have a good shot in just a moment."

"How so?" Les said.

"See that small iceberg over there between those two gigantic ones?"

Les looked where he was pointing.

"I'm going to whip around one of the big bergs and come back through the cove at high speed," Mike said. "They'll lose sight of us for a few seconds, just long enough for us to hide behind that little berg. When they sail by, I'll blast them."

"It's worth a try," Les said. "Whatever you do, do it before *Quasar Two* gets here."

Mike raced through the channel between the two massive icebergs and the *Starrider* followed close behind. Once they exited the channel into the open water, he cut the speed, turned 180 degrees, and drove headlong back inside. The *Starrider* passed them going the opposite way at high speed. The big ship then had to exit the channel, turn completely around, and reverse course. This gave Mike almost a full minute to get out of the area.

"Any pilot in his right mind is going to figure we're running for the hills right now," Mike said with a broad smile. He piloted over to the small iceberg and brought the *Quasar* to a complete stop on the far side of it. "Here's where we blind-side them."

Having lost sight of the target, the *Starrider* indeed made the mistake of assuming Mike was still running away. Approximately thirty seconds later, it sailed past the waiting *Quasar*, now only about a hundred yards off its port bow.

"Now," Les shouted. Mike hit the trigger and the beam of laser fire roared across the side of the *Starrider*, cutting a deep gash in the hull a few feet above the water line. He raised and lowered the gun turret slightly, cutting a zigzag line of destruction all along its side. Nuts and bolts and pieces of metal flew in all directions and showers of sparks sailed into the water. The big ship had no chance to return fire. It scrambled for the safety of one of the big icebergs, no longer trying to fire back.

"Nice going, Mike," Les said. "You're making it look easy."

Mike looked over at Les and winked. "I'll bet this is the first time in his lousy life that Greg Fannin has found himself at someone else's mercy rather than the other way around."

Les laughed, his long blonde bangs falling over his gray eyes. "You're probably right."

Mike looked out at the icy water ahead. He felt exhilarated. It was another of those little victories that gave him the encouraging feeling that he might make it home to Jan after all.

The other *Quasar* had now appeared on the radar screen. It was some twenty miles away and was closing fast.

"I wonder where those jokers have been," Mike said pointing at the blip on the screen.

"I don't know," Les said. "I'm just glad they weren't here."

"Let's hide again," Mike said. He spotted a large ice wall nearby and steered slowly toward it. Again using the smaller lasers mounted to the *Quasar's* roof, he cut out a tunnel in the ice. They then carefully backed the *Quasar* inside. That accomplished, they sat quietly at the controls, engine idling, listening. Nothing happened for twenty minutes and finally they decided that the danger had passed, at least for the moment. Mike cut the engine off to save power and they took advantage of the opportunity to take a much-needed breather.

CHAPTER 26

▼

STARRIDER SEEKS CLOSURE

Les and Mike sat at the console and kept a constant watch out the tunnel entrance for any sign of the *Starrider* or *Quasar Two*. Two hours passed uneventfully.

At around three that afternoon, Dr. Spellman's voice came over the radio. "This is *Starrider*," he said. "We'd like to discuss our unconditional surrender."

Les and Mike looked at each other in total shock.

"Can you hear me *Quasar One*? Over."

"Think it's some kind of trap?" Mike said.

"Probably," Les said. "But let's hear what they have to say."

He opened the microphone. "*Starrider*, this is *Quasar One*. We didn't copy that, will you please repeat? Over."

"You've used our machinery to its greatest advantage and done severe damage to this vessel," Spellman said calmly. "We feel that our only recourse is to make a deal with you. We're prepared to make you both very rich if you'll help us. Over."

"They're lying," Mike said. "There's no way in the world they're going to let us get away with all we've done to them."

"I'm willing to listen," Les said. He opened the microphone again. "How do you propose to do that, *Starrider*? Over."

"Our hull is filled with crystals we've mined here," Spellman said. "In our day they are as valuable as diamonds in your day. If you will join us in our attempts to get home with *Starrider* intact then we'll give you each five million dollars in U.S. currency upon our return. Over."

"Five million," Mike said. "Now I know they're lying."

"Yeah," Les said. "I'm not biting either. But, let's hear them out."

"How could we help you, *Starrider*?" he said. "Over."

"There appears to be a way to get a large vessel like ours back to our present through the vortex by using a talisman of some kind," Spellman said. "We've noticed that some of the pirates we have encountered have them. The talisman is usually in the shape of a model ship that spins around when the vessel nears the vortex. We believe it's made of radioactive gold. Over."

Without opening the microphone, Mike looked over at Les with a surprised look. "Then it really is radio-active."

"If you will help us find such a talisman," Spellman said. "I promise you we'll make it worth your while. Over."

"If you don't have one then how did you get here in the first place?" Mike said. "Over."

"We stumbled through during a hurricane," Spellman said. "Over."

Mike remembered what Roscoe had once told him about Evan Jonnsen and his hurricane-vortex theory. All of a sudden it began to make sense. "Can't you get back home the same way? Over."

"Perhaps," Spellman said. "But we'd rather go an easier route if possible. The first trip through almost destroyed us. We really need a talisman. Over."

Les looked at Mike. "Five million smackers."

"Forget it," Mike said. "They're lying and you and I both know it. Hey, I don't want to go to the future with them under any circumstances. If not for Jan, then I might consider it. But there's no amount of money in the world that will make me forget her. Let's tell them no deal."

"I don't know, Mike," Les said. "We've been awfully lucky to have survived this long. Maybe giving up now would save our skins."

"Les, I want you to search that sixth-sense of yours. Reach out with all your strength and then tell me what you think."

Les looked into Mike's brown eyes and pondered what he had said. "That's a good idea. I'll give it a try."

Mike watched as Les closed his eyes and began probing the sixth sense. After a few seconds he wore the same expression as the night he slept in the pirate cemetery. For a long moment, Les sat deep in thought. Suddenly his eyes shot open. "Oh no!"

Mike's eyes got wide. "What? What is it?"

Les looked down at the *Quasar*'s control panel. An instant later it lit up. The vessel powered up on its own and started moving forward out of its hiding place.

"What the hell is going on?" Mike reached down to the throttle and attempted to reverse them back into the tunnel but got no response from the controls.

"They've taken over," Les said. "They must have figured out our new combination somehow."

"Oh no," Mike said. "I'm afraid all those overrides I did on the ship's computer may have broken-down our defenses and left us vulnerable."

"We should have stayed off that radio too," Les said. They both tried desperately to regain control of the ship but couldn't.

"We've got to do something fast," Mike said. He dropped to the floor and crawled under the console to check the combination. "The code numbers are lit up in red," he said. He reached over and tried to turn the little dials.

"Can you change the numbers?" Les said.

"No, they won't move. We no longer have control of the ship." He looked up at Les with a helpless expression. "They're going to pull us out in the middle of the cove and blow us right out of the water."

They looked up at the radar screen and saw that both the other *Quasar* and the *Starrider* were approaching. The bigger ship was less than half-a-mile away.

Greg Fannin's voice came in loud and clear. "So my friends. It looks like the ball is back in my court. It's too bad you decided to be my enemy. We could have been such good and wealthy partners. Now, I'm going to have to kill you. I'll tell you what though. Just to show you what a nice guy I am, I'm going to give you a couple of minutes to jump overboard before I come over there and shoot you."

Mike looked out the window and saw the *Starrider* come slowly around a corner and into the cove. It was coming at them slowly, apparently wanting to savor every moment of what was about to happen.

"Sorry boys," Fannin said with a boisterous laugh. "I'm afraid you're just a little too primitive to be playing with me. Come back in a few hundred years and try again." Others could now be heard laughing with him. "I'm going to enjoy this more than you can possibly imagine."

"They aren't getting me without a fight," Les said. "We still have laser rifles."

"I've got a better idea," Mike said. "Do you know where there is some fishing line?"

"Fishing line?" Les said. "What do you want to do, catch a last meal?"

"No," he said. "I'm going to catch the biggest sucker ever born."

"I think we still have some fishing line in the tackle box."

"Good," Mike said. "You try stalling them and I'll go find it." He picked up the gold ship off the console and headed below decks to find the tackle box. Les got on the radio.

"Where's the five million dollars?" Les demanded.

Fannin laughed. "Surely you don't think that offer was serious. You stole my boat and then tried to sink my *Starrider* you son-of-a-bitch. Now either jump into the water or I'm sending my men aboard to bring you over here. If you like, I'll even give you a tour of the *Starrider* before we string you up."

"How generous," Les said. He stood at the console and watched the giant ship come closer. The *Starrider* and *Quasar Two* were now crawling forward from the middle of the icy lake formed by the towering icebergs on all sides. About a dozen crewmen were out on the decks holding laser rifles. Les noticed that the large gun turret on the *Starrider*'s bow was pointed right at him as well.

Down below decks, Mike had found the fishing line and was tying the end of it firmly around the little gold ship. He fed out about thirty feet of line, cut the end off and tied it to his belt. He then took the slack and balled it carefully into his pocket. He walked back upstairs. "I'll go out and talk to them," Mike said. "You stay in here and keep trying to break us free from their hold."

"And just how am I supposed to do that?"

"You're a smart guy," Mike said. "Besides, we'll never know if you don't try."

"How are you planning on buying me the time?"

"With this," Mike said. He held up the fishing line with the talisman dangling from it. "I have a feeling I can get this Fannin idiot to bend over and lick himself on the butt to get me to give him this."

"Stall him as much as possible then," Les said. He got down on his hands and knees and crawled back inside the console.

"Get your asses out here!" Fannin yelled from outside.

Mike stepped out onto the deck and looked up at the towering *Starrider*. The big vessel had pulled up alongside **Quasar One** and was only about ten feet away. From Mike's point of view, the deck of the big ship was a few feet above his head. He looked up to see about a dozen laser rifles pointed down right at his nose. Trixie barked once from somewhere below decks.

"So we meet at last," Fannin said as he stepped to the railing and looked down at Mike. He was older than

Mike had pictured, maybe about sixty. His face was pock-marked and weathered, and his gray hair fluttered in the breeze. In his steel-gray eyes Mike saw the look of an experienced killer. Fannin's very appearance made Mike grimace. At that moment a cold gust of wind blew across the deck. It was already quite cold, but this gust was unusually bitter. Mike glanced beyond the deck of the *Starrider* and saw that it was getting foggy in the distance behind them. He could see a thick mist swirling a little as it spread across the water.

That might be the vortex, he thought. It could be the miracle we need right now.

Again, the breeze kicked-up for just a moment. Nobody on the *Starrider's* deck seemed to even notice it.

"Where's that other jackass," Fannin said.

"Who?" Mike said.

"Never mind," Fannin said. "I'll find him myself after I eliminate you." He lifted a laser rifle and pointed it at Mike's head.

"Recognize this?" Mike held up the little gold ship. He leaned over the railing and held it above the water. "Kill me and the only talisman you'll ever see goes straight to the bottom."

Fannin's eyes widened and he lowered the rifle.

"I believe this is what you've been looking for," Mike said. "It's your ticket home." He rolled it gently around in his hand some six feet above the icy water.

"Don't you drop that thing," Fannin said.

"Put down your rifles and we'll talk," Mike said. "As long as at least one of you is pointing a weapon at me then I'm holding it over the water. You shoot me and you're all stuck here forever."

There was a long pause.

"All right," Fannin said. "Put your weapons down." The other crewmen looked around at each other and grudgingly did as they had been told.

Mike noticed that the breeze was picking up a little more and was now pretty steady. It was obvious to him that the approaching vortex was the last thing Fannin and his crew expected right now.

Meanwhile, at the console, Les was anxiously trying the change the numbers of the combination. The *Starrider's* computers had them locked-in. The small red lights on the numbers seemed to indicate that Les had no control over them at all. Suddenly, the lights flickered.

"What the hell?" Les muttered. He slowly rose up, careful not to be seen, and peered outside. Beyond the decks of the two other ships he spotted the approaching wall of fog, now only a hundred yards away. "Oh man," he whispered. "We may be on the verge of getting the luckiest break of a lifetime."

Les squatted back down and looked at the red indicator lights on the combination console. "Do that again," he muttered. He sat holding his thumbs up to two of the dials. A moment later the red lights dimmed just a little. He tried to change the little dials but they still wouldn't move. "Come on," he said. He pushed with his thumbs, but the dials refused to budge.

He continued to sit and wait, intently watching the red indicators. They went completely dark. He spun the two little dials and they moved. He quickly reached another and moved it too. An instant later the power returned and the indicator lights were green. "Thank you, Jesus," he whispered. He quickly crawled behind the wheel.

A moment later Mike felt the boat move just a little as it shifted into gear. He put on his best poker face to try and hide his relief from the many eyes looking squarely at him.

"Okay," Mike said, trying to sound defeated. "Here's the talisman." He tossed the little ship onto the deck of the *Starrider*. The sailors all stood a moment just staring at it. Then, almost as if someone had fired a starting gun, they all bolted to be the first to pick it up.

"Hit it Les," Mike screamed as he got a good hold on the railing. Les punched the *Quasar*'s throttle and started away. A mere instant before the first set of fingers reached the talisman, Mike yanked on the end of the fishing line and the little ship flew from the *Starrider*'s deck and straight into his hand. He then scrambled inside the cabin just an instant before a barrage of laser fire came. *Quasar One* roared away.

"Get them," Fannin screamed. After a moment when nothing had happened, he turned and looked through the windshield at the pilot. "Didn't you hear me?"

"She won't start," he said.

Mike was watching out the back of the *Quasar*'s rear window as Les steered them toward the cove's exit. "Why aren't they pursuing?"

"They haven't realized that the nuclear engines won't work for some reason," Les said. "Once I got us free from their grasp I noticed ours wasn't working either. I switched to the conventional engine and it worked fine. I guess you noticed when I put her in gear."

"Yes," Mike said. "I didn't know how you did it but I wasn't going to complain."

"The other *Quasar* is headed our away." Les looked out the back at the approaching boat, just in time to see its missile launcher lock into place on its deck. "And it looks like they really mean business." He looked over at Mike. "You seem to have a knack for outrunning these guys so why don't you drive?"

"Okay."

Les slowed down a bit and they switched places. Once Mike was comfortably in the pilot's seat he powered-up the laser turret.

"Look." Les pointed at the floor where Mike had dropped the talisman. It was on its side and seemed to be moving about under its own power. He reached down, removed the fishing line and set it upright. Immediately, the talisman turned and pointed itself back toward the *Starrider*.

"Oh no." Mike looked over his shoulder and behind them. "We're heading the wrong way."

The *Starrider* was just now getting powered up and still had its back to the middle of the cove. Mike saw his chance to get past it if he could turn around quickly enough. *Quasar Two* was already in hot pursuit and was attempting to cut them off. Suddenly, they heard a loud explosion and saw a large puff of smoke erupt from *Quasar Two's* deck. An instant later a missile screamed past, missing the stern by inches. Les and Mike looked back to see it strike an iceberg the size of an apartment building and blow it to bits. When the steam and smoke cleared there was nothing left but millions of ice cubes floating in the turbulent water.

"Well, now we know what the missile can do," Mike said. He zigzagged a couple of times and then banked a sharp U-turn back in the direction of the *Starrider*. The move caught *Quasar Two* by surprise and they sailed past them. The talisman on the floor slowly turned with them and pointed straight ahead once they were headed in the right direction.

Mike punched it and sped them up even more. A moment later they were racing past the *Starrider*'s stern on the opposite side of the cove. Several men on the big ship's deck fired at them with laser rifles but they were too far away to have any effect.

The radar indicated a lot of open water ahead and Mike steered for it. Just after they cleared the cove, the talisman started spinning around. It spun faster and faster until it became a blur.

"Look at that thing," Les said. "I think we may have finally found the doorway home."

The *Quasar*, still travelling at breakneck speed, went airborne momentarily, seeming to sail off a short cliff, before landing in rough water and starting to rock about violently. In a matter of one second they went from a cold, sunny day to a warm, stormy one. There were no icebergs anywhere.

The transition to the next dimension caused *Quasar One* to slow down. The engine revved as the boat bounced up and down on the rough surface, shaking Les and Mike about violently. Once Mike was able to get his composure, he reached for the throttle to slow them down. Before he could, the engine died. He tried restarting but it wouldn't turn over. A few moments later a hard, pounding rain started falling and the outside temperature started to plunge.

"Damn," Mike said. "Can't we ever enter a new dimension on a nice day?"

"I'll try to get the nuke power back on," Les said. He hurried down below and opened the compartment housing the nuclear engine. Once he had repeated the steps that worked before, he came to the disheartening conclusion that it wouldn't work either.

"Any luck?" Mike said when Les came back up front.

"No," he replied. "We're dead in the water. But I believe Fannin is in the same predicament. All we can do now is wait."

The heavy rain and rough seas reduced visibility to only a few dozen feet. There was no way to tell where they were or if there were any other craft around. The two of them armed themselves with laser rifles and spent the rest of the afternoon watching the water around them.

About two hours later darkness had fallen and they still had not seen any sign of danger. The weather and sea had calmed. "I think we may be in the clear," Mike called out to Les from the back railing of the *Quasar*. "I don't see any lights anywhere."

"Me neither," Les said. He was on the roof and also saw nothing. The rain had slackened to a fine mist and the only sound was the lapping of the waves against the sides of the boat.

"How's the sixth-sense?" Mike said.

"Nothing," Les said. "I don't think there's anyone within miles of us."

"I'm glad to hear that." Mike took the shoulder strap of the rifle off his neck and set it down on one of the cockpit cushions. "I'm ready for some dinner, a hot shower and some serious sleep."

"It doesn't look like there's anything we can do but wait the rest of the night," Les said. "I just wish I knew what happened to the *Starrider* and the other *Quasar*."

"Maybe we left them behind," Mike said. "After all, we have a talisman and they don't. Maybe they couldn't follow."

Les sighed. "I sure hope so. I'm tired of fighting." A little over an hour later, they were both asleep.

Mike awakened shortly after sunrise the next morning. He sat up and peeked out the porthole. The sky was still cloudy but the rain had stopped and the surf had calmed considerably. He got up and decided to step outside to the rear deck and stretch his legs. Les got up a few minutes later.

"Apparently it didn't hurt us by not being able to electrify the deck last night," Mike said. "I don't see any signs that we were visited by sea creatures. I still slept with a laser rifle beside me though."

"I guess we got lucky," Les said.

"Maybe that's a good sign," Mike said. "We still don't know where we are. Maybe we've finally made it back to our present day."

"That sounds a little too good to be true," Les said.

"Wishful thinking I guess," Mike said. "I'll go try to get the engine started." He walked up to the controls and attempted to power them up. The dashboard lights came on a moment later. "We've got power."

"Good," Les said. "Let's get moving."

Mike flicked on the radio and heard faint sounds of chatter.

"Hey," he called out. "I haven't heard anything like that in a while." He started turning the dial and continued to hear weak and distant sounds of conversation, most of it so faint he couldn't even distinguish any of the words.

He turned off the ship to shore radio and flicked on the FM radio. Static came fluttering in but when he began turning the dial he saw the red indicator light trying to flicker on. He kept turning the dial and a moment later the little red light came on and stayed on. What he heard next caused his heart to leap for joy.

"Hope you had a great Labor Day weekend, Miami," a radio disk jockey said. "Tuesday morning and it's back to work. Here's an old classic on Miami's music FM…"

"I don't believe it," Mike said.

"What?" Les said from below decks. "What don't you believe?"

"I think we're home." Mike turned up the volume.

"That's Miami radio," Mike said. "We're listening to FM radio from Miami."

Les looked at him in total disbelief. He reached over and turned on the ignition. The *Quasar* roared to life.

"Let's do a quick check of the radar," Mike said. "If the *Starrider* is around, maybe we can spot them before they mask." He turned on the detection devices and a number of other boats appeared.

"Wow," Les said. "Look at that. There are boats everywhere."

"See anything that might be *Quasar Two* or the *Starrider*?" Mike said.

"No." Les pointed at the radar screen. "I don't know about the other *Quasar*, it could be any or none of these. But there's definitely no sign of the *Starrider*."

"We'd better be careful," Mike said. "They may be just over the horizon and masked."

"You've got that right. It looks like we're about fifty miles due west of a large landmass. I believe it's south Florida. Let's head for it." He looked at Mike and smiled. Mike smiled back but it quickly faded. "What's wrong?"

"I wonder what year it is," Mike said. He sat down in the seat and almost looked faint. "I'm not sure I'm ready to try to find Jan again."

"What are you talking about?" Les said. "You've been waiting for this day forever, how could you possibly not be ready?" He looked outside as the sun peeked through the clouds. The bright morning light shimmered off the ocean like a beacon. "It's going to be a beautiful day," he said. "A beautiful day to go home." He pushed the throttle forward slowly and the *Quasar* began moving.

"Look," Les said. "There's another boat."

Mike's heart jumped into his throat and he stood up and glared in the direction Les was pointing. A couple of hundred feet off the starboard bow he saw the boat. It was a yacht with about a dozen people milling about the deck in bathing suits. "That's not *Quasar Two*."

Les smiled. "No it isn't. In fact, I'll bet if you walk out on the deck and wave at them they'll wave back." Mike stood looking into Les' eyes for just a moment.

"I'm going to try it," he said at last. He slid the Plexiglas door open and stepped out onto the side deck. As he walked up toward the front he noticed some of the people on the yacht looking his way. He held up his hand and waved. Several of them waved back. Mike kept waving, unable to stop himself. This was a simple pleasure that he had missed more than he could possibly imagine. A moment later every person on the other boat was waving back.

"How about those Dolphins," someone yelled.

"Did they win?" he called back.

"Yes," one of the men said. "They beat the Raiders in the opener last night."

"All right," Mike said. "Go Dolphins."

"Nice boat," another man yelled.

"Thanks," Mike said. He went back inside with tears in his eyes. "We're home, Les. We're really home."

Les increased the speed a bit and the mighty *Quasar* began to hum as it bounced across the waves. They were still out of sight of land but wouldn't be for long. The radar screen revealed even more boats ahead closer to shore. It was going to be a nice, warm, late summer day and they were among the lucky people out enjoying it.

The *Quasar* sped along, leaving the yacht full of football fans behind. Up ahead, another boat sat idle in the water about a quarter-mile away, soaking up the warm Florida sunshine. Les gave the boat a passing glance as they drove past, not really noticing it. He didn't realize it was *Quasar Two*. The enemy vessel powered-up at that moment and was quickly in pursuit.

"You look like you're feeling better," Les said as he noticed the broad smile on Mike's face.

"I'm nervous as hell," Mike said. He was staring off in the distance to starboard. They were both shaken back to reality when laser fire struck the back of the boat and jolted them violently.

"What the hell was that?" Mike said.

"Oh no," Les said. "It's the other *Quasar*!" He gunned it and veered a sharp right just as another shot came and hit the water a few feet from the stern.

"Damn," Mike said. "Here we go again."

"Why don't you take the wheel," Les said.

"Okay."

Without slowing down, Les stood up and stepped out from behind the wheel. The moment Mike got seated but before he had a chance to start steering, another jolt came from behind and rocked the *Quasar* violently again. He looked in the rear-view mirror and could almost see the men on the other *Quasar* smiling. "All right," he said. "Let's settle this thing right now."

"I can't understand why those idiots made this boat with no firing capability from the rear," Les said. He was using the controller on the console to try to turn the laser cannon in the direction of the pursuing vessel. It wouldn't go past ninety degrees.

"They obviously know that," Mike said. "They're staying right behind us." He veered sharply to the right; narrowly missing a big orange buoy, then immediately cut a hard left. *Quasar Two* followed close behind, continuing to stay in their blind spot. An instant later there was another loud crash as more laser fire hit the back of the boat. "We can't take many more of those."

"At least we know now that there is only one missile," Les said. "If they'd had another one they would have destroyed us with it on their first shot."

"Hopefully we still have ours," Mike said. He reached down and lifted the shield above the firing switch. When he moved the setting to "ready", a large launching mechanism raised from below and locked into place on the deck in front of them. Then they heard the missile loading itself into firing position.

The two boats zigzagged for several more minutes with *Quasar Two* continuing to shoot again and again. Mike was able to avoid them, but was growing continually frustrated by the inability to fire back.

"At this rate it's only going to be a matter of time before they finish us off," Mike said. "I just can't get around on them!"

"All we can do is keep trying," Les said. He looked ahead and could now see the Florida coastline.

Another blast hit the water just a few feet to Mike's left. As he continued to veer from side to side, trying not to form a pattern in his evasive maneuvering and trying to keep them alive just a little longer, he saw Jan's face in his mind clearer than he had at any time since he first disappeared. Over the months his memory of her beautiful face had faded. He couldn't remember exactly what she looked like anymore. Now, suddenly, he saw her face in his mind so clearly that it was as if he was looking right at her.

"Don't be afraid to ask for help," she was saying. It was two years ago, the night before they buried his mother. He was trying not to let her see him cry but he was losing the battle. He and Jan had only been dating a couple of weeks at the time and for some reason he feared that any sign of weakness might change her feelings about him. She put her arms around him and held him tight, reassuring him that everything was going to be okay. "Never be afraid to ask for help from your friends when you need it," she said. "That's what friends like me are for. Never be afraid to ask for help."

Another loud explosion of water narrowly missed them on the port side and Mike veered to starboard. "Don't be afraid to ask for help", he heard Jan say in his mind again. He looked down at the radio. "Mayday, mayday," he said into the microphone. "I'm under attack from a foreign vessel. Help me please."

"This is the Coast Guard," came a reply. "What's happening out there?" The voice sounded awfully familiar.

"Joe Sanders? Is that you?" Mike said.

"Yes, this is Joe Sanders. Who's this?"

"Mike, Mike Thompson, remember me?"

"Mike Thompson," Joe said. "It can't be. I thought you were dead."

"No, not dead," Mike said. "At least not yet. I've been marooned on a deserted island. Listen, I need your help."

"You've got it old friend," Joe said.

Mike quickly gave him his coordinates and told him of their predicament. "A few more hits and we're dead."

"We've got you on radar now," Joe said. "We're on our way."

Quasar Two continued firing at Mike and Les as the Coast Guard ship neared the area. Once they could see the two *Quasars*, Joe got on the radio.

"Attention unknown vessel," Joe said. "This is the United States Coast Guard. Cease firing immediately. You are in violation of federal maritime law. Cease fire immediately."

"This is *Quasar Two*," came a terse reply. "This matter doesn't involve you. Stay out of it or we'll roast you like a holiday turkey."

Joe glanced at his fellow sailors. "Who does this jerk think he is?"

"*Quasar Two*," Joe said. "This is your last warning. Cease fire immediately."

"This is you're last warning Coast Guard," came the response. "You are out-gunned, out-classed and in the wrong. Get lost!"

"Nobody comes into my territory and talks like that to me," Joe said. He charged straight for the two *Quasars* and fired a shot from the deck cannon that hit the water some fifty feet away from the two vessels. There was a loud splash and water shot high into the air.

Mike was watching intently in the rear view to see what *Quasar Two* was going to do next. "Come on you idiot," he muttered, "do something stupid."

The Coast Guard vessel fired again, this time a little closer, but still well off the mark. "Joe is being careful not to hit us by mistake," he told Les. "That's going to lower his chances of taking them out for us."

"It's up to you," Les said. Mike glanced over at him and made eye contact for one second. He then darted his eyes back at their attacker in his rear-view.

"I believe in you," Les said. "One shot. You can do it." They both watched as the Coast Guard vessel fired again at *Quasar Two*. This time it was a narrow miss.

"I warned you," was the only verbal reply from *Quasar Two* before it suddenly broke off the pursuit of *Quasar One* and turned on the Coast Guard.

"There's the opening I need," Mike told Les as he banked a sharp left toward the other *Quasar*. As *Quasar Two* bore down on the Coast Guard vessel, Mike got it squarely in the cross hairs. He then flipped the switch to "Fire". "Hits away," he said.

Quasar One slowed abruptly as a bright fireball burst from its deck and zoomed straight toward *Quasar Two*. Les and Mike watched the smoky cloud approach its target.

The missile flew straight into the cabin of **Quasar Two** and erupted into a giant ball of fire. The windows flew from their mountings, and flames poured out of every opening. Moments later there was a loud explosion as the vessel blew into thousands of tiny pieces. Mike and Les felt the concussion against the side of their boat as they sailed past. Back on board the Coast Guard vessel everyone cheered.

"That's it," Mike said. He slowed down and steered the **Quasar** alongside the Coast Guard cutter and put her in neutral. Then he ran out on deck to greet the Coast Guard crew.

"Mike," Joe said as he came out on deck. "Boy am I glad to see you."

Mike reached across the railing and shook his hand. "Not half as glad as I am, old friend." He introduced Les to him.

The other sailors gathered around and Joe quickly reminded them of Mike's disappearance. They all remembered him.

"How long ago was that?" Mike said.

"Three months," Joe said. "You've been gone all summer."

"Only three months," Mike said. He looked up at the blue Florida sky above. "Thank you, God."

Les couldn't help but notice the sailors admiring the **Quasar**. "Where did you get this incredible boat?" Joe said.

"It's a long story," Les said.

"Oh, Mike," Joe said. "Your house got sold. I guess you'll have to stay with me for a while."

"Okay," he said. Then the adrenaline started flowing again. "What about Jan?"

"Oh wow," Joe said. "I haven't seen Jan for a while. She sure cried at your funeral."

"Funeral?" he said. The other men on the cutter broke into laughter.

"Yeah," Joe said. "We held it at sea on a beautiful June day. It was really nice. You should have been there." They all laughed. "I'm sorry about your boat."

"What happened to it?" Mike said.

"They gave it to Jan and she sold it," Joe said. "It needed repairs and she said that she couldn't stand to look at it again."

Mike looked over at Les. "Let's go home."

"Sounds good to me," Les said.

"You guys can head over to my house if you want," Joe said. "I still live in the same place. There's a key hidden under the plant on the patio."

"Thanks, Joe," Mike said. "We'll see you when you get home."

They got back in the cabin and Les took the wheel. As they cruised closer to Miami, the familiar skyline and ocean front houses came into view. Mike sat and watched as the shore drew nearer, feeling a whirlwind of emotions from excitement to nervousness. He looked over at Les and saw an expression that said he was feeling the same way. Mike reached over and put his hand on his shoulder. "We got through it."

Les turned and looked at him.

"You don't seem very happy," Mike said.

"I didn't want to say anything back there," Les said. "But it's going to take me a while to come to grips with all of this."

"What do you mean? We're home, alive and well and we have the *Quasar*."

"Yeah," Les said. "And don't get me wrong, I'm thrilled to be back. It's just that I've now been gone for six years."

"Oh," Mike said. In his excitement over learning that only three months had passed since his own disappearance he had totally forgotten that Les had vanished so long ahead of him.

"We're a team," Mike said. "We're going to come out of this better than ever, you'll see."

They reached the harbor entrance.

"We can tie up at a marina I know," Mike said. "Go that way." He directed Les toward the spot and they were soon cutting off the engine and drifting up to the wooden dock. Trixie came running out on deck when the boat slowed down. She also seemed ready to go ashore.

Mike got out and tied them off. "Joe's place is just a couple of blocks from here," he said. "Let's go get a drink."

"Okay," Les said. He reached down and got the talisman and the bag of gold off the floor. After a moment he remembered to take the keys out of the ignition as well. Mike picked up a piece of line and made a leash for Trixie. They stepped out onto the dock and started walking, both of them in somewhat of a daze.

When they got to Joe's house, Mike found the key underneath the potted plant and the two of them stepped inside. There was a large pitcher of iced tea in the refrigerator and some leftover pizza. They warmed up the pizza and sat and watched TV the rest of the afternoon.

"Did you call her?" Joe asked when he stepped inside upon arriving home from work.

"He hasn't gotten up the courage yet," Les said.

"Well what are you waiting for?" Joe said.

"I... I don't know," Mike said. "I guess I'm waiting for her to get home from work. Plus, I think it would be better if you prefaced her and then put me on the line."

"Well let's get this show on the road then," Joe said. "What's her number?"

Mike recited it from memory and Joe dialed. The next few seconds were the most nerve-wracking of Mike's life.

"Hello, Jan?" Joe said. "This is Joe Sanders. I'm doing fine. Yes, it has been a long time. Listen, are you sitting down? Well, sit down because I have some news for you. I'm not going to tell you until you sit down. She doesn't want to sit down," he whispered to Mike. "Are you sitting now? Good. We picked up a lost traveler in the ocean today. He's an old friend of yours. Yeah, he's right here."

Joe handed Mike the phone and he took it in a trembling hand. "Hi Jan", he said. "It's me, Mike."

"Mike," she said. "Mike, is it really you?"

"Yes, Sweetheart, it's really me," Mike said.

"Oh Mike," she said. She paused and Mike could tell she was crying. "I can't believe it. Are you all right?"

"I am now," he said. "I've been stranded on a deserted island for the last three months, hungry, thirsty and missing you something terrible."

There was a long pause. He stood trembling, scared to death she was going to tell him something that was going to break his heart like she was married or something. All he heard was her crying.

"Jan, I can't tell you how badly I've missed you," he said. Tears were starting to stream down his face.

"I thought you were dead," she cried. "I haven't slept a whole night all summer thinking about you." There was another pause while she cried.

"I want to see you," he said.

"I want to see you too," she said. "Where are you?"

"I'm at Joe's house," he said.

"Don't move. I'll be there in a few minutes," she said.

"I'll be right here," he said. "I love you."

"I love you too," she said. She hung up the phone and Mike stood in a daze.

"Did she hang up?" Joe said. He nodded his head.

"Then hang up the phone," Joe said.

Mike stood motionless, still in a daze.

Joe reached over and wrenched the phone out of his hand and hung it up.

"She's coming here," Mike said. "She said for me not to move. She's coming here."

"I think she'll understand if you move across the room and sit on the couch while you wait for her," Joe said.

Joe and Les escorted Mike to the couch and a few minutes later Jan's car pulled up in the driveway.

Mike went to the door and stepped outside.

Jan jumped out of the car and ran to him. They threw their arms around each other. "I've missed you so much," he said.

"Don't talk." She kissed him.

"Kind of mushy, huh?" Joe said to Les. They were standing at the window looking outside. "I guess I'd better go drag them in here before a cop drives by and sees them." Les looked over at him and they both broke up laughing.

CHAPTER 27

▼

A MEETING OF
THE MINDS AND HEARTS

Over the next several weeks, Mike was able to regain his old job at the Department of Natural Resources and get things almost back to normal. He was pleased to learn that his efforts on the day of his disappearance had not been entirely in vain. The police had stepped in and prevented the race to Seaway Island, mainly because of what had happened to him.

For Les, the return to a normal life had been much more difficult. Even though his time in the Bermuda Triangle had been shorter than Mike's, he had been through a different part of the mysterious vortex, a part where more time somehow got away. Over six years had passed and the world had basically forgotten all about Les

Harrison. His boat repair shop and everything else on the block was now a shopping mall.

Worst of all, his friends had scattered, gone without a trace. Through Jan and Mike, Les made new friends and started all over. It was a long process. Things were made a little easier when the bag of gold coins they had brought back fetched fifty thousand dollars when sold. Only the talisman had been withheld from the sale, and it sat safely in Mike's safe deposit box.

Mike gave Les his share of the gold and he used it to buy a small boat repair shop not far from the marina. By the third week in October, Les was in business and the *Quasar* was sitting safely in storage at the shop. He and Mike agreed to jointly own the marvelous souvenir of their adventure, and Les spent the next several months repairing it and getting to know it inside and out. They hoped to sail in it again one day.

Several weeks later, Mike took Jan out for a Saturday night "snuggle cruise" in his new boat. "I think my life is finally going to start falling back into place," he said.

"Our lives." She smiled.

When they reached the same spot where he once talked of defeating the Bermuda Triangle and outsmarting the tabloids, Mike turned off the engine and walked to the back of the boat. Jan smiled as he sat down next to her.

He couldn't help remembering all the lonely times on the island when he dreamt of being here with his girl. Somehow, that seemed ages ago, in a different lifetime perhaps. He was glad he didn't have to explain the happiness he was feeling; he'd never find the words.

"I love you so much," he whispered.

"I love you too," she said.

Mike dropped down to one knee. The very sight of him made her eyes swell with tears of happiness.

"I want you to be my wife, Jan," he said with a smile. "Will you marry me?"

"Yes," she replied.

He stood, reached into his pocket and pulled out the diamond ring he had chosen just for this very moment. It was a perfect fit.

Tears began trickling down her cheeks as she hugged him tightly. "You know what this means don't you?" she said. "No more travels into the Bermuda Triangle for you."

"Not without you anyway," he replied with a smile.

"Like I said, no more travels for you." They both laughed.

LaVergne, TN USA
11 October 2009
160446LV00003B/4/A